DOWN FROM CASCOM
MOUNTAIN

DOWN FROM CASCOM MOUNTAIN

a novel

ANN JOSLIN WILLIAMS

BLOOMSBURY

New York • Berlin • London • Sydney

Published by Bloomsbury USA, New York

Portions of this novel appeared previously, in slightly different form,
in *StoryQuarterly* 42 under the title *Cascom Mountain Road*.

All papers used by Bloomsbury USA are natural, recyclable products made
from wood grown in well-managed forests. The manufacturing processes
conform to the environmental regulations of the country of origin.

LIBRARY OF CONGRESS CATALOGING-IN-PUBLICATION DATA

Williams, Ann Joslin.
Down from Cascom Mountain : a novel / Ann Joslin Williams. —1st U.S. ed.
p. cm.
ISBN: 978-1-60819-306-6 (hc)
1. Wilderness areas—New Hampshire—Fiction.   2. Accident
victims—Fiction.   3. Widows—Fiction.   4. Loss (Psychology)—
Fiction.   5. Teenage boys—Fiction.   6. Friendship—Fiction.
7. Psychological fiction.   I. Title.
PS3623.I556293D68 2011
813'.6—dc22
2010034477

First U.S. edition 2011

1 3 5 7 9 10 8 6 4 2

Typeset by Westchester Book Group
Printed in the U.S.A. by Quad/Graphics, Fairfield, Pennsylvania

For my mother, and in memory of my
first teacher, my father, Thomas Williams

He took the Cascom Mountain Road, the rounded mountain itself appearing time and time again, always a little startling, as if it had a tendency to move to different points of the compass.

—THOMAS WILLIAMS, *The Followed Man*

PROLOGUE

THERE WAS THE SOUND of rain falling, but no rain. The sun cut paths between tree trunks, laying narrow stripes on the ground as the three young people climbed. The forest ticked as it dried. Above, through the high branches, the sky was light and changing, letting go of its pale mist, blue seeping in. They hiked in single file. A breeze moved through the wet leaves, releasing drops in a flurry, nearly as loud and sudden as an explosion of wings. Earlier, a mile or so back, they'd jumped a partridge. It had burst from the ground, drumming into flight. Put them all on edge.

The terrain grew steeper, rockier. They breathed heavily, felt the strain in their muscles, each step placed and tested for traction. Over a rise, the trail flattened for a stretch.

"What's that?" the tall boy in front asked, voice jittery, slowing his pace. He was looking at something farther up the trail. Then he said, "No, never mind. Just that funky rock there."

As they picked their way over the area—a web of slippery roots and shadows netted over an outcropping of granite—they came to the junction of another trail. The tall boy stopped suddenly and turned, causing the others, the girl in the middle and the boy behind her, their crew boss, to bump into each other.

The tall boy raised his hands. "Whoa," he said. "We're at a crossroads. Where's he supposed to be?"

"Just keep going straight," the girl said. "We stay on the Clark."

"Come on," the crew boss said softly, urging them on. "Let's just get this done."

The dead boy lay on his stomach in the middle of the trail, legs splayed and slack, knees turned out like a frog's. His arms went straight from his sides, as if he'd fallen from a height, though this wasn't the case. More likely he'd just tripped and passed out. Hypothermia. It had been a cold, wet night. Mixed with alcohol. A glass liquor bottle lay on its side near the boy's outstretched arm.

There was a stink, urine and booze, and the girl put her hand over her nose and mouth. He wasn't very old. Maybe their age. Seventeen, eighteen.

The dead boy's face was in profile, a sharp cheekbone and a thin blond beard. The flesh was wrong, off, ashy. The eyes were closed as if he was sleeping, but he was obviously not asleep with that skin and the way the body lay, impossibly sunk against the contours of the ground.

The crew boss wore a red bandanna around his head like a pirate. Sweat glistened on his face, and wet hair stuck in curls to the back of his neck. He crouched near the boy's head and squinted, as if trying to see to the bottom of a stream. The girl stood behind him. Her shadow covered his back. When she stepped to the side and sunlight fell on his shoulder, he turned and looked at her as if she'd just laid her hands on him.

"Guy's wasted," the tall boy said. The others looked to see as he picked up the bottle—Jack Daniel's—and held it by the neck daintily with two fingers. "Totally." He turned the bottle upside down and pretended to pour it out. "What, no friendly drop for me?" he said. The girl shook her head and gave him a pleading look. Making light of things was what you had to do in order to get through, but still, it bothered her.

"Where's the girl?" she asked. There was supposed to be a girl waiting with the body. The girlfriend. This morning a hiker had found them on his way across from the lean-to on South Peak. He said the girl was strange-looking. She had refused to come down with him.

The tall boy put the bottle on the ground and scanned the woods. The others peered into the woods, too. The forest was brown and green and gray. There was a stand of birches, and their eyes kept returning to it, drawn by the white bark.

They all knew that the missing girl was an albino. Her name was Anna Kimball, and she had no pigment in her skin; it could be dangerous for her to be in the sun. All three of them had seen her at the lodge the night before. She was a wisp of a girl, her hair straight and long down her back, pure white, so white you thought she was an old woman from behind. None of them had gotten a good look at her eyes, but the cook had. See-through blue, pink at the edges, and slightly off-track, as if unhinged in their sockets. He said it was hard to look at her.

"Great," the crew boss said. "One dead. Now one missing." He stood, cleared his throat, pressed his lips together. His eyes watered as he looked at the body, at the dead boy's black T-shirt, and the strip of flesh where the shirt bunched up from the waist. "We need to get a search party, and someone needs to wait here with the body for the coroner."

"Goofer's dead," the tall boy said. It was their term for guests who stayed at the lodge, especially the annoying or foolish ones. "Obviously," he added.

"Rules," the crew boss said.

The tall boy kicked the bottle. It rolled off the trail, bumped against a downed tree, then wobble-rolled until it hit a root, bounced, and landed upright and intact at the base of a rock.

All three of them stared at the bottle.

"So," the tall boy said after a moment. "Where's ghost girl?"

Cascom had its stories: a forest fire that burned the summit bald; a hurricane that took down the tall spruce in the Cathedral Forest, destroyed homes and roads, and set farm animals free, including some pigs that evaded capture and, over time, bred and grew into dangerous boars with long tusks and bristled fur. The last of them had been shot in 1969. Its horrible head was mounted above the cash register in a country store south of the township of Leah. There was the tale of a young couple who wandered off-trail and froze to death on a winter climb. They were found huddled together in a snowy grave, their side-by-side footprints a map of a futile journey. It was said that their ghosts were responsible for mysterious footprints that appeared in the fresh snow of open fields. The prints went in spirals from the center of the fields, then disappeared, no paths leading in or out.

"I can start looking," the girl, Mary Hall, said. "I'll head up to the top." She knew the mountain better than anyone. She'd grown up not three miles from this spot.

"I'll head down, organize a search party," the crew boss said. He swept the bandanna off his head, wiped his face with it. "You wait with the body," he told the other boy.

"Oh, fine," the tall boy said, squatting, arms dangling between his legs. "I'll hang with the dead guy, make sure he doesn't try to get away." He looked around, peering into the woods as if he was being watched. There was nothing white, except the birches and the sunlight, casting shapes on the ground.

The crew boss turned to Mary. "Stay on the trail," he said. "I mean it. I don't need you lost too." His hands shook as he tied his bandanna around his head again.

As Mary climbed, the crew boss's voice echoed in the valley. *Anna.* The word rebounded in the woods, sounding more like

Mama, then as the distance increased, became even more form-less and hollow, like the bleat of an animal, like the cry of a fawn Mary had once heard.

On the exposed granite summit, she stopped and looked out. The only white was in the long streaks of quartz braided into the rock over on South Peak. They'd been told that the girl's eye-sight was deficient. There were dangerous ledges, chasms to fall into and disappear. Mary took a drink of water from the bottle in her pack and searched the valley, scanning the openings—cuts made in the forest—until she found the rectangle of lighter green where her parents' house stood on a hill above a field. Her parents were there, probably drinking coffee on the front deck, and not knowing yet that their daughter had seen a dead person. Maybe they'd worry for her. Or maybe they'd view this experi-ence as valuable, something to learn from. Her father, the natu-ralist, would likely point out, as he often did in his books and lectures, the respect one should have for nature, for the moun-tain's extreme conditions. For the way hypothermia, especially if urged along by exhaustion and cold, not to mention alcohol, could sneak up on you.

A mile to the left of her parents' clearing was a tan area, the sandy parking lot in front of the lodge. The lodge itself was hid-den, but the red-shingled roof of Lo-House was visible, stand-ing out like a maple tree turned early, like a dab of red paint. Lo-House was the crew's quarters, where they all slept. Where they often sat on the roof to talk and watch the Perseids. To the east of the lodge was the pond, a flat gray coin sunk into the land. Far to the south the valley dipped to Four Corners, where four counties met in the middle of nowhere, and only a checkmark-shaped scar in the otherwise blanket of green revealed where the old Gough farm sat, the buildings themselves hidden inside the walls of wilderness.

The sun was coming on hot now, and she raised her face to it.

If the albino girl was alive, if she wanted to live, she'd stay in the woods out of the sun. Mary could imagine why Anna wouldn't leave her boyfriend and return with the hiker this morning. Maybe they'd set off last night for fun, following the flashlight beam, hoping to make it to the top. Hoping to see the whole dome of the night from the summit. The night would be the best time for Anna—the soothing darkness. But they were drinking. Or he was, swigging whiskey, and they were climbing. It wasn't a long climb—an hour and a half—but it was steep, and they grew tired, breathing harder. Somewhere along the way he fell, wouldn't get up, too drunk, or passed out. Maybe she curled next to him and fell asleep. Or maybe they chose to lie down in the secret dark and tangle themselves together right there. When she woke up, he was on top of her, a heavy weight. His body was cold now. She struggled out from under him and tried to turn him over. She put her hand in front of his mouth, no breath. She took hold of his shoulders and shook him, but she already knew. Then she climbed on his back and lay on top of him. She reached her arms out to match his, her fingertips to his wrists. It had been her idea to go up in the dark. He loved her, and look where she'd led him. It wasn't easy for people to love her because they could never really see her. They looked past her, through her. He wasn't like that; he wasn't afraid. He said she was his white dove, his snow angel. She loved him. And now he was dead, and she didn't want to live. She rose, left the body.

Mary stood on top of the mountain, thinking, She's gone already, I know it. I'd be gone.

Turkey vultures circled above the summit, their huge wings draped gracefully on the air. They rode the updrafts, glided long distances. She knew how ugly they were with their naked, featherless heads, but from here, soaring, they were kings. When the shadow of one passed over her, she lifted her arms, making her own shadow wings on the rock. She began her descent, letting her shadow tip and soar across the ledge until she reached the woods again, where she disobeyed the crew boss and left the trail for the denser, darker places where you would go if you didn't want to be found.

Hours later, coming down under hardwoods, Mary's eyes ached from looking so intensely into the forest, and her voice was hoarse from yelling at every turn.

"Anna!" she yelled. "Aaa . . . Naaa." Only the tinny echo of her own voice came back.

In Clark Pastures, a small clearing, the sun beat down on the dry grass, drew up the odor of wicker. A crumbling stone wall ran alongside the clearing and away into the woods like a train. She decided to follow the wall. That's what you'd do if you were in the woods, making your way somewhere, or lost. You'd find something man-made, a sign of civilization. You almost couldn't help but follow it.

But after three ridges through brush, arms and legs scratched and bleeding in spots, she was relieved to come to the end of the wall, and out of the forest. Deerflies zigged around her head, tormenting her as she crossed a field, back to the road just below Four Corners, a quarter mile or so south of the Goughs' farm. She'd have to walk all the way back to the lodge on the rutted road. She'd been gone a long time; the crew boss was probably worried. And worse, she'd found nothing, no one—no lost girl. She'd wanted to be the rescuer. But this hadn't happened, and now she was late.

"Anna!" she called out once more, imagining the word riding on a current of air, slipping between the trees to the girl's ears.

The sound of a motor came from behind her. It was an old Rambler she recognized, the Goughs' car, and driving it was the tall, black-haired Mrs. Gough. The car moved slowly on the steep road, and Mrs. Gough, with her narrow face and curving Roman nose, gazed directly at Mary, but she didn't acknowledge her. The woman's eyes were blank and brooding. Her hair was so thick it must have been heavy, a weight on her long, thin neck. She was either exotically beautiful or sort of hideous. It was hard to say. "Stay clear of that Gough woman," Mary's mother had once remarked, "she's nuts," and the word *Gough* had sounded like *cough* the way her mother had pronounced it with an irritated, raspy breath.

Just as the car passed, a face popped up from the backseat, a dark-haired boy, maybe four or five years old. He stared out the rear window. Mary waved, though the boy was barely visible in the ashy dust that rose and puffed behind the car.

Tobin watched until the girl on the road was out of sight, then he turned and hunkered down again. A section of his mother's hair fell over the back of her seat. The frayed ends swung above his knees. He spread two fingers, making scissors, and slid them toward the ends. When his mother cleared her throat, he froze, and found her looking in the rearview mirror. The mirror cut out only her eyes, the bridge of her nose, and part of her forehead like a bandit's mask. Her eyes were fierce and dark, and he thought about ducking to the floor where she couldn't see him. Her head jerked so her mouth came visible in the mirror for a moment, then the eyes were there again, though turned back to the road. He pulled his scissor fingers back. The car struggled on the incline as she gunned it forward. Dust clouds followed them. It was hot. His mother wouldn't roll down the windows because of the kicked-up dirt, and now she was smoking, making his nostrils burn and his scalp prickle. He felt woozy and lay down on the sticky seat.

"A foolish boy drank himself to death last night," his mother said. "They found him on the mountain." His mouth sprang full of bitter saliva and he pressed his fingertips over his lips to keep it in. The car bounced, churning over the ruts. He was supposed to tell if he was going to throw up, but he didn't dare open his mouth.

"I heard some people talking at the market." She spoke as if she were reciting what she might say later to his father. "He was on the Clark Trail. He was young. Now he's dead, quick as that. Plumb dead." He heard the intake of smoke, the tiny tap-pop as her lips pinched, then let go of the filter. She blew out quick. "Exposure to the elements. The elements got him."

The *elephants* got him. He pictured huge, wrinkly gray elephants crashing through trees, then an elephant foot raised above the head of a small boy.

"There was a girl with him, but they hadn't found her yet," his mother added, and for a second he thought maybe it was the girl on the road, and maybe the elephants were after her, too, but the image bumped away with the rutted road, and he knew it wasn't that girl, and there were no elephants on Cascom. If the motion and the smoke weren't making him feel awful, he might have told his mother about the element-elephants. Sometimes she liked things like that—words, switched around, made silly.

Then his mother turned, glanced at him. "Damn it," she said. "Not again." He gripped the edge of the seat as she jerked the car to the shoulder of the road. She was yelling, and he felt the warm liquid on his chin, and there was a sour smell. Then she was at the door and pulling him out by the collar and the back of his pants. "All over the seat," she snapped. "How many times?" She dragged him out of the car, let go of him. He sat on his knees in the gravel. His shirt front was covered.

"*Damn* it all," he heard her say. "You walk the rest," and then the doors slammed and there was the grind of the tires. He was sad, stricken, looking after the car as it continued up the hill, then turned off at the row of mailboxes onto their road. His father would be mad. He wasn't supposed to upset her. He was never supposed to vomit in the car, but the car always made him sick. A crow cawed twice, then flapped away above him. He felt like an object, like one of the things his mother left in a random place for no reason he could understand—a teakettle under the kitchen table; a mesh bag of his white socks, all rolled into tight balls and hung from a tree branch in the backyard, as you might suspend suet for birds; books stacked between plates in the dish cupboard. A pillowcase of his father's things—a comb, several paintbrushes, one L.L.Bean hiking boot, a compass, a photograph of his father holding up a photograph of Tobin as a baby—stashed in the barn behind the pigsty. But he was not a thing, and she put him here because he was sick in the car, so that was a reason, and it gave him a measure of relief to find logic in her behavior, since more and more there seemed to be none.

On his feet now, he looked into the woods. He kept his eyes open, *no blinking!* until the trunks of trees and the spaces between them began to blur and shimmer. This was his new secret skill. The world lost definition quickly, then it was as if he could slip out of his body, rise up above it. There was the sound of someone hiking up the road. He blinked, shook himself out of the trance, scrambled into the ditch, and lay flat. He wouldn't let the girl see him with his soiled shirt. He wouldn't let her know that he'd been put out of the car by his mother. Moisture seeped through the knees of his pants. She came up, feet scuffing, louder, breathing hard on the steep road, then going past. Finally, when he was sure she was far enough away, he crept out of the ditch, staying low on his hands and knees. The girl started up the second hill. Her long braid swung back and forth behind her. The nausea was gone, but there was still the odor of throw-up, mixed with the muggy smell of mud. The girl walked fast. Then she stopped, knelt, and did something with her shoe. Tying a lace, he supposed. When she stood, she lifted her arms out to her sides and waved them up and down, slowly, as if pretending to have wings. She tipped side to side, soaring. Then she was just hiking again, steady and fast. But for a moment she'd done something else, been something else, pretending. He started up the road, keeping a long ways back from the girl. Closing his eyes, he lifted his arms and let them hang on the air as he walked.

Mary continued up the hill, passing the turnoff where dust still floated above the gravel from the wheels of the Goughs' car where it had veered off Cascom Mountain Road for Four Corners. She hiked another half mile, coming to the top of the last precipitous rise, a blind spot where her father often tooted the horn to warn oncoming vehicles. It was a place where the front grill of a car could seem to leap out of the sky above you as if shot from a ramp.

"Beep beep," she whispered, staying close to the ditch until she was over the top and on flat ground again. In a few yards she came to the logging road. She noted the old wooden sign her father had carved with their last name. It was arrow-shaped at one end to point down the narrow road, which was the way to her parents' house. She ought to have hiked in, asked if they'd heard or seen anything, but she was already late for dinner duty, and anxious to get back. Maybe the girl had turned up at the lodge by now.

As she came to the head of the logging road she paused, looked at the strip of tall grass that grew down the middle of the road, like a Mohawk. The road curved slightly, then vanished into the dimness of the woods, and she imagined what it would be like to find a strange, pale girl there, looking back. Goose bumps rose on her arms.

Once, when she was a girl, she'd camped in the middle of the logging road all day, waiting to see if her parents would find her. Why she was often compelled to run away, pretend to be lost, she didn't know. It was as if she needed to purposefully chal-lenge them to notice that she was gone, to come look for her, but more often than not she grew bored or frightened and gave up, grass imprinted on her knees, and went home, not missed, not even questioned. Mary, at seventeen, envisioned herself as a little girl—blazing eyes, determined, tight mouth—crouched in the grass, waiting to be found.

The logging road was empty, and she recalled all that had happened today—the dead body and the weedy smell of alcohol mixed with urine, the girl out there somewhere. The girl who must be devastated, in disbelief, heartbroken, traumatized. If she could only find her, she'd hold her, comfort her.

As Mary turned back to the main road, a small dark-haired child appeared at the horizon, coming up the hill she'd just hiked. It was the Gough boy, his head bobbing up, then a bit more, then more, like a buoy rising on waves. It puzzled her to see him, not in the car that had passed her farther back, but here and alone. His mother must have left him off for some reason. It wasn't far from the turnoff to his parents' farm; he couldn't be lost, but he seemed too little to have been left by himself. Was he following her? What worried her most was that he'd chosen a path smack in the middle of the road where no driver would be able to see him until it was too late. When he saw that she saw him, he stopped, ducked slightly. He stood still, like a startled animal, unsure. She smiled to assure him, but the sound of a motor, coming fast, alarmed her. She strode toward him, put-ting herself in the center of the road to shield him, so the driver might see her first.

Tobin felt tingles. The girl had her hand over her heart. He real-ized that a truck had roared around them and gone down the hill. He realized that the girl was still coming toward him, telling him to get out of the road. He felt how it was warm and wet between his legs; he'd wet himself. He spun around and ran back down the road, back toward the turnoff for Four Corners and away from the girl and his embarrassment.

Weeks passed before the county gave up the search for Anna Kimball, believing that she'd left the mountain, but the crew couldn't give up. They took off in their free time, hoisting an ax or scythe, and headed into the wilderness, perhaps under the guise of clearing a seldom-used trail. It was impossible to stop searching, to believe that they'd never find her. They zigzagged, switched back, straying from the trails, continually scanning the dizzying spaces between the giant beech, poplar, and hemlock. They headed toward light, areas that opened into clearings of yellow grasses and rises of granite, gray stud lichen crunching under their boots. No one called out her name anymore.

They were lured into crevices, hacking at thickets of dwarf spruce and using their feet, scuffing so their toes might come against something soft, human. They circled boulders, trudged just a little farther upstream. In their minds they saw the albino girl, her white hair, her luminous skin and floating eyes. Birches loomed from the woods time and again, causing them to flinch, sometimes even when they *knew*, they could *see*, it was only the chalky white, peeling bark—a stand of ghost trees bent in a low arc, slender trunks and branches like arms, taunting them. They saw her body draped over rocks, the brook surging around her, perhaps one waxen foot bobbing in the current. They saw her at the bottom of cliffs, arms splayed, a tiny ivory moth flattened against gray rock. From behind thick pines she leaned out suddenly, hair so long it swept the ground. She lurked just in back of them, or at the outskirts of vision, dashing in a translucent blur across the steep slopes. They saw her in the sweep of headlights going around sharp curves on the mountain road. They saw her in their dreams—creeping past a window, pressed against the wall behind a door, standing at the end of the bed. She brushed their necks with white fingernails, startling them awake.

CHAPTER 1

MARY STOOD IN THE FIELD below her parents' old summerhouse. Back up the hill, sitting on the front deck with a mug of coffee in his hand, her husband waited for her. She expected he was amused, wondering what his new wife was doing down there in the field, arms out, head back, as if she were embracing the sky, and Cascom Mountain with its sparkling ledges, full of mica. She was speaking to the mountain, telling the hills and ridges and rising face of granite that she was back, maybe for good. She imagined her parents' spirits in the breeze, in the window-eyes of the house behind her, pleased with her return, happy she'd found someone. Even the bright rock face of Cascom seemed to beam with approval.

Air shifted across the valley, fingered the collar of Mary's shirt, found its way through buttonholes. She shut her eyes and felt the mountain taking her in, listening. Then she turned and started up the hill to where Michael sat, raising his coffee mug as if to toast her, or the morning, because the sky was clear, and it was a good day for a hike.

"If you make the lunch, I'll carry the pack," he said.

"You have a deal," she said as she passed by.

CHAPTER 2

T HE FIRST TIME she brought Michael to the mountain, they'd come in at night, the headlights pushing through the dark and catching on the bare branches of hardwoods that grew close to the road. It had been early spring then, April. Buds were swollen and reddish. In another warm week they'd twist open, green. Mary drove, though Michael had been at the wheel most of the day on the highways, heading north from Boston to New Hampshire. In the township of Leah, when they'd stopped for gas and he went in to pay, she slid over to the driver's seat.

"You better let me drive," she said, when he came back. "These roads get hairy."

She rolled up her window against the bite of chilly, gasoline-tinted air, and waited as he went around to the passenger side, tucked a six-pack of beer behind the seat and got in.

"So, you think I can't handle it?" he joked.

"You could." She gave him two quick pats on his knee. "But I'm the expert. This is *my* territory." They'd been kidding each other lately about whose territory—city or country—was the fiercest. He was the city boy, she the country girl, though she was no stranger to cities, having moved back from the West Coast, San Francisco, only months ago to live with him in Boston.

On the main street, tall, arcing streetlights bent over sections of new sidewalk, too stylish and out of place for Leah. There weren't many cars or people; it was early in the season. A neat, low-roofed shopping plaza sat where Correlli's Market used to be, and the diner, which changed names almost every year, now advertised pizza on a huge, illuminated sign. At the end of Main Street, the old brick mill, perched at the edge of the dam, was now a real estate office.

Mary couldn't help but comment on these changes. Michael diligently gazed at each thing she pointed out, but remained quiet, scratched his head with both hands, combing his fingers through the thick, dark curls above his ears. When he was out of sorts, the skin below his eyes gathered in little tufts, aging him. He was only twenty-nine, one year older than she, but she could imagine how he'd look as an old man—nose a little sharper, a thickening around the neck, deeper sun-worn wrinkles at the corner of his eyes. Maybe his hair would thin at the crown. He might get a belly. None of this bothered her. There was a gentleness, a kind intelligence, she'd rarely found in others in this man. Still, she'd learned that when he ran both hands through his hair at once, he was keeping things back. Usually it was minor things, like early on, when she'd asked the age of his previous girlfriend. "Why don't you want to tell me?" she'd said, reading the gesture. It finally came out: the girlfriend had been older, fifteen years older, and as time went on (they'd dated for a year when he was twenty-seven), he'd realized that he longed for someone closer to his own age, someone who'd grown up listening to the same music, someone he could start a family with later on. He'd hurt that woman, let her down, made her feel unattractive, all for what he called small-minded reasons.

"First," Mary had said, "I think going out with an older woman shows confidence. And second, people break each other's hearts all the time for all sorts of reasons. You didn't feel right in the relationship. You did what you had to do." He'd nodded, but still, she could tell that he was conflicted.

"Everything okay?" she asked now.

"Perfect," he said. "Why?'

"No decision making tonight, all right? Just look. Enjoy."

"I'm enjoying," he said.

"Leah's a little off the beaten track, but Plymouth and especially Northlee are lively."

"I wasn't thinking about business," he said. She thought she detected a slight edge in his voice, a bit of defensiveness, something she'd noticed cropping up in his tone from time to time. As if to cover for it, he added, pleasantly, "I'm enjoying the ride."

They often avoided disagreement, as if to assure themselves that getting married had been the right thing to do. They'd been married only six months, known each other nine. At some point they'd have to stop being so careful with each other. So far, their disagreements were mostly trivial. Once they found themselves bickering over how to slice tomatoes for a salad, until they realized what they were doing and compromised—half in wedges, half in thick slices—and laughed, gasping, when she doled out the salad.

"I hope you like it," she said now.

"Of course I'll like it," he said.

"The chimney probably needs pointing up, and I wouldn't be surprised if we'll have to put on a new roof."

"Hey babe, I'm your handyman," he said, then hummed the melody from the old song "Handyman." It was a joke between them. Her mother had always told her to marry a handyman, meaning a man good with tools. A man who could fix things. Her father had been like that—the naturalist writer, as good with a chain saw as a pen. "Come-ah, come-ah, come-ah. Yeah, yeah, yeah," he sang, and she laughed when he stumbled over the lyrics, "na ad a na na busy twenty-four hours a day."

They crossed a small wooden bridge, the tires rumbling over the planks, then onto bumpy pavement on the other side. Here, the road inclined, rising above the little brook they'd crossed over several times as it zigzagged its way down the valley. As a girl, riding in the car, she would press her face to the glass, watching the banks grow steeper, the trunks of trees acting as the only guardrails.

"So, there are bear out there?" Michael asked.

"Yup," she said. "Bear and moose and coyotes. Bobcats. Once, when I was about seven years old, I rescued a fawn from a bobcat."

"I'm not surprised," he teased her.

"I only scared the bobcat off, really. I thought I heard a baby crying down in the valley and went running to save it. I was positive it was a baby; it really sounded like a kid crying *mama*. My dad heard it, too, and came after me. He knew I was in danger of running right into the middle of things."

"The bobcat's claws?"

"Yes, but it ran away, and my father crossed the brook and came back with a fawn. It was all torn up and bloody. We brought it home, fed it with a bottle, and kept it overnight until the game warden came for it. The warden was going to put it back in the wild when it was strong enough. *Mama*. It was just like that. I was so sure I was going to get a baby."

"You've always wanted a baby," he said, like a statement more than a question.

"Maybe so," she answered, amazed at how in such a brief time this man regularly made observations about her that felt suddenly, unexpectedly true. They hadn't talked very specifically about having children, only that they would eventually. But first they needed to explore their plans of where to live—the house on Cascom, year-round, or just summers?—more clearly. There was also the matter of income to consider, though she'd inherited a little, and sold her parents' small winter house in southern New Hampshire for a good sum, all of which she'd put away solely for paying the taxes on the mountain house. In the last couple of years the taxes had risen. It had gotten more difficult, especially to take care of the place from afar. It seemed a miracle she'd met Michael, who'd not only drawn her back to the East Coast but had agreed to help her take care of the house and now spend the summer, maybe longer, with her there.

"Let's get our kids a fawn," he said.

"Or a bobcat!" she suggested.

After a moment, Michael said, "You've had such a different life than I have, Ms. Country Woman. There were no bobcats in my childhood. Unless you count my father." He gave a short laugh, but there was sadness in his tone.

They'd shared a lot about their families, her parents' early deaths, but the subject of his father was a tricky one. She knew that part of why they had no wedding ceremony was to avoid his father.

"*Elope*," Michael had marveled. "A fine, old-fashioned word. Romantic."

"It sounds like something elands do," she'd said. She was glad they'd eloped. Her parents had done the same, though perhaps for more bohemian ideals.

The road turned to gravel, rocky and loose, chattering under the tires. Mary swerved around larger obstacles when she saw them in time.

"I've always wanted a garden," Michael said. "Chili peppers and cilantro. And I was thinking we could do basil, make our own pesto."

"I love pesto," she said.

When they came upon another car, its headlights blinding them, Mary slowed.

"Come *on*," she said. "Uphill has the right of way." The other car made no sign of giving room. Mary pulled over, close to the ditch, and let it pass. It zoomed by without hesitation.

Then she said, "When I was a teenager we used to borrow the truck from the lodge and drive like hell. Fifty, sixty miles an hour on these roads."

He nodded, and kept his eyes ahead. If he was nervous at her speed, he didn't say so.

There was no reason to hurry, yet Mary felt an urgency to get there, as if she were late for something that might fall apart without her. The house could wait. The mountain had always waited. She'd flown east to check on the old place several times over the last two years, shoving open the old, warping doors, vacuuming up hundreds of dead flies, patching what she was able. She'd pulled weeds, cut down poplar saplings, and mowed the fields. The wilderness was eager to swallow everything, creeping in like water, spreading over and into every possible space, reclaiming openings, filling them in. Even the granite was vulnerable—grasses and scraggly bushes dug their roots into splits and crevices, wedging the rock apart. The house was all that was left of her parents, their history, her childhood. Her dream for a long time had been to find a man, return, start a family, and re-create all that had been lost.

"What was with that guy back there?" Michael asked.

"A tourist," she said. "A road hog. Somebody staying at the AMC probably." The Appalachian Mountain Club lodge was the only other building past the turnoff for her parents' place.

"No, I mean that kid. Didn't you see him? He was up on the bank, holding a sign, I think."

"Really? I missed it."

"Kind of a desolate place to be hitchhiking."

"I didn't see him," she said.

She shifted down, using her whole body, lifting herself off the seat by the steering wheel, because she was too small for this big truck, though it had been her idea to buy it: used, dented on one side, but under 100,000 miles, and had reminded her instantly of a good-natured mutt you might find at the pound.

"He looked kind of ominous, looming there, out of the woods."

"I was busy avoiding that jackass. What did the sign say?"

"Couldn't read it."

The back end of the truck skittered sideways. Mary turned the wheel out of the skid and shifted down once more as the grade got steeper. The truck inched along, vibrating when it hit washboard.

Mary accelerated as they came to the last incline on the steep road. When she beeped the horn, Michael jumped, then laughed when she explained the blind spot and how her father had always tooted the horn here.

Now the surface leveled off, and she pulled hard, turning sharply onto the logging road that led to her parents' house. She braked, the headlights beaming on the wooden sign atop the post, and came to a stop.

"There," she said.

"'Hall,'" he read out loud.

Though she remembered the crack, severing the letters her father had chiseled and painted long ago, it hit her hard to see it again.

"That split, it's getting wider," she said.

"I could fix it." He reached across, lifted her long braid from her neck, and let his hand slide down its length. Then he rubbed the back of her neck with his thumb and fingers. "Or make a new sign."

"A new sign?" she said.

"Well, yeah," he said. "One that says Walker."

"I don't know." She was surprised at the tentativeness in her voice, and when Michael took his hand away from her, she felt a surge of guilt and worry. The sign had stood as it was, as her father had made it, for over thirty years.

She felt instantly ashamed for deflecting his offer. She knew she was possessive of this place, and bragged about her father, his books and brilliance, too much. Maybe Michael felt he could never live up to her expectations. But of course he would. He already *had*. He'd married her. They were in love.

"It's just that there's going to be a lot of work," she said. "I'm almost afraid to see it."

She let the clutch out and the truck rolled forward, rocks thumping under the tires. The swath of tall grass, the Mohawk, growing down the middle of the old road, whooshed underneath, and branches scraped the doors, flicked the windshield. The tires sank and chugged through soft mud near a bog where there was the froggy smell of stagnant water.

She slowed where the logging road ended at an outcropping of ascending ledge. Under the headlights, it was gray and full of sparkles, rolling toward them like a waterfall. Weeds grew out of cracks, and there were gravelly patches where the stone had eroded and gathered in impressions. Off to the side there was a turnaround where other cars gave up. Mary eased the truck forward.

"You're kidding," he said.

"Nope," she said, a little embarrassed by the glee in her voice. It had always been fun to show this to outsiders.

"Is this even a road?"

"Sure. It used to be, anyway. In the guidebooks they call it the original Cascom Mountain Road. Some of the older books even mention my parents' house. Call it a 'hunting lodge.'"

She took it slow onto the first low apron of granite. The truck climbed upward, rolling over humps, the tires holding on the open rock as she turned the wheel quickly back and forth, picking her way with precision, avoiding areas that jutted out and could scrape the muffler.

"Oh, geez," he said when the truck tilted far to one side.

"Hang on," she said.

At the top, the headlights streamed into nowhere, fading out in the dark, and then the truck nosed downward and they were rolling fast, descending again on the logging road that had reappeared on the other side. At the bottom of the hill Mary turned in to a grassy area and stopped. The headlights, bright and fixed, seemed to lift the house right out of the darkness. It could have been grown from the wilderness with its dark-stained boards, tight as a dense forest under the eaves. The shed roof slanted up and away toward its high peak, as if the whole structure was leaning forward, toward something—toward the dark expanse in front of the house where there was a closeness, the presence of Mount Cascom.

She turned off the ignition, and the headlights dimmed. It had been a long trip. She wasn't ready to climb out into the night. Not quite ready to feel the cool air, and hear the stillness, the near silence of the world after the reverberation of the truck all day. The engine, cooling, made a sound like a quick eruption of water drops, drumming a metal surface.

"Are you ready to go in?" Michael asked. Gently asked, having some idea what a strange and difficult thing it might be to move from the snug dome of the cab to the heavy, still air of an unlived-in house. To face the rooms of the house her parents had loved and lived in and would never walk about in again. Mary looked at the dark yard; the headlights had imprinted in her mind the image of the weeds grown up against the heavy planks of the old door, and the limbs of birches, downed from an ice storm last winter, lying like skeletons, broken and scattered in matted yellow grass.

As she lifted the handle of her door and started to get out, he took her arm, pulled her back, and held her tightly; then he let her go.

That night they spread blankets and cushions on the floor in front of the woodstove, not wanting to leave the fire, nor crawl between the freezing sheets of a bed. It was cooler inside the house than outside when they'd first pushed open the old stubborn door, and as Mary had led him from room to room, turning on switches, illuminating the dark spaces, it seemed as if the lights themselves had begun to cut the cold. Their breath and voices, the tap of shoes across wooden floors, and his expressions of awe, which had pleased her, loosened the muffled, stilled air. Musty odors that had floated up from rugs and curtains had become barely noticeable.

The light from the flames sent shadows darting up the walls and across the wide boards and heavy beams of the ceiling. Mary turned on her side to find her husband's face, his dark eyes watching her. He grinned. They were still giddy with love, with the newness of it, of marriage, and it was a wonderful feeling, though—and they'd both remarked on this—there was a long road ahead. There were "the realities," as Michael had called life's ups and downs—the disagreements, boredoms, habits—that would eventually come upon them, irk them. There would be challenges, but they would face them. They were smart, they were aware. They weren't so young as to not be prepared. They'd deal with whatever came up. They would be as honest as possible with each other.

Over his shoulder she saw the long wooden table surrounded by chairs, and for a moment pictured her mother and father sitting in their usual places. She wished they could have known him.

He pushed the blanket off her shoulder, and away.

"Want to look at you," he said.

She put her hand on his chest, urging him onto his back, and straddled him. Her shoulder away from the fire was cold, but the other burned. The flickering light turned his skin into tawny hues, and as she ran her hands through the small swirl of hair in the center of his chest, the gold band on her finger—still unfamiliar—caught her eye.

"Are we married?" she asked.

"I believe so, Mrs. Mary HallWalker," he said, running their names together as one. He bent her down, kissed her mouth, her neck. Hands on her waist, he lifted her slightly. The feel of his erection, the tip of his penis, angling for her, made her flood, ready, craving to have him inside her.

"We have to be careful," she said.

He sighed with exaggeration, teasing. "Okay. All right. Don't go anywhere."

She climbed off him as he reached for his duffel bag.

Later, Michael spooning her, she lay awake, going over all the work the house needed—possibly a new roof, or maybe just a few shingles; water-stained ceiling boards replaced, or just repainted; gutters cleaned and straightened where snow had pulled them from their hooks.

"Michael," she whispered, marveling at her ownership of this name, hers to speak into the dark, and amazed once more that his body lay against her, matched to hers. She knew he was sound asleep, but she wanted to test out the words. "Do you think you could live here, move in, for good?"

"I'm not sure," came his voice close to her ear, surprising her. He sounded groggy, as if he'd willed himself up from a deep sleep to answer her.

"It's okay," she said. "No decisions this trip."

"No decisions," he whispered back. "Enjoy."

CHAPTER 3

B Y MID-JUNE THEY'D LEFT BOSTON to try it out on Cascom for the summer. They had sublet the apartment in Somerville. Besides enjoying the peacefulness, the isolation of the mountain, the plan was to start looking for a property, somewhere more accessible, like Leah or Plymouth, to build a music studio. Maybe an old barn to convert. Mary had studied the drawings above Michael's desk in the apartment back in Somerville. His longtime dream was to set up a studio with state-of-the-art acoustics—kind of a retreat with living quarters for top-notch clients, or rich ones, who could afford to put a lot of time and work into their projects. He'd feed, house, and record them all for a flat fee. Michael had the credentials to attract the best; he'd earned a good reputation in Boston as an excellent engineer and musician. Though he wouldn't discriminate where making ends meet was a priority. All he needed was startup money (he could sell his portion of the studio he shared with his friends Paul and Lisie in Boston), and a place to do it. In the afternoons they'd been taking road trips, scouting out the nearby towns, seeing what was out there, dreaming. Michael hinted more than once that Mary would make a fine assistant in the studio. She could sing harmony, learn the sound board. Help him out with the business. In their spare time she could write songs, record them, because he believed this was her calling. She'd grown up singing, playing the guitar, and writing songs. Her parents had urged her toward the sciences and journalism, following in her father's footsteps. They'd viewed her interest in music as a hobby, not a serious career.

In California, after college, she'd lived with a folk singer for four years. From their tiny apartment in the Haight, she and Joe traveled up and down the West Coast, and later to gigs across the country from Colorado to New York City. She helped lug instruments and equipment, feeling invisible. Joe started to get a name for himself, and though she sang harmony with him occasionally, he was the star. When it came to making records, he asked other singers, more famous ones, to record the harmonies. He wrote all his own songs, so never took an interest in appropriating lyrics or melodies she wrote. Writing songs and singing was her first passion, but next to Joe's talent, the idea had started to feel absurd. He was good. Very good. Eventually, he went on the road alone, stayed away longer and longer. She suspected he'd slept with other women, and later he admitted to it. It had been a long, painful, and somewhat humiliating retreat from that relationship. After they broke up, she'd pieced together a living, teaching English as a second language at community colleges in the Bay Area, waitressing, and occasionally singing in coffee houses and bars. But whenever she considered taking it up professionally, she felt inadequate, defeated.

Now with Michael, the idea of working with him, making music again, became more and more appealing. The return of a dream. Maybe she was supposed to sing and write songs, after all.

It seemed magical that they'd first met at a folk festival on the East Coast. They'd spent the weekend together. When she was back in San Francisco, they e-mailed each other two or more times a day. He wrote funny stories, mostly about his friends Paul and Lisie dealing with musicians—they took no crap. Or the landlord who never fixed anything, but the rent was so cheap Michael didn't want to complain. There was the opera singer next door who drove him crazy, practicing scales at all hours. *Why aren't you the one singing to me?* Sometimes Mary would scroll to the bottom of his notes first, eager to see how he'd sign off. *I lose my breath thinking of you.*

Michael had made the first trip, flying to San Francisco for a long weekend. And then she made the second trip to Somerville and stayed a week. Then she came again to Somerville, and then he again to San Francisco. In all there were four visits before she was sending her belongings on a truck, and flying east in September to move in with him.

"It just makes sense," Michael had said to her. "I want to wake up with you every day. I don't want to go on like this for a year, or however long, and you want to leave California anyway."

"It's so fast, though," she pointed out. "We've known each other for, like, four minutes."

He laughed. They were standing in Golden Gate Park next to the buffalo paddock. The buffalo were bunched together near their shelter with their heavy heads and thick bedraggled coats. They didn't look happy, they looked forlorn and out of place. Longing to go home.

It did make sense, and it didn't, but life was roaring along and the steady, measured, well-thought out decisions she'd always made seemed relentless, and in truth rather useless, when she examined how lonely her life had become. Until Michael. He'd grinned and looped his arms around her, pulled her in.

Now, to have come home, to have married Michael, to live in the house on the mountain she adored. She'd done it! They were here.

CHAPTER 4

W<small>E'RE HERE, MARY THOUGHT</small>. It was June, spring, and she stood in the field looking up at the mountain, the early morning sun setting the glass in the distant fire tower ablaze. Back up the hill, sitting on the front deck of the house with a mug of coffee in his hand, Michael waited for her.

She turned and started up the hill toward the house. Michael raised his coffee mug as if to toast her, or the morning, because the sky was clear, and it was a good day for a hike.

She smiled and came up, eyes on him, noting the bandanna tied around his forehead, holding his floppy black hair away from his face. She noted the blue canvas shorts and unbuttoned blue and green plaid shirt, the white T-shirt underneath; the scrunched white socks and low hiking boots, and the way his feet were placed on the deck, knees apart, relaxed. The fine dark hair covering his legs. His grin, as he took a sip of coffee and smiled again. The smudge of dirt across his cheek because he'd been working in the garden all morning. He planted five different kinds of lettuce, and would have gone on to plant carrots, arugula, and the pink, orange, and red zinnias that she'd requested because she loved a garden with color.

He would have gone on setting onions and peppers and dill. Would have continued to slide a two-by-four through the soil, cutting even rows, sifting seeds through his fingers. He would have spent the whole day in the garden, if only she hadn't suggested that with good weather they chuck all the work and climb the mountain.

"If you make the lunch, I'll carry the pack," he said.

"You have a deal," she said as she passed by.

To get to the trail, they walked the road to Cascom Mountain Lodge. As they came through the parking lot, Mary felt excited and anxious. Here was the lodge where she'd worked so long ago as a teenager. In a way, she felt as if she was introducing Michael to a family member. But it was just an old building in need of new clapboards. There were lots of cars in the parking lot, day hikers or guests staying the weekend. As Mary pointed toward the red-roofed Lo-House across the way, where she had lived when she was on crew, a teenage girl emerged from the side door. The girl was slender and had long blond hair that she gathered into a ponytail, shaking her head back, securing it with an elastic pulled from around her wrist. She wore jeans and a knee-length sweatshirt, obviously one of the young crew members. As she started across the lawn toward the lodge another girl, a redhead, came from Lo-House.

"Callie, wait up," the redhead called, then skipped toward the blond girl, swinging her arm around the girl's shoulder. The blond, Callie, laughed, and they skipped together. Two girls, both glowing with youth, beauty, solidarity. Mary was impressed. In her day, she'd been the only girl.

Deep in the woods, the trail grew steeper and she followed Michael, letting him set the pace. She could have run; she was electric with energy. She used to sprint up this trail. Instead, she went along behind, step by measured step, entertaining him the whole way with her history: how she climbed the mountain when she was only two years old, in baby shoes! (Though, okay, from the other side, and on an easy trail. But still, her father said he never had to carry her.) How, as a teenager, when she worked at the lodge, she made out with the crew boss on the roof of Lo-House. How there was a dead boy, and the albino girl.

In the Cathedral Forest, where few remaining giant spruce towered above them, the air was cool and felt good against their sweaty skin. Breathing deeply from the climb, they paused on the trail and peered into the forest: eerie to imagine getting tangled in there. Blowdowns, piled and crisscrossing each other, made the spaces between the trees so dense and dark that no one, not even animals, could pass except on the narrow trail. Mary thought of the crew boss so long ago, and how determined he'd been to search here for the missing girl, though even he hadn't gotten very far from the trail, trying to cut a path through the brush. *Ghost girl*, they'd called her, and the name stuck; even new generations of crew used the term, though the truth of its origin—a real girl named Anna Kimball—had been lost.

At the top of a wooded rise they paused for the earliest glimpse of the summit, still far off, more squashed seeming from this angle, dazzling against the sky. The trail opened out into bright sunlight, the huge dome of bare granite rising before them.

"There was a fire," she told him. "In the 1800s. The wind swept the flames up into a giant tornado, burned everything off. That's why the summit is as clear as it is. They call it Old Baldy sometimes, which I think sounds mean."

"Where's the fire tower?" he asked, looking up the slope. His neck glistened with sweat, T-shirt collar soaked.

"Too steep to see it from here," she said. "We still have a ways."

"Will we be able to go up into it?"

"If the fire watchman is there. If he's in the mood for company. But I don't know him. He's new."

Soon they left the trail and followed the secret path toward the lookout spot. *Secret* because it wasn't marked, though people who knew Cascom knew it well, and actually, Mary observed, it was a pretty well-worn path at this point. True, the weather-beaten spruce had given way to years of suffering, their branches forced aside, pressed back. Mary led them through the opening as if through a door. Beyond the trees, a narrow swath of granite parted the low blueberry bushes, guiding them toward the sweeping ledge above the cliffs.

The valley rolled out below, rising and falling over ridges mottled with various tones of green. There was the light green patch, the lawn in front of her parents' house. Her house. Mary and Michael's. *Their* house. Far beyond the valley was Cascom Lake, a giant puzzle piece of gray-green. Beyond that, the hazy edge of the world.

"This is an amazing view," Michael said, and she felt as proud and happy as if she'd created it herself.

She stooped to pluck some red bunchberries, something else to show him. Berries that were basically tasteless, but edible and juicy. Michael went ahead, forward, toward the edge. A breeze moved across the ledges, a low hum through branches, cooling her forehead, neck.

"Water?" Michael asked.

She glanced up in time to see him shrug the pack off his shoulders, swing it around, and begin to undo the buckles to get at the water bottle. He was very close to the edge. Somehow the strap slipped from his grasp. He did a sort of corkscrew on one heel, the other knee up, batting the pack like a soccer ball. It responded, rose, but then it went off, to the side, away. He reached for it. "Oh."

CHAPTER 5

MARY SCRAMBLED ACROSS the steep ledge, then plunged through a wall of scrub. The trail appeared for a few paces, but she veered off it, and headed for what she thought would be the base of the cliff. She came out on a narrow shelf of dirt and sparse blueberry bushes; this shelf thinned into nothing, and there was no way down from it. A snarl of junipers and low weather-beaten pines grew below. The stunted growth was thick, impossible to see through. She called his name. He didn't answer.

Out in the valley there was the tiny cut in the land, which was the field in front of her parents' house. She drew a line from there to herself, then up the slope to the ledges behind her. The rock seemed to lean toward her, a wall of gray granite laced with cracks. She was sure she was standing directly below the spot from which he'd fallen. But she couldn't find him. She couldn't see where he'd landed.

Noises came from her throat, whimpers, and when she realized she was making sounds, she turned them into his name. "Michael." *No, please, God.* "Michael Michael. Michael." She backtracked, and then her feet went out from under her and she slid a couple of yards on her side down an outcropping of sheer granite so steep it put her on her feet at the bottom, and she didn't stop moving. She yelled his name and ran with her hands out, pushing branches from her face. The woods opened, and she came out on a large expanse of easy sloping rock that descended into a crevasse filled with scraggly dwarf juniper. She looked up again, up toward the mountain to the cliff, and up into the sky above to see where he'd come from, where he'd come down. She saw how far it was, the span from up there to where she stood. All this time there had been her voice calling his name, and then it changed when she saw that distance. His name was in her mouth, but now it was a different sound, like a howl.

She looked up to the cliff, then down to her feet. Where was he? It was as if he'd flown away. He'd never landed at all. This was where he should be. It was here, only here, this open tract, with dirt and blueberries and all things peaceful and fine and good. The sun glinting in flecks of mica.

She started to run uphill; she had to see from the top again. To see what she'd missed, to discover some other place he'd rolled, or landed, and come to rest. Or perhaps he was on his feet, and only bruised, and he was climbing now, at this very moment, back to the top. He'd be sitting on the ledge, waiting for her, the blue pack, the one he'd reached for, the one he'd fallen after, right next to him.

"Please God, no," she said. *Don't let this be happening.*

She zigzagged across the slope, going up, calling his name again. The cliff towered over her, and the sky above seemed unnatural—white, almost, making the jagged edge black against the sky. She got up close to the wall; it was cool and smelled of dank water and moss. She inched along, keeping a hand on it, then suddenly came out on the trail that they'd climbed together only a short time before.

She took the trail. Her muscles felt nothing of the incline. She ran up and then off the trail, crossing once again under the ledge, onto the narrow shelf, still yelling his name. She had to look again. Nothing there. She went a little farther to the end where the shelf seemed to disappear and saw that there was a way down. She slid on her butt, jamming her heels into the clefts of tumbled-down boulders, until she came to a shallow drop-off—the rock protruding in an overhang above brambles. She sat down, dangled her feet, and shoved off. Branches snapped under her weight, and she hit the ground, landing hard in a crouched position.

Beneath the underbrush there was the pack. Blue. Open at the top. It sat upright, as if someone had placed it there. It hadn't been damaged by the fall, but she didn't touch it. She could hear her own breathing. She was no longer calling his name. She just stared at the pack. Then she stood up, too fast, with a head rush. Everything went white, and she thought she was going to faint. She put her hand on a boulder. Her fingers dipped into a crevice; it was wet. She thought it would be water, but her fingertips held blood. Bright red, oily blood. And then she saw red spatters on leaves and looked hard into the bushes a few feet below on another tier of land, and then she saw blue and green plaid cloth, his shirt, and then flesh, his leg. She threw herself toward him. A tangle of branches caught her at the waist, lifted her off her feet, and dumped her on the ground. Then she was with him, next to him.

He lay on his back, eyes closed. One arm crossed his chest. The other arm lay above his head and was crooked in such a way that she knew it was broken.

She put her fingertips on his neck to find a pulse, but she was shaking so hard she couldn't feel anything. She slid her hand under his neck. She didn't dare move him, afraid his back was broken, or his neck. Warm liquid spread over her hand; she didn't look. With her other hand she used her fingers to pry his mouth open, and she put her mouth on his, breathed out; his lungs inflated. She tasted blood. She could barely breathe herself. She pressed his chest with the heels of her hands, pushed hard, not worried any more about broken bones, or breaking any. He could take it. She pumped his chest, then put her mouth on his again, forced air into his lungs. She turned her ear to his mouth, heard nothing, felt nothing. Smears of blood stained his T-shirt where her hands had worked. *This was just a little hike, a day hike.* She leaned the heels of her hands on his chest again, pushed. It seemed impossible that his arm, which could snag her as she walked across a room and draw her close, was angled above his head like this.

She didn't want to leave him, but she had to. If she could get help, then maybe they'd revive him, take him down, helicopter him out. She took off her sweatshirt and put it under his head.

"I'll get help," she said.

She ran, careful to look ahead at each spot where her feet would land, finding her way over rubble. The trail was steep, and now, a half mile down, she was deep in the valley, under the towering hardwoods. She left the trail on a shortcut—the old ski trail. It was grown over and full of bushes and saplings. The sound of the brook grew louder, and she knew she was about a mile from the road, from the lodge. Then she saw someone.

He was far off, heading up the slope under a grove of tall white pine. She stopped running and stood still. She watched him move up the hill. He had no pack. He was dark-haired, and wore a plaid shirt, and for a strange moment, she thought it was Michael and he'd awakened, found himself lost, alone, but it wasn't him; he couldn't have made it here from where she'd left him. The figure turned slightly, heading diagonally away from her; he didn't see her. He didn't see her at all. From the glimpse of his face she could tell that he was young. She could not make herself call out; to say anything at all was to confirm things she wasn't ready for. And also, he was just a boy and far away, and getting farther away. What could he do, anyway?

She turned and started to run down the hill again, then stopped. Michael was alive, and she should go back. Yes, she'd made a mistake, and he was probably just now waking up, and he'd be cold and worried. She hurried back to the trail. He'd be sitting up when she got there. He'd be holding her sweatshirt to the back of his head where there was a bump and the cut. She remembered how cuts in the head always bleed a lot, so there's more blood than you think there should be, even when it's not that bad. He'd look dazed. Then she pictured his arm, his crooked arm and how bent it was, and knew he couldn't be sitting up. She stopped, turned around, and ran back down the hill, down the mountain, and on, across the brook to the old logging road and finally into the parking lot in front of the lodge.

There were people in the front yard, lounging on lawn chairs. She heard her own voice, yelling. The people got to their feet. They started coming toward her. She'd made the connection, and now she lost her legs, collapsed in the middle of the gravel parking lot. Hands touched her shoulder. She pushed a bottle of water away from her mouth so she could speak. So she could tell them where he was. So they would hurry because he was still alive. He was alive.

Even after the EMTs arrived at the lodge and looked her over and put bandages on her abrasions, she hoped. Hoped that the rescue team—the EMTs, and the young people who worked as crew at the lodge, and the guests who joined in, and all those people with knowledge and medicine—would go up there, find he was alive, breathing. Fix him. Revive him. A miracle. She prayed. She asked one of the young crew, the redheaded girl, if it was possible. The girl took her hands. The girl said anything was possible, but the girl's eyes told her that it was not possible. Still she hoped. She wouldn't let the girl phone anyone.

She hoped until they brought him down. They carried him on a litter. Silently. Reserved. It was dark when they came. They carried him from the woods. Three young men and the blond girl, her free arm lifted like a wing to keep her balance, helped to bear him. They looked like they were carrying a boat.

They set the litter down behind the ambulance. Guests, staying at the lodge, looked on from the lawn. There were children too, and adults keeping them back. She heard voices say, "That's her." And, "It's her husband."

They'd covered him in a gray plastic blanket and tied him to the litter. His face was serene; he could have been sleeping. It was Michael's face, her face, the one that belonged to her. His dark curls, shiny as iron, a little gray in them. Salt, a little salt. Thirty gray hairs, she'd told him once after pretending to count. There was a matted area, greasy and dark. Blood. She felt sick. The redheaded girl put her hand on her shoulder, steadied her.

One of the young men who'd helped carry the litter came to her. He wore a uniform, and she guessed him to be a forest ranger.

"Ben," he said, introducing himself. "I work in the fire tower."

His words sounded underwater. He had the lilt of a New England accent. Her eyes couldn't leave Michael's face, the curves at the corners of his gentle, frozen mouth.

"I'm so sorry, Mrs. Walker," he said. "There was nothing you could do. Nothing any of us could do."

She tore her eyes away, looked hard until she registered the forest green uniform with yellow and red insignia patches on the breast pocket. A white T-shirt showing at the collar underneath. He touched his chin, pulled on it. In one earlobe there was a small gold hoop earring. His mouth, bowed, childlike, opened, closed, opened again.

He said, "He hit his head. I mean, it was quick. He probably didn't experience any pain."

It was the wrong thing to say. It was as absurd as the fall, the reaching for a blue backpack that took him out of sight, out of his *life*, *their* life. Just a day pack, because this was an easy climb. Just a little jaunt up the mountain. They'd taken only one bottle of water. Two apples, two ham sandwiches, a candy bar to split. When they stopped for water, she gave his butt a squeeze, and he said, "Hey!" then grabbed her by both arms and pulled her to his chest, into his damp T-shirt. His skin was cool, and he bit her lip, then more, so she'd press her mouth closer, and she did. As close as she could.

That anyone could think there was no pain involved in Michael's death was wrong. It was not true. She'd seen his face, just the side of it when he realized that he'd lost his balance, that gravity had hold. There was knowledge that he'd lost already and was going over, and that it would hurt, whether he actually felt any of it or not. The pack had slipped somehow. It slipped from his fingers, and he grabbed for it. She reached for him, but she was several yards away, so grabbed nothing. His body twisted, corkscrewed on one foot, and went over. He cried out. He knew what was happening. He knew. There was pain. The fire watchman cowered, and she realized she was glaring at him.

The EMTs lifted the litter, slid it into the ambulance. She didn't know what to do.

"Mrs. Walker," the redheaded girl said. There was that name. A joke really; it was his mother's name. Not hers. But it was her. At this moment it was her. "Can I call someone for you?" the girl asked.

There were Michael's parents, but she wasn't ready. They were on the Cape, far away. Safe. Safe from this for now. She shook her head.

They told her she was to go with the ambulance, but first she was led away from the parking lot and the people. She was led back across the lawn, between the lawn chairs. There was the redheaded girl on one side, and the blond girl—the one who'd helped carry Michael—on her other side. The blond girl smelled like suntan lotion and put her hand around Mary's arm. There was authority in the girl's fingers; she was strong, and Mary thought the girl was much like herself when she was a girl and worked at the lodge too. In the girl's eyes she saw something, a brightness, a confidence, that trained-in detachment. Then the girl's eyes filled and her mouth trembled. Mary felt sorry that the girl had had to see someone dead. *Michael* dead? This wasn't real. She could wake up at any moment in their bed and sigh and breathe relief. Just a horrible nightmare. He'd reach his arm out, draw her in.

They came around to the side of the lodge, and just as they were going to turn to walk up the steps into the kitchen, she had the inclination to look toward Lo-House. It was lit by the outside lights. Her eyes were drawn to its red-shingled roof. There was someone sitting on the peak of the roof. He was looking at her. There was something familiar about him. The boy she'd seen in the woods.

"Who's that?" she asked.

"Who?" the girls said, looking.

"Just Tobin," the redheaded girl said. "Tobin Gough." The name gave Mary a quick flutter of recognition. The redheaded girl held the screen door open, and they urged her to go inside.

The kitchen had been enlarged. She hardly recognized it with its new gleaming ovens, many dangling pots and pans, and a long butcher table. There was a microwave on the counter. The night's dishes were piled high next to the sinks, stacks of unwashed white dinner plates and bowls. She remembered the routine of scrape and stack, then rinse. There was a bucket overflowing with scraps. Saved for the farm across the valley.

"You still have a pig bucket," she said. "Is it?" She was unsure if she remembered right; the name of it—*pig bucket*—had come back to her from such a distance.

The girls looked at her.

"I used to work here," she told them. "A long time ago."

"I'm so sorry about your husband," the redheaded girl said, as if she couldn't let Mary wander too far away from it.

Out the window she saw the roof of Lo-House. The peak was empty now, and another surge of loss came through her. The redheaded girl handed her a cup of tea. Mary was shaking and couldn't hold the cup. The girl took it back and put it on the table, then she laid her hand on Mary's shoulder.

"I wonder if I've seen your name," the blond girl said after a moment. "On the old crew signs upstairs."

"*Callie*," the other girl said, as if scolding the blond girl for bringing up something trivial.

The girl's lips tightened into a frown of embarrassment. "I just wondered what year," she said.

Mary tried to remember, but nothing was coming to her. Her mind wasn't working; it was as if she were gazing across a vast field of gray wheat under a white sky—nothing. *Michael? This can't be true. Let me wake up.*

"I've been looking them over," the girl said. "For ideas." She stooped slightly as if to catch Mary's eyes with her own, to hold Mary from drifting, to keep her focused. The girl's eyes were gray, smoky.

"Callie's in charge of painting our sign this year," the redheaded girl explained.

Mary remembered the signs. They were hung along the walls between the guests' rooms. Each wooden plaque was a document of the year, the name of each crew member, and where he or she was from. She remembered the sign from her year—elaborately painted with trees growing up the sides, framing their names.

Boughs wove between the words, and yellow and green leaves overlapped and sprouted through letters.

"It's the one with the birches," Mary said. The girls nodded in recognition.

The girls looked at her with expressions of interest and worry and pity. The kitchen came into focus behind them, then the dark sky out the window, and then all that had happened. They let her cry.

The EMTs came around, ready for her. "Who can we call?" they asked.

She couldn't answer. Any movement toward action was another loss of hope. She wanted to wake up and start the day again, lying next to Michael. She wanted to watch the sky grow light out the window once more as the sun came up, moving shadows farther and farther down the mountain until the whole ridge, all that exposed granite, was bright and ready for them.

CHAPTER 6

T HEY WERE SAD ABOUT THE MAN, and especially sad for the woman, Mary Walker, but after the ambulance and everyone was gone, they joked and cleaned up the dishes and set the tables for tomorrow's breakfast and decided it was a good night for a swim. They hiked down the hill to the pond. Callie couldn't wait to dive into the water. She wanted to get under and swim as far as she could without breathing.

As crew, they worked hard, mowing the fields next to the lodge, shoveling lime into the outhouses, digging drainage ditches, and cleaning rooms in the lodge. They served breakfast and dinner, and cleared trails on Mount Cascom. Sometimes they led hikes, doled out moleskin for blisters. The man, Michael Walker, was their first dead person. Tonight Lewis the cook had stood at the kitchen door, pulled on his goateed chin, and stammered out a few words about staying open with feelings, and that he and his wife Barb were available if anyone wanted to talk.

They were sad, but they didn't want to talk about it. Callie dove in and swam out to the middle of the pond. Marlee, Rabbit, and some teenage boys staying at the lodge for the weekend splashed to the float and began a game of King of the Raft. Callie kept treading water from a distance. The game could be rough. Marlee enjoyed the fight, but Callie didn't like being touched by so many hands. Marlee was eighteen, two years older than Callie. She had fiery orange-yellow hair and her eyes were the bluest of any Callie had ever seen. When Callie first met her, she found it difficult to look at Marlee without blinking.

In the darkness she could only see the silhouettes of bodies as they stood or flew from the raft. They weren't supposed to disturb the guests up at the lodge, and sound carried across the water. Still, there was a lot of splashing and an occasional squeal followed by a chorus of *shh*'s.

Callie floated on her back. She liked the weightlessness, and the rumbling underwater sound in her ears. It made her feel removed from the world, in a dream, womblike, where her thoughts felt close and safe inside her head. The air was full of sweet smells, honeysuckle and cut grass. For a second she let herself think about Mary Walker, but it was hard to imagine what the woman could be feeling. She thought of Mary Walker's husband, who was alive only nine, maybe ten, hours ago, and how strange it was to think of that short gap of time between being alive, and then not, and how that gap was growing wider every minute. She'd seen him alive. She'd noticed the couple as they'd passed through the parking lot on their way up the mountain. She remembered how they leaned against each other, the woman's shoulder to his arm because she was shorter. How the woman had hold of his arm, smiling, talking to him, and how he listened, then stopped her, wet his thumb on his tongue, and smudged something off her cheek. That seemed like it was ages ago. Tonight, the woman was completely changed from then; her face was drained, gray. Any brightness in her eyes had flattened and dimmed. She moved with hesitation, staggered, like someone knocked nearly unconscious and trying to shake it off.

Callie had helped carry the body down. It was strange—a dead man's body, useless. She'd felt woozy at times, trying to keep her stomach calm by thinking of other things: her mom's long pigtails and the crooked part down the back of her head; her dad in his black-and-white sweater from Peru with the leather patches on the elbows. Little Evangeline, rosy-cheeked and giggling hysterically over any funny face you made. Cyndi's toenails clicking on the hardwood floors as she trotted into Callie's bedroom at home, white-tipped tail waving side to side like a metronome. But the man was dead. There was blood in his hair. At one point they'd stopped to rest, setting the litter down, stretching their arms. The boys, Rabbit and Spencer, continued their patter about silly, unimportant things—a way to keep them from the truth of what they were really carrying—until Ben the fire watchman had caught up with them and everyone got quiet because he was solemn and seemed distant.

Now she kicked her feet up and let herself hang in the water until her legs drifted deeper and only her face was above the surface. When she scissored her legs again and swept her arms out, her hand brushed against something. She struggled to right herself, swallowing a mouthful of water.

"It's just me," came the voice of the crew boss. "Spencer."

"You scared me," she said, spinning herself around. "Don't do that. God."

"Sorry," he said. He slid in front of her and dipped his chin and mouth under the water, his face hazy in the dark.

She was in a cold pocket, but surges of warmer water came against her legs as he pedaled, making currents below.

"I didn't know you'd come in," she said.

It was unusual for Spencer to join them. He really wasn't that much older, he just seemed older because he was the crew boss and because his wispy blond hair was thinning on top.

Spencer was the first crew member she'd met on the day she

arrived at the lodge. He'd shown her to Lo-House, where she would live. There was something about him, about his masculinity, that made her feel shy, awkward. He had a friendly smile and was good-looking, though his eyes were a little close together, making his nose seem even longer. But there was a confidence about him—the way he carried off his big nose made him more attractive in a way. When he told her he was going to Harvard, she could tell he was impressed with himself. Spencer lived in the main lodge—the crew boss always had a private room in the main lodge. She didn't know much else about him. She'd never really talked to him about anything except what work had to be done around the lodge. She knew he had a girlfriend in Cambridge. He was always getting calls from her and sometimes the cooks teased him, calling her "the fiancée," even though he wasn't engaged.

"Gorgeous night," he said now. "I mean the moon." They both looked up at the bright moon. "It's been kind of rough, otherwise," he said. From the raft, Marlee squealed and the others hushed her. "How are you taking it?"

"I'm okay," she said. "Just sad for that lady, is all."

Spencer rolled over and floated on his back. Callie's arms were growing tired from treading water, so she decided to swim in. When she snapped her legs and fanned her arms out in a breast stroke, her fingertips accidentally touched and brushed down the length of Spencer's side.

"Oh," he said in a pained way.

When she came to shallow water he was right there, reaching for her arm as she got to her feet, and then pulled her into him. His skin was warm; it felt almost hot in contrast to the cool air, but her knees began to shake. She was afraid the others would look across the water and see them.

"You're cold," he said. His lips moved above her ear. Then he let her go, reached for a towel, and swung it around her shoulders, drawing her against his body once more. "I've wanted to do this for a long time," he said.

"I'm freezing," she said.

He ran his hands over the towel, up and down her arms, trying to warm her up. "I just can't stop thinking about you," he said.

"You can't?" she said. Her teeth chattered.

He hugged her closer. She felt his penis pushing against her. "No," he said. "I can't."

They heard the others splashing, swimming in. Spencer let her go; she slipped out of his towel and moved quickly across the sand to where her own towel was.

Tobin was sitting there on a log. He was scraping the sand between his feet with a stick.

"Hey, Tobin," she said, reaching for her towel, wondering if he'd witnessed her with Spencer. She tried to sound nonchalant, but her voice was breathy. "How come you don't swim with us?" she asked. "If you want," she added, not meaning it to sound like it was a kind of criticism. He was sort of an odd duck. He didn't work at the lodge, just came with his father in a truck to get scraps for their pigs, and sometimes hung around, watching everyone like he wanted to be friends but couldn't figure out how to join in. He was nice enough, just awkward. His dark, thick hair was always half in his face.

"That man," Tobin said. "He was dead?"

"He was," she answered, remembering that Tobin had been there, watching from the roof of Lo-House. "It's so sad."

Marlee was by her side in the next moment, hopping around in the dark, drying herself off, searching for her flip-flops.

"Colder than hell," Marlee said. "I'll bet ghost girl is out tonight."

Callie shivered. The ghost girl was a creepy story, and true, everyone said.

Tobin got up and moved toward the path, back to the main road.

"Are you walking home?" Callie asked. "Don't you want a flashlight or something?"

"No thanks," he said. "I can see in the dark all right."

"What, are you a bat?" Marlee said.

"Bats are blind," Callie said. "They have radar."

"It's called echolocation," Tobin said, and perhaps embarrassed, added, "Actually, I mean. It's like sonar."

"Just a joke," Marlee said. "No need for a lecture, Mr. Brain." Then, perhaps realizing her tone, and because she wasn't an unkind person, and a lot of awful things had happened that day, she added, "Get home safe."

As Marlee and Callie got ready for bed, Marlee was quiet where usually she'd be analyzing everything, going over the day, discussing every detail about the dead man and Mary Walker. Callie couldn't stop thinking about being on the beach with Spencer. She had flutters. Her skin felt tight and clean. She combed her hair out, flipping it up and down, trying to dry it. Marlee sat on Callie's bunk, staring at her.

"Spencer's got it bad for you," she said. "I've seen it coming for a long time."

"You think?" Callie wondered if Marlee had seen them on the beach.

"Do you like him?" Marlee asked.

Callie thought she did, suddenly. "Yes."

That night Callie waited for everyone to fall asleep, although she thought she saw Marlee raise her head as she went out of the room. Callie was surprised at herself, taking the initiative. But it seemed she couldn't stop herself even if she tried. Also, she had this other feeling, an urgency, that it was now or never.

She crossed the field barefoot and in her long T-shirt, feeling the damp grass between her toes. Spencer's windows at the back of the lodge were dark. She wondered if he was asleep. It didn't matter; she knew he wouldn't turn her away. She knew that if she knocked on his door and went inside, she'd be taking a big step forward in her life, a transformation. She stopped for a moment, looked up at the stars. I'm here now, she thought, as I am. In a little while I will be changed, though no one will know. It will be an invisible change. For a second, she wavered, thought to turn back. But no. It was time.

She stood on the cool granite step, tapped on the old wooden door, and waited. In a moment she heard footfalls coming across the room inside. An outside light went on above her, and then the door opened.

"Hey," she said. She couldn't see his face inside the dark room at first, but his hair, curly around the back of his head, looked almost as white as his T-shirt. He leaned into the edge of the door, sighed, and stood still. For a second she wondered what was wrong, then he took her wrist, tugged her inside, and led her across the room. When he switched on the light, she saw how her feet had left footprints and pieces of wet grass across the pine floor. On a table there was a blue knapsack. She recognized it as the one they'd brought down with the dead man, and she wondered why Spencer had it here. Neither of them spoke, and then his mouth was on hers, kissing her, while his hands inched her T-shirt up and over her head, and tugged her underwear down until she stepped out of them. He stood back, his hands on her shoulders as if to hold her in place, and looked at her. She didn't like being naked alone, so she moved toward him and pulled at the waist of his undershorts.

Later that night she crawled out from under Spencer's arm and tiptoed across the room. She found her T-shirt and underwear, pulled them on. The door creaked, but he didn't wake, and she latched it softly behind her. Then she ran. When she got to the middle of the lawn between the lodge and Lo-House, she stopped and looked up at the brilliant eye of the moon. The breeze lifted her hair and came up under her T-shirt, filling it for a moment. She was sixteen and no longer a virgin. A man wanted her, maybe was even in love with her. But she wasn't with him. She twirled around, letting her arms swing out. She twirled until the dark woods, and the moon, and Lo-House and the lodge were going faster than she was. She was filled with a mysterious power, with magic. She turned until she couldn't stand up and collapsed in the wet grass, shut her eyes, and spun in the darkness of her head. Then she remembered the dead man they'd carried down the mountain, and she rolled onto her hands and knees and saw the black woods out there at the edges of the field. She shuddered, suddenly afraid. She imagined the ghost girl darting out of the woods, white hair flying, coming after her. She leapt up and ran toward Lo-House. She ran with a chill at her back, knowing she'd given all the demons in the world the right to chase her down the minute she'd dared to mock love.

CHAPTER 7

WHEN HE DISCOVERED her in the field, she was lying on her side, facing away from him. He was at a distance, but he could tell she wasn't dead because her arm moved. Still, the sight of her on the ground made his stomach clench. She wore a pinkish colored dress and he couldn't see her face, so it made him think of the painting of his mother that hung over the mantel in his father's house. In the painting his mother lay in a field, posed for his father, in an imitation of Wyeth's *Christina's World*. In his father's painting, his mother's dark hair hung down her back almost to the ground. Her dress was the color of bleached lobster shell. He didn't like to look at the painting, because sometimes it seemed as if her shoulder was canted more than others, as if she were slowly turning, and soon he might find her frightening eyes glaring at him.

Mary Walker was nothing like his mother, and she wasn't old like Wyeth's Christina with her clawed hand and thin crippled arm.

She didn't move as he approached her. The grass was flattened like a nest around her. She looked like a stunned bird, like one that had flown into a window, fooled by reflection. One arm was folded across her chest, and the other stretched out in front of her. There were red welts, probably insect bites, on her arms. He wondered how long she'd been in the field, and why she'd returned to the mountain. It was just three days ago when her husband fell. The morning heat, muggy and hazy, lay over the land, muting the world.

The sun was rising, and the tall yellow grass glistened. Sweat trickled down his side. Her hair was dark and short, and some of it stuck straight up from the top of her head. Her hair had been long before. There were scratches and nicks on her legs. A bloodstain, the size of a palm, bloomed through the material of her dress near her hip. It scared him. Her eyes were closed. He knelt next to her, touched her shoulder.

"Michael?" she said.

"No," he said. He knew it was her husband's name. Maybe she was dreaming.

She rolled onto her back. Her eyes were green, not looking at him. The buttons at the neck of her dress were open, and he saw the ridge of her collarbone and the place where the skin dropped into a pocket—the curve where her breasts began, whiter skin.

"Are you hurt?" he asked. "There's blood."

She raised herself a little, swept her hand over her hip.

"I walked into a branch," she said. "Or maybe it was the sideboard." She shut her eyes and let out a short burst of air, a quick sob.

"You should get up," he said, and put his hand around her upper arm to help her, felt the bone right through her flesh.

She turned her eyes on him, full of water, green. "You're the Gough boy."

He looked away. The buttons on her dress were tiny and thin, like shavings from the inside of a shell. She called him a boy and he thought to correct her. He was fifteen, almost sixteen, and already through high school, having been put ahead.

"I saw you," she said.

He felt a wash of anxiety. *Where? What did she see?*

Then she said, "You were up on Lo-House. On the roof," and he knew she meant the other night when they brought her husband down. She'd looked right at him, suddenly, almost as if he'd called out to her. But he hadn't made a sound.

"Please," he said. "I think you should come with me. I can carry you." She was small, like a girl, but he wasn't sure if he could lift her; he'd never carried anyone. And then there was his leg, and the pain that sat ready—a greedy, low-grade throb, hip to thigh. His father had once carried his mother out of the woods. It was a long time ago. There was snow, and his mother had been naked.

"I remember you," she said. "When you were little."

He just wanted her to get up. He took her hands and drew them together. Her wrists were thin. He pulled her into a sitting position, got her to her feet, and lifted one of her arms over his shoulder. She was light. A breeze trailed over the grass, making it ripple like waves. She'd chosen the center of the field. The trees on the other side, where the road went on up the valley, were a long way off.

"Can you walk?"

She took a step. She was missing a shoe.

"Do you remember me?" she asked. "I stayed with you once when you were little."

Of course he remembered. But he wasn't sure he wanted her to remember.

"You played the piano," she said.

"You've lost a shoe," he said.

She made no acknowledgment, but leaned against him, not putting as much weight on her bare foot as they walked. Her wrist, where he held it over his shoulder, was lean and flat, like holding a strap. He glanced at her face. Tears came from her eyes and made streaks in the dirt on her cheeks, but she didn't make a sound. He looked at her feet. A rivulet of dried blood ran down her calf and curved around her anklebone, disappeared under the instep of her bare foot.

"It's all right." He didn't know what else to say.

"I'm going to be sick," she said. She pulled her arm off him, and he reached for her, to steady her, as she bent over, away from him. One hand lay on the small of her back, on the knobs of her vertebrae. The other hand felt ribs. She spit, nothing else. Then, still leaning over, she picked up the hem of her dress and wiped her mouth. He held on to her and waited, then took her arm again, draped it over his shoulder, and they walked.

"I didn't think I'd still be here," she said. "And the sun." She squinted into it. He thought she was staring at it too long, and he wished she'd look away. He just wanted to get to the trees, and then through them and out onto the logging road beyond. The poplars made a dense green and gray wall. When he was a kid, he pretended that once you slipped through the trees and came out into the field, and into the hot sun, the yellow grass, you'd stepped into another world.

"Last night," she said, her voice soft, almost no sound. It made him think of the word *pianissimo*. They walked a few more paces before she spoke again. "I was so sure Michael was lying next to me. He was talking to me. 'You listen to me,' he said." She touched her ear.

Tobin's scalp tingled. He registered a smell, an odor that had been wafting, and he hadn't been able to place until now—alcohol, coming from her breath, her skin. He looked toward the trees. The poplar leaves fluttered, turned over as they do when it's supposed to storm. They went from green to silver to green.

"I'm sorry," he said. "Sorry." The man was dead. She was dreaming, or drunk.

She cocked her head, looked at him. Her lips tightened like she was trying not to cry. She had the greenest eyes—pine green, and filled with needles of other greens, like she was looking at him from under the cover of firs.

"I thought he was alive. " Her breath became short, staccato; she was crying.

He could hear the ache in her. He understood why she might have come to lie in the field in the night. Maybe to die. But he wouldn't let her. He would not let her.

CHAPTER 8

S HE WONDERED IF TOBIN had perhaps on some occasion
come here when her parents were still alive, because he
brought her inside and led her down the hall to the bathroom as
if he knew where it was and had been in the house before. In the
bathroom, he made her drink water, keeping one hand on her
the whole time. Then he let go of her, stood her to the side as he
leaned over the bathtub. He passed his hand through the stream
and turned the knobs. Her mind was fuzzy—Tobin here, a teenager. He was five or six years old when she'd stayed with him.

The bathroom mirror throwing back the opposite window
and a bit of the yard outside, the pine boards of the back wall—it
was all wrong to be here. She leaned against the door frame.
Her arms itched from mosquito bites. Tobin stood up, his hands
dripping. She looked toward the rack, wanted to hand a towel
to him, but couldn't will her arm to reach. There were the two
towels—hers and Michael's.

Tobin's mouth was open slightly as if he'd said something and
was waiting for her to answer. He ran his hand over the top of
his head, fingers combing and lifting dark hair in spikes, like
ruffled fur, now settling back on its own. His eyes were dark and

heavy-lidded, so he appeared sad or sleepy. She remembered the long eyelashes, still like a little boy's. Then he looked down at her feet, at her one bare foot and one with the shoe. She knew there was blood and dirt. She shut her eyes and the world shifted. Tobin had hold of her again.

"Mary," he said. He gripped her shoulders, held her up. "You're shivering." The tub was filling, water pounding. "Go slow," he said. "It might be hot. You can add cold."

She touched her throat, the collar of her dress. Tobin backed away, closed the bathroom door behind himself. She heard him go down the hall, then outside. The screen door creaked and clunked.

She stepped into the tub without undressing. The one shoe became heavy underwater, the lace snaked out. The canvas darkened. She toed the shoe off, lowered herself into the water, and it did feel good. She undid some of the buttons and pulled the dress down and off, and let it float at the foot of the tub, the pink cotton swelling with air. Dried blood from the wound near her hipbone washed away and revealed an abrasion surrounded by a bruised area. She remembered trying to put the whiskey bottle away, stumbling into the corner of the low cabinet, glasses clinking inside.

Now it was just her and silence, an occasional drip, a ripple of water. There was the sink, the hot water heater, the toilet. Sunlight wavered on the wall above the mirror. The mirror, covered with steam. The room like always; she couldn't bear it. Michael should open the door. Kneel next to the tub, one hand dangling in the water, touching her leg, talking to her. There should be something cooking, rosemary and garlic. There should be music.

Her arms were limp under the water. She lifted one and laid her hand on her breast. Michael's hand on her breast. She couldn't stand it and slid her hand away. She still had her underwear on. Ridiculous; she wriggled in the water, struggling to pull them off. It was odd to do something so practical, as if for that one second of work she forgot her life. Forgot everything. But she didn't want to forget. She didn't want Michael to grow blurry, or fade away. She shut her eyes. He'd drawn some designs, a new room, small, just off their bedroom. His eager face, as if he were seeing the future in that room. His arm, pointing to where the window would be. Then his voice—*We can plant marigolds in the window box.* Then, *I want to make your belly grow.* And that same voice whispering close to her ear, lips kissing her neck. Or reaching into the pocket of his shirt, pulling out a guitar pick. *This is a flat pick, in case you didn't know.* His grin. Sleep was trying for her, making her head fall to the side, her chin drop, but she kept jerking awake.

Later, rising out of the cooled water, she dried herself with the towel that was hers, not Michael's. Tears started again. She gripped the edge of the sink, unable to breathe.

The funeral was in two days. She'd come back to get some clothes and close up the house. Tonight she'd go back to Worcester, stay with Michael's friends Paul and Lisie. Friday they'd drive her to the Cape, where Michael's parents had made all the arrangements.

Outside, Tobin stood next to the garden, his hands in his pockets, a young man now. She remembered him as a brilliant little boy, though fraught, weighed down. A disturbed mother. She'd been asked to take care of him for a few days. Mr. Gough had come to the lodge, asked for a sitter, and she'd volunteered. Later she learned that they'd gone to have his wife's mental health evaluated. Mary remembered how bright Tobin was, how so many facts and ideas rushed from his complicated little boy's mind in a frenzy. He'd recited all the presidents' names and their years in office. He'd talked about glaciers and granite. He had a quirk, making an exaggerated shrug after each bit of information as if ashamed, or bewildered by his own knowledge.

At the piano she'd watched his small fingers bounce and flutter over the keys, amazed at how he conquered the stretches. It was a sort of lullaby, she remembered, for her. When she began to hum along, putting her voice to his melody, he'd stopped playing. She remembered thinking that she'd broken his trance, but then he laughed and started again. "What are the words?" he'd asked. "Let's invent some." If they had, she didn't remember them now.

In the bedroom, her parents' old room, she rummaged through the closet, pushing things aside, then decided on a shirt—a flannel shirt that was Michael's—and her own jeans. The shirt was large on her and soft, and she wished she could disappear inside it. She ran her hand over her head, around the back of her neck, smoothing her wet, newly cropped hair. Yesterday, imagining Michael's hand sliding down her braid, lifting it, she'd grabbed the scissors, hacked it off. As she passed the mirror, she thought she saw a boy. A dark-haired boy in a flannel shirt, with wide confused eyes, looking back at her. Once again she was nauseated and made a run for the toilet.

CHAPTER 9

Two days after the funeral, Mary found herself sitting in the truck outside the apartment back in Somerville. It was hot. Sweat pooled under her legs, against the vinyl seat. Squashed insects on the windshield had smeared further when she'd tried to use the wiper fluid. People were out walking, heading for their cars, watering plants, strolling, dogs on leashes. It was a sunny Saturday.

This morning at Paul and Lisie's house, she'd awakened in a rush, as if some giant hands had scooped her up from the bottom of a lake, bursting through the surface, and on up into the bright sky. She felt weightless, almost giddy, comprehending again what she'd come to realize as she'd driven away from Leah four days ago. Adding things up, calculating, counting days, she'd grasped the truth.

She felt like laughing, then caught sight of herself in the side mirror. Her face was having nothing to do with her thoughts—mouth pulled taut in a painful frown. She looked exhausted, drawn, pale, eyelids swollen.

Mary. It was Michael's voice, as if he sat right next to her. And then a different voice. Michael's mother. His mother at the funeral, telling her something. Something with an edge, with a rough note, from grief, or anger, or both. She'd said *Mary*, and Mary had separated herself from her own name. Mary was someone else. Michael's mother was speaking to someone else, and being led away by Michael's father. The father, whose nose and mouth resembled his son's, opened the car door and the mother got inside. The mother's eyes were the color and shape of Michael's eyes. The mother's eyes were full of tears and gleaming, and not as angry as the voice. Then Mary had walked up to the car as it started to pull away. She knocked on the trunk. The car stopped and the driver buzzed the back window down. Michael's mother's eyebrows pinched together in question. Michael's father leaned across his wife.

"Mary?" he said. "What is it?" and Mary imagined how odd she must have seemed to them, the wife of their dead son. The wife they'd never met, suddenly smiling.

"You're not in this car," Michael's mother said.

Mary knew this; she was meant to ride in the car with Paul and Lisie. She glanced back to the line of cars queuing up. Paul was there, a tall bearded man, hard to miss, standing next to his car. He was watching her, hands in the pockets of his black suit pants. Mary bent closer, leaned into the car window.

"I thought you should know," she said to Michael's parents. "I wanted to tell you some good news."

Michael's father shifted uneasily, and the driver, whose arm had been draped over the seat back, waiting to see what was holding them up, turned to straighten the rearview mirror. Michael's mother began to cry, and Mary felt her own throat go dry, then she reached in and touched the woman on the shoulder. The silk material of her dress was surprisingly warm and damp. Mary drew her hand back.

"I'm pregnant," she told them. The moment she'd uttered the

words and saw the baffled expressions on their faces, an icy sweat cut down her back.

Now, she looked away from her image in the side mirror and leaned out of the window. A breeze cooled her forehead. Pregnant. She was pregnant. Her period was at least two weeks late, maybe longer; she was never good at keeping track. She remembered Michael teasing her about how often she had had to get up to pee lately. These last days she'd felt sick almost every morning, and not just sick from stress, but a more specific kind of ill feeling, like motion sickness. They'd made love several times without protection. True, they were usually careful, but something had happened to them on the mountain, and they'd just sort of let go, allowed everything. Pregnant. The word kept repeating in her mind, but its meaning seemed elusive, even though the giddy feeling was with her, too.

Now she dared to look up at the windows of their apartment. She and Michael had looked out those windows hundreds of times. She remembered when she'd first moved in. She was terrified that it was all a mistake, that once she actually left San Francisco, arrived in his town, he'd get scared, send her back. He'd waved to her from that window, shoved it up, stuck his head out. *Welcome home!*

How generous he was about where her stuff would go when it arrived. He didn't care, just as long as he had his desk in the corner and his instruments around him. She wondered if she would have been so accommodating if it were him moving into her apartment. He didn't care about things like that. He cared about time. Having time and space to work when he needed, and she was more than happy to give it to him. And the house on the mountain was going to be perfect.

It had been just last October, when Mary had rented a car and made the trip to Leah from Somerville on her own. Michael couldn't get time away from the studio, and she wanted to check on the house one more time before winter; once snow fell, it would be difficult to get in. She'd left early in the morning and managed to get back to Boston by evening, proving to Michael that a commute, if necessary for a while, was entirely possible.

"It's still there," she told Michael as she took off her boots and hung up her wool coat in the hallway. He was in the kitchen and she marveled at the coziness of the room, the warm light in this colorful alcove—bright yellow walls with lime green trim (a previous tenant's paint job), red colander atop the fridge, blue casserole dishes on open shelves, ivory-colored mugs hung on brass hooks, stacks of plates of all sizes and colors—and then the smells of garlic and tomato sauce. Cello music, Jacqueline du Pré's, floated from the CD player. He stood at the stove, stirring with a wooden spoon. Another pot steamed, readying for pasta. He'd set the table with place mats and cloth napkins. A salad, which sat in the middle with thick slices of tomato neatly circling the rim of the bowl and wedges of tomato set out on top in a pinwheel, made her laugh. A bottle of red wine was open next to two wineglasses. He wore jeans, belted, with a button-up blue shirt, one he wore on special occasions, tucked in neatly. He was newly shaved and showered, his dark curls combed back and still damp.

"Taste," he said, holding the spoon up, one hand under it to catch drips.

She opened her mouth, but he kissed her first, then again, a bit slower.

"Delicious," she said, then tried the sauce from his spoon. "Superb."

"Pour wine," he said, "and sit."

She did, and took her chair at the table. He stirred his sauce, turned and lifted his wineglass in a silent toast. They both took sips. Then he put his glass down, came to stand in front of her, took her glass from her hand, and put it on the table. She let him, bewildered, smiling. Then he was on one knee in front of her, holding her hands, and asking her to marry him.

A young, slender black man came out of the front door of the apartment building. He started down the steps, unbuttoning his shirt, as the heat must have caught him by surprise. Maybe he lived in one of the three flats in the old house, but she didn't recognize him. Holding the lapels of his shirt, he aired himself, fanning the shirt open and closed, exposing flashes of his wet, dark chest.

"It's hot," she said to him as he stepped onto the sidewalk. He nodded, maybe a little suspicious of a woman parked here in front of his building, and now talking to him. "I live here," she said, pointing up at the windows. "But it's sublet for summer."

"Oh," he said, and nodded, pursing his lips in a way that said, Okay, that makes sense. He ran a hand over his tight curls and around to the back of his neck. Then he was studying her face. "Are you all right?" he asked.

She remembered what she looked like. "Allergies," she said, and smiled, sniffled as if giving proof.

Then he brightened, came closer. "We just moved into 3B, above you."

"I hope the tenants are okay. Quiet," she said. "They seemed nice."

"Oh, they're nice folks," he said. "Hey, but did you have trouble getting the landlord to fix things?"

"No, not really," she said. "I mean, my husband took care of stuff pretty well."

Her throat constricted slightly and she coughed.

"You're lucky," the man said. "I call the guy, he won't come. He promised us new paint, new fixtures. Supposed to be done before we moved in, but obviously that didn't happen."

For a second she pictured the yellow and green walls of their kitchen, the beige ceiling above the bed, the weird three-pronged light fixture that was painted a bright purple and how they'd come to love it, lying there in bed, talking, staring up at their ugly, funky chandelier. And then Michael, sitting at his desk. Sometimes she'd stand in the doorway to his office and just watch him. He often stayed up late—his back to her, headphones on, papers spread out on his desk, the room dim but for his desk lamp. She'd watch, quiet, marveling. *That man . . . in that room . . . is my husband.* He'd let her watch for a while, she felt, then he'd grow tired of the game, or self-conscious, and without turning, he'd stretch an arm behind himself. He wouldn't beckon, just hold his arm out like that, until she came forward. He always seemed to know she was there, no matter how silent she tried to be, tiptoeing from the bedroom, holding her breath. *You can trust me*, his open arm seemed to say.

"We're up in New Hampshire for the summer, maybe longer. We have a house there. My parents' old summer place."

The man smiled. "Blackflies is what I think of when I think of New Hampshire." He wiped the sweat from his forehead with his fingers, then flicked his wrist toward the ground. "I'll bet it's cooler there, anyway, huh?"

"I might give up the apartment," she said, casting her eyes to the windows up there. Even in the heat a chill went over her head. Who was she now? What would she do now? She ran her hand up under her bangs. "Also, then we thought we might want kids. Actually, we're going to. Have a baby, I mean."

"Hey, congratulations," the man said. "That's great."

She smiled brightly as if everything was right in the world. "Yeah," she said. "It's pretty exciting. The house is roomy, acres of land. It's safe there. I mean, in the country." And then out of the blue, "My husband wants a boy. But I don't care what we get."

"Either's nice," the man said. "Right?"

"True," she said. "We'll love him or her no matter what." She was anyone, engaging in everyday patter, sharing easy, acceptable anecdotes.

He nodded and made motions of heading off. So she did too, straightening in her seat.

"Good luck with the landlord," she said as he began down the sidewalk. He waved, and went on.

She started the truck and pulled away, thinking, *Pregnant.* Michael would laugh, and then he'd snag her in his arms and squeeze; he'd be thrilled. *Pregnant.* The giddy feeling drained out of her. She put her hand over her mouth, pressed, unsure if she might be sick, or start crying again. A single mother. A baby, alone. This was impossible. Then not impossible. She would just do it. *Michael, oh God, Michael.* Unbelievable that he wasn't here to share this. His legacy. Their child to continue on. When the baby came, there'd be no time for anything—no despair—only forward momentum into the future. What an incredible gift Michael had left behind.

Continuing down the street, the old landmarks came and went by, and were gone behind her, like leaving a dream. Rooftops, shingles and peaks, seemed to bend forward, lean in from the bright sky, then stand back as the truck passed. And as colors and structures disintegrated behind her, she had the overwhelming feeling that she had to get north as soon as possible. Back to the green. Back to the house.

"I need to be there," she said out loud, her tone incredulous, as if someone had doubted her.

It took another two weeks to get back to the mountain. Two weeks of living in a fog of sick grief. A looming presence, like something down below her, underwater, and she could never quite swim away from it. Then, a sunbeam striking a shaft through cloudy water: the knowledge that she was pregnant.

Paul and Lisie were kind and told her to stay as long as she needed, even though truly they didn't know Mary all that well. They were Michael's friends, new acquaintances to her. She wanted to tell them about the baby, but didn't, afraid almost that to speak of it again would transform it from what it was—a fragile seed that needed to wait for the snow to thaw, the ground to turn warm and rich and nourishing.

She imagined the baby, lying on its back, its chubby legs and arms waving. The toothless smile—her own smile, Michael's smile, shining back to her. The little fingers grasping her fingers, tugging. She put Michael's eyes in the baby's face, dark, warm, shining with love. One day she drove the truck to Somerville again, but didn't stop, circled the block. In the rearview mirror she imagined a car seat and the toddler strapped in, his gaze toward the window, little mouth popping open, making sounds of delight, music to his tiny, perfect ears. Then, sleeping, cheek on his own shoulder, little flutters of his lips as breath puttered out. Thick eyelashes, dark tassels, spread out on the peach-white skin below his eyes, on his perfect skin.

In a dream one night the child was a dark-haired girl, still with Michael's dark, aching eyes, and the girl spoke to her, asking for something, though Mary couldn't remember what when she woke up.

Then the fog of grief began to shift toward something else, toward a desire to live, to push on, to get started on a new life. She said good-bye to the perplexed, worried faces of Paul and Lisie, and drove north finally. On the seat next to her, the girl again, maybe seven now, seatbelt across her small frame, kicking her feet up and down, laughing, pressing her forehead to the window, gazing into the woods that bordered Cascom Mountain Road. Two dark braids, draped over her shoulders, over the straps of her denim coveralls. As Mary drove she smiled at the imagined daughter, or sometimes son, or at the empty seat beside her. She felt the sprout inside her tingle, and a wave of nausea. She shifted down on the steep incline, wheels skittering across washboard, headed home, home, home.

CHAPTER 10

S IX DAYS PASSED. She'd slept a lot. This was good. Anything to get through more hours. Though waking was always another moment of agony as the truth of her life—Michael's death—would surface in her consciousness again. Sometimes it came slowly—there might be a fraction of a second where all she knew was sunlight on the floor, specks of dust floating in the beam—then, seeping knowledge, awareness again.

Tobin was outside, sitting on the picnic table. He came every day, keeping an eye on her, she supposed. Her head felt heavy as if she couldn't quite wake up all the way, and there was a pressure behind her eyes, a wooziness, almost like a hangover, though she'd had no more whiskey since the night she'd stumbled into the field. She hoped she hadn't done any harm to the baby.

Out the front window, the sun hung above the mountain to the right of the summit, lowering fast. The tower, tiny as a diamond from this distance, stood atop the granite dome. She wondered if the new fire lookout was up there. He seemed youngish—maybe thirty—for such an isolated sort of occupation. When she'd been on crew, the fire lookout had been an older guy; he'd lived in Hi-House, the small lookout's cabin that sat just below the tree line, making his daily hike to his job in the tower. He'd helped in the search for the missing albino girl.

The hills were a puzzle of deep greens—the hardwoods mixed with pine. The bright yellow-greens of the birches that had survived the ice storm last winter, though there were far more dead—their skeletons stood out like etched Y's—interspersed throughout the hillside. And in the front yard, the old stand of tall white birch had been destroyed. They all bowed over, snarls of dead branches hanging down like hair, like women bent over a stream, washing their hair.

At the edge of the field, blackberries and brambles moved in, saplings grew taller, and bushy trees blocked the view of her father's little field—one he'd cleared farther below—a window in the forest to watch animals cross through. The growth made her anxious. All of it made her anxious. The roof needed fixing. The gutters, the chimney. The pump made noises; the water sometimes drizzled, then burst from the faucet as if it was plugged. The front deck was peeling, boards rotting, falling in. Pine boards under the windows in the bedrooms were gray, stained and moldy from condensation over the winter. Rocks had tumbled from the stone wall at the edge of the driveway. There was hardly any cut wood in the shed. *I'm your handyman.*

"You must feel like an orphan," Michael had said to her when she first told him that both her parents had passed. It was the day she met him. They were in line for beer at the folk festival outside Boston. She nodded, embarrassed at the blur that came to her vision. She'd just made the trip east to check on the house, then taken a detour to join friends at the festival. Later she told him about the house on the mountain and how it was nearly impossible to stay more than a night there; it was just too sad, yet she was compelled to keep the place.

"I understand," he said. *I understand.* Her own father, who should have understood the love she had for the mountain, for the house, had told her that she should sell it. *You can't take care of it from the West Coast. You have your own life. Do something with all your talent.*

The house was the only place to call home. It was unique and gorgeous, like no other place in the world. She hadn't planned on living on the West Coast forever. And maybe all her talent was mediocre. Though at the time she still played guitar, wrote songs, and had even been hired twice as the warm-up act in a bar in San Francisco, she figured she wasn't good enough. What other talent her father might have been referring to was a mystery. "That must be one of your other daughters," she'd joked to him. She sat at his side in the hospital room. He was hooked up to apparatus, tubes stuck in one arm, breathing tubes in his nose. His skin was milky gray, and he'd become thin.

"Mary is my daughter," he said, too seriously, his eyes traveling around the room. It was the morphine, she realized. Disoriented, he was telling her, or someone, who his daughter was.

"It's okay, Dad," she said, daring to touch his forearm gently. His skin felt too soft and cool, like the underbelly of a newborn puppy.

"It's nearsighted," he said, his voice suddenly hard, angry. "Those corrupt, lying bastards!" She wondered who was with him now. Maybe Republicans. Or some other evil the drug was inventing. "It's death to the ecosystem," he said, and she knew he was fighting his lifelong battle to preserve a species, a river, or a forest, still. "Franny," he said, his voice lowered suddenly, soft, sad. It was her mother's name. "Franny, ask Mary to call me. I have to tell her."

"It *is* me. *Mary*," she told him. "I *am* here."

"Can't keep it from her any longer. Must tell her the truth."

"The truth?" For a second Mary worried—was there some secret?

"I'm ill. Quite ill."

"I know," she said, and then she was crying, but trying to hold it in, hand over her mouth, tears streaming.

"Can't bear seeing you hurt," he said, and Mary wasn't sure if he was apologizing to his dead wife for being ill, or to Mary for her tears.

"It's okay," she said.

Then the morphine haze seemed to break open, and he looked right at her, his gentle brown eyes clear and beaming.

"Oh, Mary," he said, as if she'd just arrived. "Hello."

Now, Mary stood before the living room window. There was the mountain, ever present. Her parents were gone. Michael had died up there. It was hard to breathe.

In an instant, the sun sank to the ridge, then started to dip below it. The world was in motion. Michael had noted this, how it was as if you could see the earth revolving in these moments when the sun dropped so quickly. Time was passing. She was twenty-eight, alone. Pregnant. She calmed herself, put a hand on her belly, breathed. She would do this, be a mother, love her child, find a way.

She could be her own handyperson. It was easy enough to replace deck boards, hammer some nails, stain and waterproof. Clorox would take the mold off the windowsills. She could lift rocks, clean up the stone wall. There were plumbers and roofers in Leah she could call. Tomorrow, perhaps, she'd see what sort of lumber was in the shed. The trees were eerily still. No breeze. No birds.

In a last glimmering beam, the sun vanished behind the mountain. White spots traveled in her vision across the slopes, dimmed hills, and up to the sky, wherever she looked. The mountain was in shadow now, though the sky was still bright. When she shut her eyes there was a sunspot inside her eyelids, doubled and black, floating. When she opened her eyes, it appeared white again. A ball of light, shifting with her eyes, or her eyes following it. But then it grew, limbs spanning from its sides, coming toward her. A white figure. Mary's knees gave a little, and she braced herself against the window. It was a girl, white-haired and impossible, running up the hill, coming toward the house in a hurry. And now at the screen door and saying her name, saying, *Mary, Mary, Mary?*

CHAPTER 11

MARY DIDN'T LOOK WELL. Her eyes were sunken, and dark circles pressed into the skin beneath them. She'd gotten thin, too thin—collarbone protruding, cheekbones sharp, jaw narrowed. Her hair was chopped short and uneven, the braid gone, cut off. Callie didn't know what she'd expected, but when word was out Mary Walker had returned to the mountain, Callie thought it was good. The woman had come home, as if that meant *healed*. Now Callie realized that Mary wasn't healed at all. Of course not. She wondered why Mary was here, and not with family or friends.

"Mary?" Callie said, through the screen door. "Mary? Mary, I'm sorry if I startled you."

Mary came forward finally, pushed the screen open, and let Callie step inside. It was dim in the room. Callie had the urge to flip a switch. She'd never been inside the house, but she and Marlee had looked in the windows once when no one was here. They'd tried the doors, too. If there had been an easy way in, they would have explored the place. They'd done this at other remote, seldom lived-in weekend houses. They never took anything or did any harm. At one place farther down the mountain, an old cabin with no sign of life, they'd climbed through a window. It seemed like an okay thing. It was interesting to see how other people lived. Mary Walker's place was unusual. Callie knew that it had been Mary's parents' place first, so maybe it was all their stuff here: odd metal sculptures, wiry figures on the wide sills; tracings of fish in wooden frames; fishing poles in a rack on one wall; an animal's bones laid out like a puzzle on a board; a large, faded rag rug and worn-looking stuffed furniture. A long wooden table took up half the room and was surrounded by eight chairs. "A big family, or a lot of company," Marlee had said. There was other furniture too—heavy wooden shapes that resembled the trees they were carved from: a coffee table with trunklike legs; a chair that looked like the middle of a huge tree, the stub of a branch still jutting from its side. Shelves crammed with books lined the walls on either side of the fireplace. The picture window was huge—a set of twelve large panes. These people loved a view. Callie knew that there was a main bedroom down the hall, past the bathroom. She and Marlee had looked in those windows, too.

"I'm Callie," she said to the woman's back. Mary had gone to the front window and was staring out at the darkening mountain. "I work at the lodge? I met you, before," she added feeling awkward, because, of course, Mary knew *that*, but maybe she didn't remember her name, and Callie didn't want to embarrass her. "I'm really sorry about your husband."

"Thank you," Mary said and turned. She smiled, a vague sort of trying smile.

"If there's anything we can do," Callie said. "Please let us know. Spencer, the crew boss, wanted me to tell you you're welcome anytime. Any meal."

Mary shifted her gaze from the side windows to the picture window, as if measuring the distance between them.

Callie thought she should just go. The woman was distracted.

But she'd come to give Mary the knapsack—Michael Walker's blue knapsack. She'd gone to Spencer's room, decided it was time to deliver the pack, since Spencer kept forgetting, or putting it off. "Take it," he'd said, obviously relieved to have someone else deal with it. Now it seemed wrong to have worn it on her back.

On her way across the valley Callie had gone through the pack. She'd just cut through the lower field and come onto the old wooden bridge that crossed over the brook. The brook was low, a soft gurgle, flowing around the protruding rocks. The sand and underwater rocks looked golden brown. She sat down, dangled her legs off the edge, and opened the pack; a faint odor of turned food wafted out. There were soft apples and smelly sandwiches inside plastic containers. She decided that it would be rude to return the pack with these things, so she tossed the apples into the brook, then dumped the sandwiches after them. She snapped the covers back on the sandwich containers and stuck them in the sack. There was also a candy bar and a bottle of water. She left those. Then she wondered if she'd done the right thing. Maybe Mary would want that food. The food she and her husband had packed together and planned to eat. Callie watched the bread separate and float downstream. She didn't know where the apples had landed and sunk to the bottom. It was too late. It would be crazy to want rotten food, she supposed.

In the smaller pocket there was a red Swiss Army knife, thick with blades and tools; a baggie of tissues; a tube of Neosporin; a pen. A little round case opened into a small mirror. Callie looked at her mouth, her eyes, one then the other, then snapped it closed. Then opened it again. What did she look like? What did Spencer see? He said she had faraway eyes, the kind that made you think she was seeing things no one else could see. She wondered if this were true. Sometimes she could get so deep into her thoughts, she was gone, not seeing. Spencer said she had beautiful breasts. She held the mirror above her chest, trying to see herself. Something flashed behind her, caught in the mirror. She flinched and turned. There was nothing. Maybe a bird. Then she stood, slung the pack on her back, and began up the hill.

"I have your knapsack," Callie said. She shrugged it off and held it out to Mary. Mary stared at it blankly. Callie put the pack on the end of the table. "I threw out the food. Sorry."

Mary seemed not to have heard her, and unbuckled the straps. She looked in the bag quickly, then unzipped the smaller pocket, took out the tube of Neosporin, and dropped it back in the pocket. She held the Swiss Army knife in her palm for a moment, then laid it on the table.

"I gave him that," she said. "For his birthday."

"It's nice," Callie said. She felt foolish, not sure what to say about a dead man's present. "When did you work at the lodge?"

"A long time ago. I was seventeen."

"I'm almost seventeen!" Callie said. She felt her cheeks go hot. She'd spoken with too much excitement, as if it were some amazing coincidence.

Mary raised her eyebrows in affirmation and smiled warmly. Callie noted what a pretty woman Mary was, or could be, if not so washed out with pain. She had strong dimples that made her look cute, almost girlish, but there were lines at the corners of her eyes. Smile wrinkles, Callie's mom would call them, though right now it was hard to imagine the lines from smiling.

"Tell the crew boss thank you for me," Mary said.

Mary ran her hand over the back of her neck, and up into her hair. Callie couldn't believe she'd cut off her beautiful long braid.

Maybe Mary didn't want to talk anymore, but Callie wasn't sure it was right to leave yet.

"I looked at your crew sign," Callie said. "The one with the birches."

"You did," Mary said.

The way she answered sounded more like a statement than a question, and Callie felt as if she'd been deflected, then continued anyway.

"It was kind of cool to see your name," she said. "You were Mary Hall, right?"

Mary's eyes had fallen to the things on the table, the knife, and Callie wondered if Mary was listening.

Then Mary said, "The crew boss painted it. He was sort of my boyfriend that summer."

The words "sort of" made Callie curious, though she thought she knew what Mary might mean. She remembered the initials painted in thin black strokes at the base of one of the birch trees. The white paint of the tree trunks was thin, and the grain of the board showed through as well as some of the ferns and bushes he'd arranged behind the birches. It seemed the artist had intended the tree to be transparent—a see-through tree. A ghost tree.

Mary reached for the knife, slipped it back into the small pocket of the knapsack.

Callie remembered seeing Mary and her husband that day he died, and how happy they seemed. They were married, so there was no "sort of" about it. It was a mystery to think how the right two people found each other. She wondered where her own husband might be out there in the world, and what he was doing right now at this exact moment. He was someone she didn't even know yet, probably.

Mary held something small, pinched between her fingers, something else she'd found in the little pouch of the knapsack. Her mouth was open, like she was saying "Oh," but she wasn't saying anything.

"What is it?" Callie asked.

Mary's eyes had darkened, and it looked as if she might cry, but then a smile, and then she laughed. Laughed! Callie couldn't help but laugh too, even though she didn't know what was funny, but it felt good. A relief. It was nice to see. Mary clenched whatever it was in her fist, held against her chest.

"It's a joke," she said. "Between Michael and me. It's a flat pick."

"Like, for guitar?" Callie asked.

Mary opened her hand to reveal the triangular shard of tortoiseshell-colored plastic.

"He puts them everywhere," Mary said. "When I first played a guitar in front of him, he couldn't believe I didn't use a pick. I strummed with my thumbnail."

"You play guitar?"

"Not anymore. Not really. No."

"Ben plays guitar. The fire watchman. He's really good." Callie had seen Ben, guitar strap over his shoulder, reach deep into his trouser pockets, or tap his chest pocket, searching for a pick. He always had one with him.

Mary's smile evaporated. She dropped the flat pick back into the pocket of the knapsack.

"Are you going to stay here?" Callie asked. "Do you have friends—" She stopped. It wasn't coming out right. But it seemed like there should be someone here with her. "I mean, will you go back to Massachusetts now?"

"I can't," she said. "We sublet our apartment in Somerville. When I was back there, I stayed with friends. There was the funeral on the Cape and everything. It was weird being down there, but not at our place. People living there. Our stuff's in there. What could I do?"

Mary looked at Callie as if she might have an answer. Callie nodded, though she wasn't sure she understood all of it. But she understood enough.

"Well," Callie tried, "you need to live somewhere, right?"

"Right," Mary said. Callie felt she'd been helpful; it seemed she'd given the right answer.

"Come, sit," Mary said. "I'll make tea."

They had talked for a long time. Mary told her all sorts of things about when she was on the crew, the only girl. Back then she'd had to fight to do the same jobs as the boys, like clearing trails, going on rescues. Otherwise, they'd have had her in the kitchen mostly. Callie was glad to let Mary reminisce; it seemed good for her. Her face brightened, and a sort of splotchy blush had crept from her neck into her cheeks.

"And you grew up here, in this house?" Callie asked at one point, and Mary took herself further back in time to when she was a little girl, wandering the woods, taking her dolls on excursions. Once, she pretended to get lost and waited for rescue. But when no one came, she became paralyzed with fear. She bawled and called out, until a stranger—a tall, bearded man who'd been logging—came out of the woods, took her home. Another time she'd rescued a fawn, half-eaten by a bobcat. Bobcats on Cascom! Her father, she said, had written about it for a magazine.

"His name was Cecil Hall," Mary told her, indicating the bookshelves behind where she sat. "He wrote books about nature. All those." She pointed to one full shelf. "He was well known in his early days, but had kind of slipped the minds of the literary world. That is until he died, then there was a little flurry of interest, but mostly accompanying his obituaries. Actually, one of the first things I learned about Michael was that he'd heard of my father."

"How did you meet your husband?" Callie dared to ask.

"I was in line to get a beer at a folk festival, actually. I remember thinking that this guy in front of me was attractive, and the next thing I knew we were having this discussion about the difference between poetry and song lyrics. He thought one of the songwriters had misused a Jane Kenyon poem by setting it to music. Anyway, I must have told him that my father was a writer and his eyes got wide when I said his name. 'Cecil Hall?' he said. 'The essayist? The guy who writes about the environment?' I couldn't believe he'd heard of him."

"That's cool," Callie said. "So random, I mean." Jane Kenyon, she'd have to look her up.

"It was cool," Mary said. "Then when I told him that my father had died over two years before, he looked like he was going to cry." Mary paused, then said, "My father died of cancer. My mother died two months before him. A stroke. I think my father just couldn't take losing her. I don't know."

"I'm so sorry," Callie said. She couldn't imagine losing her parents, ever.

"It seemed impossible," Mary said. "One, then the other. Practically both at once. Like a flood tore through."

Callie remembered a news clip she'd seen on television—the aftermath of a broken dam that had sent water surging through a canyon. A whole village vanished.

Mary looked so sad, but then she continued her story.

"Michael was a complete stranger to me, but he took hold of my arm, I guess to urge me forward because the line in front of us had moved ahead, but then he didn't let go. It was as if we were bound by a shared sadness. He told me that he'd read my father's work in college and heard a tape an instructor had brought in of my father on NPR. He even considered going into environmental law at one point. He actually started out in law, until he found it wasn't for him."

"He liked music instead?" Callie asked.

Mary nodded. "He didn't leave my side all day. Later we met up with each others' friends and we all went to dinner. I don't even remember talking to anyone else. We were oblivious. I don't know, we just hit it off. I think, also, that Michael knowing about my father, and being so genuinely sad to hear of his death, worked inside me like some sort of spell."

A spell, Callie had thought. It sounded so romantic and beautiful.

Now Callie glanced out the window. A few stars had pushed through the murky, dark blue sky. She'd walked the road with Marlee many times, coming back from some of their night prowls. But she'd never done it alone. At night the old stories about Mount Cascom spooked her. Once, walking with Marlee, their flashlight beams stretching out on the dirt road in front of them and illuminating the tips of overhanging branches, Callie found herself imagining the ghost girl waiting for them on the road ahead. She lifted her flashlight, shining it farther ahead, but there was nothing ever there, just the rock-pitted dirt road, or the short white posts of the railing on the bridge over the brook, and more washboard road curving on up to the lodge. But still, what if you looked up and there, wavering like mist, was a ghost with long white hair? Hair so long it dragged on the ground behind her. Then you'd see that her eyes were nothing but black hollows, burned out by the sun from an eternity of roaming the mountain, they said, lost without her lover, crazed with jealousy for the living. When a pair of shining eyes suddenly appeared, fixed in their flashlight beams, she and Marlee screamed and clutched each other's arms, only to realize in a second it was just Peggy, the cooks' old calico cat.

Maybe she could call Marlee. Marlee could borrow the truck and drive up and get her if she wasn't on front desk duty. Or maybe Ben would come; he had been there at dinner. Maybe he'd decided to stay the night rather than trek back up to Hi-House. He'd been staying a lot lately. Maybe because of Marlee. She wasn't sure.

The first day on the job, when she and Marlee were unpacking their duffels in their room in Lo-House, Ben and Rabbit had come over from the room across the hall. Ben started singing, holding his walkie-talkie to his mouth as if it were a microphone. He wore the fire watchman's green uniform, which looked odd with his pierced ear, but cool, too. He had a playful grin that could make you laugh at nothing, sometimes to Callie's embarrassment. Marlee stood on the ladder to the upper bunk, making up her bed, and Ben sang to her, inventing the melody.

When Ben finished on a high, off-key note, he took a bow. Rabbit clapped and made his ears move up and down dramatically; it was how he got his nickname. Marlee ignored them, jumped down, and laid her palm on Ben's uniformed chest, pushing him aside as if he were a curtain in her way. Ben caught Callie watching him, pulled his shoulders up in an exaggerated shrug, and made a clownlike disappointed face, then grinned at her. She smiled back, but slowly, unsure of where her allegiances should lie. Then he did a funny thing: he cocked his head and raised his eyebrows at her as if in question, and she wondered what his question might be. He kept his eyes on her—sparkling, dark eyes—and she felt a pull in her stomach, charmed. Then he looked away, and that was that, though a rush of heat came to her face, as if she'd said or done something revealing.

Now, Callie wished she hadn't left so late in the evening with the pack, and she wondered if Spencer was worried. He wanted her to come to his room tonight as usual, after the rest of the crew were asleep, but she wasn't sure she wanted to. Maybe tonight she wouldn't.

"Can I use your phone?" she asked Mary. "Maybe I can get a lift back."

"It's not hooked up. Disconnected," she said. "I forgot to pay the bill."

"Oh. I can walk."

"I'll get you a flashlight. Tobin can walk you."

"Tobin Gough? Is he here?"

"He was."

But when they went outside, there was no one around.

"I'll drive you," Mary said.

Callie wanted to be braver, wished she could say that she didn't need a ride, but with the woods getting darker, the trees blending into a black wall, she agreed.

It was weird to climb into the cab of Mary's truck, to be lit up momentarily by the interior light, and watch this small, sad woman become efficient, take control. Mary worked the gears, and Callie realized that Mary was barefoot. She backed the truck up, threw it into gear. Callie didn't know how to drive yet. She was just learning on an automatic. Watching Mary, though, she decided that she too wanted to drive a stick shift. She wanted to look that good, and be barefoot on the pedals, and have that kind of confidence.

Just as the truck swung around, the headlights flooding the yard, they spotted Tobin. He was sitting on the roof of the house, his legs hanging off the low eave. Mary stopped the truck and looked at him. She didn't seem fazed about him being up there. Then she rolled down the window and leaned out.

"Go home now," Mary told him. Her voice was gentle. "I'm all right," she said. Callie thought Mary's tone was reassuring, though there was something false in it—a note of trying to convince herself as much as Tobin perhaps.

Tobin raised his hand and nodded, and Mary shifted, pressed the gas, and they pulled away.

CHAPTER 12

Mary heard music, the high resonance of a fiddle, when they pulled into the parking lot. People were gathered on the front lawn, sitting in the grass or on lounge chairs, or standing in groups. Torches lit on posts sent fluctuating light across the lawn and over faces. Now the people were clapping. Several young people stood in a half circle at the front of the crowd, poised with their instruments. Mary recognized the fire watchman among them. He held a guitar, his green uniform shirt unbuttoned over a white T-shirt and the guitar strap over his shoulder. An acoustic guitar, old, no pick guard. He stood with his arms crossed, elbows resting on the top of the guitar, and watched the redheaded girl as she spoke to the crowd. His stance, though a common one for guitar players, reminded her of Michael and the way he'd pause like that between writing lyrics, or deliberating a recording, or after trying out a new song and looking at her, waiting for her response. Her throat felt tight, and she had to take a long slow breath and blow it out. She wasn't sure if she could do this.

"Come listen," Callie said. "You have to hear Marlee sing."

Mary was glad the attention was on the musicians as she and

Callie crossed the parking lot. She walked warily, not only because her bare feet were tender on the gravel but because she was conscious of the area, this spot where the litter had been set down only twenty-seven days ago. That was June, now it was July. It seemed impossible.

She and Callie came onto the lawn and the grass felt good under her feet, cool and damp. The music started again, a guitar and a fiddle, and the redheaded girl, Marlee, sang in a clear, sweet voice—a bluegrass song—and the boy on fiddle, who Callie said was called Rabbit, joined her in harmony. Then he did a funny thing with his ears, wiggling them forward and back without touching them. People laughed and clapped.

"How he got his name," Callie remarked.

Mary listened to the music and remembered these sorts of nights when she was a girl working here, and how there was always guitar playing and singing and how nothing had changed.

The harmonies, that satisfying blend of tones working together, and Marlee's voice rising and dipping, pausing for the guitar, and then the fiddle, it was beautiful, pure and natural, and Mary thought, Michael will love this. *Would have* loved this.

Callie bobbed her head in time with the beat, and Mary felt the tug of something dire, telling her, *Everything has changed.* Or back to the way it was—*You are alone*—but she didn't want to hear it.

When she was Callie's age, love had seemed inevitable; the power of her own desire assured her it would come. But then it didn't come, or came falsely in short-lived or unhappy relationships. So lucky, she and Michael had said, knowing how rare it was to feel sure of someone, to love someone so confidently. It had astounded her at times—how blessed, how baffling—that he felt the same way. He was so sure of himself. *I want to marry you, Mary.* On his knee. *We should get married.* Then, laughing. *That's a question, in case you were wondering.*

Callie said she'd be right back and moved off, then returned with a sandwich and a paper cup of lemonade. She handed them to Mary. The sandwich was roast beef and tasted good—mayonnaise, crisp lettuce, and soft bread. Eating for two, she realized. *I'm two.* At the thought of this she felt a heaviness in her lower belly, a pressure, not unlike an ache she'd often felt just before her period. The crew boss came up, a rugged-looking guy with blond hair and a prominent nose. Callie introduced him as Spencer, and he leaned close so Mary could hear him over the music.

"Please come any time," he said. "You're more than welcome."

"I appreciate it," she said.

Then Spencer turned to Callie, said something close to her ear. His hand, Mary noticed, brushed the small of Callie's back, but she didn't turn toward him, or make any gesture of acknowledging whatever it was he was saying to her. Her eyes were on the guitar, on the fire watchman's hands, his fingers picking fast. She seemed mesmerized.

When the musicians took a break, and Callie went off to help Spencer with something, the fire watchman laid his guitar in its case and came toward her.

"It's good to see you," he said. "Again. I mean, I hope you're okay. Got to be hard." She remembered his New England accent and the gold hoop earring. He shifted from one foot to the other, nervous. "I wanted . . . I was going to . . ." If it were another time, she might have felt pressure to help him out, urge him to finish a sentence, make him more comfortable, but now it didn't seem of any consequence. "I hope you're . . . I'm just so sorry for what happened." When he gave up, straightened his cap—lifted the bill up, then tugged it down, setting it straight again—she felt sudden compassion.

"You play well," she told him.

"Oh. Not really. Enough to get by," he said. "Nice of you to say."

"Well, you do." For an instant she was a girl again, luminous, bantering with a shy young man, one who smelled of woods and rain and played guitar. She noticed his olive brown skin, and the shadow of a closely shaved beard. Shiny, prominent cheekbones. He was maybe thirty, or younger. She felt suddenly weak, exhausted, wanted to fall against him. But what crass emotions were these, appearing in the face of everything else?

"Time," he said finally, succinctly. "It really does help."

The platitude, too many times said, drove her back into her own dark weight. A twitch of anger.

"Can you tell Callie good-bye for me?" she said, and took a step back.

"Sure," he said. "Listen," he said. "I wanted to tell you something."

But she didn't want to listen, didn't want to be told anything, and kept moving toward the truck. She just had to get away. Now.

"If I can do anything," he said. "Let me know." These familiar lines, though well meant, felt like one more stab. The stab of cliché. She didn't want to be mean, but she had to go.

She jammed the truck into gear, backed up, lurched ahead on the dark road. Gears clawed. There was too much air, or no air, like water in her lungs. Too many people lost. Who was left in the world who really knew her? She shifted, grinding gears again, shoved the stick mercilessly until the engine caught.

CHAPTER 13

A CROSS THE VALLEY, Tobin stood in the dark outside his father's house. His father, visible through the brightly lit windows of his studio—a separate, smaller building near the house—was perched on a stool in front of his easel. Tobin assumed the painting was of the field, yellows and greens. His father had been working in watercolor for a while, not his best medium—all landscapes, and lately the subject was the field in back of the barn. He had tacked several of these paintings to the walls inside the studio.

As Tobin neared the screen door, his father dabbed at a tray, the brush seeming to spring from one color to another. Then he raised the brush and pointed it toward the paper, halted. Tobin wondered what it was his father saw, what he felt, because then the man's shoulders fell, he lowered the brush and hunched over as if he'd exhaled every last bit of breath. His ponytail, short and gray, hitched up on the back of his collar, and spiraled like a pig's tail.

His father's shirt, a blue button-up, was neatly tucked into his corduroys. His belt disappeared under his sagging belly. He looked neat and disheveled all at once. There was paint in blotches on his sleeve, as if he'd leaned against a wet painting.

Tobin moved closer to the door. His father's forehead was prominent, shining, giving way to thin gray hair. He'd had a ponytail for as long as Tobin remembered. The hippie doctor; the back-to-the-lander, people called him, though that was long ago. Now his father was just a sixty-three-year-old guy—much older than most fathers of kids his age—with a ponytail, and a crumbling farmhouse with rooms upon rooms of musty odors, some closed off to save on heat. He had owned some pigs since Tobin was little, for no other reason than he liked pigs. Thought they were smart, which was why he never slaughtered them. They were Chester Whites, long backs, big flopped ears. Now he worked part-time in Leah at the clinic, and spent his free time trying to paint landscapes; but he wasn't very good. Tobin turned away to the barn.

The pigs, four in all, were inside for the night, rooting around in their pens. Their sour smell hit him. He'd never get used to it. He didn't hate the pigs, but they seemed coarse and soulless to him, preoccupied with themselves in a way that was creepy, like they were planning something. Their eyes were tight, straining marbles that looked right through him. When he was a boy he'd liked to hold the piglets, until a sow had rolled over on one and suffocated it. He couldn't stand to touch the babies after that, they were so pathetic and rubbery.

Seeing they'd been watered and fed, their snouts buried in the trough, he closed the barn door, slid the bar across, making sure the bar was perfectly centered.

On his way back he stopped once more to watch his father through the screen door. He knew he should go in and say something, but now his father was painting again. His hand jiggled from the wrist, the brush hitting the paper in short bursts, amber splotches. It would be wheat. Grass. But it wouldn't be right. A few days ago his father had complained, "I see it in my head. I see every slope and shadow. I see it exactly, but somehow it won't come out that way." He'd squinted at his work. Tobin had squinted too. It was a field, blond and tan and yellow, and in some areas it actually did look like grass, but mostly the paint had been too full of water, seeping heavily, drying in stains.

His father stabbed the brush into a jar of water, let it go, then wiped his hands on his thighs, scratched the back of his head, and tugged at his ponytail.

Tobin knocked lightly on the screen door.

"Hey, T," his father said. He motioned for Tobin to come in. Tobin put his hand against the screen to push it open, but stopped. The studio had always smelled of musty paint, and oils, and turpentine. Smells that made him uncomfortable.

"Where have you been off to these last days, coming home late? The lodge?" his father asked, reaching under the small lamp pinned to the top of his easel, switching it off.

"Mary Walker's," Tobin said through the screen.

"Who? A girlfriend?"

Tobin felt the wings of embarrassment brush his face. "No, Mary *Hall*. You know, only now her name's Walker."

His father pinched the bridge of his nose as if he had a headache.

"That's right," his father said. "The husband was Walker. Mary Hall's Mary Walker."

Tobin nodded, though his father wasn't looking at him but staring at his painting, the water-warped paper.

"Poor woman," his father said softly. "She's suffered a lot of losses. More than someone her age should. Both parents nearly at once. Now a husband. Though it's hard to lose someone you love at any age." And Tobin knew he was thinking only of his own loss because sooner or later everything had to do with Tobin's mother—her absence—though she wasn't dead, just not here.

"Pigs are fed," his father said.

"I was going to do it."

"What are you doing there? At the Halls'. You aren't . . . I hope you aren't *intruding*."

"What?"

"I'm sure she's got people," his father said.

"I don't know. I guess."

"Probably doesn't need a boy hanging around. Does she?"

Tobin didn't answer because he'd already turned from the screen door and started across the yard toward the dark house. His father could be such an asshole.

In his room upstairs he sat on the bed, pulled off his shoes, aligned them, then lay back without undressing. He stared at the water stains on his ceiling. One was shaped like a small wooden boat. When he was a kid he'd discovered a huge boulder in the woods that was shaped like a boat. He'd named it the *Hemingway* after his mother once read him *The Old Man and the Sea*. Sometimes he imagined getting a stepladder, climbing up with a palette, and filling in the stain with details. He'd put in silver oarlocks and make the lines of smooth, curving gunwales. He'd paint grass under it, the tall straw of late summer. Wind beaten, and in waves, like water. He could paint grass. It wasn't that difficult to master. He'd taken a watercolor class in school. He enjoyed painting; it was like music in a way—learn the basics, then forget them. Let the image or melody take over. Though letting things take over scared him, too. He shivered at the thought. Watching over Mary these last days had made him feel good, confident, necessary. Her roof was easy to climb. He felt secure up there. The low eave was only an eight-foot drop or so. After Mary had told him to go home and drove away with Callie, he'd jumped off. He landed in a crouch and waited as an ancient pain rode down his leg, traveling the bone. Waited for the pain to shift, shoot up the other way, hover at the hip, then evaporate. Then, as he started away, a voice in his head said, *Go back, touch the wall of the house. If you don't touch the wall of the house, something bad will happen.* Consequently, he'd had to go back and touch the house. He hated that, but he couldn't move on until he'd done it. Did that make him crazy? Too risky not to do it, though. He knew the voice was his own, not any demon. But still, when the commands came, he gave in. As long as no one noticed, and it didn't veer him too far off course, maybe it was okay.

He turned the lamp off and sat up, looked out the window. Fireflies pulsed in the yard—a flickering sea of stars. Bats criss-crossed in the darkness. They swooped fast, from one side then the other. Up from below the eaves, then down, then gone in the darkness. Beautiful, sure and swift, though he knew their faces were ugly—mouselike. People called them flying rats. But they could fly—mammals that had flight. Graceful, silent, though he knew they were making sounds—sounds too high-pitched for human ears. Tones for direction, bouncing off objects, telling them where everything was. Other pitches for communication. He marveled at that—secret timbres going on all around you, but you didn't even know.

This wasn't his childhood room, not the one he'd slept in as a boy. That room had been closed off. It was still filled with his childhood things, books, toys. Fouled with memories. He liked this room better. The old iron headboard, a desk under the window, a couple of straight-backed chairs, a sewing machine on a side table no one had used in years. He liked that there wasn't much of anything in the room, and had chosen it to sleep in whenever he came home from school. Now he was done with school, done with Exeter Academy. He was supposed to be look-ing into colleges, but where and what for? Freshmen in college were older than he was. College frightened him. He didn't want to go anywhere.

Far off he heard the brook. The water rushing, that continuous sound, it was like wind coming down through the hardwoods, or a motor humming. Soon he didn't hear the brook or the crickets anymore. He heard Mary's voice, soft, calm, *tranquillo*. And her kind eyes, which were a certain green. Paint drops in a glass of water, sinking, then dissolving. More drops. And more, changing the water to the silvery green shade of poplar leaves. Roundish leaves, fluttering against each other, tapping, like fingernails on piano keys. Then there were his mother's hands—her too-long fingernails, painted dark maroon, and clicking with each note, fastening to each note, to Clementi's sonatinas, ticking like insects in the grass. Then her long dark hair, draped over her arms and across the keys, and then placing her forehead on top of the piano. Her hands still moving, now pounding with her palms, thin arms, elbows sticking out, flapping up and down. The thrum and clang of too many keys at once. *Stop, Mom. Stop.*

CHAPTER 14

CALLIE MOVED SLOWLY, careful not to wake Spencer. She lifted the sheet, placed her feet on the cool wood floor, and eased away from the bed. Spencer sighed, rolled onto his back. He didn't reach for her. Sweat tickled her skin, evaporating. Somewhere in the lodge a faucet came on, water shuddering in the old pipes, then off. She waited a moment more, then tiptoed across the room, found her long T-shirt, and slipped it over her head. She felt across the floor for her underwear, picked up his boxers and a pair of jeans. The belt clanked when she put the pants down, and she froze. Spencer didn't wake. She left without her underwear, stepped out into the warm night air, closed the door gently, and ran.

The grass was wet and slippery under her feet. She slowed, taking gingerly steps so she wouldn't fall. It was her habit to run all the way to Lo-House, slip through the side door, and take the stairs to the upper floor cautiously, staying to one side so the boards wouldn't creak. The stairs angled over the cooks' suite of rooms, where Barb and Lewis lived, so she had to be especially careful. Once on the upper floor, she'd creep by Rabbit's room, then slip into her own. It was always a relief to get into her own bed, safe, comfortable. Still, she couldn't stop herself from going to Spencer's room whenever he asked.

If Marlee was awake, she never let on, but she knew, of course. The other morning, as Callie hid under her covers, groaning and pretending the alarm hadn't just gone off, Marlee had said from the upper bunk, "A wee bit of a late night, eh?" Callie grinned at Marlee's pretend Scottish accent, but didn't answer. Then Marlee came down the ladder and sat on the edge of Callie's bunk. She sucked in her upper lip and scratched the tip of her nose. "I hope you're using something," she said, her tone suddenly serious. "And you know what I mean."

Callie did know. "Condominiums," she'd said and smiled. Marlee squinted at her, then let herself smile at the joke. "Just checking," she said. "Just be careful. You don't want to get anything. You know, like diseases or babies."

Spencer liked her body. He would say this. Once, during the day, she'd ended up in his room and he undressed her slowly, pulling her bra straps from her shoulders one at a time, pulling them down, then up again, then down a little farther, then up again, as if wanting to get it right, relishing it.

His attention did intrigue her, made her feel pretty, and also as if there was something hidden, unobtainable, in her. Then in another way it made her feel dishonest. It was always just sex. She thought she'd learned what he liked, gauging his moans and sighs. Sometimes he'd simply place her hands where he wanted them and she'd rub, jerking him off, her arm growing tired. It was as if she wasn't there, only her arm, the muscles aching, her hand sliding up and down, sometimes sticky, sometimes slippery. He'd kiss her, poking his fast tongue into her mouth, pushing it around her gums, like he was probing for a loose tooth.

Sometimes the inside of her legs hurt where his hips crashed against them again and again. At first he'd keep his eyes on hers, staring at her, and she'd look back. Should she smile? Should she make a face of pleasure? What was he looking at? It seemed he was looking at her, eyes shining with need, with love even, but then his eyes would turn blank, glazed, and she knew that he was inside his head, inside his own pleasure completely separate from her. With his hands pressed into the pillow on either side of her, he'd pound harder, rocking his body forward, his head thrown back, eyes now squeezed shut. Pounding, pounding, until she got dry, and chafed, and she'd hope he'd finish soon. Then he would, and with always just the same pinched moan, then the collapse on top of her, his body quaking slightly. She'd run her fingertips down his back softly and he'd fall asleep.

Still, she couldn't stop herself from coming to his room, lying in his arms. She liked it when he ran his hands all over her body, caressing her in the dark. Liked it when it seemed he couldn't get enough of her. She could leave if she wanted to, but it was interesting, this detached experience. Whatever drove her to his bed, she couldn't quite name. Not love, but less lonely.

Tonight he'd left the lights on as they undressed at the foot of the bed. She wanted to shut them off, but he held her back, gripped her arms when she moved toward the switch. He said, "No. Stay there. I want to look." She felt aroused, but also embarrassed, like she was acting, not being Callie, but someone in a movie. Then he guided her to the middle of his room and had her stand there while he lay down on the bed, hands behind his head. He still had on his undershorts; she could see the cucumber shape of his penis, lying crosswise. It quaked like an animal trapped underneath the material. She started to come toward him and he said, "No. Stop. Stay there." So she stood there naked in front of him, letting him look at her. Then he asked her to turn around, and she did. He was quiet, and she stared at the wall across the room, at his bulletin board with photos of his family,

and of a girl, that one in Boston that he went to see and the cooks
called his fiancée. She felt him looking at her, at her back and her
bottom. She wondered if her bottom was too big. She leaned on
one foot, then stood straighter, making the weight even for both
legs, hoping her bottom looked smooth and not lopsided.

The girl in the photo was pretty. She smiled at the camera,
chin-length brown hair falling forward as if she had picked something up from the ground and was just standing upright when the
photo had been snapped. She looked very happy and pleasant and
her smile was wide and friendly. There was a neatness about her
clothing, about her smooth hair and her wide jaw—something
Callie couldn't quite define. It reminded her, though, of the very
popular girls at school. The ones who were cheerleaders and prom
queens. The ones who were wealthy and went out with the boys
who were just like them—neat and rich and wholesome. Those
girls were sometimes nice to her and a couple of them were on
the ski team with her and they said once that her hair was pretty.
Like angel hair, one had said. Callie had tried, but never felt
comfortable with those girls. They would hate it here. There was
no television. No computers, except for one in the main office.
No one carried a cell phone, except on their days off. Those girls
didn't know Callie, maybe thought she was naive. They would
never imagine her to be standing here naked with a guy—a guy
who was older and in college.

"Spread your legs," he said. She did, but only a little. She felt
foolish, and was about to say so when he came up behind,
reached around, and took her breasts in his hands. "You are *so*
sexy," he said. He pulled her back against himself, keeping one
arm firmly across her chest. His other hand was on her bottom,
and then he slipped his fingers into her from behind, and she
flinched, tried to pull away. Something trickled down the inside
of her thigh, and for a moment she worried that she'd peed, but
it wasn't that, and when he took his fingers out and ran them

across her stomach they were wet and sticky, and she was surprised at how her body was doing that even when she was also thinking that she didn't really like this.

Now, out in the night, she was about halfway back across the lawn when the door to Lo-House opened and someone stepped out. She stopped, bent low and made her way to the edge of the yard under the trees. She wasn't sure who it was, until he passed near the night lantern. She knelt down, let her fingers spread into the grass, and lay on her stomach as Ben started across the lawn, coming in her direction.

He walked with his hands in his pockets, shoulders hunched. Then he hung his head down and crossed his arms in a hug around himself. He wore his fire watchman cap. He stopped a few yards from her and turned his cap backward, looked up at the sky. Maybe he'd decided to head up the mountain after all, having already slept awhile on Rabbit's bottom bunk, which he sometimes did. But he didn't have his pack, or flashlight.

She felt like laughing, or jumping out and scaring him, but there was something about the way he stood, his arms around himself, tight, like he was holding himself together. And it was late to be out, alone, lonely.

When he spoke, Callie held her breath. He seemed to be talking to the sky, or himself. The grass was prickly on her legs. She strained to hear what he was saying, but now he sighed, then after a moment he turned and went back across the lawn and into Lo-House.

The night lantern glowed and sent hazy orange light up the clapboards. She lay with her cheek against the grass. Her T-shirt was damp all the way through, but the air was warm, and she felt a bit like she was floating in the pond.

She waited, giving Ben time to go up the stairs, and wishing she'd been brave enough to come out of the shadows, to approach him, share the night sky with him.

All at once she felt immensely, deeply sad. It was the *dark-gloom*. That's what she'd named it. It came, not for anything really specific. It was a dreadful feeling that descended over her out of nowhere. No rhyme nor reason—just intense sadness, like tons and tons of black sky pushing down on her back, pushing her into the ground. Mary Walker was in grief. Dark-gloom was for nothing.

Mary's dead husband. She couldn't stop picturing him. The blood in his hair. His twisted arm. That face. Unmoving, finished. Dead. Mary, all alone, never able to touch him again.

Her parents hadn't been too keen about her staying at Cascom when they heard she'd been a part of carrying a dead body down, but they tried to understand. It was her job; she'd taken all sorts of courses in rescue and first aid. She liked it here. Still, a part of her was homesick. She missed her sister's smell, her no-tears shampoo and soft lotion, especially when she sometimes crawled into bed with Callie, asking to "tell stories" together, a tradition the two sisters had invented long ago. Callie longed for her mother's smile and her "Glop," Callie's favorite pasta and vegetable dish. Her dad, his deep belly laugh, and *How're my girls?* in the morning.

She was such a different person now, here, on this mountain, from who she was back home. Not a virgin anymore, though nothing really seemed changed because of that. Except, maybe, her childhood was farther behind her, and that meant that time was going by, rolling her forward toward the end of things, toward sad things she'd someday have to face.

She waited for Ben to have time to get to his room, followed him in her mind's eye up the creaky stairs and into the room he shared with Rabbit whenever he stayed. She watched him shed his clothes, his khakis dropping to the floor, his feet stepping away from the pants. His sturdy legs sliding under the covers. His dark, olive-golden skin, like the silt at the shore of the pond. Then she watched him shut his eyes, watched as his mind wandered toward sleep. She gave him a dream of rippling water and honeysuckle in the air. She put herself in his dream too, standing at the edge of the pond, bright in the sunlight, so he might turn to see her for the first time in a new way. A spell.

CHAPTER 15

THE KNAPSACK SAT ON THE TABLE where she'd left it, upright, holding its shape as if it were stuffed, though there was hardly anything in it.

At the lodge, Spencer had apologized for keeping it so long. He'd faltered and looked to Callie for help. Callie said, "We didn't know when you were coming home."

Home. The picture window, backed by darkness, mirrored nearly the whole room. There she stood in the reflection. A muddy image, dim face. She walked to the middle of the living room, paused in the center of the round rag rug. As a kid, the rings of multicolored braids had made her want to run in circles around and around. She remembered her parents waltzing. She was just a little girl, doing her own sort of ballet with them, laughing and spinning until she was dizzy. Her mother stood on her father's toes, and he walked her with his feet. And there was the reflection of her parents in the window—a twin room with another pair of dancers. There was the little girl in the reflection too, looking back and forth between the window and the room, wishing by magic that one pair of dancers, the impostor set in the reflection, might take off on their own. As the music played and her parents danced, she drew closer to the window, nearer to her own reflection, until she saw right through herself to the dark ridge of the mountain.

Crickets chirped, little rusty hinges, twisting her thoughts inside their choppy loops of music, making her mind repeat things: If only she'd been standing closer to him, she could have grabbed his arm, his shirt, yanked him back. She saw herself reach out, get a grip on the back of his T-shirt, pull. If only. The mirror image in the window reached, grasped, pulled back nothing. There was a blue object in the reflection, and she turned to face it.

It sat there on the table, gaping at the top. She snatched it up, swung open the heavy front door, and hurled the pack outside. She heard it land somewhere on the dark lawn and slammed the door. The door boomed, windows rattled. When she turned around, she saw him. He stood at the end of the long table, his chin raised in concern. Then he was gone. It was just shadows on the wall, a sweater over the back of the chair in the dim lamp-light. The corner of the sideboard. Still, her heart fluttered and prickles flew up her arms.

In the bathroom she brushed her teeth, washed her face, peed. Turning to flush the toilet, she froze, stared into the bowl. Blood.

"What?" she said. "Oh no." *No, please don't let this be true.* But she knew it was true. This was the heaviness, the ache, she'd felt, off and on, all day. So familiar, yet she hadn't made the leap until now. Her period. Nothing more. She flushed, watched the bloody toilet paper swirl away. In the cabinet above the toilet she found a box of tampons, took care of things. Numb and worn out, she couldn't think of anything to do but go to bed.

CHAPTER 16

A WEEK PASSED. Days went slowly, but nighttime was its own eternity. Sometimes she went to the cupboard, gulped whiskey, hoping it would put her back to sleep. Tonight she'd slept fitfully, then awoke to a bright light shining through the window. A flashlight? Startled, she sat up, confused, until she realized she was staring at the moon. It was amazingly bright and low, setting all the room in a bluish light. She got up, slipped on her flip-flops, went outside, stood in the grass, and opened her mouth to the sky to swallow the moon whole. Inhale the light.

In other times she might have been a little afraid of the night—the dense forest at the edge of the field, the possibility of whatever startling animal noises, or scary things one's imagination might conjure. But now that seemed ridiculous. There was nothing more to frighten her. She was utterly alone, and somehow this gave her absolute power. Come and get me, she thought.

She took the logging road toward the main road, the same way she and Michael had gone that day before their hike. She walked in the Mohawk, letting the tall grass scratch and brush against her legs. The flip-flops didn't offer much protection, but the occasional dull pain of a pebble or stick caught under her heel didn't bother her. She was made of stone. She was impenetrable. Nothing, absolutely nothing, could harm her.

It was even brighter when she came out onto the gravel road, wider, more exposed to the moon's light. There was her father's sign, the arrow-end pointing back down the road she'd just come from. Michael had glued it together and tacked support pieces across the back to keep it tight. You'd never know there was a crack down the middle of *Hall*. She'd had a plan to surprise Michael, make another sign that said "Walker" and nail it to the post below her father's sign, but that hadn't happened.

The tank top and knit shorts she'd slept in stuck to her back and sides in the balmy, muggy air. She turned left toward the lodge, imagining the pond, the cool water, sliding over her skin. She remembered those nights she swam there at seventeen, feeling alive, blissful, content. She'd been strong, and well liked for her level head, for how calming she could be in the face of trouble.

She remembered swimming in the pond with the crew boss. Nick's little brother had been killed earlier that summer, before they'd come to work at the lodge. Hit by a car. Nick had told her about it one night when they'd gone swimming, just the two of them. They'd swum out to the middle of the pond and climbed onto the raft. The air was cool, and they lay close to each other so their shoulders touched. His skin felt rubbery. She was in her bathing suit, but she felt naked almost. The stars were glittering, and she looked at them while he told her about the accident. "He was on his bike," Nick said. "He loved that bike. He'd been asking for it for a year—a Schwinn ten-speed—and my dad got it for him on his birthday. He was constantly washing the thing, polishing it up. Rode it everywhere. He had a headlight and reflectors, but some idiot didn't see him."

When she asked, "What was his name?" he began to sob and couldn't say the name, though each sob was a try. She didn't know what to do, so she sat up and laid her hand on his chest. She kept it there while he cried. His body jerked and trembled. She kept her hand on him like that, until he was done, and they slipped quietly back into the water and swam to shore. As they found their towels in the dark he said, "Jim. Jim's his name."

Back then, his grief wasn't something she could feel herself. In fact, his anguish was a conduit, a way to get close, to kiss him.

The tall lights over the parking lot were on, illuminating the sandy ground, the several cars. The lodge windows were dark. Everyone was inside, asleep. She crossed through, feeling a bit too visible, then beneath the trees and down the path to the pond. At the shore she kicked off her flip-flops. The sand felt soft and pleasantly cool as she dug her feet in. Then the water too, lapping around her ankles. For a moment she hesitated, cowered. Dark water had always scared her a little. She waded in to her knees. The raft was a dim square shape out there on the water. The moonlight was amazing still, showing even slow rills, lazily sliding into shore. The pond was spring-fed, always alive, fresh.

She waded further, ready to submerge herself, sink to the bottom, hold her breath as long as possible, when there was a sound of splashing, water displaced, showering down, and a form rose from the depths out there, dragging itself up, crawling onto the raft. Mary came out of her trance, all strength vanished, her limbs weak, and a noise came from her mouth, a gasplike squeak. In the same instant she knew it was just a person, not any monster, just someone else out for a swim, and embarrassment washed over her. But the someone else shrieked in return and flattened herself to the raft. Mary, too, had involuntarily ducked her shoulders under the surface to shield herself. The figure on the raft spoke.

"Who's there?"

It was a girl's voice, the tone of it alarmed but also stern, attempting authority.

"It's Mary," she answered, and felt the incongruity, that weird distance that occurred when she pronounced her own name, separating herself. "Mary Hall," she clarified. "From up the road."

"Mary," the voice, young and airy, acknowledged. "Mary Walker?"

Mary Walker? She'd nearly forgotten. A name no longer viable. Unnecessary.

"Yes," Mary said, straining to see out over the water to the girl-shape on the raft. She thought she recognized Callie's voice, but she wasn't sure. "And you?"

"It's Callie," the voice said, now whispering, perhaps aware of sound carrying across water to the lodge, where others slept with windows wide open.

"I'm coming out," Mary said and pushed off.

Wet, cooled, on the raft, knees drawn up, sitting next to Callie, Mary returned to herself, no longer an apparition, a force harder than darkness. She now had to be human and real and speak with the girl. No acting. No trance. But still she felt removed from herself, from the Mary who'd lost a husband and for whom everyone felt sad. What if she was still part girl, part seventeen, on the raft in the pond, full circle, backward in time. Back when Michael didn't exist.

"Water feels great," Mary said.

"Are you okay?" Callie asked, softly.

"Yes." It came out in an exhale. "I'm fine," Mary said. The girl was so sensitive, so aware of what Mary had lost, of where she really was in time, of what she might be feeling, but Mary wanted to deflect any sympathy, any reminders of her loss. "Can you believe this moon?"

"I know!" Callie said, that lovely tinge of pure excitement in her voice. "And it was so hot. I had to cool off."

Drops pattered onto the wooden surface of the raft, and Mary realized that Callie had twisted her long hair into a ponytail, wringing out the water. She wore a T-shirt, the sleeves plastered to her arms, and now she pulled the bottom of it out, stretching it over her knees to make a sort of tent. Mary twisted the hem of her tank top, wringing it out.

"I'm usually scared to swim at night," Callie said. "When I was little I couldn't go in water, you know, lakes or ponds, at all. I was afraid of things down there."

The moon, Mary noticed, was lowering behind the crowns of the trees that surrounded the area above on the embankment. It was still bright, but Callie's face was in shadow. From a distance they'd be two dark figures, sitting on the float in the middle of the pond. The raft was like an island, private, safe. It felt familiar. Perhaps she'd slipped back in time again.

"Not fish or anything. Fish are supposed to be there. I was afraid of things that weren't supposed to be there, like logs, or once at this girls' camp at the lake there was an old raft, I don't know what it was doing there, but it was lying on the bottom. Just thinking about it still gives me the creeps. I couldn't swim over it, and it was right on the route we were supposed to take to swim the daily quarter mile. I was going for my senior lifesaving badge. No matter how much I told myself it wasn't going to rise up to get me, or my toes wouldn't even come close to brushing it, I just couldn't do it. I'd swim close, then panic. It was, like, totally irrational."

"This is uncanny," Mary said. "Was it Nawayee? The camp?"

"You know it?" Callie said.

"I do. I went there. And I know the thing you're talking

about. I was never sure what it was—a boat, a raft. I didn't even like going over it in a canoe."

"Holy crap," Callie said. "You went to Nawayee, too?"

"Nawayee, oh Nawayee," Mary said, half singing the words of the old camp song. She couldn't help but laugh at Callie's incredulous delight.

"Awesome," Callie said. "I was in Birches and then Ashes."

"I was in Birches too, but I skipped Ashes and went to Skyhighs. I was an aide for a summer, too, before I came to work here."

"Cool," Callie said, twisting her hair up again, more drops pattering onto the wood. "That's so cool."

"Canoeing was my big thing," Mary said.

"Me too. I canoed all over. The Penobscot in Maine. And lots of other rivers. Talk about things underwater; once on the Baker River we floated over this doll, a big plastic baby doll, lying on the bottom on its back, like arms reaching up and everything. I screamed my head off. But I guess everyone did. We thought it was a baby."

"That's awful." Goose pimples rose on her arms, and she realized that her hand had flown to her belly.

"It was only a doll," Callie said with gravity, as if she thought she had frightened Mary. "How long did you work here?"

"Just two summers," Mary told her. "Then I went to Pinkham Notch at the base of Washington. I didn't like it so much there. Mostly because I had a boyfriend back home and I just wanted to be with him."

"Was he the boyfriend, the one you met here? The one who painted the crew sign?"

"No, no. That ended when summer ended."

"Oh," Callie said. She sounded disappointed. Then she said, "Remember Sunrise Rock? It was *so* beautiful. I loved watching the sun set over the lake."

"And the singing. All the singing."

"Someday I want my daughter to go there," Callie said.

Mary, too, had imagined that one day her own daughter would go to Nawayee, like so many of the other girls who had that history—a mother, or aunt, or grandmother who'd gone there before them. Now, here was Callie. They were like doppelgängers, or just girls on the same path, one older than the other. Mary ahead, Callie behind. Then she remembered how Callie had participated in the retrieval of Michael's body. Mary wanted to apologize, but she also didn't want to dwell there. An apology wasn't really the right word for what she wanted to say to Callie. More like, concerned. Concerned the girl had to witness Michael dead. And then Mary realized this other similarity between them—Mary, too, at seventeen, had seen a young man dead.

"I wish," Mary found herself saying, "that you hadn't had to see my husband dead. I hope it doesn't ruin your time here."

"I'm all right," Callie said. She was quiet for a moment, and Mary began to worry. Was she all right? Then Callie said, "Sometimes I have this thing, but I've always had it. It's hard to explain. I call it dark-gloom. Hyphenated."

Mary felt cold suddenly and pulled her knees up. "Dark-gloom? That doesn't sound comfortable."

"I've had it a little bit here," Callie said, and Mary thought she detected the smallest hitch in her voice. "I don't know why I feel it. It just comes."

"I think I understand," Mary told her.

"Do you have it, too?" Callie spoke with that same hint of eagerness. Perhaps she hoped for another similarity between them. "I mean, oh gosh, I'm an idiot. Your husband and all. I'm so stupid."

"No, you're not. I like that you named it, your feeling."

"It's kind of like being lonely even when I'm not alone. I've never told anyone about it before."

"Do you have a boyfriend?" Mary asked, remembering the crew boss, his attention to Callie that night she'd driven Callie back to the lodge.

"No," Callie said. "Not really. Maybe Spencer, sort of."

Mary felt like a girl again, trading secrets with a girlfriend. If only you could slip back in time, alter the trajectory you'd made into the world, recompose your life, be an influence on your younger self. But what would she change? She would have tried to know her father better, especially as an adult. She would have learned to kiss her parents and tell them she loved them. She would have opened herself up to the world more. She would have studied music with more dedication. She wouldn't have been so intimidated by everyone and everything and would have noted to herself that she was talented, kind, worth knowing. Michael had told her these things. She'd tried to believe him. *God, you have a beautiful voice. You should sing more.*

If she could go back, they wouldn't have climbed the mountain. They would have made love without protection; they would have made love with abandon, and she would have had a baby. *A baby.* It had been such a sweet hope. It had gotten her through those first weeks. Now it was only an apparition, lying on the bottom of a stream.

The moon had sunk farther below the trees, and it was time to plunge back into the dark water and swim over invisible things, fear rising up to meet them, dark-gloom pressing down upon them.

Callie leapt out in a canon ball, making an enormous splash that rained up onto Mary's legs. Mary laughed and followed Callie in.

Swimming next to each other, paddling near one another, made the dark water less creepy, and Callie said so herself—*That was easy. Not so bad*—when their feet touched the soft, silty bottom and they waded in to shore.

"Sleep well," Mary said, keeping her voice low.

Then they parted, Callie toward the lodge, and Mary began the walk up the gravel road. The remnants of the moon still made the world white-blue and full of shadows. Mary turned back once, but Callie had disappeared, gone beyond the lights in the parking lot to Lo-House. And Mary walked on, feeling gentler somehow. The sky was growing darker as the moon sank, and soon the day would come on. As it would. As it always did, no matter how much it had taken away from you in all the days before.

Somewhere out there was her crew boss, Nick. Nick's brother was named Jim, and he'd died as a child. That young death must have been absorbed over time. Probably still painful for Nick, wherever he was, but the loss might have dulled with time. *Time heals*, she remembered Ben the watchman saying, as had so many other people. Cliché or not, it was true, perhaps. Would Michael's death ever feel dulled, absorbed, less? Though what had started to bother her was how distant their life together already seemed. The familiarity of it was receding. It had been such a short time together. Barely anything. In some ways it felt similar to the way she'd noticed San Francisco had been eclipsed so quickly once she left California. Details faded promptly, and her new life in Somerville—their funky apartment, the weird three-pronged dangling chandelier over their bed, the walk to the corner market, Michael's music, singing with him, all of it—had become truer, more familiar, almost instantly. The years in San Francisco seemed like the memory of an ancient dream, a hazy era in her life. But Michael wasn't an era, or a period of time. He was a man. Her lover. Her husband. Flesh and blood impossibly disappeared.

Nick had kissed her that night he'd told her about his brother's accident. They'd climbed through the window, out onto the roof of Lo-House. He'd put his arm around her shoulders.

They'd looked up at the sky, at the glorious stars, and he'd thanked her for being there, for listening. Then he'd run a fingertip along her jaw, from her earlobe to her chin. He'd said, "I don't think you know how beautiful you are," and he'd gently tugged her lower lip down with his thumb, "and sexy." Then he'd leaned in and touched his lips to hers, just grazed her lips, then pressed, open mouth, ravenously.

For a second she felt it now, the butterflies, that plunge in her belly. She was seventeen again. They'd been crazy about each other, but summer would end, they'd part—they'd always known that. Mary imagined Callie, kissing her crew boss, Spencer, and remembered briefly how lonely that could feel.

Just before the turnoff to the logging road, she heard the rumble of a car coming up the mountain, the engine straining on the steep hill, tires grinding or slipping at one point. As light skimmed down the telephone wires and headlights began to illuminate foliage at the top of the rise, Mary stepped off the road. It gave her a shiver, the thought of being seen on the road, so late. She crouched behind bushes. Whether the shiver was for herself or the poor driver who might be taken by surprise by the sudden appearance of a bedraggled and ghostlike figure, walking the road in the middle of the night, she wasn't sure. The car passed, unknowing. When the red glimmers of its taillights disappeared around the bend, heading for the lodge, she stepped back to the road and went on.

CHAPTER 17

MARY WATCHED from the front window as Tobin slipped between the dead birches and out into the front yard. He carried a chain saw in one hand. When he caught sight of her, he smiled. She liked his smile, how it expanded very slowly across his face—all teeth, and then gums. Dimples. A smile that kept growing, uncontrolled. Almost too uncontrolled, as if her attention set something loose in him. She went out to the front deck.

"I'll cut the trees," he called to her. "Clean it all up." He motioned toward the birches.

They'd discussed this before, but taking them down made her sad. The trees had stood since before she was born. Now, most had split or bent in the ice storm last winter.

"Any way to save the one?" she asked. There was one that still had life in it, a few branches of green leaves, though it had been as crippled as the others, and severely bowed over.

He didn't answer right away. He turned, looked at the stand of trees, looked back at her.

"It's got a lot of dead wood on it, and bugs will get in, and rot."

"I see."

"I'll try," he said.

The grass was damp, just beginning to dry out, and there were good smells of hemlock and cedar as Mary went around the house to the garden. It was cool, but it would be hot later. Weeds and stray tall brown-eyed Susans and white daisies grew against the house and grasshoppers clacked on some open granite near the truck.

The chain saw started. Not an unpleasant noise, a stop-and-go whirring, whining sound she knew so well from her childhood. Her father cut saplings and branches, keeping the place clear, the views open. She was thankful that Tobin wanted to cut the dead birches. Thankful he was doing something more useful than walking on the roof. Though sometimes tracing his path across the roof with her ears, her eyes on the ceiling, listening to the thud of his footfalls, was reassuring. When he stopped pacing, she'd know he sat on the highest eave, gazing at the mountain.

Under the mass of weeds in the garden, the soil was dusty, parched and lightened as if flour had been added to the dirt. She took a few steps forward, knelt low, and separated some of the tall grass and chickweed, pulled some up and shook the loose soil off. She leaned back on her heels, queasy, and recalled the whiskey she'd had last night. The feeling passed, and she pulled more weeds. Then there were green shoots in even lines. She stopped pulling, her fingertips trembling as she parted grasses to see better. A few feet over, the feather tops of carrots. And leaves of lettuce—scraggly, purple-fringed lettuce. Michael's plants had come up! Here was another row, and another. She squatted, pulling out strands of grass, then pressed her hands into the dirt near darker leaves—spinach. So dry. They needed water. She hurried, careful to step between the rows, across the yard for the hose. She cranked the outside spigot and water hissed and sputtered, then opened into a fan of fine spray. Rainbows glistened through the mist as she dragged the hose to the garden's edge. A cloud of dust rose in a puff when the drops hit the powdery soil, then the dirt darkened. The plants glistened.

When puddles began to form, she stopped watering. It panicked her for a moment to think that she might have drowned them. But when she went close to inspect, she saw that all was fine and the lettuce seemed greener, cleansed, almost visibly revived.

The chain saw coughed, shuddered, then buzzed evenly, biting into wood. She dropped the hose in the grass and looked at the garden, at the little plants gleaming, droplets of water clinging to their fragile leaves. She felt peculiarly moved and sad, but also giddy; Michael had sent her a sign. A task. Get busy. Here are things to take care of.

She worked the garden, pulling weeds, shaking soil from roots, uncovering rows. The sun beat on her back, burning her shoulders, but she couldn't stop. She'd fix the garden. Put it all back the way it should be, clean, even rows. Give light to the sprouts. Mulch. She could cut the grass, gather it, lay it between rows, smother the weeds. When her legs began to hurt from crouching, crab-walking, she dropped to her knees. Careful not to pull the wrong things. Not anything Michael had planted. He'd planted seeds and they'd grown. *I want to make your belly grow. We could make pesto.* Yes, basil. Basil would need to be planted. She panted, sweating, felt a moment of vertigo; the ground spun, but she dug her fingers in, gritted her teeth. Nothing was going to stop her from this. And when she was done, she'd go to her father's little field, clear away branches. The deck needed staining too. Drainage ditches should be dug alongside the road. The gutters—

"Mary," came a voice behind her. She turned slowly, dizzy. A man walked across the yard toward the garden. Cold thorns pricked down her arms. He was all the shades of Michael, a blurry photo of him, but not him—same size and gait. Her stomach felt weak. There were the short sleeves of an olive green T-shirt. The slightly bowed and pale legs. His light blue eyes held hers with an expression that seemed to know that she was not understanding who he was, but that she should know. He held his chin forward as if to say, *What's wrong with you? You know who I am.* Her heart rattled. Then as if a downpour had suddenly and abruptly stopped, it came clear. Michael's father. Clayton Walker.

CHAPTER 18

THE TREE THAT Mary said she wanted to save, the one with some life to it, was not in good shape, but it did have several live branches dense with its heart-shaped, toothed leaves. The tree's main stem had cracked, though not all the way through. Still, the tree lay open—a wound, revealing the light heartwood underneath. Insects had probably already tunneled in there. Too bad he couldn't straighten the tree up, tie a sling around it, let it graft back together. He didn't want to take the whole tree down. Not if Mary wanted to keep it. It had been a beautiful tree, bright white with crosshatches of black that looked almost like letters or symbols, as if the tree was speaking its ancient secrets. He'd leave it; maybe it would be all right, for a while it might.

The chain saw started with one easy pull of the cord, and he set the blade first against the delicate limbs of the downed trees, slicing through little branches clean, then into thicker stems, rotating the blade forward and back, letting it slowly sink, the motor whining louder as he drove the saw in. After trimming off the branches and throwing them into a pile, he began to cut the trunks into logs—manageable sizes for Mary's wood stove.

Birch burned fast and hot and was good for getting a fire going. In the fall, as it turned cold, Mary would want this wood. He could even lay a fire for her now so it would be ready for the first cold night. And then he imagined himself there with her, watching the flames take hold.

The other day, she'd come out on the front deck while he was sitting on the eave above. They'd talked a little, her looking up at him, smiling, shading her eyes with one hand, like she was saluting him. There were moments when you wouldn't know from her demeanor that her husband had died, then a darkness would seep across her face, an eerie sort of closing down, and he knew she was swimming in murky waters somewhere inside her mind. He tried not to look at where the V of her T-shirt pointed toward her breasts. Once, a flash of dark lace, the edge of her bra. In the shade of her hand he saw her mouth, the dimples— *angel wells*, his mother used to call dimples.

In that moment, looking down at her, and her smiling up, her mouth raised to him, like a baby bird, almost, he wanted to fly down, swoop down, nudge his face up under her shading hand, put his mouth so close to hers that he could feel her moist breath, then they'd press their lips together. He'd felt mildly guilty for imagining this, but who didn't imagine kissing someone when you were talking to them? He'd imagined it with girls at school, and Callie or Marlee at the lodge. It didn't mean anything, really. It was just interesting to wonder what lips might feel like, taste like. He hadn't kissed a girl since ninth grade. Valerie was older by two years, and her tongue tasted exactly like what he thought toothpaste would taste like if it was mixed with lemons. Sour fruit and peppermint. Most girls in school had regarded him as a freak because he was so much younger, fifteen as a senior.

The top half of one tree had broken off, but still hung by a few threads. Its crown swept the ground. He went after the trunk at the base. Light-colored bits shot out in a spray. Papery pieces of bark, white and pinkish, flew up in the wind like snow. An image of his mother, naked and running across a snow-covered field, came to him. Her feet broke through the crust up to her shins; it sounded like paper, tearing in little bursts. She ran wide-legged as if on snowshoes, the dark fur patch between her spindly legs. Her breasts, pale and heavy, swayed, and her arms swung wildly, sometimes paddling the air as if swimming. She'd gone into the woods, thrashing at the silvery, ice-covered branches, not far from where Tobin had stood, mesmerized by this manifestation.

The tree shuddered from the saw's vibration, and the trunk jerked from its stump and fell. Branches whipped across his face. He jumped back. It felt as if someone had slapped him. His cheek stung. The branches had fallen around him like a net, jabbing into his back and pressing against his chest. A hawk circled over the lower ridge of the mountain. He breathed to calm himself, smelled mint, knelt slightly and dropped the saw. It plunked nicely onto the grass in a space near his feet. He straightened and used his palms to push at the tangle of twigs, but the branches were tough; they bent and didn't break, then flew back into his chest. For a second he felt trapped—his arms pinned inside the snag of wiry branches, twigs, and dead leaves near his face and eyes. It didn't want to let him go. He peered out between the cross of branches.

He'd peered out through branches when his father had come running after his mother. His father had called to her and carried a blanket, his long winter coat flapping behind him, boots crunching. When he dropped the blanket, he stopped, went back. His toes caught under the crust, and pieces of it flew up, clattered, and spun across the hard surface. The blanket lay in a heap. He snapped it up, billowing. Moments later, Tobin watched his father come out of the woods, carrying her in his arms, wrapped in the blanket. Her legs hung slack, feet bare, swinging. He took her into the house. Tobin looked at her footprints, the holes in the crust; there was blood on the sharp edges, little curves of it, bright red. He followed the trail of foot holes to the house. There were her footprints and also his father's interrupting hers, and tracks in a quick spiral where his father had backtracked. Drops of bright blood peppered the crust, like hard, red berries shot into it. Inside the house, water sloshed, and he knew that his father had put her in the bathtub to warm her up. "Cordelia, Delia, why?" he said. Outside water dripped from the eave of the house, pattering hard against the crust; it sounded like a fast metronome. Across the yard, the studio door hung open, and the pedestal where she'd been modeling was empty except for the pink wrap she must have been wearing for the portrait. Behind the bathroom door his mother was quiet, but Tobin pictured her lying in the tub, legs curled to the side, and his father sponging warm water over her. His father saying, "My silly girl," and not seeing, not understanding, refusing to see that she was crazy, going *crazy*.

That morning he found Mary in the field, he'd drawn her a bath. It was all he could think to do. Now he found a way to stomp at the base of a branch, and finally it snapped, freeing him. He hoisted the branch to the side, tossed it away, and sawed more branches, heaving them toward a pile. Sweat ran down his face. Every now and then, pain wiggled its way from his lower back and down his leg, and he tried to ignore it. The calcium between his vertebrae, building up, squashing the vulnerable nerves, was like the rot in the tree, he thought, eating away. One doctor had suggested cortisone shots, but they didn't help. His father, the retired doctor who never wanted to think of Tobin's injury as Tobin's mother's doing, maintained that it would likely heal on its own eventually.

Maybe Mary was watching him. It made him feel stronger to

think so as he heaved branches atop the pile. He glanced back toward the house. The front window was full of reflection—cumulus clouds hanging over a watery mountain. Then her face moved through the reflection, close to the window. She was watching him! He cracked a small branch off the trunk with his hands. When he looked again, a different face in the window. A man. Taller than Mary. A brownish shirt. Clouds drifted in the reflection, making the features impossible to discern. The watchman uniform color. Ben? Jealousy swept him, surprised him, made his breath shallow. He looked for the hawk, but it was gone.

The good tree stood before him, leaning over, bowing to him, pathetic with its sparse clusters of leaves. *Take me down*, it said. *If you don't, something bad will happen.* He snagged a high branch and pulled it down hand over hand, got hold of a larger branch, and put his arms around it. Twigs snapped against his chest, gouged him. He hugged the mass tighter, felt a breeze pass over him. Leaves rustled. Something—a leaf or twig?—brushed his neck lightly, like the tip of a feather, and a sinister weight fell to his belly. There was something in that brush that was cruel, and he wanted to defeat it.

He remembered his mother, crushing his shoulders with her hands, holding him against the wall, screaming like a crow on fire. All for no reason, none that he could figure.

He pushed off with his feet, rose with the branches as if on a pulley. The tree resisted, tried to hold him aloft, shuddered, moaned, the wood tearing inside. He held on, bounced, and then the tree snapped, popped, the moist heartwood burst open, and the top half of the trunk came down in a crackling sweep. He fell away. The trunk, still attached, hung on only by a few shreds of wood, bobbing. He took hold of branches and yanked them back and forth. The branches cracked and whooshed, breaking against other branches. Then he let go as the main stem crashed to the ground. He felt exhilarated, a spurt of vengeance.

Out in the valley, the hoarse shriek of the hawk. The bird floated in the sky, nearly still, then forward, in a slow arc. The tree lay there, a few branches still swaying. It would have died anyway. It was going to die anyway, just a matter of time. It had been infected, bent over like that, opening tiny cracks to rot and bugs, weakening it. The leaves would have dried up not long from now. It would have died. Or the next snows would have brought it down.

But Mary had wanted it. It was the last living one, the last one from the ancient stand of birches that had stood since she was a girl. The birches, she'd told him, her parents had loved, *she*'d loved. He'd failed her.

Nothing could be done now. Slowly, he lifted the chain saw, started it up, and let the blade dig in. When he dared to look toward the window once more, there was no one there at all. Mary was gone. There was no man there. It was as if he'd let a ghost get the better of him. Or worse, and a bolt of fear turned him cold, his mother's poison had come loose in his blood.

CHAPTER 19

"YOUR PHONE ISN'T WORKING," Clayton Walker said. "I've been trying. I decided just to come. I took a room at the lodge last night."

He wore khaki shorts, the olive green T-shirt tucked in neatly, so much like Michael. His low hiking shoes looked stiff and new. White socks gave way to thick calves. His legs were covered with dark fuzz, much like Michael's. He looked perturbed, unlike Michael, and took a step forward.

She had the urge to run into the woods and hide. Somehow she moved toward him. She should have shaken his hand, but her arm wouldn't rise. Abruptly, he took her wrist. He had the hose suddenly, and he turned the spout to open it and water dribbled out and onto her palms. He used his other hand to smooth the dirt away, until he'd rinsed her hands nearly clean. His fingers stopped on her wedding ring for a second, then he let go, walked back toward the house, dragging the hose with him. She followed him across the yard, watched as he coiled the hose, fast and efficiently over the hook, putting it up where she stored it.

"I scraped the hell out of my muffler on that road," he said, tipping his head toward his car. It was some sort of compact white car, parked close to her truck. She hadn't heard his approach over the noise of the chain saw. She didn't know what to say about his muffler, amazed that the ledges hadn't deterred him.

The shape of his jaw, a similar cast of features—she could easily see Michael in all of it. Handsome. Yet they were very different looking men. This man was slender, delicate boned, higher cheekbones. His mouth was like Michael's in that the lips were slim and made a long tidy line, drawn up at the corners like checkmarks, though on this man it didn't look as if he were thinking pleasant thoughts. She remembered making these observations before at the funeral when she'd first met him.

He was one of those older men you notice because he was fit and neat and had so much thick white-gray hair. Older? Fifties? His name was Clayton. Should she call him by his first name? Or Mr. Walker? She touched her forehead, trying to think. Her fingers were cold and wet. She pressed her palm to her cheek, and it felt good, cooling.

He finished coiling the hose and wiped his hands together, looked at her.

She should say something about his car, but she couldn't think of what. Then she remembered the garden.

"Look what I found," she said. She pointed to the garden. The chain saw, which had been silent for a time, whirred on again, and she had to speak louder. "Michael planted them."

Clayton looked toward the garden. She couldn't read his face. He nodded, looked at her wearily, it seemed. He didn't understand, perhaps, that the plants had just been discovered. That they were his son's doing.

"Can we talk," he said.

His silhouette before the picture window—it could have been Michael standing there, looking out for the first time, exclaiming, as Clayton was now, saying, "This is an amazing view."

"Yes," she said. She sat, the old vinyl couch cushions exhaling. She'd given him a glass of water, and he held it with both hands, a palm under it.

When his eyes fell on her belly, needles pricked across her back, and she remembered in an abrupt, heated rush. She should have found a phone, called Michael's parents. Should have let them know, but it had slipped. She'd forgotten. Or—and she knew this was probably more accurate—she hadn't been able to bring herself to tell them. Had avoided it, buried it, pretended she'd never told them such an uncertain, unproven thing. Though she had been sure then, at the funeral. All those weeks. She was sure then. But she'd been fooling herself.

"How are you feeling?" he asked.

She shook her head, working to formulate the words. An image of Michael's mother came to her—Lucy at the reception after the funeral, peering between the shoulders of somber, black-suited people across the crowded room—an expression of disdain and alarm and deliberation, like an animal stopped in its tracks, deciding whether to pounce or flee. Mary, the unknown wife, had taken their son away from them. She'd ruined their lives. The only son. But, then, surprise! she'd give them a grandchild. Only now she'd have to tell Clayton there was no grandchild after all.

"Oh. Mr. Walker," she began.

"Clayton," he said. She remembered now that he'd asked her to call him by his first name before, at the funeral.

"Clayton," she began again, but he cleared his throat and spoke again.

"Leah's a quaint town," he said. "I went by the lake. Lots of whitecaps today. Windy. Sailboats were flying." Mary nodded. "I used to take Michael sailing when he was a boy."

"Really?" she said. They'd never talked about sailing.

Clayton turned back to the window. "Where did he fall?" he asked, a slight hitch in his voice. It made her throat ache.

She looked toward the window, the mountain, thinking, *There.* Then thinking, *The ledges above the Clark Trail,* though it was not on the Clark Trail exactly. It was not any trail because they'd hiked off it. Michael next to her then, wiping his neck, saying, "This is an amazing view." *Water?*

She felt a sob working its way out and pressed her fingers over her mouth.

"I want to see where," Clayton said.

She went to stand next to him. Tobin, down below, bent over, tossing branches into a pile. She looked up toward the mountain, pointed. Took a breath.

"See how there's that upside-down triangle of dark trees way up, just where the trees stop? See there's that white streak in the granite, the quartz?"

"No," he said.

She didn't know how else to describe it. "There are binoculars somewhere," she said.

"No, Mary," he said. "I mean, I want to *see* it. I want to go there."

Clayton's eyes were on her; he meant this. He wanted to see the exact spot where his son had fallen and died.

"Give me directions," he said.

"I don't know," she said. "It's not easy to find."

She tried to think of how to tell him, but the more she thought of the trail, the rocks and small passageways through junipers, the more she saw herself, running, branches lashing and stinging. Thickets grabbing her ankles. She saw the ledge overhead, dark and looming. Then she saw Michael tipping, heard that slipping sound of bits of rubble moving under the treads of his boots. She saw his arms loose in the air, then his body going over. His body, dark against the white sky, slow, heavy, coming down as if she were below, looking up. If only she had been below, she could have broken his fall, reached, caught him in her arms.

Clayton put his hand on her back, guided her to the couch. "Sit," he said. "Breathe." He sat next to her and took her hand. "Shh," he said, and smoothed the top of her hand with his.

She stared at the top of his hand, the ridges where the bones fanned from his wrist toward his fingers, a few dark hairs on some of his fingers, slighter than Michael's. For an overwhelming moment she saw her father's hand.

Clayton cleared his throat. "I keep thinking he's going to come around the corner or something," he said, softly. "The phone rings, and I think it will be him. I guess because I didn't see him very often, it takes longer to sink in. I can't really even picture him correctly. I mean, I see him as a grown man, then I get an image in my head, some random thing usually, and he's still a kid. The other day I was digging in the garden behind my house, and I remembered once when he was about five or so and he came into my office with a metal box, one of those round cookie tins. He was collecting objects to put inside and bury, like a time capsule. He had one of his matchbox cars and some other little toys. There was a letter he'd written to himself, for when he'd dig the box up five years later, but he couldn't resist and dug it up only a few months later."

Mary imagined Michael, one of the little-boy photos she'd seen, writing his letter, folding it neatly. A message to his older self, one who couldn't wait for the future. The future, she thought, that never came. The future, too, that had somehow driven a wedge between Michael and his father. Though growing up, he and his father had been talking, being a dad and a kid. What had happened?

"I gave him a pipe to put in his time capsule. It was my grandfather's. He'd carved it himself. There were elephants linked by tails and trunks around the bowl. Mikey had often admired it."

"That was nice of you." *Mikey.*

He made a small huff, and his mouth twitched. "He's gone,"

Clayton said, almost as if it were a question. One she should answer, or affirm. He held her gaze, his eyes full.

He is gone. Gone forever. Mary heard the words in her head, and for an instant the meaning of them became true to her, truer than they had been. He would never be in the same room with her, pick up his guitar, and play again. Never sing nonsense lyrics to her—lyrics about a girl named Mary whom he loved. She would never hear his voice out loud. She would never be able to tell Michael that his father had come to see her, and that he wanted to see the place where his son had fallen. It would interest Michael that his father wanted to see the ledge. It would have fascinated him. She wished she could tell him.

"The letter," she said, suddenly desperate to find out all she could. "What did it say?" She was also aware that she was delaying what she needed to tell Clayton, and she knew it was going to be like telling him his son was dead all over again. When the EMTs had asked if they should call Michael's family, she'd done it finally. Lucy Walker had answered. Lucy, who had never warmed to the idea of Mary, the son's new wife, whom she'd only ever spoken with on the phone. Mary asked to speak to Mr. Walker, but then Lucy must have heard the break in Mary's voice. Lucy was crying before Mary had even said anything, and then Clayton was on the other line shouting at his wife to be quiet, to let their daughter-in-law speak, so Mary just said it outright: *Michael's dead.*

She needed to say now, *There's no baby.*

"I don't remember exactly," Clayton said, and coughed. "I remember other letters, though." Clayton's voice had changed, gone deeper, pained. "More recent." Clayton's shoulder jerked as if he'd startled himself with these words spoken out loud.

"Recent?"

"There are other things, important things, we should talk about," Clayton said.

She looked up to find his stern face. Again, his eyes fell to her middle. Her head pounded, and she felt nauseated.

In the next moment she was making her way to the bathroom, hand over her mouth. She shoved the door closed and vomited into the toilet, then held the edge of the toilet seat, weak, exhausted, eyes shut. After a while she heard him come to stand outside the door.

"Morning sickness?" he asked.

She flushed the toilet, careful to stay bent over the bowl. Finally, the nausea passed and she felt better, though her face was hot. She wet a cloth with cold water and held it over her eyes. Her bangs were damp and clumped, and she noticed how they'd grown out a bit, now dragging over her eyebrows. Then she brushed her teeth. She sensed him still outside the door. It wasn't fair that she should have to deal with Michael's father without Michael here to help her. This shouldn't be her responsibility. Not alone.

When she came out, he had returned to the living room.

"Crackers might help," he said, and smiled a sweet, familiar smile. It made her weak. "The baby," Clayton said. "It's all that's keeping Lucy going." He wiped his eyes with his fingers, faced the mountain again, defiant, it seemed, ready to confront the thing that had killed his son. "She still thinks about the other baby, you know, the one put up for adoption when Michael was in high school."

Mary stared at him, felt her blood drain. "Other baby?" she said.

Clayton looked surprised. "He didn't tell you about that?"

"No," she said, barely a whisper.

"Oh, sorry," he said. "His high school girlfriend. She gave the baby up for adoption. We didn't even know if it was a boy or girl. Water long gone under the bridge. Sorry he didn't tell you about it. He probably didn't want to remember."

She had the sense that Clayton felt a certain pride, maybe for knowing more about Michael than she did. Well, of course he did. She'd known Michael nine months. Only nine months. Still, she felt hurt. Why had Michael kept that from her? She wondered if he would have ever told her.

"It's hard not to think of it . . . of the past," Clayton said.

Mary didn't know what to say. Somewhere out there was Michael's kid. Clayton and Lucy's grandchild. A whole other, invisible, disappeared life that no one would know.

"This is why," Clayton said. "Why it's just so important to us. To be a part of this baby's life."

Mary's skin could have been glass, exploding into shards across her back, up her neck. Her forehead felt compressed. Woozy. "Clayton—"

"What are you going to do?" he asked. "Where are you planning to go?" She felt like she was coated in wax, looking out through a gauzy, thick material, paralyzed. "You can't possibly winter here," he said. "How will you manage that road? A baby takes a lot. Needs things. You can't go about things like it's just you anymore."

She couldn't tell him the baby never existed. She couldn't. A lie might be better. Miscarriage.

"The thing is, it *is* only me. I lost—"

"It isn't *only* you anymore," he blurted out. It sounded like something he'd prepared to say ahead of time. "It's incredibly selfish to think—" He stopped, chin trembling. "Not just you," he said, almost as if pleading. "You have someone else to think about. Look, Lucy and I thought about this. We want you to come back to the Cape. Let us help you. For the baby's sake."

"You don't understand."

"I think *you* don't understand. If you can't properly take care of it, there are *legal* things." His voice was ice. "If you're not fit, not competent, well then . . ."

131

Her hand fell to her stomach as if to shield herself, as if for a moment there was a baby. She understood now what he might be capable of, how he would take the baby if he could, deem her incompetent, or do whatever it took. Again she felt lost in a wave of disorientation, protecting, guarding something that wasn't even real. Michael should be here, dealing with his father, damn it. Then she was aware, again, Michael was never going to be here. She was on her own. And Clayton was hoping for something that didn't exist.

"I'm not pregnant, Clayton." Then in frustration, the truth. "My period came."

Clayton stared at her, eyebrows pinched.

"I'm sorry," she said. "I'm so sorry. I wanted it more than anything. I truly thought I was pregnant, then. My body was different. My period was late. Michael and I hadn't used any protection, so I just thought . . . I really believed—"

"Why are you saying this?" His voice weak, a whimper. "Why?" he said, pleadingly, as if she were a bully, being cruel for no reason.

"I was wrong. I got my period."

He gestured toward the hallway. "But you have morning sickness."

"No," Mary said. "It wasn't."

"What?" he said. "What?"

"It was a shock to me. A complete shock. I couldn't even believe it. I should have told you before. I really should have called you. I just . . . I just . . ." But there was no real answer.

"Dear God." He shook his head, wiped his face, shook his head more. It was as if he was rejecting what she said, refusing to believe her. "Are you sure?"

She nodded, but suddenly she wondered if she was sure. Yes, she was sure. It was her period. In Boston, she'd almost bought a pregnancy test, but then she was too afraid. Too afraid to find out that it might not be true. Then it wasn't true anyway; she started menstruating. Now a doubt rose. In college, a girl on her floor, shouting in relief when her period had arrived, but it must have been implantation bleeding, because the girl eventually dropped out and went on to give birth, after all.

Clayton raised his chin, stared out the window. His lips tightened, then parted, then tightened again. He crossed his arms and uncrossed them. He faced the mountain, shaking his head in tense bursts as if to deflect, or deter, the truth.

She waited, watched, as his body came to terms with it, arms finally limp, hanging at his sides, shoulders lowered.

"My God," he said. "I'm sorry. I'm very sorry." He looked at her, eyes watery. And she knew he finally understood. "You must be devastated."

She nodded. She felt exhausted. Weak. She wanted to put her arms around him, have him hold her up, but he looked away. Took a deep breath and crossed his arms again.

"Or perhaps you're relieved," he said.

"I wanted it," she said. "I wanted to die when it wasn't—" She stopped, not knowing what word to use to finish the sentence.

And Clayton, so like Michael, raised both hands and slid his fingers through his hair on either side of his head, then down, hands locking at the back of his head. With elbows jutting out in front of his face, he sighed. Then dropped his arms again. He stood as if in a trance for quite a while. She didn't dare speak, didn't know what else to say.

"Who's that kid?" Clayton asked.

Tobin, in the yard below, faced away from them. All the trees were down. He hadn't been able to save any, not even the one she'd hoped to save. Now there was a neat stack of white logs with bright, freshly cut ends. He'd sawed the stumps of each tree close to the ground. Off to the side was a tall pile of brush, mostly wiry dead branches, but some green—a few green from the one tree.

"He lives across the valley," she said.

"Is something wrong with him?"

Tobin stood, arms at his sides, opening and closing his fists as if his fingers were numb or stiff and he was trying to wake them up. Then he squatted, fell to his knees, and began patting the grass as if he'd lost something.

"Clayton," Mary said, softly, reaching to touch his shoulder. "Listen, I'm—"

But Clayton wasn't listening. He made a fist, punched the window, a quick jab. The glass cracked, held a second, then shattered, shards falling inside and out.

CHAPTER 20

MARLEE'S LEGS DANGLED from the upper bunk. It was early and Callie was still groggy, wishing there were more hours to sleep. Marlee swung her legs slowly as if treading water. Callie swiped her hand through the air, trying to grab one of Marlee's feet, but missed.

Marlee jumped off her bunk and landed in a squat next to Callie's bed. "Rise and shine," she said.

Callie pulled the sheet over her head. "Go away. I'm still sleeping." When she looked again, Marlee was near the dresser and pulling her nightshirt over her head. She twirled it around her hand, tossed it back up on her bunk, and stood naked. She never seemed to have any modesty. Callie rolled onto her back, trying not to look. She didn't like to feel shy when she herself was dressing, but often turned her back to Marlee, or pulled clothes on discreetly, never exposing her whole self at once. This seemed odd in a way, especially when she could stand naked in front of Spencer. Marlee dug around in her drawers, lifting clothing, shoving it back in. Callie inched her feet out of bed and sat, yawned, pretending to be uninterested in Marlee's body, but at the same time wanting to observe. Marlee looked like she'd been spattered with orange-tan paint drops on her shoulders and chest. She was slender, waist hardly discernible from her narrow hips. Light freckles swam down her legs in an orange lace. With her bright orange hair, it made Callie think of some exotic orchid.

"This?" Marlee said. She held a lime green T-shirt up under her chin. "Or this?" She lifted a navy shirt with her other hand.

"Blue," Callie said. Marlee's breasts were larger than Callie's and of a different shape; the nipples seemed placed off-center of each breast and tipped upward like little acorn hats. When Callie stood in front of the mirror, her own nipples were exactly in the center of her small breasts. If she put her index finger under her breast, it reached only to her second knuckle. She wondered if they would grow more. She had never thought about what her own nipples looked like until one night Spencer commented on them. He said that they were huge and covered most of her breast. She must have looked upset because he quickly explained that, to him, this was beautiful.

"They get so perky," he said, circling her nipple with a finger. She'd looked down at her own chest, at the tip of his finger going around one erect nipple, and squirmed away. Maybe it was the way he stared at it, like it was his discovery when it was her body, a part of her that she should have known about, or did, but hadn't ever thought of that way. The word *perky* was unpleasant and wrong.

From where she lay on her bunk, she could see the mountain out the window. The summit rose up over the rooftop of the lodge, vivid, almost two-dimensional, laid against the blue sky. It seemed closer, clearer, from this view. The fire tower on top was brilliant, its edges well defined even though it looked no bigger than a pebble on top of the world. She wondered if Ben was up there, or maybe he was still in Hi-House, below tree line, getting breakfast before he'd run up the granite to the top. Maybe she'd go up there later, after chores. She and Marlee had run up the mountain once.

It was an amazing feeling to know you could do that, even though in some places they were only hiking fast because it was way too steep to really run. That time they'd done it, she and Marlee had been panting so hard that they couldn't talk once they made the top. Ben waved from inside the tower, and they went up the metal steps and through the hatch. Ben said, "You crew are crazy. And fast!" Callie and Marlee had smiled at each other. They felt good. Their muscles were strong, their legs taut and sturdy. Their biceps bulged from all the work they did around the lodge. Marlee's eyes were as blue as the sky, and her bright orange hair was wet and sticking to her forehead. Her T-shirt clung to her breasts and her nipples showed through. Callie saw Ben glance there and away, and Marlee saw him do this, and she turned her back to him as if to save him the embarrassment, and she said, "I can never get over this view." And Ben looked out at the valley and distant lakes and all the green and said, "Yes, I'm the luckiest man on Earth." When she was sure they weren't looking, Callie glanced at her own chest; her nipples stuck out too.

Marlee was dressed now and twisted her hair up into a clip. They heard Rabbit moving around in the room across the hall.

"I'm up," Callie said, not moving. "Now I'm up." She flopped back on the bed.

Marlee laughed. "Late night?" she said.

She hadn't gone to Spencer's last night, but she had been out, looking at stars, maybe looking for Ben. Hoping he'd come aross the field like before.

Marlee said, "You know, he still has that other chick in Boston, don't forget."

For a half second she thought Marlee meant Ben, and disappointment surged. Then she realized.

"I know," Callie said, though she hadn't thought much about the girlfriend they'd all heard of at the beginning of the summer, the girl in the photograph in Spencer's room. She hadn't imagined Spencer was still sleeping with that girl, too. But he had gone to Boston on his days off. Perhaps she'd thought Spencer had given that girl up for her.

There were footfalls outside their door.

"Time to serve the goofers," came Rabbit's voice. Spencer had asked them not to use that term for fear the guests might hear it, but Rabbit had started bringing it back to life. Callie liked it when they shared their own language; they were friends, a group, and she was part of it. She'd learned that washing pots was diving deep. To ream was to clean rooms, and the other night Marlee had placed a knife next to the sink to be washed and said, "Careful, land shark on your left."

After Callie dressed, Marlee opened the door. Ben stood next to Rabbit. She could hardly believe it. He had stayed over; he had been at the lodge last night. He was tucking a white oxford shirt into blue jeans, not his usual uniform of green khakis, his belt still hanging loose. Callie watched his hand slide below his waistband, smoothing his shirt in. Then in a second he had the belt buckled and was grinning at them.

"Don't you have a job?" Marlee asked him sarcastically.

"I'm on daze," he said, meaning days off. "Got stuff to do. Breakfast first," Ben said. "So come on you two, get a move on. I'm hungry."

"I'm not going to wait on you," Callie said, trying to joke, then felt silly, because of course she wouldn't wait on him, nobody would; Ben always helped out in the kitchen when he stayed over. Embarrassed, her cheeks went hot.

"Dead guy's dad checked in last night," Rabbit said.

"Really?" Marlee said.

"He seemed spacey, out of it."

"His son just died," Ben said, not angrily, just matter-of-factly.

"I know," Rabbit said. "I told him we were really sorry and everything. I told him I thought his daughter-in-law seemed like a strong person, and he said something like, 'I don't know. I guess she has to be with the baby coming.'"

A *baby*? Callie and Marlee looked at each other. Marlee raised her eyebrows.

"Whew," Ben said, still tucking his shirt in. "That's got to be tough."

Callie looked at Ben, surprised at his reaction, because she thought it might be a happy thing, too. But why hadn't Mary mentioned this in any of their conversations? No wonder Mary had cringed when Callie told her about the doll on the bottom of the river.

Marlee said, "I wonder if she knows he's here."

"Does now," Rabbit said. "I gave him directions to her place."

Callie followed behind Ben as they all tromped down the narrow, hollow stairs and out into the morning sun. Crossing the yard toward the lodge, Callie noticed a bit of the hem of Ben's shirt, bunched and hanging over the belt in the back. She reached out and slid her fingers into the waistband of his pants, pushing the shirt in.

"Hey!" he said, turning, laughing.

"You were untucked," she said, amazed at herself.

He grinned at her, then walked on.

She knew red blotches must have sprung out on her cheeks. When they reached the lodge, Spencer was already there with the cooks, helping to spoon oatmeal into serving dishes. He didn't look at her. They never let on that there was anything between them around the others, but there was something different about the way he didn't even give her a hint of a smile; his mouth was tight. Maybe because she hadn't gone over last night. She felt light and happy, and she didn't want him to ruin her mood.

The kitchen was warm with the smell of oatmeal and blueberry muffins. Barb and Lewis were in their usual high gear, spatulas in hand, ordering and directing them—Lewis grumpy and Barb smiling and teasing him. Soon the crew flew out of the kitchen and into the main dining room with platters of scrambled eggs, bacon, and muffins. The long wooden benches were crowded this morning with the weekend guests. Some stayed in the lodge, some in tents in the nearby campsites. People began passing serving dishes, the room full of chatter. At the far end, guests laughed hard at something Rabbit told them; they called after him as he went off toward the kitchen to hurry back and keep them entertained.

Ben passed behind her, carrying empty serving dishes, bringing them back to the cooks for refills. She felt energized by his presence, aware of where he was at every minute. Even when she couldn't see him, she felt him as if something rushed from his body to hers—an invisible force. Then Spencer put his hand on the small of her back to move her forward so he could pass behind her. She stepped away from his hand abruptly, then wondered if he'd noticed or just thought it was the fluid movement of waiting on people, slipping between the tables, back and forth. It wasn't like he had to touch her to get by, though. She felt irritated with him, and annoyed with herself for suddenly finding him so repugnant. His eyes seemed washed out, set back too far in his face. His T-shirt clung to him, revealing his enlarged, overworked pectorals. It bothered her that she'd let him slide his fingers under the hem of her T-shirt and slowly draw down her underwear. One night she couldn't find her underwear, so had left his room without them. When she came the next night she found him with the underwear on his head, his ears and hair sticking out through the leg holes. It should have been funny, but it wasn't. She'd snatched the underwear off his head angrily. He'd laughed.

Now Spencer was tapping a spoon against the coffee urn to call the room to attention. Guests quieted and faces turned toward him to hear the day's messages. He gave the weather forecast, then turned to Ben, who announced the level of fire hazard—medium to high—and advised that smokers be especially careful, and no smoking in the woods at all. Spencer announced that to-day's bag lunches could be picked up after breakfast and that dinner was at seven as usual.

He told them that Peggy the cat was missing, and asked for everyone to keep an eye out for her. The crew already knew that she was gone, probably caught by a coyote. It was unlikely she'd show up again, gone now for a week, but you never knew.

"Join us at the campfire for music and ghost stories," Spencer went on. "We'll supply the marshmallows, but you have to bring your own sticks. Perhaps Ben will grace us this evening, tell us some *real* ghost stories?"

Ben leaned with one hand against the wall next to Marlee.

"Only after the parents are asleep," he said, winking at some little kids who giggled. "Don't want to scare them." He smiled at Marlee, who grinned and nodded.

Spencer concluded with, "If you have any questions, please don't hesitate to ask our crew." He gestured toward where the crew stood, lined up next to the kitchen door. As he named each of them, they nodded or waved or bowed. This was the procedure every Saturday for the new weekend guests. Barb and Lewis stuck their heads out the kitchen door for a quick introduction and applause from the tables, then they were gone.

"They're not allowed out of the kitchen," Spencer said, and the crowd laughed. Callie thought about how many times she'd heard Spencer say this very thing, like it was a punch line, week after week. He grinned at the laughter, his scalp reddish as if sunburned through his hair. Yet he wasn't a bad person, she reprimanded herself. He was kind and he cared about the lodge and the guests. He was proud of the crew and how well they worked together. Still, as they all moved to sit down at the crew's table and he gave her a look, knowing and soft, she turned away full of disgust that she had let herself, her body, be touched and fondled and that she had given it over to him and wanted that, but did not love him.

CHAPTER 21

H E WAS SURPRISED when Mary bounced a ladder on the eave and climbed up. An image of his mother, following him, climbing to the barn roof, chasing after him, made him unsettled, but this was Mary. She hoisted herself onto the eave.

"How are the stars tonight?" she said as she inched her way toward him. She was slow coming up the angle of the roof. He saw how she kept low, maybe afraid. He sat at the high edge, his feet hanging over, and wondered if he should get up, move back. But she came all the way, though on her hands and knees for the last bit. Then she sat next to him, let her legs off the edge like his. She wore shorts. The shingles were gravelly and her knees were bare. She wiped them, then brushed her hands together, getting the grit off. "I'm not a monkey like you. I need the ladder. Mind if I join you?" she said.

"Sure," he said. "Can't see anything, though." The night sky had been full of vivid stars earlier, but now they were diminished, cloud cover thickening. He wasn't sure he liked being called a monkey; it sounded childlike. "Can hardly see the mountain."

"Maybe it can't see us," she said.

He wasn't sure what she meant. She sat only a foot from him, leaning back on her palms, away from the edge. Her skin shone in the darkness. He smelled alcohol. The legs of her shorts were bunched up on her thighs, and he imagined pulling the hems straight, making them even. Then he thought, Stop it. It doesn't matter if they are uneven. Not everything needs to be aligned.

"My parents used to come up here a lot," she said. "Sometimes they'd bring me along. We'd watch for meteors."

"Best in August."

"I wanted to thank you for cutting down the . . . those trees," she said. "And the logs. The stack, I mean." Now he was sure he smelled alcohol, and her words sounded round, slow.

"I'm sorry about the one," he said. "It probably wouldn't have made it."

"I know that," she said. "You're right."

It relieved him to hear her say it. She lifted herself a little, pulled a leg of her shorts straight. The air was humid, and his hands felt clammy. It was very still. Not even many crickets, like they'd shut down, turned off, like the stars. A wind came on, then died just as fast, and he was glad because he didn't want her to get chilled and leave. He was glad she was here, sitting next to him.

Mary was quiet, then she said, "Michael's father. He thought I was pregnant. I thought I was until a couple of weeks ago. I got my period. I don't know why I didn't call him when I knew."

It took him a moment to understand what she was telling him. Menstruation wasn't a subject anyone had ever spoken to him about directly, and the suggestion of her being pregnant was hard to work out, seemed impossible almost. Her husband was dead.

"He was devastated," she said. "It really hurt him."

She was telling him this because of the window this afternoon. When he'd heard the glass shatter, he'd thought it was her, throwing herself, or something, against the window. It crossed his mind, as he ran back up the hill, that she might be angry with him because he'd cut down the good tree. He was relieved to see through the window that she was okay, and then also he was relieved because there *was* a man there after all, and not Ben, and he hadn't imagined it. The man held his own hand, wincing. As Tobin approached, Mary had put her hand up like a stop sign and said emphatically, "An accident." Then, when he bent to pick up triangles of glass from the ground, she said, "Please don't." The man also told him to stop: "I'll take care of it. You'll cut yourself," the man said.

Now there was cardboard taped over the missing window.

"You said 'an accident,' but it wasn't?"

"He didn't mean to," she said.

Tobin tried to think of something more to say, but he figured she was right. He'd helped Mr. Walker tape up the cardboard, then the man, arms around himself as if holding himself together, gauze wrapped around his cut hand, had gone to his car, driven away, off to the lodge for the night.

"Can you hear that?" Mary asked. "The music?"

A waft of fiddle music rose, then fell. And then a faint voice singing; they were playing at the lodge. The air currents determined how loud or soft the music could be heard. And also the valleys and hills, like waves rolling, letting sound rise over the top, then carrying it down, making it disappear into troughs. The forests, too—coniferous, deciduous—in their thicknesses, their leaves or needles, decided what range of tones would be revealed, as if corralling the music, releasing it in increments.

Then she said, "I remember when I stayed with you. You played the piano for me."

He didn't play anymore.

"You were good," she said.

"No," he said. "Not really."

"You should play that song for me sometime, if you remember it." Mary was quiet, and he felt terrible. He'd do anything else for her—cut trees, stack wood.

"The piano's out of tune. No one plays it anymore."

She nodded. "Where is she now, your mother?"

"A group home. In Concord."

"Do you see her?"

"Not since I was eleven. He made me go down there, to the state institution where she was living then."

Tobin remembered walking the grounds of the institution, seeing the crazies talking to themselves, wondering if they thought he was a crazy, too. *If you talk to yourself, in the woods, alone, are you crazy?* His father didn't like the word *crazy*. "Ill," his father had said about her when he finally took her away for good. "Ill," like it was a bad case of the flu.

"He thinks she's better, but it's just meds."

"I'm sorry, Tobin."

Yesterday he'd wandered into his father's studio, startled to see that the painting on the easel wasn't of a landscape, but the head and shoulders of his mother. His father was imagining her from his memory. It was her, so similar to the earlier paintings, yet off somehow. The lines weren't as neat or pure, and the shape of her jaw was wrong, softened. Her collarbone arced down slightly and impossibly. The eyes were completely wrong—the lids, golden half-shells, smooth and curved over the oval of her eyes in a way that made her look angelic. His father's memory was as skewed as his skill.

Tobin could paint better than his father. He envisioned Mary nude, lying across a bed, modeling for him, and his cock twitched, and even though she surely couldn't know, his face burned and his knees began to shake.

Mary swung her legs back and forth. In the dark her bare feet were shadowed, grayish, flying up. A bat swooped near them and was gone, then another. Mary's legs went faster. It made him nervous. He tried to study her face, but it was too dark.

"I'd like to read your father's books sometime," he said, hoping to distract her.

"Sure," she said. "You can borrow them."

Her hands were still behind her—her weight away from the edge—but she was being reckless, body rocking. She was drunk, he knew.

"Please," he said, stretching his arm out in front of her like a fence. He braced himself, ready to push her back if she rocked too far forward. When she didn't stop, he put his hand on her thigh and pressed down hard. Maybe too hard, but she stopped moving her legs right away.

"We were going to do so many things. There was so much I didn't know." She sucked air, a sob. "I should hate this mountain."

It was just a mountain. It wasn't alive. It wasn't looking at them. No one was. Even though she'd stopped pumping her legs, he kept his hand on her thigh, felt the bare skin under his palm. Usually, he didn't care for how alcohol affected people. With Mary, it made him responsible. She wasn't in control. Not herself. He'd guard her.

"How could he fall? Goddamn him," she said. "No one *falls*. You don't fall off Cascom."

"They do, though," he said. "I guess. It can happen." Had anyone before? Not that he knew of. He wondered if he should put his arm around her, but didn't. He let his hand stay where it was on her thigh.

Finally, she took a long, shuddery breath and was quiet.

His hand was still on her leg, and she didn't seem to mind it being there. She breathed, sniffed.

He tried to think of something else to talk about. He thought to remind her again of when she came to stay with him. How they'd discussed a book he was reading, *The Swiss Family Robinson*, and they'd drawn plans for a tree house. It was going to be a *glorious* tree house, she'd said, with many rooms and secret closets and escape hatches. It would be high up in a pine tree, so no one could get into it if he was inside with the ladder pulled up. It would be a good hiding place.

She'd told him about the girl who'd disappeared on the mountain. She said maybe the girl didn't want to be found. The way Mary had talked about the girl made him think she was talking about herself. He made up something on the piano that was like Mary's sadness for the missing girl.

Then his father had returned with his mother, and Mary left. In a day or two his mother was just the same. Not cured. Not at all, maybe even worse. He remembered how he'd hoped she'd come back changed. Like the way he imagined she was before his father brought her to the farm, before Tobin was born. The way his father had described her—lovely, brilliant, gentle. But that person was missing, too.

"I always wanted to live here," Mary said. "I wanted to be like my parents, I guess. But I don't know why. Michael indulged me, but I don't think he really wanted to be here. Shit, I feel like I'm losing my mind. I'm going crazy."

"You are not *crazy*," he said, a bit too emphatically. He hated that word.

She was quiet. He hoped she wasn't making the equation that he was sure other people made. The mother was crazy. Was the son, too? If he was, he'd asked himself since he was a boy, how would he know? When would he know? He didn't *have* to do the stupid, trivial things that came to his mind. He could stop. He wouldn't let it control him anymore. Mary helped. Talking with her, his thoughts seemed to slow down, arrive in an easier cadence. He felt stronger, more in control. It was good to be around her.

"I wish you could have known Michael, Tobin. You would have liked him. He was such a good guy."

He heard the admiration in Mary's voice, and how her love was still so present. He thought about how death could lock love in place forever. Mary would always be in love with her husband, maybe. Tobin wondered how that could ever change. The dead had the advantage.

"He would have liked you, too," she went on. "He was a fantastic musician. We all could have played together. Shit. I can't imagine singing without him."

He felt dismal. "I'd like to hear you sing," he said.

"Oh," she said in a sad voice. "I feel so . . . empty. It's impossible."

"Someday, maybe," he tried.

His hand still lay on her leg. His fingers on her thigh, and then a couple of fingers disobeyed him and tapped her thigh, like he was playing notes. She wiped at her face. He knew he should take his hand away, but now the voice in his head said he might need to tap each finger, one after the other, as in a scale. He tensed the muscles in his arm, trying to paralyze his hand, willing his fingers to be stiff.

She breathed deeply, and there was the odor, again, of alcohol. Tap, tap, tap. It started with his thumb, then next two fingers. *Stop. Don't do this. You don't have to*, he told his fingers. A noise—a whispery whine—from his own throat startled and embarrassed him. Maybe she was intoxicated and wouldn't notice. His fingers played up the scale on her thigh, then back down again, coming dangerously close to the hem of her shorts where fingers could slide up, underneath. He stopped tapping. The tapping was done, but then his hand rested there on her soft skin. His hand moved, his palm curving, over her knee, caressing her knee, then back to her thigh, tips of his fingers skimming just at the hem of her shorts.

She placed her hand on his hand to stop it, and gently squeezed his fingers. Then she patted the top of his hand twice before lifting it from her leg and placing it back on his own leg, where she pressed it slightly as if to make it stick there.

"Good night," she said softly, and scooted back from the edge, turned around on her hands and knees, stood, and went toward the ladder.

CHAPTER 22

Everyone had gathered at the pit, and Spencer had lit the fire. Callie imagined the campfire from above, as if she were floating up, looking down on the fire with all the guests gathered around it. From above, the fire wavered and glowed and appeared as a red-orange eye, blazing out of the dark field. She drifted in her mind's eye toward the lodge, just a couple hundred yards away.

From the front it was broad and barnlike, with softly lit rows of windows. Lamps outside turned the weathered clapboards into gray, shadowy stripes. Below some of the bright second-story dormers there were tracts of roof where shingles had fallen off, leaving dark gaps, checkered, like spaces between teeth. From above, the roof sagged, old beams bowing under time and weight and weather. Barb and Lewis had told her how heavy snows, and then ice dams, trapped the melt every spring—no place for it to go but through the roof. Ceilings had leaked and were patched, but the brown stains were impossible to cover with paint, and showed through. Paint was peeling all over the lodge; it needed work. It was an ancient building—a firetrap—Spencer often reminded the guests, pointing out where the fire extinguishers were kept on every floor. Then Callie drifted toward the mountain, and up through the black night, until she was hovering over Hi-House where Ben lived. No lights on there, because he was "on daze." He was supposed to come share ghost stories, but he wasn't here yet, and she wondered if he would come at all. She willed him to come to the campfire where she sat, hoping, waiting.

Late-arriving guests drifted in from the darkness and took seats around the campfire on logs laid out in a circle. The fire burned in the middle. Rabbit and Marlee had been playing, but now their instruments were stored in the cases behind them. The singing was over and people sat, knees drawn up or cross-legged in the sand, leaning their backs against logs.

If Callie looked into the dark outside the circle for too long, she felt blind, especially if she stared into the fire first. It was humid. The air felt heavy enough to float on and was tinged with the smell of bug spray. Inside the circle, the sand farthest from the fire was cool, cream colored and rippled with shadow pockets, like beach sand. Spencer knelt close to the fire, poked at it with a stick, then placed a short log in the middle of the blaze. The fire shuddered, cracked, then flames curled around the log and flared up, bright again. One by one, he dropped used marshmallow sticks—green branches, skinned and whittled points—into the fire. After roasting marshmallows, the children had been put to bed. No ghost stories for them after all.

Callie stretched her legs in the sand, dug her bare heels in, feeling the coolness of it. She thought about all the nights she'd come out late, crossing to the lodge, dashing by this pit, then across the grass to see Spencer. Though lately she walked slowly, or stopped, or even turned back. Sometimes she just stood in the middle of the yard, looking up at the stars. Hoped to see one streaking so she could make a wish. Wishing Ben would come.

Tonight the stars were dim, grains of salt melting in black liquid. Firs stood tall and dark and pointed against the sky along two edges of the lawn. The other side rose into a black hill, a mass of hardwoods, no definition in the darkness. Callie let her hair fall forward on either side of her face and peered out, as if between sheer drapes. She admired her tanned legs, and how they showed the contours of strong, worked muscles. She felt self-conscious suddenly, wondering what sort of expression she wore. She tried not to think about her face, stitched her eyebrows together, and concentrated on the flames. She let her gaze linger on a corner of a log, and then a woman's sneaker, the rubber edge separating from the canvas.

There was the sound of soft voices as the guests talked to one another, and the fire crackled like paper crumpling. Peepers near the pond whirred out a barrage of high notes. Marlee hummed a tune, and Rabbit said, "Oh, yeah. I know that one. What's it called?" And Marlee said, "Ben will know." Callie's ears felt as if they'd opened wider.

Barb and Lewis were the last to join the circle, greeted with words of praise for such a good dinner—rosemary chicken and stuffing. Green beans and cranberry sauce. Chocolate pudding for desert. The cooks took seats inside the circle, holding hands. Barb and Lewis looked alike—thin faces, eyes close together over long thin noses. They could be made from the same mold, except for Lewis's goatee, which Callie and Marlee had decided made him look like a beatnik. Lewis smiled at Marlee and said, "Did we miss you?" meaning her singing. She shrugged. And Lewis said, "Shoot. Will you guys play again? Please?"

Marlee said, "If Ben shows up. He can play guitar better than I can."

"I doubt that," Lewis said. "I mean, you play fine."

Barb nodded, agreeing with her husband, and pulled Lewis's arm around her shoulders.

Callie pretended not to notice that Spencer was constantly glancing in her direction. She peered out between the curtain of her hair, looking at the fire, then through the flames, where Marlee sat on the other side. Marlee drew in the sand with a marshmallow stick. She looked serious, deep in thought, her face illuminated with firelight.

An elderly man, whom they had dubbed Salad Man because that was all he ate, said, "Ghost stories. Who's got one?" When no one answered immediately, he said, "Marlee? I seem to remember a story you made up last year."

"Oh, I don't make them up," Marlee said dramatically. "The ghost girl is a *true* story." Some of the guests made silly sounds— ghost oohs. "Just don't go into the woods at night," Marlee warned. "She'll be right behind you, but when you look, no one will be there. She moves very fast."

Spencer placed another log on the fire, and sparks shot out. Callie felt Spencer's gaze on her outstretched legs, then traveling up the length of them. She glanced down, noticing how the seam of her shorts dipped slightly, making a shadow in her crotch. She drew her legs up and wrapped her arms around her knees. Spencer looked away, poked the bark off a log. The last time they'd slept together she'd woken up in a wet spot, something that had never happened before. She lay still, confused and uncomfortable, feeling the damp sheet beneath her bottom. For some reason she felt embarrassed, until she grasped, with irritation, that it was his fluids leaking out of her. She'd never been so relieved to sneak away, back across the dark lawn, to her own bed.

"Once a man did see her," Marlee said. "He stayed too long on the summit and got caught in the dark coming down. First he heard the sound of twigs snapping, then a loud crash, and he thought he'd flushed a partridge, but the noise didn't stop. It kept pounding, like there were twenty partridge flapping their wings. He ran, but he couldn't see in the dark and tripped, got the wind knocked out of him. When he looked up, there she was.

"She wore a long white gown. Snarled white hair, leaves and

twigs stuck in it. The man tried to run, but then she was right in front of him, blocking his way. She raised her arm, pointed at him."

Marlee pointed at the fire, making her eyes wide. She held this pose, just long enough for everyone to see how it would look. Callie felt prickles go up her back.

"She opened her mouth, and out came a horrible hawklike screech. It went on and on. Then, finally, she said, 'Look at me.'" Marlee made her voice different when she said what the ghost girl said. She made the ghost girl's voice like a little girl, pleading, whispery. *Look at me.* It was sad. The guests were quiet. Marlee's eyes seemed glazed, distant, as if she'd fallen into a trance.

"Okay, so what happened to the guy?" a man finally asked.

Marlee sighed, relaxed, stretched her arms out in front of herself, as if the story was over; they weren't going to get any more.

"Guess he lived to tell," someone else said, and the guests chuckled softly, unsure.

Marlee wore a grim smile. She reached down, brushed something off her toe, glanced at Lewis and Barb. Callie wondered what was wrong, and when Marlee looked her way, she tried to ask with her eyes. But Marlee seemed to be looking just past Callie, or off to the side.

Lewis gestured above Callie's head and said, "Ben, do you have any stories?"

Callie turned. Ben! He was standing right behind her.

Ben shrugged and sank his hands deep into his pockets.

"Aw, I don't know," he said. He looked down as if studying his boots, tugged at his earlobe, at the one earring, then stepped over the log and sat down next to Callie.

"Well," he said. "Before I worked here I was over to Three Mile Island on Winnipesauke for about, oh, seven years."

Sometimes Ben's accent was more evident, and with his storytelling mode it was strong, charming, Callie thought. He gave a little smile toward his boots. So handsome. So kind and humble. I love him, Callie thought.

"And before that I worked on Mount Washington in the huts at the Lake of the Clouds for three years. The White Mountains are chock full of stories. There are crosses up there along the trail that loom right up out of the fog, scary enough. It's a dangerous place. Weather changes in a flash. Temperatures drop. Cascom may be a little mountain, but still it can be dangerous."

Callie thought of the cliffs up there, how steep they were, and of what had happened. Then Ben leaned back against the log, stretched his arms along it, one around the back of where Callie sat, so his arm was basically encircling her shoulders, though not quite touching her. She saw his hand on the other side, his fingers curled slightly, hanging off the log. She felt brilliant, pleased and proud.

"The fire lookout before me just about went crazy, trying to keep the ghost out. He'd wake up in the morning and find his food broken into. Not like an animal. Not like mice nibbling or bear or anything like that, either. If he had a whole loaf of bread, he'd find it half gone, and the twisty all tied on neat. Leftover soup, pot empty. I suspect he thought he was sleepwalking. Or sleep-eating."

Some of the guests laughed. Ben chuckled and looked directly at Callie, he smiled at her, winked. It felt as if a meteor had flown between them.

"He rigged up some pots and pans to hang over his door outside. If someone came in at night it would make a racket. Nothing happened for a while, then one morning he found all those pots and pans piled up, all neat on his front stoop. And wouldn't you know, his food was gone again.

"Next, he laid a trap—a beaver trap or some such thing—at the base of the steps, covered it with brush and leaves. Next day? He found the trap had been snapped, but nothing there, until he inspected closer to see long strands of white hair caught in the teeth of the trap. It was as if she'd got her hair stuck in it, and ripped it out getting free."

Callie watched Ben's face, his high cheekbones disappearing under the brim of his cap. His lips. He'd stretched his legs out in the sand, crossed his ankles. She'd put her legs out again too, and their legs were almost touching. Then he shifted, and his knee came against her leg, then away. She'd felt the material of his pants, the pressure of his leg against her leg, and even though he wasn't touching her now, she still felt it.

"Story goes that he never caught her, but sometimes he'd wake up and there she'd be, perched on the end of his bed, just staring at him."

"What about you, Ben," a lady asked. "Have you seen her?"

"I may have," Ben answered, mysteriously, but before he said more, people were craning their necks, looking around Ben. Someone was coming up to the campfire out of the dark. The man had bright gray-white hair. He came to the edge near Ben and stood behind the logs, outside the circle.

Spencer nodded to the man. "Join us, Mr. Walker?"

Callie startled at the name, felt her heart speed. Walker. Like Mary. Mary's father-in-law.

"That's all right," the man said. "I just wanted to speak with you for a moment."

Spencer got up and the two moved away from the campfire. After a minute, Spencer came back.

"He'd like to meet the crew," he said, and motioned for them to get up. "You, too, Ben."

Marlee stood, using the top of Lewis's head for support. Lewis laughed and ducked, then slapped her on the thigh. Marlee said, "Hey!"

Callie felt annoyed with Marlee suddenly. Marlee could be a flirt, and men got stupid around her. It diminished them somehow. It didn't seem right to be laughing and making jokes with Mr. Walker so near.

They gathered around the man, and Spencer introduced them.

Callie extended her hand to Mr. Walker. "Hello," she said, feeling as if somehow she knew him, or they shared a bond, but the man didn't see her hand. She let it drop. Marlee noticed and gave Callie a secret raised-eyebrow look, joining them together, and Callie felt guilty for being annoyed with Marlee two seconds earlier.

"I want to tell you," Mr. Walker said, his gaze traveling from Spencer to Rabbit. "I appreciate your help. What you do is a hard job."

"We're sorry about your son," Rabbit said, adultlike.

Callie remembered what Rabbit had told them, that Mr. Walker said Mary was expecting, and she wondered if Mr. Walker was happy about that or not. He'd be a grandfather, without his son. She wanted to say something about it, but she felt confused that Mary hadn't told her about it herself. Maybe it was too painful.

"I appreciate your interest in Mary, too. Spencer has told me that you invited her here. Brought her things." He looked directly at Callie, and she felt proud.

Mr. Walker put his hand over his mouth and kept it there like he was going to cough, but he didn't. He took his hand away. There was white gauze wrapped around his other hand.

"I'd like to see the place," he said. "Where he fell."

"If you want," Spencer said. He didn't sound convinced.

"I could take you," Callie said, surprising herself.

"Yes," Spencer said. "Callie knows where it is. She can be your guide. If you're sure."

Mr. Walker nodded several times, then walked away quickly, and everyone watched him. They heard a noise, like a gasp, and he walked faster toward the lodge, then he was near invisible in the dark, then visible again under the night lamps.

CHAPTER 23

WHEN MARY HEARD THE RUMBLE of a vehicle coming down the road, she went to the screen door, thinking it might be Clayton. The car pulled into the driveway, not Clayton's rental but an old car, rusty around the wheels, dents in the passenger-side door where another car must have tagged it, pulled in next to her truck. The driver, wearing a baseball cap, waved to her through the windshield and got out. She almost didn't recognize Ben out of uniform. He went to the back of the car, opened the trunk, and lifted out two heavy-looking paper bags, kneed them up into his arms, then elbowed the trunk lid closed.

"These are for you," he said as she came across the yard. He didn't stop, and headed for her door. She followed, held the screen open for him. He went in and put the bags on the dining room table.

"I thought maybe you could use some things. I was in town on my day off."

"You didn't have to," she said. She looked around. "My purse is somewhere."

He put his hands up. "This is on me," he said. He looked at

her for a moment, his eyes dark, serious, waiting, she guessed, for her to accept his offer. "If you'll let me."

When she didn't say anything, he pulled at the rim of one of the bags, looked inside.

"I wasn't sure what you might like, so I got what my mother calls staples. Rice, potatoes, pasta, tomato sauce, cheese, green beans. Pickles. Here's some chocolate," he said, up to his elbow in the bag, rummaging around inside it. "A baguette. And here," he moved on to the other bag. "Toilet paper, Tootsie Rolls. Better put these in the fridge," he said, handing her a box of Popsicles.

"I should pay you, " she said. The box was cool and damp. She looked at the colorful picture on the box. "Popsicles?"

"Assorted flavors. I didn't know what you might, you know, have cravings for," he said. "We heard you were—" He glanced at her middle. "Mr. Walker said—"

"Oh, no," she said. "No, I'm not. I thought I was. Huge mix-up. I'm not. He knows this. When did he tell you?"

"Oh, sheesh. Sorry. He didn't, actually. It was Rabbit who said, but now I see. That was before Mr. Walker came to see you. I guess he told Rabbit that you were."

"It was a terrible misunderstanding. I had thought—But I wasn't. Here," she said, "let me pay you."

"Please," he said, and raised his hands up as if to say *stop*, then placed them, one atop the other, over his heart, "it's on me."

She smiled, tilted the box toward him. "Popsicle?"

They sat on the front deck. Ben's eyes were shadowed under the bill of his cap. He made small talk—the dry weather, the fragile woods, how they needed rain. The best Popsicle flavor—grape.

"It's nice of you to think of me," she said. "And on your day off, to boot."

"Happy to," he said, and laughed.

Ben brushed his hand through the air near her arm, and his fingertips grazed her skin. A mosquito hovered. He grabbed it out of the air, squeezed and opened his fist, wiped the dead mosquito on his pant leg. She looked into his grinning face, then her eyes disobeyed her, grazed his chest. Pectoral muscles made smooth mounds under his T-shirt. His arms were tan, smooth looking. Heat rose in her cheeks. And then a horrible feeling, like she was betraying Michael.

"I can see that field from the tower," Ben said. He gestured toward her father's little field farther down in the valley. "When I first saw it I thought it looked like one of those crop rings, like an alien ship landed, pressed out an amoeba-shaped spot."

Mary remembered how her father had cleared the land in such a way as to produce the best sort of opening to encourage wildlife movements—the irregular shape allowed for longer perimeters, and more vegetation around the edges for shelters or escape areas.

Ben gazed out from under the brim of his baseball cap at the mountain, at his fire tower on top. Mary looked, too. The granite was bright, shining and bold against the blue sky. Then she remembered the cliffs, felt a tightening in her stomach. She looked away. And then there he was, reaching for the knapsack, torso twisting, that sound he made. That simple, vaguely self-conscious, *Oh*.

"How are you doing these days?" Ben asked. He turned his eyes on her, as if he'd sensed what she'd just remembered. He scratched the back of his head, up under the cap. Then he lifted the cap off his head, set it back on his head. His hair, she noticed, had been newly shorn.

"I'm better," she said, surprising herself. Was she? "I've got a lot to do. A lot I want to fix. The little field is growing in. I need to mow and cut back the brambles. There are a thousand things to do."

"Good," he said. "That's good. Busy is good."

He nodded several times, apparently to show strong approval. Strangely, she did feel affirmed. She wouldn't mention that she hadn't actually done much of anything. Only a little in the garden.

"Will you stay?" Ben asked. "Or back to Boston in the fall?"

"I don't know. I can't think ahead. I guess plans should be on the agenda."

"Or not. Just be, maybe. Just be until you know what you want."

"I spread my parents' ashes in that field. That's what my father wanted."

Ben nodded more.

"Michael's buried on the Cape. That's what his parents wanted. I couldn't protest. But I wish . . . now I wish . . ." Then it seemed ridiculous. Why would Michael care where his ashes were scattered? Maybe he wouldn't even want them here. Here on the mountain that killed him.

"You would have liked his ashes spread here," Ben said, as if he'd read her mind. "It's a nice field. Magical, almost." He gazed into the valley. "The way it breaks open the forest like that. It's like a window. A window looking into another world." He looked at her, smiled, shook his head at himself. "Or just a nice little field to watch animals pass through."

"All those things," she said, grateful he understood what it meant to her.

"They might have given you some of his ashes."

"They didn't cremate him. Even though I know that's what he would have preferred, but at that point I just couldn't interfere. I felt so . . . I felt . . ." She stopped. No reason to try to articulate it. "Listen, I should have thanked you before," she said. "You helped carry him out. I think I was rude to you."

"No, you weren't," Ben said. "Don't even think about it. I just wish there was something we could have done. I wish I'd gotten there first. I should have."

"First?"

"The crew got there before I did."

It occurred to Mary, suddenly, that this was true. Coming down from the tower would have been a lot quicker than the crew hiking up.

"I mean, they're just kids," he said. "They handled it well, but still it was a difficult situation for them. That Callie, I really worried about her, but she seems all right. Did you know she volunteered to guide Mr. Walker up there, to the place?"

"Wait, why didn't you get there first?"

"I stupidly went to the wrong cliffs," he said. "So *stupid*."

Mary's heart started to pound and her skin flushed hot, then icy up her back. The *wrong* cliffs? He should have been there *first*? What was he saying?

Ben's eyes were on her face, then he glanced downward, and she realized that her hand had flown to her own chest in shock. Her thoughts snapped. What if he'd gotten there sooner? First? Her lungs felt compressed. Michael was lying there alone. She'd left him to get help.

"It was a mix-up," Ben said. "I've wanted to tell you."

"What?" she squeaked. Tears stung. What if he'd gotten there, done something, some CPR, something? He was trained for that. "What are you saying?"

"I was sure they meant the ledges that you get to from the Clark, but on the *western* rim." He spoke slowly, calmly, seeming to have registered her growing panic. "I haven't been working here that long. The big ledges are over that way. It never occurred to me that it was the other ledge."

A noise came out of her mouth—a rough sob, jagged and cutting her throat. "You could have done something," she cried.

"Oh, Mary," he said, shaking his head.

But she couldn't hear anymore. She hit him, more of a shove against his chest, below his collarbone, with the heel of her hand. He barely flinched. She shoved again, harder. Made a fist, ready to punch. He put his hand up, took the punch in his palm, then gripped and held her fist so she couldn't pull it back, nor throw it forward. He got her other hand too, and pressed them together. She struggled, but couldn't get free, and then she saw through the blur of tears his serious eyes, dark, unfazed, patiently waiting for her to stop.

"I'd let you do more," he said. "But it really does hurt."

"He might have been alive," she cried, though she knew it wasn't true. She dropped her elbows, weak. He didn't release her hands, unsure, then finally he let go, palms out, still cautious. "You could have given him CPR."

"No, Mary," he said, sympathetically, in a way that made her anger ebb. "That would be wishing."

He reached for her hands again. She'd twisted the hem of her shirt, rolled a fist into it, knotting it around her hand. He pulled the cloth free, drew her hands forward, anchoring them on top of his knee with his own.

"I never should have left him," she said. "I should have tried more."

"Mary, you listen to me."

For a dizzying second she heard Michael's voice, the way he'd say that sometimes when she was afraid, when he wanted to assure her: *You listen to me. You are smart. You are beautiful. You can really sing. You can do anything.* The millions of reassuring things he'd said to her always started with, *You listen to me.*

Ben's tone was like his hands, warm, heavy, gently pushing down, telling her mind to stop backtracking, stop rethinking, stop. She tried to listen.

"He was already gone. You know this. You did what you could," he said. "You tried to revive him, but you knew he was gone, didn't you? You do know that. Don't take yourself anywhere else with blame or wishes. There was nothing you could do.

"And Mary." He squeezed her hands, shook them a little. "Mary," he said again and waited for her to look up. "It was an accident. You had no way of stopping it, or anything else. An accident. Out of your control."

Mary found herself nodding. She felt like a child, a little girl, looking into her father's eyes, hearing one of his pointed lessons. *That fawn was pretty torn up. You did all you could. And that fawn really took to you, Mary. It trusted you. But Nature's fickle, cruel, indifferent. It probably wouldn't have survived on its own anyway.*

"I know," Mary heard herself say.

"An accident," Ben said. "No other thing but."

She nodded, hearing him. She said, "You couldn't have done anything either, I guess."

Ben sighed, perhaps relieved. "It's true," he said. "Thank you for knowing that. I'm not one to feel guilty over things I couldn't have changed."

"I understand," she told him.

They sat quietly, looking out at the mountain, breathing. His hands still on hers.

"He's with God," Ben said. "Keeping watch over you. Probably following you around, making sure you're okay." He gave her a soft, sweet smile that made her eyes sting.

She didn't really believe in God. Though she'd prayed a lot in her life. She'd prayed to Cascom Mountain, too, as if it were an all-knowing, powerful being. It was comforting to think that Michael, or his spirit, might be out there, worried for her, following her.

Her nose itched, but she didn't want to undo the weight of his hand.

"So, when is Callie taking him up there?" she asked. "Clayton. Mr. Walker."

"Tomorrow, if it doesn't rain, but I think it's supposed to. It always does on my days off."

She smiled at him. He smiled back, then gazed out at the mountain.

"I lost my girlfriend last November," he said. "I wanted to tell you."

"Lost?"

"She died. Only twenty-five." He looked at her, lips tightened. "Like your husband. So young. Ridiculously young." He blinked several times in a row.

"I'm sorry, Ben. What happened?"

"Her heart just stopped. We were skiing, and I left her to take another run. She headed down. Apparently she was walking into the lodge when she collapsed. By the time I got down, there was an ambulance just leaving. I figured someone broke a leg skiing. Some people told me a girl had been taken away. A girl with a red jacket and long blond hair, and well, anyway, it was her. They were never able to revive her. It was a fluke. A heart condition no one suspected, though she'd had rheumatic fever as a child."

"It's awful." Mary said, and suddenly tears slid down her cheeks, into her mouth, dripped from her chin. "That poor girl."

Ben slid his hand from hers, patted his chest pocket, then his pants pockets back, then front pocket, until he found what he was looking for, a white handkerchief. As he pulled it out, other things, coins, some tiny silver bolts, came with it, bounced and clinked across the bench and deck.

"It's fresh," he said, handing it to her. "I went to the Fluff n' Puff while I was in town this morning. What else are days off for besides laundry and a haircut?"

She laughed and wiped her cheeks as he gathered up the spilled things from his pocket, collecting them into his palm. The bolts, pennies and dimes, paper clips; some things had fallen through the crack in the deck.

"Oh well," he said, peering between the boards. Then he reached for something next to her foot. He held up a flat pick. "Can't lose this."

When she looked up at his face, she wanted to see Michael's face. But it was a different man—light brown skin, from sun or heritage, she wasn't quite sure. High cheekbones, a shadow across his eyes from the bill of his cap. He leaned back, stretched his legs out and crossed them at the ankles. The flat pick, it was like Michael speaking to her, saying, "Hey."

"I guess I wanted to tell you about Maggie," Ben said, "because, well, I know what it feels like. And for a long time I blamed myself for not being there with her. I could have helped her maybe, I kept thinking. I could have helped. What if I didn't take that last run? You know?" Ben kept his eyes on the mountain. "Then when this happened," he said, indicating the mountain, the granite up there.

"No, stop," she said. "Now you're doing it. We can't change anything."

"Thank you," he said. "It's odd, but I haven't told anyone else around here about Maggie. I feel safe telling you. Less alone, I guess. Grief, side by side, diminishes each. I read something like that somewhere. You know, it's just we're not the only ones. We're not alone."

"I suppose," she said, tears seeping out again, feeling suddenly defensive. "Though I feel selfish, too, about my grief, about Michael. It's mine. I can't share it."

"It's okay," he said. He lay his hand on her forearm, squeezed. "I understand."

Those simple words—*I understand*—were so kind, so affirming. Ben was right. Safe. She felt safe.

"Here comes Tobin," Ben said, drawing his hand back.

Tobin came through the woods from the logging road, then

into the yard near the brush pile. When he saw them he stopped, looked away.

"He comes every day," she said.

"Probably has a crush on you, I'll bet," Ben said. She felt her face flush.

"Tobin," she called to him. But Tobin had turned his back, now patted his shorts pockets as if he'd just realized he'd forgotten something. He patted them several more times, both hands going at once, until it didn't seem quite normal. Then he turned abruptly and went back through the trees, gone.

"Poor kid," Ben said. "He always seems so preoccupied, off course. It's like he lives in his own world."

Mary stared at the trees where Tobin had disappeared, knowing that it was likely Ben's presence that had deterred him. She felt overcome with the desire to go after him, to take the boy in her arms and just hold him, let him know she would never let anyone harm him. But she didn't go after him, and remained seated next to Ben on the deck, the face of the mountain before them.

CHAPTER 24

T HE TRAIL WAS WET, muddy in some places; it had rained hard for two days—much-needed rain, as Spencer had told the guests each morning they awoke to another day trapped inside the lodge. The rain had also postponed Callie taking Mr. Walker up to the ledges until today. He'd stayed in his room or in the reading room, Callie noted, and had not gone out to see Mary again.

Now they hopped from rock to root, sometimes splashing into puddles. Then, as they got higher, the ground dried out some, and Callie let Mr. Walker go ahead of her. She sensed that he wanted to lead. Maybe she'd set too slow of a pace. She heard him breathing heavily, not used to climbing, though he seemed in good shape. His hiking shoes were covered with mud, the backs of his legs splattered with mud dots. The legs of his shorts, like hers, were wet from the ferns and bushes that swept against their sides as they hiked the soggy trail.

They'd hardly talked, and this made her uncomfortable at first, but now it felt good. They'd established silence. It was okay. Just hike. Move along.

She wondered how he would react when she took him to the

ledge, and wondered why he needed to see it. Perspective, perhaps. Get a feel for how and where, so he might envision it, and then believe it.

The sun beamed overhead, and they hiked over shimmering dapples of light on the ground. Sweat ran from her temples. She lifted her arm, pulled her short sleeve out, and used it to wipe her cheek.

"It's not far," she said.

Mr. Walker stopped. "Water?" he said, and turned so she could open his pack and dig out the water bottle. She handed it to him, but he put his hand up. "You first," he said.

She hardly ever drank water while hiking. It was something she was proud of, not craving it, even though Spencer had said that was silly and that even if she didn't think she did, her body needed it. She pulled the top on the bottle, took a drink, not wanting to disappoint Mr. Walker in any way, and handed the bottle to him.

He drank, then asked, "Where do you go to school?"

"St. Paul's. In Concord. I'll be a junior."

"Good for you," he said. "An excellent school, I hear."

She shrugged. "It's okay, but my parents really can't afford it." She found herself in the habit of saying this. It was true; her grandmother paid for it. But also some people thought that kids at St. Paul's were rich and snotty; she didn't want anyone to think she was like that. Even Marlee had made jokes about Callie going to an uppity school and being a rich kid. And even though she explained to Marlee that this wasn't the case, there was that wedge between them. She knew Marlee had grown up in an apartment complex with her mother raising three kids alone. Going to St. Paul's hadn't been Callie's idea—her grandmother wanted it—but Callie had always worked hard to keep her grades up; it wasn't everyone who got accepted to St. Paul's. Still, Marlee had a way of making Callie feel guilty for her privileges. Marlee had worked at Kmart all through high school, whereas Callie had never worked until now. Marlee could sing, though, like Alison Krauss, or even better. Like Emmylou Harris, or someone like that. She could be a famous singer if she wanted. Callie imagined going to see Marlee in concerts and being invited backstage to meet the musicians. Maybe Ben would become a famous musician one day, too. Callie had no idea what she would become in the future. She liked to write poems and kept a journal now and again. She loved music, but couldn't play more than chopsticks on the piano. Maybe, she decided with enthusiasm, she'd ask Ben to teach her to play the guitar. Ben. Just the thought of him, and spirals of light, silver light, wriggled through her whole body.

Mr. Walker handed the bottle to her. She screwed the top on, and he turned his back to her so she could put it into his pack.

He started up the trail again. "Where do you want to go to college?" he asked.

"I haven't decided," she said. She hadn't wanted to think about it. She wondered if there was a college where Ben lived. She wanted to go there, wherever it was.

Little pulses vibrated in her belly when she remembered Ben, his knee brushing against hers at the campfire. His arm behind her, resting on the log they both leaned against. Winking at her. Mr. Walker was probably waiting for her to say more, but she didn't want to talk about school. Then, remembering Ben's leg, brushing against hers, more pulses, only this time between her legs.

"My son went to U-Mass for undergrad. Then UC Berkeley for law school," Mr. Walker said after a while, through deep breaths. The trail had turned steep and rocky. They hiked from one side of the trail to the other as if going up twisting, uneven stairs. She followed his way, stepping on the rocks he chose.

"Mary told me he was interested in environmental law,"

Callie said. "Partly because of her father. He'd liked some of her father's essays or something."

"Well, he quit law. Music was his passion, it turns out. Turned out. Apparently, he was quite a musician. Something I missed out on. Something I regret."

Callie remembered what Mary had told her. Michael Walker was known in the music business. They were going to open a studio, help musicians make records. It had occurred to Callie that she might like that sort of job too, especially if you got to work with your husband. An image of herself, next to Ben, turning dials.

"At the top of this rise, we turn off the trail," she told Mr. Walker.

"Is that the spot?"

"No, not yet. We go along there for a bit, about three hundred yards."

He stopped, balanced on top of a rock. "I'll let you lead, then," he said. She nodded and moved past him. They cut through the spruce, and onto the smaller trail that soon disappeared as it wove its way over open rock. The sun beat down and felt good on her skin. She turned a little, trying to see Mr. Walker's face, but he looked at the ground, following her. Soon they came to the cliff.

"It's here," she said, stopping about thirty feet from the precipice. He passed her and went forward. She wanted to tell him to be careful, but didn't. Let him do whatever he needed to do. He halted a few feet from the edge and leaned forward, stretching his neck, one foot forward, but the weight on his back leg, anchoring him. She knew what he saw: a long drop to the tops of junipers. And rocks, boulders all over, some partially hidden under branches. A long fall to the bottom, and no soft landing. It was rugged terrain, strewn with sharp rock edges, stiff juniper needles, jagged branches, down to steep abrasive granite that would put a body into a slide toward more rocks. Surfaces that would make a body bounce, send it into the air, then down, roll it, catapult it over craggy trees, and into thorny scrub, just as Callie had imagined it, time and again.

Mr. Walker moved back a few steps, and straightened. He gazed out at the hills and valleys, chin raised slightly, looking farther out where there was a lake, blue and flat, sunk into the green far away. She sat down Indian style on the ledge and watched him, wondering what he was thinking, or if she should say anything. He tipped his head back, eyes toward the sky; she worried that he might lose balance, but she also didn't want to interrupt him. He gazed out again for a long time, taking it in, figuring it out, she guessed. Then he came and sat next to her on the ledge. He shrugged off his pack, took out the water bottle.

"If you don't mind," he said, and took a drink. "I'd like to go down there, down below, and see the bottom."

"Okay," she said, and started to get up.

"I'd like to go alone," he said. "If you could just give me directions."

"Oh," she said. "Sure."

Relieved, she explained how he had to go back to the trail, descend about two hundred yards, then turn into the woods. She explained that the trail wasn't marked, but if he kept looking up, he'd see the ledge above and he should follow it for about ten yards, then he'd see where there was a streak of quartz. It was there, below that, approximately that spot, near a big boulder.

"I'll find it," he said. "Wait for me here?"

He'd been gone about five minutes. She had no idea how long he'd be. She stretched out on the rock, bunched her extra shirt up, laid her head on it. The sun felt good on her face and legs. The sky was a vast blue lake. Some huge puffy clouds stood at the edges, almost like mountains might look upside down, reflected in water. She thought of dark-gloom, then how the sky was the reverse, all blue and white. Maybe there was a way to reverse the feeling of dark-gloom.

Mary came to her mind, and how she'd said she used to play guitar and that her husband had played guitar. The image of Michael Walker's face, still, like wax, haunted her. And how the body, though lifeless, had jiggled and bounced on the litter as they'd carried him. She didn't want to think about this.

Then she heard Mr. Walker call to her.

"Callie?" came his voice again from down below. She rose and went as close to the edge as she dared, looked over. At first she didn't see him, but then he waved his arms over his head. He stood directly below, up to his waist in junipers. "Was it there?" He pointed over the tops of the little trees.

"Yes," she called back.

She watched as he moved down into the junipers, then deeper, where she knew he'd stepped off an outcropping of granite, and then it was just the top of his head, the gray hair showing, then he was gone, as he disappeared under the scrub to the small clearing where she and Spencer and Rabbit had found Mary's husband.

Then movement, a flutter of blue in a different direction. Someone. It was Mary. She stood in a small clearing of gray lichen-covered granite farther down, below the spot Mr. Walker had disappeared in. Then she crouched, hands on the ground between her legs, like in a game of leap frog. Was she hiding? She was frozen, almost not real, like a mirage made by leaves and branches. She wore a light blue summer dress, not hiking clothes. Then the dress moved in a breeze, fluttered between Mary's knees, making her real, truly there, and Callie felt a chill because there was a not-real quality to what she was seeing. Mary shifted, still crouching, but bringing her knees close together so the dress was tucked between them. Mary would know that someone had guided Mr. Walker up here. She'd be aware of her presence, wouldn't she? It seemed the minute Callie thought this, Mary turned her gaze upward.

The expression on Mary's face was so startling that Callie ducked and moved away from the edge, back up the granite slope and out of sight. She must have scared Mary, being so close to the edge of the cliff, but it was also like she'd caught Mary at something. Mary hiding, spying on Mr. Walker.

CHAPTER 25

WHEN SHE SAW CALLIE on the ledge, a chill passed through her. She almost called out, but then Callie moved back from the edge at the same moment. Mary took deep breaths, calming herself, and crept farther into the brambles below the ledge out of sight, careful to move branches slowly, silently. She crouched, her hands braced on the granite between her feet. She had a good view through the junipers. Seeing this place again was more painful than she'd anticipated.

This morning, when the sun had come out after two days of rain, she guessed this would be the day Clayton would make the climb. She wasn't sure what she needed to witness, but something had driven her up the mountain. She'd waited off-trail at the junction, certain that eventually they'd come through. She felt like a girl again; she'd often avoided other hikers, secreted in the woods until they passed. There was a thrill in being invisible, listening to conversations, presence unknown. Sure enough, Callie and Clayton hiked by. They were silent, Callie leading. Mary had followed not far behind them, feeling more shame than anything else.

Callie had stayed on the ledge above, while Clayton went

down alone, and now stood in the middle of the small clearing by the quartz-strewn boulder, his eyes on the ground. He put one hand on the rock just as she'd done. It made Mary shiver, but there wouldn't be any blood left after the rain. Then he squatted, put his hands on the ground in a position much the same way as hers now. He stayed like that for a moment or two, then lay down on his back.

Seeing Clayton with his arms at his sides, toes skyward, made her shake. The anxiety of trying to find Michael, beating her way through the scrub, finding him here in this obscure spot, washed over her again. Her body was in spasm. She felt resentful that Clayton was here, putting himself in Michael's place, this sacred place.

Clayton raised his arms, reached for the sky. A moment later, he let them drop, useless. When he began to writhe, inching his hips side to side, his legs bouncing, she rose slightly, concerned suddenly, ready to thrash her way to help him. Abruptly, he stopped, lay still again, moaned—a deep, low moan. She knew what it was like—that grinding, agonizing grief that would not let you be, would not let up, would not let you change what had happened. With his bandaged hand, he scraped handfuls of dirt and debris from the ground, let them sift over his stomach and chest.

She looked at him now, lying there as if he were trying to take in, experience, the death of his son. The man loved his son. He was devastated. Whatever had happened between Michael and his father to estrange them could hardly matter now. If only Michael could have known this, *seen* this, maybe all would be forgiven. She felt angry with Michael, suddenly, for not loving his father when he could have. Then angry with Clayton for allowing himself to be driven away.

CHAPTER 26

C ALLIE SAT UP as Mr. Walker came back across the ledge. There were twigs and pieces of dead leaves and dirt stuck to his shirt. He saw her see this and gave himself a feeble brush across the chest. A smudge of dirt crossed his cheek, streaked by tears, she realized. He sat down next to her on the granite. She sat quietly, waiting for him to speak.

She wondered if Mary was still below, and if Mr. Walker had seen her. He didn't say anything, and she felt she shouldn't betray Mary's presence. He brushed at his shirt again, then cupped his hands over his knees. His fingernails were full of fresh dirt, the gauze on the one hand grimy.

"I don't feel any better," he said and gave a short laugh. She looked at the side of his face as he gazed out at the land. Small gray curls of hair clung to his temples in his sweat. She remembered how Mary's husband had curly hair, only black. She remembered the dark blood in it, greasy.

"No, there's not much that helps," she said. "It never goes away."

He looked at her. His eyes were a pale blue-gray.

"Have you lost someone?" he asked. His voice was gentle.

"No," she said, embarrassed. "No one."

She felt her face grow hot. She had spoken cryptically as if she'd suffered a great tragedy. And she'd meant it to sound that way, like she knew of such sad things, as if she, too, had experienced something tragic and secret and mysterious. Like Mary losing her husband. But why would anyone want that? Darkgloom came over her. She thought of her family, how she couldn't imagine anything happening to any one of them.

"Mary told me about her parents," she said, trying to make a reason for her obscure remark. "They died one right after the other. She said they loved each other that much. Grief brought on her father's cancer, she said. He was totally healthy until his wife died, then he got cancer."

"I knew they both died a while ago," Mr. Walker said.

"She's a cool person," Callie said, and even though it didn't quite fit what they were talking about, she was glad she said it.

"It's *different* to lose a parent." His voice sounded mean, like he was scolding her. "Parents are supposed to die first. A father should never have to survive the death of his son."

She wanted to say something that would cheer him, like maybe about his grandchild. Instead she nodded and looked at her feet. She didn't like the way his anger was directed, like it was at Mary, and Mary hadn't done anything wrong.

"It's probably different for her, too," Callie said, surprising herself. "Different from her parents dying." She tried to make her tone lighter. "I mean, she loved him more than *anything*." She felt her eyes sting.

Mr. Walker's expression softened. "Come on," he said, then he patted her on the shoulder. "Let's get back to the lodge. I've had enough of this mountain."

They rose, and she followed him back across the mantle of granite toward the trail. She looked out once, but didn't see anyone. She hoped Mary would know that she wouldn't say anything to Mr. Walker about seeing her hiding down there. Mary was her friend.

Mr. Walker went on ahead. Leaves and debris stuck to the back of his shirt and shorts. There was dirt ground into his elbows, too, and she wondered if he'd slipped, taken a tumble.

She wished Mr. Walker had wanted to go up to the summit where Ben would be in the tower. Maybe Ben would come down to the lodge for supper tonight. A thrill spiraled in her belly again, but then she remembered that the end of the summer would come and she would have to leave. She thought she might die of grief.

A surge of nausea came over her. Not for the first time today. She didn't want to think about it. No. She shook her head as if to keep the thoughts, the feeling, away, wishing nothing had ever happened between her and Spencer.

Ben. She remembered seeing him out walking that night on the lawn between the lodge and Lo-House. She'd crouched low, remained hidden. He'd seemed so sad. Maybe if she saw him out walking alone at night again she'd let him know she was there, pull him down, tell him that she loved him. That she always had.

CHAPTER 27

A FTER CALLIE AND MR. WALKER left the ledge, Mary appeared as Tobin knew she would. Although he hadn't
known exactly where she'd positioned herself, he knew she'd
been there all along, concealed by craggy, weather-beaten spruce
and dense brushwood. He watched as she shrugged herself from
the undergrowth, walked a few paces, shaking out her legs. It
surprised him when she started hiking up the trail toward the
summit rather than down, no longer following the man and
Callie. He waited until she was a good distance ahead, then went
up, but not on the trail. He hurried around the base of the cliff
and zigzagged through clusters of low ash and shrubby haw-
thorns until he found open, easy-sloped granite and ascended
there. Over a bluff he caught a glimpse of her ahead. He stayed
back, off to the side, so she wouldn't see him. Like her, he knew
how to follow someone without being detected.

She walked easily up the steep slope. Her dress caught wind
and filled, then snapped back between her legs, clinging to her.
She was so unreal, like a sea anemone, opening then closing, in
that quick movement of skirt and legs and wind, only not in
water but on a tundra of granite, sky all around her.

Now she rested, and he stopped too, waited. She put her hands on her waist, arms akimbo. Then she ran a hand through her hair, over the top, and then up from her neck, cooling herself. Her hair had grown out some since he'd found her in the field.

When she moved he moved. She hiked fast. Sweat ran down his sides as he kept pace with her on his parallel trajectory up the mountain.

He remembered how she'd swung her legs on the roof, recklessly almost, as if she didn't care if she fell. He would not let her fall. If she got into danger, he'd appear, but right now he'd be invisible. He'd be her secret lookout and protector.

Off-trail wasn't easy going. He had to circle around boulders or crevices full of wind-worn junipers. As she got farther ahead, he felt his heart beating rapidly from trying to make up time, but also from anxiety. He didn't want to lose her.

Then she left the trail to the summit and headed toward Hi-House, where Ben lived. The trail descended for a few hundred yards into a sheltered bit of land where the spruce grew taller, though their crowns were stooped and deformed, beaten by the constant wind. The tangle of scrub between the trees here was too thick to pass through; he'd have to take the trail, so he waited uneasily until she was far enough ahead. It was kind of silly, following her. He could catch up, say hey. But somehow he felt he should stay out of sight, give her room, and he didn't want her to think he was stalking her, or anything weird, or crazy. He cringed. He was only following her. Not *stalking*. Following her to protect her, to make sure she was okay.

When Hi-House came into view, he halted and edged himself into the bushy, sharp-needled branches that scraped his skin and jabbed through his clothes.

Mary climbed up the steps to the door of Hi-House and knocked several times. When no one came, she went down the steps, and around to the side of the building. She stood on tip-toes, to look through the filmy panes of the one window. Then she turned, looked toward the summit where Ben would be if he wasn't here.

There was no way to follow her up the granite without being seen. He could reveal himself now, but that might be embarrassing. He'd wait for her here behind the trees, until she came down again. And hopefully she'd come back this way, because there were plenty of other trails, though none as direct to her house.

He waited, listening to the wind through trees. His mind said, Snap three branches or something bad will happen. He took hold of a twig near his back, snapped it off. Then another.

"Stop," he said out loud, knowing how ridiculous it was, how nothing bad would happen. Snapping branches wasn't going to change anything in the universe. But then he snapped the third, just in case.

The sun was high when she returned, Ben with her. They moved slowly over the steep granite, making sure the treads of their footwear took hold with each step. He heard them talking, but couldn't make out what they were saying. He was amazed to hear Mary laugh. Ben had made her laugh. He bit his lower lip, leaned forward, straining to hear.

Ben said something about the solar panels attached to his tower. Mary asked a question. Ben responded. The rock was sheer. Ben stopped and reached back for her. She gave him her hand as she inched her way down a steeper section, then let go. As she passed by him, she used Ben's shoulder for support. Irritation worked its way up his spine, and he wished he had caught up with her, said hey, said, I saw you hiking up. He should have climbed up with her. Now Ben was with her.

At school, he'd gone through a horrible spell of jealousy,

wanting the girl who'd kissed him, but she wanted someone else, and with jealousy came paranoia—the worst of the mind-distorting emotions. He refused paranoia. He would not indulge it; it was too close to his mother's disorder.

At Hi-House Mary turned toward Ben, said something, then moved off. A few yards down she called back, "Come by when you can."

"I will," Ben answered, and waved.

Then Mary swiveled, her dress billowing, and moved toward the trailhead, and then was gone. After a second, Ben fished around in his pocket for keys and let himself into Hi-House.

Tobin backtracked, moving quietly away from Hi-House. He wasn't too many minutes behind Mary. If she needed him, he'd be there.

CHAPTER 28

Mary stood on the rock in the middle of the brook, slipped off her sneakers, pulled her dress over her head, stepped out of her underwear. She was sweaty from the hike; the sun was hot. Water roared, churning around and through the large aprons of smooth granite, rushing into the pool below. Her parents had discovered this place when they first bought the land, before Mary was born. Over the years the three of them had come here to swim, but it had been a long time since she'd been here. She hadn't even had a chance to show it to Michael. They would have skinny-dipped, and stretched out in the sun on the warmed rocks.

She scanned the woods on either side of the brook and downstream where the brook curved and disappeared out of sight. The woods were thick, dark behind the closest trees—their leaves verdant. The water in the pool seemed thick too, tinted only by the wavering bottom—molasses-colored rock below, lit from the hard-penetrating sun. A trout darted away in a brown flash.

Things were still dry despite the recent rain, Ben had said, when she asked him about a fire permit to burn the brush pile. Still, water pounded, dropping from a three-foot ledge above the pool, shooting down the rock in a narrow slide as it always had.

There was no going slow into this freezing stream. She crouched low, edging her way down the steep rock toward the water. The granite was silky from years of erosion. She pushed off.

The cold took her with such a start, she felt weak, barely able to paddle her arms or legs. She came to the surface in a hurry, struggling to get a full breath. But then there was air, and the thunder of the waterslide, and the bright sun, all in a comforting din around her. She moved her limbs, letting her body get used to it, enjoying the numbness.

In a crevice, where the water shot between rocks, she grabbed hold on either side, finding the little handholds she remembered well—dimples carved by the endless torrents of water—and let the surge pound on her chest, push and roll into her stomach, lifting her body gently up and down.

She spread her legs, felt the flow of fast water rush between them. She thought of Michael's fingers, touching her, just right, just fast enough. Then Michael inside her. Their bodies one, connected, allowing everything, making a baby, even though they hadn't spoken about it. And she'd believed a baby had been made, but it hadn't. She wondered, now, if he'd thought about his other child, the one he never met, as they'd made love without protection.

The frozen water beat against her chest and spooled around her neck. A sob came unexpectedly from deep in her throat, and then more, and she let them come, let herself cry hard and loose and horribly.

When at last she let go of the rock, floated out, then stood up in the shallower water, the tears stopped. She made her way out, up on the warm rock again, her skin still vibrating with the sensation of rushing water and lay down in the sun.

Her parents had lain in this exact place. They'd loved each other and taken chances, buying the house, hardly any money. They'd found this secret pool. Maybe it was here, in this very spot, on this flat, smooth rock, that her parents had conceived her.

It occurred to her that she could do anything now. Get pregnant. It wouldn't be any less absurd than Michael's falling from a ledge. She put her hands on her cold stomach, and her imagination leapt into the future, beyond any man or method, to the warm weight of a baby in her arms.

The sun felt so good on her skin. She shifted, adjusted her position on the rock. The brook was loud, soothing. She turned her head, looked toward the bank.

Tobin stood there. She shielded her eyes against the sun, rose slightly on one elbow, and drew her dress, which had served as pillow, to herself, held it over her breasts. Tobin made no acknowledgment, no expression of surprise or embarrassment. His face was serene. Strangely, she felt no urgency herself. They merely looked at each other. The usual unwieldy lock of his black curly hair had fallen over one of his eyes, and now he pushed it away from his eye, a gesture she'd seen him do many times. Perhaps it was the sun, so warm, like a covering on her skin that made her only mildly uncomfortable with her nudity. And the rock, so smooth, holding her in its slight curve and basin. Or it might have been Tobin's lack of expression—a composed observer—that made the moment more a curiosity than shock. Then, maybe realizing what he was seeing, maybe blushing, he turned away, walked back into the woods, and was gone.

For a while longer, she kept her eyes on the bank—the stand of young poplar, smooth gray stems, branches thick with green-gray leaves—where Tobin had disappeared. Reluctantly, she wiggled into her underwear, rolled the dress into a band to cover her breasts, then lay back again against the rock, shut her eyes. The sun. Sun. A warm, reassuring veil. Water, rushing around the island of rock. Drifting. She felt as if she were traveling downstream, bobbing gently through the sluices, passing whoever stood on the edges. Mother, father, Michael. On toward wherever.

CHAPTER 29

TOBIN WALKED FAST, away from the brook, away from Mary, his face burning. Across the field, through more woods, until he came to the boulders. He stopped, aware of how hard he was breathing, as if he'd run a mile. He had often run here, gulping air until his throat hurt. Back then. He'd run through the woods, pushing away the branches, sometimes hands above the head, wading through bushes high as his chest. Notes, stacked in triads, sounded in his head. Each footfall made a reliable tempo, working against chaos, until he reached safety.

He remembered the rhythm. He was seven.

In the woods . . . there were boulders . . . and he had named them. The one that was full of white quartz and was shaped like a giant whale was Moby. He sat on another boulder, which was flatter on top and long and boat-shaped. This was the Hemingway. Through trees and bushes and roots only a few yards away, Moby swam alongside his boat. The sea was calm, but it could get dangerous, and so he was ready, but right now he was safe in his boat. The sun whittled its way through the billowing sail of green leaves, making glints of light that rippled and sparkled on the surface of the sea. A soft breeze hummed and rattled through the leaves above, and he lay back on the flat of the boulder, in the bottom of his boat, and let the waves carry him. He closed his eyes. He was far out on the ocean, safe in his boat. Moby would protect him. His mother wouldn't find him here.

This morning she was nice to him, and when she was nice the going was more treacherous, unpredictable. She tousled his hair and told him to sit at the table, brought him a bowl of cereal. She sat across from him and made a small, sad smile. Her eyes were sad too, like she was truly sorry for everything, like she regretted how he ducked and cringed when she was near.

"My little button," she said. "Play for me."

He started to get up, and she said, "No, finish breakfast first. Then play something beautiful for me."

So he ate more cereal, swallowing hard, not chewing enough, forcing it down his dry throat, then took his bowl to the sink as he knew he was supposed to, and turned on the water to rinse his bowl, remembering to turn the faucet just enough so it wouldn't splash, and she said, "Leave it, Toby. I'll get it later."

His cheeks felt red hot. He was keenly aware of how far she was from him in the room. This was the niceness getting ready for meanness. The back door was there, open already, just the screen door, easy to push open. The living room was over there, maybe easier to get past her that way, and then to the front door. But now he was following her into the living room where the upright piano stood against the wall next to the locked French doors. The thin white curtains let in dusty light. She carried a mug, and he watched her hands holding it. Watched her arm to be ready if the muscles should tighten in a way that meant the mug might be flung from her hand. Her hair covered her back, all the way to her bottom, like a shawl. She wore a bathrobe, white with lace at the neck and ruffles at the cuffs.

She reached the piano and tugged the bench back for him to

sit. Then she lifted the cover. The keys were like teeth, he always thought, teeth with black spaces—the flats and sharps—between them. But the piano never bit him. It had this big mouth with teeth and it was gentle and let you put your hands inside its mouth, and then it sang.

She reached over his shoulders and played a few notes, then a happy C chord. He didn't feel so afraid now. She loved music. She could play anything in the stack of piano books on top of the piano—Beethoven and Brahms, Chopin and Schumann. She played the music exactly as it was written. Exactly every note. She had just the right bounce to her staccato; the perfect touch on the grace note; every trill fast, complete, never blurred. She played without moving her upper body, without looking at her fingers, and her expression was always stern, as if to keep the music down, under her hands, not allowing its effect inside her. Her fingers were precise machines, synchronized and pro- grammed to follow the score. She never improvised, or made up anything of her own, but she'd always encouraged him to do so. She always encouraged him to invent his own melodies, to pre- tend he knew only the first bars of any master's work, and then go from there. *What would come next if Beethoven had died before he finished writing this?* It was hard to wipe away his memory of the melody he'd heard before, but soon he reveled in his ability to reorganize compositions until they became his own.

This morning she moved away from him and went to the chair across the room behind him. She gestured for him to play. He didn't like this because his back would be to her. But once he started playing, he could leave his body. If she came up behind him, he'd be ready for it; he wouldn't even really be there.

So he played. The song was about coming into the field. It was how the field sounded in his head with its tall, blond grass and warm wheat smell. How it felt when he came into the other country behind the poplar trees. Sun on his skin. Then he passed through that country and into the cool shade of the woods on the other side. And deeper and deeper until he came to Moby, and he ran his hands along Moby's rough head, and looked into the indentation, which was an eye the size of his fist. Then he was swimming, the sea was rough, but he was strong and Moby was there, and he made it to his boat. He climbed aboard the Hemingway, safe. The song was peaceful, the notes slow, high, only a few accidentals where there was knowledge of danger, of huge waves, or sea creatures down there in the black water. When he finished the song, he came back from his other world to the living room, turned, and she was looking at the ceiling, her head resting on the back of the chair, her arms draped over the arms of the chair. She said, "Thank you, Toby." She said, "You are my smart little boy. I'm so lucky."

He got up cautiously. She didn't move, so he left her there. He walked out of the room and across the foyer, glanced at her portrait over the mantel, hair rising on his arms because the figure had shifted further, turning her head, ready to flash horrible eyes on him. He got out of the house and crossed behind the barn, and then onto the road toward the field, and into the deep woods, until he was here, exactly where he'd imagined. Safe onboard the Hemingway. He looked up into the trees overhead and then over at Moby. He was here. Not a song-dream. This was real.

She had called him smart, and he knew that she meant very good at music and making it up. There were other times she'd been nice too, and he brought them to mind. Sitting next to her as they watched *The Wizard of Oz* and comforting him with a hug when the flying monkeys came. And one time when she drove him to school and he'd thrown up in the back of the car, she surprised him and didn't get mad. Instead she was kind and took him into the lavatory to wash him and said, "There, there, you'll feel better once you're not moving."

She was usually nice when his father was around, but it was an off-nice—accidentals and dissonant backward inversions, pinging inside flowery chords.

Once she came to his room in the night and lay down beside him. He pretended to be asleep, and she put her hand on his forehead like feeling for a fever. Then she put her hand on his stomach under the covers, and he flinched and she said, "Shhh. It's all right. Go to sleep." But he couldn't sleep at all with her hand on him. And he remembered how the sow had rolled over on the piglet, killing it. He lay awake all night, too scared to sleep, feeling small and trying to keep to his side of the bed. Where was his father? Why didn't he come get her?

If he could only figure out the pattern, the order in which things happened. If only he could envision and follow the melody of her exactly, the chord structure, never vary, but it was impossible. Sometimes she despised him, his body. And it was as if she wanted to squeeze out the boy inside. Sometimes, even if she had him by the shoulders tight, he floated up, outside his body, almost like looking down from above.

His father was always nice. But his father loved her and wouldn't see how she was. Though lately he must see, because she was throwing things in his studio, and she put some of his paintings, the portraits of her, her naked body, in the fireplace and lit them. Then went to get more. His father stopped her and held her, smoothed her hair back from her face, letting the paintings burn, lighting their skin in flickers and shadows.

The paintings burned, and Tobin wished it was her burning up. The oils made bluish flames and slithered down the painted cheeks, the oily neck. The painted eyes turned black and opened up to flame underneath, eaten from the inside out.

Safe on Moby, the sun came through the leaves, lighting them up from behind making little green lanterns. Moby had led him way out to sea. The waves were rough, but he was safe in his boat. He was safe now. He was seven years old. Not yet eight when his mother stormed into the bathroom when he was in the shower, made him stand naked on the toilet seat in front of her. Not yet nine when she slammed the piano cover down on his hands, leaving bracelets of black and blue on his wrists. Not ten when he climbed to the roof of the barn, and she followed, began to climb.

Even now, at fifteen, standing alone in the woods, the trees grown up even more around the boulders, the sound of the brook and Mary naked, far behind him, he can still hear the wheezing note in his mother's heavy breathing as she climbed. The swear words as she scrambled onto the first low roof, then up the wooden ladder. But then he was already lifting out of his body, just outside it, and rising higher, leaving the barn roof for the hazy stars above.

CHAPTER 30

MARY WOKE TO THE SOUND of pounding rain against the roof. She went around closing windows. The cardboard Clayton had taped over the broken pane was holding up so far. Outside, a gray cloud hid the entire mountain, right down to the edge of the yard at the bottom of her hill. Mist hung in the air over the grass, lowering slowly over the stack of birch logs. Puddles had formed in places in the yard—the ground couldn't absorb the rain all at once. The brush pile nearby looked smaller, heavy with water and beginning to break down under its own weight.

Rain splattered off the deck, and she was glad to see water beading on the wood—the coat of paint she'd put on the other day was working. She'd always liked a good rainstorm, but this morning she thought she might not be able to stand the gloom.

She looked up, hoping there wouldn't be any leaks. But already one had started. Drops slid along the beam, then fell, tapping onto the rug. She put a saucepan under it, listened to drops clang and pop.

A vehicle was coming in. Ben? No, the white rental car.

* * *

"Didn't scrape the ledges once," Clayton announced when he came in. He went to the window, ran his fingers over the tape around the cardboard. "I called a place in Leah that sells glass. I'll pick it up today, install it. Really, this must be old glass. If you're thinking of wintering over here you'll want double-pane glass on all these windows anyway."

He glanced at the pot she'd placed on the floor to catch a leak. Then he looked up at the ceiling, shook his head.

"It's only going to get worse," he said.

It stung. It was as if he was speaking against the house, its very structure.

"You're really going to stay here?" he said.

She had the strangest sense of worry for Michael. Michael the little boy who'd grown up with this man. A man who could punch windows and make hurtful comments without an ounce of awareness. But Michael wasn't a boy anymore. He had become a man, now gone.

She picked up the pot, took it to the sink, emptied the quarter inch of water.

"Callie took me up the mountain yesterday," Clayton said.

"Oh?"

"She thinks highly of you."

"She's a nice girl," Mary said. "So. Did you go, you know . . . ?"

Clayton nodded.

Mary's stomach felt off, queasy. Maybe partly a hangover; she'd drunk some whiskey last night, hoping it would put her out. She also needed to eat, and nothing appealed to her.

The rain let up suddenly and a sunbeam shot across the living room, then disappeared behind clouds.

"I'll go to town with you," she said. "I should get the mail."

Outside, they found Tobin coming up the hill, hair matted from the rain. He nodded solemnly at Clayton when Clayton greeted him. She thought Tobin was averting his eyes from her, perhaps embarrassed about coming upon her naked.

"We're going into town," Mary told him. "Want to come?" Tobin's face brightened, obviously pleased. Selfishly, she thought he might be a buffer between her and Clayton. She really didn't want to be alone with Clayton.

They took Clayton's car. He insisted. Tobin climbed into the backseat, strapped himself in. Mary smiled at him as she got into the passenger seat, and he blushed.

In such a low-riding car Clayton had to be slow and careful over the ledges and rutted roads, but still she felt impatient with his driving. She thought he was being overly cautious. An on-coming car pulled over and stopped when it was clear Clayton wasn't going to give them the room.

"This road is a hazard," he said.

She glanced at him, saw what seemed like despair, and decided not to explain the uphill right-of-way rule. He was a youthful fifty-something, she guessed. It was strange to keep looking for Michael in his features, but she couldn't help herself. The chin, the nose, so similar. An ache went through her. Michael was dead and she was riding in a car with his father. If she'd ever looked into the future, she never would have imagined this. Michael's plan had been to get settled, established, then slowly begin the introductions to his parents. Now, she had no future with the Walkers. She might not ever even see Clayton again after today. She figured he'd called his wife from the lodge, and told her: No baby. No grandchild. Nothing of Michael left in the world. She presumed Lucy hadn't ever liked the idea of Mary—the sudden wife.

"Is Lucy doing okay?" she dared ask.

"Her sister's with her."

When after another half mile he'd said nothing more on the

subject of Lucy, she pictured the worst: Lucy crumpled to the ground, or throwing the phone across the room. A sister, comforting her.

The car bumped from gravel onto pavement, and the tires ran smoother. It had stopped raining. Clayton turned off the wipers and sped up as the road straightened, crossing the farmlands. Tobin, she noticed, had rolled down his window halfway, his face getting the full blast of air, hair blowing. He looked a little pale, and she thought to ask if he was okay, but he closed his eyes. She didn't want to disturb him.

When they came into town, Mary suggested they go to the post office first. Clayton followed her directions and pulled into the parking lot, found a spot, turned off the ignition.

"You could get the phone turned on," Clayton said as they got out. "That's something you could do while we're here. Call the phone company. I'd think a phone would be essential. You're very isolated. You don't probably get cell service, do you?"

Tobin had already gotten out of the car. He stood with his hands on the hood, his head down, face drained.

"Tobin?" she said with alarm, and put her hand on his back.

"It's okay," he said, but kept his head bowed. "It will pass."

Clayton came around to the side of the car. "You shouldn't ride in the back," he said. "Motion sickness, right? Mikey had it, too."

Mary patted Tobin's back. He lifted his head, took a breath. *Mikey had it, too.* How had she not known this? Then, Michael had never had reason to ride in the back of their car. Maybe that's why he always wanted to drive, too, so he'd feel less sick.

Tobin's floppy hair had dried, but some still stuck to his forehead with sweat. She brushed it out of the way, smoothed it back from his eyes. The flush came back to his cheeks, and now he gave her a half-smile, his dark eyes shining at her. She felt a rush of something, compassion, love, also trepidation. Tobin pressed his head into her palm, almost as a cat would. She withdrew her hand, her face hot, but couldn't yet turn away.

"You ride up front on the way back," Clayton said, nearly an order, though she appreciated Clayton's taking control, and his show of care. "Riding up front is better. Mikey had it, too," Clayton declared once more, and Mary pictured Michael as the fifteen-year-old Mikey she'd never known. A teenage boy she would have had a crush on as a teenager herself. *Motion sickness?* So much to learn about a person. There had never been enough time with him.

"You go ahead," Tobin assured her. "It'll stop in a minute."

She stepped back, stumbled a little on the curb, and went after Clayton, who'd already started down the walk to the front entrance. As Clayton held the door for her, she glanced back to see Tobin, hands still atop the car, head low, but now his fingers drummed against the roof of the car as if he was playing a fierce concerto.

She worried for him. His odd quirks had become more and more obvious to her. It was painful to see how he tried to battle them, awkwardly hiding them.

She hadn't been to the post office all summer. Not since before Michael died. Clayton stood behind her as she asked for her mail, and a squat, smiling woman went into the back room and came back with a large box, which she slid across the counter. The box was full.

"There's a package, too," the woman said. She held a piece of pink paper, reading it as she disappeared again into the back room.

There were flyers and bills, most with change-of-address stickers on them—mail that had gone to Boston first. Many were addressed to Michael. Or Mr. Walker. Or a few—Mr. and Mrs. Walker. There were several issues of the *New Yorker*, *Harper's*, and *Rolling Stone*—magazines Michael subscribed to. There were pastel-colored square envelopes that she knew were cards of condolence. She started to sort things, reaching into the box, then turned the box on its side and scooped it all out onto the counter. Clayton helped her stack the mail into two piles so they could carry it. She tossed some flyers in a wastebasket. Then the woman came back with the package, and Clayton went to get it.

They were out the door when Clayton said, "What did you get from The Red Pony?"

"I didn't, I don't think," she said. "The Red Pony? The children's store in Cambridge?" She felt her heart speed up. Something of Michael's?

Tobin sat on the curb, waiting. He got up as they approached.

"You," Clayton ordered, but with levity. "In the front seat."

Tobin obeyed, and Mary got in the back. They left the car doors open for the breeze as Clayton handed the box to her over the back of the seat. Addressed to her, twice the size of a shoe box. The label had a border of brightly colored rainbows woven around tiny teddy bears. Clayton handed her his keys so she could slice the tape, and he and Tobin swiveled in their seats to watch. She unstuck the flaps, pulled tissue paper away to reveal a stuffed animal. She lifted it out. The plush, furlike fabric was amazingly soft. Tan with white spots. She held it up, trying to make sense of it. Black button eyes. Fat legs, weighted by beanbag-filled hooves.

"A toy?" Clayton said.

And then she understood. Michael had listened to her story about the fawn. About rescuing the fawn, and then he'd bought this. Not only for her, but for their kid. Their future kid.

"Oh," Mary said, feeling a flutter of joy. "This is so sweet. I told him this thing, from when I was a kid, and he remembered. He's amazing." Her eyes burned, but she felt herself smiling as she looked from Clayton's face to Tobin's. They looked back at her, both with pained expressions. "It's good," she told them. "It's wonderful. It was this joke about what pet we might get our kids one day."

Tobin raised his eyebrows, looked at the fawn as if he thought a stuffed animal might be corny. Clayton nodded, serious eyes, then turned and started the car.

The diner sat overlooking the lake. The parking lot was full of cars, and she realized that the diner, too, was full of people, and she wasn't sure if she could go inside, be around people, but Clayton wanted lunch. And she wanted Tobin to have lunch; he still looked pale. And she noted, for the first time in a long while, that she craved something specific—a cheeseburger. The sky had clouded up again. The lake, dark gray-green, was fairly calm, though an occasional raindrop sent rings out here and there on the surface.

Before she got out of the car, she placed the stuffed fawn back in its box and smoothed the tissue paper over it as if covering a baby in its crib. Nausea returned, threatening, and she knew she needed to eat.

"You can see the mountain from here," Tobin said, pointing toward the far end of the lake. Clayton followed Tobin's finger, gazed into the distance.

The summit rose behind hills, gray and far off, the fire tower making it easy to identify. The thick gray sky had started to break, opening into separate, dark, heavy-bottomed clouds. Some blue areas showed through.

Mary sensed people in the diner, those at the windows who might be casually observing them. A man and woman and a young boy, coming in for a meal. It might look normal, like a family. It struck her how you couldn't know the misery concealed inside people.

A booth by the windows was just being cleared, and they

followed the waitress to it. Tobin stood back, waited for Clayton to take a side, then slid in next to her. The mountain across the lake loomed above the hills. That giant woman made of ridges, lying on her back, now rolling over on her side, pondering the view impassively. *There is the wife of the man who slipped off my cliffs. There is his father. There is that troubled boy.*

"That toy," Clayton said. "He thought you were pregnant?"

She felt both of them looking at her, waiting.

"No, he didn't. It was only afterward that I thought I might be. I'm sorry I told you that at the funeral. I just . . . I just wanted it. My body felt different. And, by the calendar, and everything, it made sense. My period was late," she said, explaining again.

Clayton glanced at Tobin, perhaps wondering if it was all right to talk about these things in front of a boy.

The waitress brought them water, took their order. Tobin ordered exactly what she ordered—a cheeseburger, fries, coleslaw. Clayton ordered a Caesar salad with anchovies, exactly what Michael would have ordered.

"He wanted kids?" Clayton said, more a statement than question. "You both wanted kids," he said.

"We did," she said. "Though we weren't sure when."

Something changed in Clayton's expression. His eyes took on a dulled hue, the sheen gone, dark as the lake. He'd twisted his napkin in the middle, as if wringing out a wet cloth.

"You did go to a doctor," he said. "To be sure, right? I've heard of women spotting. How do you know you're not?"

She glanced at Clayton, trying to feel strong, but again she felt lost in a wave of confusion, protecting, guarding something that wasn't even real. She thought she understood Michael's distrust of his father all the better—how single-minded this man could be, how difficult to deal with.

"The morning sickness," he said, still desperate, trying to offer up evidence to the contrary, still hanging onto hope.

"It wasn't. A hangover. I drank some whiskey. Michael had a bottle."

"*Drinking*? But that could have hurt . . ." Then, Clayton's shoulders sagged in despair, realizing again that there was no baby to hurt.

The cheeseburger was delicious, grilled perfectly. Swiss cheese. A fresh slice of tomato and crisp lettuce. The coleslaw was made with just the right amount of mayonnaise, cold, tart, and mildly sweet. A pickle spear, crunchy. The fries, excellent, not greasy or too thick. Water with a wedge of lemon. A meal. Needed. Again, here was the body demanding and receiving what it craved. A month ago she could barely swallow water. Depression, other forces, had wreaked havoc on her system, but eventually, what was necessary prevailed. She ate everything and finished before Tobin and Clayton. They both glanced at her empty plate, as if it was something to marvel at.

Back in the car, Clayton sobbed horribly for several minutes, his hands over his face. Tobin, in the front seat, stared straight ahead, clearly unable to fathom what to do. Mary waited, also unsure how to comfort him. Finally, Clayton gathered himself, started the car, and backed around.

The fawn lay in its box on the seat next to her. She thought of a sketch Michael had drawn for her in a note he'd sent her when she was still in San Francisco. It was a series of boxes. In the first picture there was a box, tied with a bow. In the second the bow was unfurled, and in the third picture, the lid was off the box and the word *love* seemed to fly out of the box. "Get it?" he'd written. And here, he'd sent her a real box. A box of love and hope. A time capsule. A gift for her—the fawn she'd rescued and wanted to keep and raise, though nature had decided otherwise.

"I need you to do something," Clayton said, looking at her in the rearview mirror.

"If I can," she said to his eyes in the mirror.

"Take a pregnancy test."

She tried not to sigh too visibly. "Okay, if that will help, I will. There's a pharmacy on the main street. Not far from the glass place, actually."

Clayton glanced at Tobin, maybe worried that he was saying too much in front of the boy, but instead he asked how Tobin was feeling so far with his motion sickness. Tobin assured him that he was fine. Being up front was, indeed, better.

"Something else, Mary," Clayton said, his eyes again in the rearview. "I need to ask. Tell me, did he . . . did he hate me so much?" She thought she saw Clayton's temple beat with a tiny pulse. "Would he ever have forgiven me?"

"Forgiven you?" she asked, leaning forward, her hand on the back of the seat near Clayton's shoulder.

"For, you know, the woman. Seeing the woman," he said.

"Who?" she said, stunned. Though what Clayton was telling her was clear enough. His eyes held hers in the mirror. She shook her head. "Honestly, he didn't talk much about you. He never mentioned anything to me about anyone."

Clayton looked ahead, clutched and reclutched the steering wheel. Tobin looked out the side window, acting as if he wasn't paying attention.

"Maybe it's just that we didn't get there," she said. "I mean, there was a lot we hadn't gotten the chance to talk about yet. We were only together nine months."

Clayton nodded, maybe able to grasp more plainly what she'd actually lost—how brief her time with Michael had turned out to be. Their future cut terribly, unfairly short.

Then Clayton said, "It was over a couple years ago now. Michael got caught in the middle. He knew, but kept it to himself." Clayton looked toward Tobin again, then away.

An affair. Michael hadn't told her any of this. Maybe he

thought it was so despicable he couldn't bring himself to talk about it. Then she felt sorry for Michael, and tried to add this bit of information into what she did know of Michael's life, and all he might have gone through with his parents. Maybe even keeping it from her because he wouldn't have wanted to bring any anger or past resentments into the happiness of their new marriage.

It occurred to her how vehemently Michael did not want to be anything like his father. She saw now how adamant Michael was about loyalty, whether they were discussing characters in movies or the behavior of their friends. In a way, Michael was always a little didactic—emphasizing the ethics of any situation, illustrating his values—especially if the circumstances reflected back on him, and their expectations of one another, the tenets of marriage, or the nature of love. He admired her parents for their devotion to one another. More than once he'd joked about her "good stock." Maybe he felt she was a good bet. He loved the stories about her father and mother, their incredible love and support for each other, even, he admitted, if it was to the exclusion of their daughter on occasion.

Michael was perceptive. Her parents had often been unattainable, and Michael had gleaned this through her recounting of events, no matter how fondly or with what amusement she'd told him stories. Once, when she was in high school, her father had driven by her in a rainstorm, unaware that the girl on the street was his own daughter, drenched, shivering, trudging home from school. There were occasions when she was a teenager and her parents left her alone for entire weekends while they went to the mountain. Mary hadn't minded and thought it brave and kind of them to trust her to take care of herself. All these incidents she'd attributed to her parents' great love for each other and her father's great distraction as a writer and scientist. She'd left some things out, though—those times when her parents had fallen into rigid gloom and silence. And the arguing she'd often listened to from her bed at night. The mythology she'd chosen to illustrate for Michael was her parents' romance, their absolute devotion to each other. But they had their problems, too. Any marriage would. She and Michael might have, if they'd had the chance.

Clayton said now, "I should have apologized to him. Now it's too late."

"You could apologize now," Tobin said, surprising them. "I mean, anyway." He spoke gently, seriously, looking at Clayton with what seemed like longing in his eyes. "You know? Just say it. We'll listen. I'd listen."

Tobin's innocence, and what she suspected was his own yearning for nurture, made something ache through her for this boy; a tiny seed beginning to uncurl. Some force of love.

Though he didn't speak, Clayton nodded, reached over and squeezed Tobin's shoulder, then put his hand back on the wheel as they drove on.

CHAPTER 31

IT WAS MARLEE'S IDEA, and now she and Callie were on the road in the dark, heading for the Goughs'. They walked, shining their flashlights up every now and then, letting the light go as far as it could in the dark, which wasn't very far before it vanished. They almost didn't need flashlights here on the open road. The sandy gravel appeared as white as sea salt.

This wasn't going to be easy. Not like peeking through the windows of empty summer homes, or once climbing through a window of the musty old Smith cabin to explore its rooms while the residents were clearly away. Or the new house on Mountain Road, that hadn't even been furnished then. This "expedition," as Marlee called it, would be trickier because Mr. Gough and Tobin might be there. And also because the moon was so bright.

"Maybe we shouldn't," Callie said, though she knew her curiosity wouldn't stop her now.

Marlee giggled. "Hey, if they see us we'll just say we were out for a stroll."

"Yeah, right. In the dark, down a dead-end road."

"Come on, Callie. This is going to be *illuminating*." Marlee clicked her flashlight off and on for emphasis. Then Marlee said,

"I heard that Tobin's mother was loony, which doesn't surprise me when you look at Tobin." This was, in part, why Marlee wanted to spy on the Goughs; there were stories about the mother, and Marlee wanted to investigate "the mysterious Goughs."

Callie laughed, but felt ashamed; she liked Tobin and didn't want to make fun of him.

"I know he's a brain," Marlee said. "Lewis told me he played amazing piano when he was like three, finished high school already. But he's sort of off, weird. Like one of those kids who's so smart there's nothing left for social skills."

"I don't know," Callie said. "Maybe he's just sort of shy."

"Ben said Tobin is moony over Mary Walker."

"Ben? When did he tell you that?"

"I don't know," Marlee said. "Sometime."

They walked on in silence.

The other day, as the crew had bustled around the kitchen, cleaning up, Callie thought she had caught Ben watching her. She was up to her elbows in the large industrial sink, scrubbing the last of the pots. He leaned against the counter, wiping his hands on a towel. She smiled at him, but he turned away so quickly she wondered if she'd been mistaken. Marlee was being her usual silly self, scraping plates, laughing, and singing, then Ben hip-checked Marlee, making her miss the pig bucket. A blob of gook fell onto the toe of her sneaker, and she started to chase him around the kitchen. Everyone laughed at the spectacle. Marlee pretended to be really angry, but she smiled through her curses as Ben circled the cutting block. He hiked his knees high like a cartoon character, looking over his shoulder, mouth open, eyes wide for exaggeration. Marlee caught the back of his shirt and held on. Ben ran in place, arms swinging, as if he really couldn't get away. It was funny, but Callie felt a little jealous, too. She wished she could be as playful as Marlee, and not so careful around Ben. And Spencer always watching her, too.

"Spence, Spence," Ben squeaked, reaching out with both arms toward Spencer, who stood at the other end of the cutting block. "Help me. Help me," he said, in a high vibrating voice, the imitation from the old movie *The Fly*—an ongoing joke, since Lewis had insisted it was brilliant and rented it so they all watched it together on the office computer one night. They were hysterical with laughter. Then Lewis had come in, and everybody scrambled to act busy. He looked mad at first, spotting the food on the floor, and pulled at his goatee, then Marlee gave him a punch on the arm and he softened, laughed, and shook his head at her with a big grin. Lewis was usually surly in the kitchen, and even his wife Barb stayed out of his way when he was cooking. But Marlee had that charm. People couldn't be around her without giving in to her mood.

Ben and Marlee were just friends, Callie assured herself. Besides, Marlee had a guy back home who everybody knew about. She talked about Jack all the time, how they were going to college together in Colorado, would probably live together eventually.

Still, she'd seen looks pass between Marlee and Ben at times, and it had made her stomach clench. But hadn't he just been watching her, too?

Callie looked up at the moon, at the shadow of its dark crater. *Please*, she thought. *Please, moon. I love him.*

Then, the other thing—the creeping fear she'd put aside—coming to her again. Her period was late. How late? A few days, maybe three by now. She felt woozy. Not for the first time. She wanted to tell Marlee, ask for advice, but maybe her period would come. She felt trim, flat stomach, fit. There couldn't be anything growing inside her. With the thought of that, a wave of nausea came over her.

"Marlee?" she said.

"Hmm?" Marlee answered.

"How do you know when, or how late can your period be before you should—"

It took Callie a second to realize that Marlee had stopped walking and stood still behind her on the road.

"Oh. My. God," she said. "Please tell me you're not." She shone her flashlight in Callie's face.

Callie put her hand up to cover her eyes. "Stop," she said with a tremor in her voice that was half giggle, half anger at the light. "I don't think I am," she said. Marlee lowered the light to Callie's feet. Callie couldn't see Marlee now—her sight was all painful and bright. "No, it's just I'm a little late."

"That asshole!" Marlee said. "I'll kill him."

"No," Callie said. She hoped Marlee wouldn't say anything to Spencer. She had to make Marlee swear secrecy. "Don't say anything to anyone. Please. It's probably nothing."

"I hope not," Marlee said. "I just cannot believe him!"

"Maybe the condom broke," Callie said. "I mean, I don't even know how it happened. Or *if* it happened."

"Yes, but you're sixteen! He's twenty-one. It's statutory rape."

"It's not like that." She wasn't sure what *statutory* meant exactly, but the word *rape* was too awful.

"It is to the law. Jesus H. Christ. How late are you?"

"Just a couple of days. It's nothing."

Marlee was quiet for a minute, then she started walking again. Callie went along beside her, wishing she'd never brought it up.

"He *knows* better. I should have stopped this long ago," Marlee said.

"It isn't all his fault," Callie said.

"It is, though," Marlee said. "You're just a kid."

"I'm not!" She was *not* a kid. It wasn't Marlee's place to stop anything.

"Christ," Marlee said. "I know you like the guy, but Rabbit is more mature than Spencer, and he's only seventeen."

"Just don't say anything to him," Callie said. "He doesn't know. I'm not seeing him anymore anyway. I don't even like him anymore." Tears burned in her eyes suddenly, and she pinched her lips together so she wouldn't cry. She'd stopped going over to Spencer's, so it wasn't fair that her period was late. It didn't make any sense. She didn't want this, or anything to do with Spencer. She didn't even want to talk about it, or think about it.

"I like *Ben*," she blurted out.

Marlee didn't say anything. Then Marlee put her arm around Callie's shoulders and pulled her close as they walked. Callie smelled Marlee's hair, lemony.

"We'll work this out," Marlee said. "Probably it's nothing. But if it's something, we'll work it out."

Callie felt a rush of gratitude. She put her flashlight in her other hand and curled her arm around Marlee's waist, and they walked together like that, hip to hip for a few yards, then Marlee released her.

"I had an abortion last year," Marlee said. "So it's not like I'm judging you. I just care about you, okay?"

"You did?" Callie was amazed Marlee hadn't mentioned it before, especially with all the stories Marlee had told Callie about Jack. How they would probably get married eventually.

Marlee reached for Callie's hand, squeezed, and held on.

"It was awful," Marlee said. "And I would never do it again. I still think about how the baby would be, like a year and a bunch of months old by now."

"Did Jack want it? Was he upset?"

"It wasn't his."

"Oh." She didn't know what to say.

"It was a different guy. Someone I thought I was madly in love with. Jack and I were having troubles at the time, not seeing each other as much."

Here was another thing Marlee hadn't told her. Some other guy, not Jack?

"I even thought about marrying Aaron," Marlee said, "but he freaked when I told him I was pregnant. If that didn't hurt enough, then there was the abortion itself. Imagine cramps magnified by a thousand. I hope you don't have to go through anything like that."

"That's awful," Callie said. "Did Jack . . . did he know?"

"I couldn't see any point in telling him. It's weird to think that for a while I really thought Aaron was the one, you know, but I sure was wrong."

Callie knew that this world of the summer would end and she'd have to leave, go back to school. As vague as it was to imagine, somewhere out there, a long time from now, she knew she'd marry a man she loved, and she'd have his baby. Like Mary.

Maybe that man was Ben. *Please please.*

Marlee had called her "a kid," and Ben was even older than Spencer. Though age didn't matter when it came to love. Love could fix everything.

They walked on, and Marlee said, "If it's only a couple of days you probably shouldn't worry."

"I think so, too," Callie said, and she believed it because Marlee was so sure and comforting.

They came to the first bridge, the brook running down below, echoing through the culvert. They crossed over the bridge and started up the hill, the water sound receding.

Then Marlee let go of her hand, and they walked on quietly, but for the sandpapery scuff of their sneakers on the gravel road.

CHAPTER 32

MARY LEFT THE HOUSE early evening before the sun set. She hiked fast, breathing deeply, pushing herself on up the Clark Trail. She felt a little weak, lungs aching, legs straining. When she was a girl, she ran past hikers, a steam engine up the mountain.

This afternoon, when they returned, Clayton and Tobin had worked installing the new pane of glass while she put the groceries away. In the bathroom she put the pregnancy test into a cupboard. She'd do it later, when she was alone. There was a part of her that felt thrown off balance; maybe it would be positive. Could it? Clayton had made her start to doubt herself and to hope. Maybe all her nausea and hunger and emotions were a sign. What if it had been only spotting? What if her period was late? She felt concerned about drinking the whiskey and tried to remember how much she'd actually consumed. But no. Stop. She knew it would be negative, and getting that confirmation was also something she wanted to do alone, tomorrow morning, perhaps.

Finally Clayton had driven back to the lodge, and Tobin, after hanging around a little longer, had been persuaded to go home. Didn't his father worry about where he was? He insisted his father was oblivious. She piled Tobin's arms with her father's books, and that appeased him.

Now she just wanted to get away from the house. From memories. She wanted to pound the mountain with her feet. She wanted to scream from the cliff. She wanted to tell Cascom to go to hell. The sky was growing dimmer. She peered into the woods, between the trees, into the depths where the light faded, turned to a dark blur. The sun had lowered, making the spaces between trees even more obscure. There were moose tracks sunk into a muddy area. Crows cawed and followed one another, one at a time, from treetop to treetop.

There was a growing irritation at what Clayton had revealed to her about his affair. She felt as much hurt that Michael had never told her, as disgusted with Clayton for cheating on his wife and putting Michael in the middle. She wondered if Michael's mother knew. Knowing Michael, how kindhearted he was, it was frustrating to realize he'd let his relationship with his father deteriorate completely, never to be reconciled. Yet, she knew Michael enough to understand how a betrayal like that would incense him.

She moved on, a chill at her back, as if she were being chased, faster, trying not to think. Not about Michael, his body twisting, reaching. Or Clayton's request that she take a test, his insistence on proof. Not about her parents, or Tobin's parents, or Clayton's affair. Not about the dead boy sprawled on the trail, or where it was he'd lain exactly as her feet trod over the same ground. Not about the missing girl. Nor Callie's dark-gloom, which she understood, and thought she felt too, right now. A deep sadness, a weight pressing on her shoulders.

Though she'd imagined standing on the edge of the cliff, challenging it to pull her over, she passed by the cutoff that led to the ledges and simply continued on, up the trail.

As she came out into an opening of steep-rising granite, a wave of warm air came off the rock, drying her skin and making her shiver. Using the toes of her sneakers, she zigzagged up the sheer granite toward Ben's cabin. By the time Hi-House came into view it was getting dark. A haze of light came through the windows. She paused and breathed until her lungs slowed almost to normal, then almost to nothing. It was as if she were not there at all. Sweat evaporated from her back, and the air started to feel cold. There was the smell of balsam, and then a waft of garlic. She pushed wet hair away from her forehead.

A breeze made a shushing sound through the scrubby trees behind his cabin. Stars flickered lightly as if just turning themselves on in the dimming sky. A tremor shook her, and goose bumps rose all over.

Ben's figure, blurred, passed behind the glass, and she realized the window was covered with condensation. She walked to the steps and stood still in front of the door, barely breathing, feeling her heart slow, making it steady. A sudden blast of wind made an eerie tone, a low howl, as it drove itself around the edge of the cabin. Then she raised her fist, knocked.

From inside came a clang, like a saucepan lid falling into a sink. "Ben?" she said.

He opened the door, his mouth open and his hand on his chest. "I just jumped about ten feet," he said.

"I'm sorry. I couldn't exactly call first."

He stepped back, holding the door open for her. The room was very warm, which was unexpected and good. The building, all one room, she vaguely remembered from her years on crew. Ben had made it look larger by dividing it into sections with furniture. There was a stuffed chair, awkward to have been carried on someone's back, or perhaps brought to the summit by helicopter, then carried down to the house as she knew some supplies were. Several small tables and wooden cabinets, very old looking, maybe even antiques, occupied walls and corners. Who knew how long they'd been here, how many fire watchmen had used them? The kitchen area took up one side of the room, and a pot of water boiled on the stove. A small oval table for dining, and two ladder-back chairs. A single cot, made up with a plaid blanket, sat snug against the back wall. A guitar case, tucked under the bed. She remembered Michael's guitar, stored under the bed back at the house, hidden by the bed skirt. She hadn't dared to pull it out or look at it.

Ben went to the stove and turned the gas off under the water.

"I don't mean to interrupt your dinner," she said.

"No, no," he said. He picked up pot holders, lifted the pot, and poured water and pasta into a colander in the sink. Then he turned and gazed at her, his eyebrows arched, obviously waiting for her to say something. She hadn't prepared any reason for coming. She'd just propelled herself here, trying to move herself in some direction, and now she was standing in his tiny house. It smelled warm and good. Garlic. Fresh bread. She noticed the loaf now, cooling on a rack.

"You bake?" she said.

"I was making spaghetti. Join me?"

Her face felt flushed and she didn't know if it was from the climb, then coming inside where it was warm, a little too warm, or also maybe because she was suddenly embarrassed at just showing up, coming as if she knew he'd welcome her. Somehow his presence was a little too real now. She wasn't sure she wanted to be here. She'd just wanted to get out of the house. Away from the possibility of Tobin coming back, or the pregnancy test awaiting, or just sitting in that house, alone.

"Making bread is an easy thing," he said. "And tastes so much better than anything you can buy." He opened a cabinet above the sink, took out two plates, handed them to her and tipped his head toward the oval table.

"I just headed out," she said, clearing the table of magazines and books. "And I ended up here."

"Good," he said.

She felt relieved to hear him say it. It was okay. He didn't mind. She felt tension too, though. She laid the plates, feeling his eyes on her. He pointed to a silverware tray on the counter and she went there. He pulled at his earlobe, the one with the earring, as she'd seen him do before, then smiled, his endearing grin.

He wore the uniform-olive khakis, but the olive shirt hung loose, unbuttoned, showing a brown T-shirt underneath. The T-shirt was tucked in; belt buckled neatly. The collar of the T-shirt was wide, pulled out of shape, and a few dark hairs showed there.

Ben stirred the tomato sauce with a wooden spoon, then left it and bent over a tiny refrigerator. There was the back of his neck, and the shoulders, broad, sure, a lot like Michael's. Her throat ached, remembering Michael's proposal dinner. The to-mato sauce and garlic in the air, just like this. No, she pushed the memory away.

Ben handed her a can of beer. She took it, wiped the rim with her fingers out of habit, and pulled the tab. It tasted so good, like brook water and sweet, and she remembered her father giv-ing her sips of beer when she was a girl. It occurred to her, if she was pregnant, she shouldn't drink. But a beer couldn't hurt. And she wasn't pregnant.

"Cup?" Ben said, pointing to an open shelf where there were plastic and tin cups of various sizes. She shook her head. He didn't use a cup either.

"I'm not much of a cook," he said. "But I'm all right at pasta. It should taste good."

The room, softly lit by one standing lamp behind the stuffed chair, was calming. The windows, steamed from the boiling water, made the room seem a bubble, a shelter so high up on the mountain. Impossibly comfortable and safe, even with the weather out there that could turn mean and harsh in a moment.

"Sit," Ben said, pulling out one of the ladder-back chairs. She sat. She couldn't think of anything to say. The aroma of the bread and tomato sauce and garlic was so fine. And the heat from the stove felt good. He opened the refrigerator, took out a bottle of salad dressing and a plastic container, snapped the lid, and doled out salad into two bowls. The sturdiness of his body made her feel safe. The body of the man in the room, moving between sink and stove, making dinner. She felt the beer all the way down her throat and into her stomach, then quick to her head. The sweat had evaporated from her clothes. Even in the warmth she felt chilled and ran her hands over her arms. He noticed and pulled a wool shirt from a hook, handed it to her. She put it on and rolled the sleeves above her wrists.

He brought food to the table and served her. She smiled, but still there were no words in her head, completely empty. He wasn't speaking either, after all. He tore bread from the loaf with his hands and ate, and glanced at her now and then. Maybe there was nothing to say right now. Just feel, taste, smell. He pushed the butter dish toward her, broke bread off the loaf for her, rose and came back with a smaller, completely unnecessary plate for her bread. The gesture touched her. He spun spaghetti around in a large spoon, deftly, smoothly. His eyes were fringed with dark eyelashes that gave him a soft look. He took a sip from his can of beer. His eyes passed over her face.

She ate, realizing how hungry she was. The bread was soft and delicious. The spaghetti sauce spicy, warming. The wind had grown stronger outside, and moaned around the outside of the cabin. The door rattled in a hard gust. She drank a long gulp from her beer, then looked down at her plate, suddenly exhausted.

"Are you okay?" Ben said. He spoke a little roughly, it seemed, as if she were acting crazy. "Mary?" he asked, this time tenderly, and she realized he was just concerned. Maybe she was even scaring him, worrying him.

"I'm tired," she said. "I feel fuzzy."

He stood up and came to her, took the beer out of her hand,

and put it on the table. Next he urged her up, led her to the bed. She went with him, wondering what was happening. Thinking, What's he doing? What am I doing? His grip was gentle. He kept one hand on her arm as he pulled the covers down and patted the pillow. Then he put both hands on her shoulders, turned her around, and sat her on the bed. He knelt down in front of her, untied her sneakers, and pulled them off. She noticed how grimy her socks were at the ankles where the edge of the sneakers caught the dirt, rubbed it in. There was the top of his head, dark short hair. She wanted to run her fingers over the top of his head, let him lift his face, and then let her be in the past, before summer, before everything. She lifted her hand to touch the top of his head, but then he stood up. He'd left her socks on.

"Get in," he said. She realized that he meant for her to lie down in his bed, alone in his bed. "Rest," he said.

She slid her feet in. He pulled the covers over her, patted them around her shoulders, and went back to the kitchen area.

"I'm sorry about your girlfriend," she said.

"I know," he said, turning to look back at her. "And I *do* know," he said gently, and she knew what he meant. That he was someone who knew—just knew—like her, what the world right now felt like.

She shut her eyes and listened to water splashing into tin or metal, gurgling from a plastic container. She opened her eyes to see him clear the last of the things from the table. Then he sat down in the stuffed chair, his back to her, and she presumed he was reading under the lamp.

The sheets were stiff and the blanket smelled musty, so she folded it away from her face. It was nice under the covers, comfortable, and she was surprised to find her mind slipping quickly, heavily. She wanted to stay awake, but her body wasn't letting her. She felt the cabin sliding sideways, falling backward with the slow spin of the earth. She put her arms around the pillow, held on.

CHAPTER 33

THEY TURNED OFF THEIR flashlights and made their way through tall, dewy grass, approaching from behind the Goughs' barn. Keeping close to the wall, they crept around the barn and stopped at the front corner. Marlee grabbed Callie's arm and squeezed, and they giggled, then shushed each other. Off to one side of the barn was the smaller building, long and narrow, like a couple of train cars. A light shone in there, and also there were lights on in the downstairs of the main house, the third building, all laid out in a triangle.

Mr. Gough, stout and ponytailed, passed by a window of the main house. They clutched each other's arms and pressed their backs up against the side of the barn. Then Tobin passed the same window and was gone, leaving the lit window empty to show some sort of white wall behind it and a cupboard door. In a few seconds Tobin came back to the window, stopped, and stood, looking out, as if he were staring directly across the yard, toward the barn and where they froze, flattened along the wall.

"He can't see us, right?" Callie whispered. "Out a lit window?"

"He's washing dishes," Marlee whispered. They watched

Tobin, his arms working, shoulders hunched forward. After a bit he took a towel, wiped his hands, and threw it off to the side and left.

There was the smell of mildew and hay and a biting waft of something harsh. A scuffling sound inside the barn made Marlee squeeze Callie's arm, but they knew it was the infamous pigs.

One evening when Tobin had come with his father to get the pig buckets, Callie had joked with him about the pigs. She was in the kitchen scouring a baking pan full of burned-on pork grease. Tobin, introverted as usual, was busy lugging the buckets of scraps out from under the counter, seeming embarrassed or self-conscious, unable to look her in the eyes, so she'd tried to engage him. "You know what?" she said. "We had pork chops tonight." Tobin stopped what he was doing as if paralyzed, then looked up, his thick eyebrows pinched, chin raised. "What I mean is," she began, "there are pork bones in there. In the buckets."

"Pork," he said, the slightest glimmer of a smile. "So?"

"You're going to make your pigs cannibals!" She smiled at him. Pigs as cannibals was funny, though also it sort of grossed her out. "It doesn't seem right," she said. "Pigs eating pigs."

Tobin's eyes glimmered, crinkled at the corners, the smallest twitch of amusement at the corner of his mouth. And then he laughed—a funny, high chuckle, accompanied by scrunching his eyes shut briefly, revealing long, dark eyelashes. Then he opened his eyes, bright as stones plucked out of water, and grinned, his dimples accentuated. It pleased her so much to have gotten this out of him. She grinned back, then with a touch of sudden shyness, she turned away, refolded a dishrag.

"They do make pigs of themselves," he said. "They eat anything. Remember Dorothy in *The Wizard of Oz*?"

She remembered the scene he was referring to—the one where Dorothy fell off the rail into the pig sty and the pigs converged on her. A horrible scene, not one you'd laugh about. But she wanted to let Tobin know that she liked him, and she didn't want him to feel self-conscious. He'd grinned, gums showing, then his long lashes flickered. He was cute, she noted. Even handsome when he wasn't hunched over in his self-conscious way.

Now Marlee said, "Come on," and they pushed away from the barn wall and ran across the yard toward the smaller building. Marlee's shadow trailed behind her on the ground like a cape, and Callie's feet traveled inside it. The air was lovely, silky, and they ran swiftly, barely a sound as if their feet didn't touch down. They were witches, riding the currents, invisible. They could see in, but no one could see out. They were powerful in the dark. A bubbly thrill went through Callie, and she felt such a warm joy, and also so much admiration for her adventurous older friend who loved her. Marlee was the wild spirit. They both were!

They breathed hard, trying not to make a sound, and crouched below a lit window. Knowing Tobin and Mr. Gough were in the main house, they weren't afraid to stand up and peer boldly into these windows.

Paintings, brilliant and bright with color, hung on every wall. Propped alongside table legs and chairs, there were stretched canvases stacked against each other. One wall was filled with small, rectangular watercolors, of fields and barns—that barn across the way. Tall, skinny spruce in the fields. There were paintings of Cascom Mountain with its fire tower—several renderings—some with bright blue skies, or gray and white, some with sunsets, bleeding pink, red, and orange. Gray stone walls crossed yellow fields of tall grass. A brook snaked between leafy banks and overhanging branches. Birch trees arched over a gravel road, their light green leaves full of fingerprint-sized yellow dabs, which, Callie imagined, represented sunlight. There was the lodge even.

The roof sagging and all the windows full of streaky reflection. It was all the land and forest, and everything they knew of Cascom.

Marlee pinched Callie's wrist gently, and they moved on to the next window. Here was a tall wooden easel, a painting clipped to it. The scene was a field with outcroppings of granite that stuck out in a swirl of sprays of grass. There were sections not yet filled in, but outlined with darker brushstrokes. They moved away and around to the back of the building and along the wall to where there were darkened windows at the one end; it was like looking in the windows of a train, the rooms long and narrow. The building might have been a chicken coop or animal stalls in some other incarnation. This room was unlit. Marlee ran her fingers along the bottom sill. The window went up with no trouble.

"No," Callie whispered, frightened, never wanting to go any further. "Let's not."

Marlee put her finger up to her lips, then laced her fingers together and held them down for Callie to step into. Callie paused, then put her foot into Marlee's hands as she'd done before at other summer homes.

Once they were both in, easily as cats, they stood still and waited just in case they'd made any noise. It smelled like oil paint and turpentine, and also mildew—the air stiff. Some light penetrated from the adjacent room, and it took their eyes a moment to adjust to the half-light, and then the shape of things started to come clear.

The woman was naked, horrible, and glaring at them. She had a long, narrow neck and draping black hair that dangled like clumps of glistening seaweed over her heavy breasts. The paint looked thick and furrowed in places. Callie turned slowly to see the same woman repeated in other paintings. Goose pimples rose on her arms; the eyes of the woman were on her from every direction. In some, the woman sat on the edge of a hard-looking wooden chair. In others she stood on a platform, arms crossed or akimbo, nude, though occasionally a pink cloth of some sort curled at her feet, or draped over a shoulder.

"Oh my God!" Marlee said in a husky whisper, and yanked Callie's arm.

Callie jumped, nearly shrieked. "Don't do that! You scared me," she whispered.

"Sorry," Marlee said, "but look." She clicked her flashlight on, drawing the beam up, then slowly down, to reveal a huge painting. It reached from the floor nearly to the beams of the ceiling. The woman stood straight, arms at her sides, one foot forward like she was about to step out of the canvas. The pink cloth lay at her feet. Nude again, hair hanging long, covering her breasts, pubic hair dark and bristly. Something was different about this one—the paint was thinner, her skin pale, almost translucent. On close inspection, the background—a window, framing a blur of autumn foliage—was visible through part of the woman's midsection, as if the artist had painted the backdrop first, then laid her transparent form over it, allowing the landscape to bleed through her ghostly form. The woman stared directly at the viewer, black eyes, no light in them, no white. It was eerie. Then, an optical illusion. Callie realized the eyes weren't open at all; the eyelids were closed, painted as smooth ovals. Thick, long eyelashes at the lower rims. Tobin was in the woman's face; those same dark lashes, hints of dimples, even though she wasn't smiling. Her mouth was crooked slightly—the trace of disdain?

"Let's get out of here," Callie whispered. "This is creepola."

The woman's eyes followed them as they scrambled out the window. The last thing Callie saw in the one quick flash of Marlee's light was another portrait of the woman, nude again, but this time lying on her side and obviously pregnant—belly distended, taut. Callie recoiled at the sight of it, worry spinning through her again, then hung her leg over the windowsill, and she was out.

They squatted, resting their backs against the outside wall, breathed for a moment, then Marlee was up and waving Callie to follow, heading toward the main house. Callie didn't want to go there. She'd had enough, but Marlee was already halfway across and running stooped over, keeping to the darker side of the yard where the peak of the house made a giant triangular shadow across the ground. Callie caught up with her, squatting below a window around the corner from where they'd seen Tobin washing dishes. They heard voices inside. Callie tried to breathe as softly as she could.

She couldn't make out the words, but Tobin sounded weary, distressed.

"Her medications make all the difference," came Mr. Gough's voice, practically right above them. The window was open, just a screen. She thought she saw the shadow of Mr. Gough's head bob within the rectangle of light that fell on the ground just past where they hid. "You'll see," he said.

"It doesn't matter!" Tobin yelled.

Callie tensed at the anger in Tobin's voice. She and Marlee gripped each other's hands. Even in the dark Callie saw Marlee soundlessly mouth, "Yikes."

"She needs us," Mr. Gough said, softly. "I need her here."

"You *use* her," Tobin said.

"Anyway, it's not your decision," Mr. Gough said. Then he coughed and said, "T, it's not like it was before. Can't you give it a chance?"

"She'll ruin everything," Tobin said. Callie could tell he was near tears. "She's crazy. Don't you remember what she did to me?"

"She's still your mother," Mr. Gough said. "She's better. I know. If you had taken a minute to visit her, you'd know, too."

"You are a *fucking* fool," Tobin snapped, crying now. Callie flinched, and Marlee squeezed her hand tighter.

Poor Tobin. She wondered what his mother, that scary woman in the paintings, had done to him. If Callie were inside, she would stand up for Tobin, tell his father to let him alone. Then came a rapping sound, like knuckles on a wood table, wall, or counter.

"Don't do that," Mr. Gough said. "Stop doing that." But the knocking continued, rhythmic, uncompromising. There was rustling, then footfalls across the room inside, and the knocking stopped.

"Please, T," Mr. Gough said, more gently. "She's not who you think she is. Not anymore. Please try. This isn't necessary. You must try . . . try not to do these things."

"Don't do it," Tobin sobbed. "I don't want her here."

Callie had had enough. This was private, personal, not something they should be listening to. She signaled to Marlee, thankful that she was in agreement, already up on her toes, ready to go. They inched themselves away, keeping low, then ran back across the yard.

The tall, itchy grass swept against her legs as she ran behind Marlee. She didn't feel mysterious or brave or fun anymore. That woman in the paintings was real. She was Tobin's mother, and she was alive somewhere. She was a lunatic and scary, and Mr. Gough wanted to bring her here. Here, to the mountain. Poor Tobin. How awful to have such a hideous mother. She thought of her own mother—longed for her mother's sweetness washing over her. And her dad, who'd smooch her on the top of her head. She missed them. That portrait, the woman's pregnant belly, distended, odd and smooth, pushed out from her body—Callie felt sick thinking of it.

When she and Marlee came out on the gravel road, they slowed to a fast walk and turned on their flashlights again. They didn't speak, as if they were unable to until they could be safely inside their brightly lit bedroom, because to speak here on the road would be to say something about the scary woman in the paintings, and to say something about her was to bring her to the dark road with them, and they were too afraid of the night and its possible wickedness. Trees creaked and moaned, and the brook gurgled down there in the blackness. Callie didn't dare shine her flashlight too far left or right, afraid to illuminate the woods. It felt like something was out there, traveling alongside them, silent in the woods, but not like the moon that kept pace with them, slipping along behind the crown of the trees. It was something hidden, something watching them from everywhere.

CHAPTER 34

S HE'D BEEN ASLEEP, though not deeply, when Ben removed a folded blanket from the bottom of the bed. He was being careful not to disturb her, not to wake her. He started back to his chair.

"Ben?" she whispered.

"Sorry," he said. "Just needed to get some sleep."

"Please," she said, and moved herself closer to the wall to give him room. "Get inside. You must be freezing."

He didn't move at first, holding the blanket to his chest, then he came back. She lifted the covers for him, and he got under, bringing a chill with him on his clothing, and smells of balsam and garlic. He lay on his side with his back to her. Her knees were close to his legs—she could almost feel where they would touch if she moved even slightly—and her face was close to the back of his head.

It wasn't long before his breathing became even and deep, and she lay awake, falling into the incessant circle—the what-ifs her brain constantly manufactured, sometimes whole reenactments, long scenes she'd imagine before she caught herself and reminded herself of the facts. Michael had fallen. She was alone.

Also there was the unremitting sensation that just under her skin there was something toxic, abrasive, wearing her down. It was grief, of course—constant, relentless, indescribable. Its presence fixed itself on her every move and thought. Even in the moments she wasn't fully aware, it was still there, like a hand on her back.

She'd tried to will herself asleep. The wind hummed a high-pitched tone as it blew against the outside walls of the cabin. Occasionally the door tapped in its frame, a stuttering rattle, and she felt a slight breeze across her face.

Here was a man sleeping next to her. Hard to believe she was in Hi-House, with a man, a stranger almost. Not Michael. Where *was* Michael? Gone, completely gone. Fading, even. He seemed so long ago.

It struck her in a rush of shivers and possibility, and like the hand on her back constantly pushing, she realized she'd carried an idea with her when she came here, though she hadn't admitted it to herself until now. Her mind said *Don't*, but her body moved. Her body moved closer to Ben until her knees pressed firmly into the back of his thighs. She felt herself grow wet all at once, the desire was so powerful. She needed him to touch her. Michael was gone, truly gone. She repeated the words like a mantra in her head—*truly gone, truly gone*—as she placed her hand on Ben's shoulder. His skin was warm through his T-shirt. Nothing she did now could hurt Michael. This was need. Pure physical need. She slid her hand down Ben's arm, feeling his skin, the fuzz of hair on his forearm. He tensed and his breathing changed; he was awake. She put her fingers around his wrist and pulled gently. He rolled all at once, smoothly, calmly, toward her. She felt his breath on her face, and he put his arm around her.

He said, "It's okay. I'm here. Sleep."

She felt the weight of his arm, and his breath on her neck,

and his sudden kindness that made her almost sob. His chest hair tickled her nose. She pressed her face against his chest, moved her hips so they were determinedly against his. It seemed to her that her body was acting all on its own, separated from reason and locked into its own biological urgency. Her body had to have this. She took hold of his hand to move it between her legs, but he didn't understand and tried to lace his fingers between hers, another affirming grip. She untangled her fingers from his, took his hand firmly, and placed it between her legs, on top of her jeans.

He didn't take his hand away. She smoothed the back of his hand, pressing it between her legs. He was still, his hand still. She spread her legs farther apart and with her other hand unzipped her pants, wriggled them down a bit, then put his hand on her belly. And then his fingers were sliding under the elastic of her underwear on their own, and down. She shuddered. The ache intensified, and she opened to it and spread her legs more. His fingers moved, and he made a soft moan. She lifted her hips as he got on his knees, used both hands, tugged her jeans and underwear down. He lowered his face between her legs, the stubble of his beard rough and his tongue moving, and she opened to him, letting her body give over to it completely. There was a sound in her ears like water rushing. She imagined the rills swirling, the current between her legs. She held her breath, went underwater, lost in it for a moment. Then her hands found his cheeks, and urged him up, to be on top of her.

"Are you sure?" he said.

"Yes," she said.

She smelled herself on his mouth, and the faint hint of beer on his breath. The door rattled, and a draft shifted the air in a cool sweep across her face. He was on top of her, heavy and waiting, and her legs were apart and she was wet, but she couldn't breathe. The water sound that had been in her ears ended abruptly.

The last man she'd made love with was Michael. If she did this with Ben, then Michael wouldn't be the last one; he'd be a step removed. What if Michael's baby *was* growing inside her? She felt Ben's breath on her face, on her mouth. He kissed her cheekbone. It was gentle, sweet. She wanted to cry as he slid his own cheek against hers, kissing her neck, and she felt his ear, cool, rubbery, and something else, hard, foreign. The earring. Something inside her turned. She jerked. Her body retracted, revolted. She pushed against Ben's shoulders, and he rolled away quickly, fully understanding or not.

Then came his voice, softly, "It's okay. It's okay."

He put his arms around her. She pulled back, then stopped when she realized that he only meant to hold her, to comfort her. It was okay. She was safe. She relaxed, and soon felt as if she were rushing away, downstream. And she went with it, let it take her. He held her and breathed into her neck, and she was calm.

"It's all right," he whispered. "Hush. Just rest."

A man, a friend, a person. A kind person, just comforting her, not asking for anything else. And it was all right to let herself be comforted. It was all right.

CHAPTER 35

AFTER THE BREAKFAST DISHES were finished and the kitchen duties were over, Callie went to the bathroom to check, because she felt wet down there, but it wasn't blood. Her body didn't feel any different. Maybe it was simply stress, or worry. Marlee had told her that could be the reason. Stop worrying about it and it would come. Okay, she wouldn't think about it. She wasn't pregnant. It was impossible. She and Spencer had always used condoms, though there was that nagging memory that one night it had been different.

Now Spencer wasn't speaking to her. He was giving her the cold shoulder, ignoring her in the kitchen, not looking at her when he gave the crew their instructions for the day. He'd caught on, she guessed that she didn't want to see him. She wasn't going to his room anymore. When he introduced the crew and told his usual jokes, she didn't laugh like she used to, and sometimes she rolled her eyes at the guests like they'd all heard it a thousand times, which they had. Spencer had put a baking pan down on the counter next to her when she was on pot duty. He said it was still scummy and to wash it again. "Dive deeper," he said, using the crew lingo in a mean way. She was beginning to hate him. She wished she'd never slept with him. Did he think he owned her? Well, he didn't. She could do whatever she wanted. It was statutory rape, Marlee said. Callie had looked it up. Weird. It made her equally angry that the law could decide something like that. It was her body. She owned it. No one, no one would tell her who she could or could not have sex with.

Next week she would have "daze," and she would ask Mary or catch a ride from someone to town. She'd maybe buy a pregnancy test somewhere. To find out she wasn't pregnant would be a relief, and then she could focus on other things.

She sat on her bunk, looking at the ends of her hair, using her fingers like scissors to estimate how much she needed to trim. A couple of inches, maybe. It was pretty long—halfway down her back—but it was thin at the ends and would look better cut straight across, blunt and neat. Maybe Marlee could cut it. Where was Marlee? They had an hour before she and Rabbit were supposed to clean up a trail that hadn't been cleared for a summer or two. She was thankful Spencer had paired her with Rabbit and not himself for trail duty over the next week. Today Marlee and Spencer were going to shovel sand onto the small beach at the edge of the pond. A dump truck had delivered the sand yesterday, and it sat in a huge pile on one side of the parking lot.

There'd been no noise from across the hall in the boys' room, but now she heard someone come up the stairs, then go into the boys' room. It could have been Rabbit, but she'd seen him hanging out with Barb earlier; she was showing him how to roll pie crust. Maybe it was Ben over there. Yes, the footfalls sounded more like boots, like Ben. She should just get up and walk over and say hello.

She stood up, checked herself in the mirror. Her heart was beating fast. The boys' room door was open. She stuck her head in.

"Howdy, Callie," came Rabbit's voice from the top bunk.

She felt her face flush. Ben wasn't there at all. Of course not.

"Hey," she said. "Guess we get to clear trail all week. Big fun."

"I don't mind," Rabbit said. He'd been reading a book and laid it facedown across his chest. "At least we get to be away from the goofers."

"I guess," she said. She felt disoriented. She'd been hopeful that it was Ben who'd come up. Plus, Rabbit could go on and on about things, and now she was stuck because already he was telling her about *A Fan's Notes*, which she'd already read, like two years before.

Rabbit went first, using his sickle to clear a path through tall ferns that bowed into the trail. Callie followed, swiping her own sickle at whatever Rabbit missed. In her other hand she carried a pair of giant clippers. Her pack was heavy from the huge water bottle Spencer had insisted she bring. To spite him, she wouldn't touch it. She was so mad at him. It seemed to her that he'd purposefully stuck her with Rabbit and not Marlee to assert his authority.

She looked forward to getting back, to evening when they'd all be together, working in the kitchen again. Ben might be in the tower. Maybe, if they got the trail done, they could pop up there and see him.

Soon she and Rabbit were under the trees and into the shade where the trail was less overgrown, except for some fallen trees they had to climb over. Someone would have to come up here with a chain saw to remove the trees. Most were huge, fat trunks, and she had to find a way through stiff, tight branches without being scraped up. Some trees had hung themselves up on other trees, and she and Rabbit walked under them easily, but fast because they looked so precarious. Most of the fallen trees were spruce, toppled by high winds last winter, their roots pulled up out of the ground. It was creepy to see their roots like that, all squiggly and reaching out in all directions, like octopus arms.

Rabbit had a small handsaw with him, and he used it now on the branches of a spruce that lay across the trail. The branches were so snarled and massive that they wouldn't be able to step through them without some clearing. Callie helped by trying to snap off smaller branches with the giant clippers. The blades bit through the little branches easily. Other branches required all the pressure she could muster, and even then she'd have to take hold with her hands and twist the branches back and forth until they broke off, or got thin enough to cut through. Soon her hands and the grip of the clippers were sticky with sap.

By the time they reached tree line, they were both sweating and streaked with dirt and pitch. They took a lunch break, sitting out on the granite in the sun. It felt good to rest, and even to drink water. She was thirsty. This was hard work, and she was worn out. The sun was hot, but as her sweat evaporated a chill took her.

Rabbit made sounds of awe, gazing at the view. He pointed out a funny-looking tree that grew from a shallow crevice nearby. It had been beaten by years of wind; its bark was scrolled and twisted, and the trunk had grown nearly perpendicular to the rock. It was amazing really that anything could grow up here, or would want to.

Rabbit poked around in his knapsack and pulled out his sandwich container. He opened it, and the smell of tuna wafted out. Before she knew it, she was gagging. She put her hand over her mouth and stood up. She barely made it to the crevice before she was vomiting next to the scraggly tree.

When she finished, she spit a few times, and then she felt Rabbit gently take hold of her hair and pull it back from her shoulders.

"You might have heat exhaustion," he said. "Here, let's get out of the sun." He tried to lead her away from the crevice and down the ledge to where the trees began, but after a couple of steps her legs didn't want to move.

"I'm fine," she said, though her head felt light and the thought of the sandwich over there where he'd left it made her queasy. She bent over, but nothing came up, just saliva. She spit again.

"You must have overdone it," Rabbit said.

She wiped her mouth with the back of her arm. Her face felt hot and her eyes had filled so it might even appear as if she were crying. Rabbit looked worried. The edges of his stick-out ears were pink from sunlight coming through the backs of them.

She felt better now and sat down where she was. Rabbit stood over her for a second, then went back up to their stuff to get her water. When he came back he put his hand on her forehead.

"Feels hot," he said, handing her the water bottle.

They'd both passed a first aid course and had learned about heat stroke and heat exhaustion and hypothermia and shock. But Callie knew it wasn't any of those things. It was just the smell of tuna. It was the thought of eating tuna, or anything. She pulled her knees up and laid her forehead on them. Rabbit let her sit like that until finally she felt better, and she raised her head.

"I feel fine now," she said. But her jaw felt stiff, like she couldn't say what she didn't really believe. "I just needed to rest."

Rabbit nodded, though she could tell he wasn't convinced. They'd worked together clearing trail before, and even harder labor under the sun. She was strong and capable. This wasn't like her, and she felt a surge of cold blood rush up her legs and into her belly as she realized that her body wasn't behaving the same as always.

"You should drink more," Rabbit said. She shook her head. "Do you want anything to eat?" he asked.

She couldn't answer at the thought of it and leaned back on

her palms, feeling the rough granite and little pieces of grit stick to her palms. She took a deep breath and blew it out, letting her cheeks fill.

"Whew," she said. "That was not fun."

"Let's go down now," Rabbit said, and went to get their packs.

She looked out at the valley, the rolling green hills, the lakes in the distance, flat and gray. There were the White Mountains far off and hazy at the horizon, where the land seemed to end as if the earth was flat and you could step off right there and fall into oblivion. She was sixteen years old, and there was a whole world out there. She couldn't be pregnant, yet the dread that she was, that of course she was, what else could it be? came upon her like wind, leaning against her, and not letting up.

CHAPTER 36

Down from the mountain, Mary took a detour, cutting across the big field where Tobin had found her that morning just a few days after Michael's death, and through the woods to stand in the center of her father's little field. An upper portion of the house was visible from here, far up the valley on its hill, the picture window shining with reflection. She turned around, surveying the new growth. Saplings grew in from the edges, and some sprouted right up in the middle, thin, spindly-looking trees, but tough and ornery. Huge branches lay across one side of the field, fallen from a tall, dying pine tree. Brambles and thorn bushes grew in every nook and cove. She looked far into the woods to where the trees lost shape in darkness. The little field was a pool of sun, bright, comforting, amid the sea of forest. She'd need to get a sickle, a chain saw; maybe Tobin could help her. She knelt, pulled some of the tall, yellowed grass aside, remembering how when she'd spread her parents' ashes, she'd stooped to see the fine particles—some of the grainy, coral-like bits larger than she'd anticipated—lying on the ground between the grass, almost as if she'd sewn seeds without turning them into the soil. Now, of course, there was no trace of them. Just grass and ground.

Standing again, alone in the field, she remembered when she was five years old and had run away from home. Not far, just down the hill and across the brook and into the big field. She knew how to get home, of course, but then, being there alone, the sun starting to thin, sifting through the crowns of the poplars, she began to feel afraid. She wanted her parents to come find her. She called out for them, but they didn't come. It seemed they had to come. They had to know that she was gone, and they had to miss her. The air grew cooler, and she bawled. Everything was a blur through tears. *Daddy!* she yelled, through heaving sobs. Why didn't he know she was lost? Maybe he didn't care. The more she cried, the longer she waited, the more it became impossible to move.

Then, through her watery vision, a man stepped out of the woods. He appeared at the outskirts of the field as if through an invisible door. She stopped crying instantly because it felt like she'd been caught in a lie. She'd conjured up someone else instead. This man wore a flannel jacket of red-and-black checks over dark olive pants. A long black beard dragged below his collar. He walked with his arms out, palms up, as if to say, What's all this about? He waded through the high yellow straw until he was right in front of her, towering above, looking down from so far up that she had to tip her head all the way back to see his face. The beard lay flat on his chest when he looked down. She could see up his dark nostrils. His eyes were clear and light and kind. He seemed very sad for her demise.

"What's the matter, little one?" he said, and then he put his hand on her shoulder. She looked at his hand. His fingers were grimy with dirt. His thumbnail was warped, yellowed, and there was a terrible dark bruise underneath where blood had pooled from some impact. She smelled tobacco and chain-saw grease.

"Are you lost?" he asked.

She didn't know how to answer.

"Well, come on," he said, and reached for her hand. "I know who you must belong to." He had a strong New England accent. This was long before the Goughs bought the old farm and moved in, so it was an easy assumption who Mary belonged to.

His hand was big, the skin on the inside of his fingers hard and cool feeling. They crossed the field, then the brook on the rickety wooden bridge, and trudged up the logging road to her parents' house, where he delivered her to her mother, explaining to her that he'd been logging when he heard the little girl crying.

After the man left, her mother was incredulous. "You were *lost*? But you knew where you were." How could Mary explain? Yes, she knew where she was, but still, she was lost.

Now, standing in the field, it was useless to cry. No one would come. Only their ashes were here, long ago dissolved into the earth.

"Hi Mom," she said. "Hi Dad."

A breeze went through leaves, a lovely, loud wash of sound.

"Michael?" she said. "I miss them."

She remembered the folk festival, meeting Michael, how his focus on her that day was compelling, though she began to feel suspicious at the same time. Maybe he was just being polite. She thought she really should shut up about her father—the great naturalist writer, activist, professor. And her mother, his muse. Maybe she sounded like she was bragging. Then, as they were leaving the restaurant, his hand upon her back, guiding her through the crowd, she apologized for going on so.

"No need," he said. "It's refreshing. You loved them."

She'd nodded, grateful that he understood.

"You could call me," he'd said, prepared with his numbers printed on a beer coaster.

"Where are my friends?" she said, looking around for Will and Carter, her ride home.

"There," he said, pointing. Will and Carter were saying good-bye to Michael's friends Paul and Lisie, and climbing into a car. "Or you could call me. It's your choice."

Maybe it was seeing Will and Carter slam the car doors, buckle up, and act as if they were leaving without her; they were pretend-ing, she knew. Maybe it was Michael's eyes on her, amused, ear-nest. Maybe it was her orphaned state that made her suddenly determined. Caution to the wind. "Okay," she said.

"Which?" he said. "You'll call me, or you'll call me?"

"Can I just come over? Now?"

They'd spent two days in bed, only getting up for food deliv-eries. Sometimes they played songs for each other, handing the guitar back and forth, sitting naked on the bed. *I can't believe you don't use a pick.*

When she was back in San Francisco, he'd sent her a letter by real mail. It was a list of all the things he wanted to do with her: Go to New Mexico. Kiss your breasts. Lift you up and carry you around. The movies. Hold hands in the movies. Teach you to use a flat pick. (You really ought to know how!) Sing you songs. Take care of you. Dance. Wash your hair. Give you a box of flat picks. (Don't you even own *one*?) *Why aren't you here?*

"Why aren't you here?" Mary said now to the field. "Why aren't you here?"

Once again branches stirred, leaves burst into sound.

She remembered the logger who had found her. His New En-gland accent: *What's the matter, little one?* And then she thought of Ben, his arms around her, the rush of wings in her belly.

As she rounded the top of the logging road, coming up from the valley, she spotted Clayton's car parked next to her truck in the driveway. She felt uneasy and ran her hand through her hair, hoping it wasn't too much of a mess, hoping she wouldn't have to explain where she'd slept last night.

He sat at the picnic table, waiting for her. His hair was neat, shining silver. When she got there, he swung his legs out from under the table and stood up, held his hand out to her, and she took it. He squeezed her hand, looked at her, then his eyebrows scrunched, and she wondered what he was seeing. She knew she was grimy from the hike, mud splattered on the hems of her jeans, dirty sneakers. She'd sweated through her T-shirt at the armpits and collar. Clayton let go of her hand.

"Have you," he started, "done it? Taken the test?"

"No," she said. "Not yet. Please, come inside. Let's get some coffee."

Clayton hesitated, then said, "Wait," and went to get something out of his car. "You forgot this," he said, holding up a box.

"The fawn," she said, incredulous that she'd left it behind. She remembered putting it on the floor of the car and getting out of the car, gathering all the mail, preoccupied with Clayton's confession and Tobin's needs. Still, guilt crept through her, taken aback that she had forgotten Michael's posthumous gift. "I'm sorry," she said, taking the box. "I'm *so* sorry." Clayton looked surprised at her apology, shrugged, and followed her inside.

CHAPTER 37

CALLIE WIPED THE COUNTERS with a rag and shut off the kitchen lights. None of the crew were in the dining room, but several guests sat at the long tables, talking or playing Scrabble. She didn't want to get hooked into any conversations with these people. They could corner you and keep you there telling you about their lives, or the hike they took, or giving you advice about where you should go to college.

Spencer was at the front desk, so she didn't pass by there, but slipped back into the kitchen and down the south stairs to the basement. The sound of a fiddle came from the boot room, a room so named because it was where guests in muddier seasons removed their boots before coming upstairs. It was a cozy room with a fireplace, couches, and an old piano that no one ever played. She knew it was Rabbit, and where Rabbit was with his fiddle, there might be Ben with a guitar. He'd come down for dinner tonight, and she hoped he planned to stay the night, but when she went into the room Rabbit was alone.

"How're you feeling?" Rabbit asked.

"Fine," she said, which was true. She hadn't felt sick at all for the last couple of days. Maybe it had been the heat, after all, though her period was still late. "Where's Marlee?" she asked.

Rabbit lowered the fiddle from under his chin and rested it on his knee.

"Beats the pants off of me," he said. "Reading in Lo-House, I think."

Rabbit didn't offer any information on Ben's whereabouts, and she didn't want to seem too curious, but then he said, "Ben went to find a guitar."

She was relieved. This meant they'd play music, and she could plop herself down and listen. She could watch Ben all she wanted, and she could sing along with the guests who would show up soon. Then maybe, later, she'd go outside, find Ben alone.

She took a stuffed chair across from Rabbit as he tucked his fiddle underneath his chin again, hit a few notes with his bow, then reeled out a melody. The music brought the guests, tromping down the stairs and soon the room was full of people. She was surprised when Spencer showed up, having closed down the front desk early, but it was Saturday, and all the weekend guests had probably already checked in.

Spencer took the couch that abutted her seat, and she crossed her legs away from him, leaning against one arm of her chair. He became engaged in conversation with some guests anyway, so didn't seem to notice.

Soon Rabbit was knocking out tune after tune, playing requests. He knew just about every bluegrass song they asked for. Still, no Ben. No Marlee.

Spencer wasn't paying any attention to her, and somehow this started to vex her. She wondered at herself. She didn't want Spencer, but when Spencer acted like he wasn't interested in her, she wanted to draw his attention back. She'd heard something, too, about his old girlfriend, the one in Boston who the cooks used to call his fiancée, and how she wanted to come visit him. Spencer had told her this information one day as if it was supposed to be a threat, but she didn't think he wanted that girl anymore, so she'd just shrugged. Now she leaned toward him, trying to catch his conversation with a middle-aged woman, but he didn't acknowledge her, nor did he acknowledge her when she added her two cents about what trail was the most difficult but the fastest route to the top of the mountain. The woman nodded at her and replied, but Spencer wouldn't make eye contact.

Somehow she'd gotten herself locked in the room, and everyone seemed to be talking to everyone else, or else singing, and she was just sitting there staring at Rabbit, pretending to be listening, but all she wanted was Ben, and Ben wasn't showing up.

Then, to her amazement, she spied Mary through the crowd, standing by the old piano. Mary's eyes were on Rabbit, then sliding to the other side of the room. She looked exhausted, cheeks drawn, but she was smiling. Callie sat forward, lifting her face so Mary would spot her, but it was Spencer Mary saw first. He waved to her.

Callie waved too, but Mary's eyes were still on Spencer as she made her way across the room, sliding behind chairs, stepping carefully over outstretched legs and around bottles of beer that people had set down on the floor near their feet. A man, the Salad Man, said something to her, and she stopped, nodded, spoke to him. The man reached into a cooler and handed her a bottle of beer. Eventually Mary made her way through the crowd and seated herself on the couch on the other side of Spencer, who quickly engaged her in conversation.

"Mary?" Callie said, looking behind Spencer's back, so Mary could spot her.

Mary's face filled with kindness, eyes shining.

"Oh, Callie," she said. "I didn't see you there." She reached behind Spencer, squeezed Callie's hand, then Spencer leaned back as if to cut them apart, and Mary made a funny raised-eyebrow face.

When Ben came through the doorway with Marlee right behind him, Callie's heart sped up. He maneuvered through the crowd, holding a guitar case at his hip like a rifle and using it to make his way toward Rabbit. The guitar case was Marlee's, covered with stickers from places Marlee had been. Marlee waved to Callie and followed behind Ben, plunking herself down on the couch next to Rabbit. A guest gave up her chair for Ben, and he lay the case on the floor, unlatched it, pulled out the guitar, and began tuning. He glanced up, saw Mary, and grinned at her. She smiled back, raised her hand hello, and Callie felt a thread of surprise, a tinge of envy. Ben and Mary were older, closer in age, and seemed at ease with people, whereas Callie felt so awkward, especially around Ben.

The threesome, Ben, Rabbit, and Marlee, were all here, and now the music would really take off, especially with Marlee and her remarkable voice. The cooks arrived, Lewis following Barb through the crowd, working their way to chairs near the singers.

Spencer and Mary talked. Callie couldn't hear what they were saying. Annoyed with Spencer, she turned her attention to the music, and to Ben.

Ben began to play, looking down, concentrating on his fingers. His forehead glistened, and he made little puckers with his lips every now and again. When Marlee started, her voice ringing out clear and pure, he bobbed his head in time, keeping his eyes on her, following her lead. They sang "Another Night," and the guests joined in on the chorus. Rabbit took a fiddle solo and everyone applauded when he finished. Marlee amazed everyone when she improvised, making her voice undulate, then break into a sort of hoarse, throaty sound that suddenly carried her to an octave higher.

Lewis clapped and yelled out, "Hoo wee."

Callie watched, torn between Ben and wanting to talk to Mary. When she glanced toward Mary, she was surprised to see how engaged Mary had become with Spencer. They were talking animatedly about something, then Callie couldn't believe it when Spencer lay his hand on Mary's arm, as if he was telling her something so important that he had to emphasize it that way. Mary nodded at whatever Spencer was saying, and she rested the mouth of her beer bottle against her bottom lip. She smiled, her eyes intense and stunningly green. Her face had flushed; the room was really warm, though. She laughed at something Spencer said. It dawned on Callie that Mary shouldn't probably be drinking. Maybe a beer was okay. Her mother had had an occasional sip of beer when she was pregnant with Evangeline. The awful worry found its way back to Callie, but no, she'd get her period any minute probably. If she could talk to Mary about it, though, she'd feel better. They could compare notes.

She turned to watch Ben's fingers spider across the frets, and then she realized that Ben was looking right at her. He gave her a big smile and bobbed his head in time to the music. Callie smiled back.

Mr. Walker appeared on the other side of the room. Chin raised, he looked over the tops of heads until he spotted Mary. Mary put her beer down immediately as if she'd been caught, but her face was calm as she rose and crossed to him. He and Mary talked briefly, and Mary patted his arm before he turned and left. Mary returned to the couch as Rabbit announced a new instrumental, something he and Ben had been working up, a tune they called "Cascom Mountain Road." The crowd clapped. Ben strummed a few chords and then Rabbit drew his bow in short bursts across the strings and launched into a bluegrass tune. The melody and rhythm reminded Callie of riding in the lodge truck, driving fast up the gravel road, the dust swirling behind, light dappling the road.

A song later, Ben put down his guitar as if he was getting ready to leave. Disappointment flew through her. Then Ben looked at her and raised his eyebrows. He made a big, clownlike frown, imitating her, she realized. She could have died with embarrassment.

Then she heard Mary say, "I used to play that old piano. When I was on crew."

"So," Spencer said. "What's stopping you?"

Mary shook her head. "No, no. Not sure I'd remember anything anyway."

"Isn't it like riding a bike?" Callie said.

Mary half smiled, pulling her lips together as if she were contemplating it.

"Hey, Rabbit," Spencer called out. "What can Mary play with you? On the piano."

Rabbit and Marlee quickly offered suggestions, and everyone was excited and encouraging. Then Mary rose. Guests moved to the side, letting her through, and a man flipped the lid off the keys for her and pulled out the stool. Mary sat, placed her hands on the keys, made a quick chord. The piano was old, but sounded fine, and before long Mary's fingers were working the keys, and then Rabbit and Marlee followed with their instruments. A lot of people recognized the tune, and in a moment the whole room was alive with song and Callie's heart felt like it would burst, it was so beautiful and so wonderful to see Mary playing and singing.

Ben got up and leaned against the piano, one arm draped over the top, watching Mary's hands, and now singing along. The song was about a soldier and a morning in May. Mary's voice, too, joined in on the chorus, a harmony line, following Marlee's voice so beautifully.

The room was in full applause when the musicians worked their way through the last notes to the end. Mary swiveled on the bench to nod to the crowd, her face rosy. Ben clapped the loudest, and lured the crowd to clap in unison, asking for more. Mary spoke to Marlee and turned to play again. Callie wished she was nearer, leaning against the piano next to Ben.

This time it was a slow song, something melancholy and moving. Marlee began to sing, and her voice was so pure, so perfect, that no one interrupted her, or dared to join in. It sounded Irish, this song; Callie had never heard it before. The words were sad, too, about a young man dying at sea. A girl left behind. Rabbit took a solo, drawing his bow slow and long over the strings. The music worked into her heart, sad and beautiful. It was like magic, like threads of moonlight being sewn by the bow, stitching through her heart. Ben looked pensive, his eyes on Mary's hands as she played. Ben, Callie thought, meet me outside tonight.

Just outside the doorway there appeared another face—Tobin. Even though he stood back, perhaps not daring to enter, Callie saw a look of awe and delight in his face, and she was sure it was the beauty of the music, the wonder at Mary playing piano. He shut his eyes for a moment and when he opened them, they were glistening. Callie felt her own eyes fill to see him so moved.

The air was humid as she crossed the yard from Lo-House back toward the lodge, grass damp underfoot. She'd waited for Marlee to fall asleep, then snuck out. Spencer's light was on. There was a faint illumination at the back of the lodge near his door. She stopped and stood still in the dark.

She pulled at the hem of the long white T-shirt she always slept in, peeling the material away from her skin. She felt cooler for a moment. The stars were hazy. The air so thick and full of water, it was like standing inside a black cloud. Sweat ran down her front between her breasts. She pressed her hand to her stomach and the shirt stuck. She tugged the shirt away, then, in a flash of daring, she pulled the shirt up, over her head, and off. She dropped it on the ground and stood there naked. The air was very warm, clinging to her. Then a breeze tickled over her skin, and she felt free and brave. Haunting. She lifted her arms over her head and opened them to the night sky. She offered herself up.

"Here I am," she whispered.

For a second she felt afraid. The ghost girl might be out here, but no, she wasn't going to be afraid. Just stories, not real. She closed her eyes. She could stand here in the dark, the open yard, naked. It was powerful. Then lonely, and the weight of dark-gloom came over her. She thought about going to the pond, swimming out, but she wouldn't yet. She wanted to remember the other feeling she'd had tonight. It came with the music, with Mary playing, singing, smiling. And all her friends, together, sharing that—the mysterious joy of music. Tobin, too, she could see he'd felt it. It had filled her up with something. Something blue, deep and kind. Blue-kindness.

She loved all of them. Marlee, Rabbit, Barb and Lewis. She loved Mary so much, too. Even Spencer. He wasn't a bad person.

Then she saw someone. She dropped to the ground, flattened herself into the grass. He walked in long slow strides, coming across the lawn, and she didn't breathe, didn't move. She was overcome with longing. She wanted to love someone as much as Mary had loved her husband. And she wanted to be loved that much, too. He might have passed right by her and never known she was there if at the last moment, she hadn't reached out, touched Tobin's bare shin, and pulled him down to the grass.

CHAPTER 38

THE MAN WHO PICKED Tobin up on Cascom Mountain Road had dropped him off in Leah, not far from the highway. He'd been walking. Now the sun glared down. He smelled hot tar and listened to the rhythmic scuff of his boots. He felt he had to keep moving, keep getting away from Leah, from the mountain, but his thoughts were tangled and none of the particulars were clear. Just go. He started up the ramp to I-93. A car came and he turned, held up his sign. The driver sped past him. He hoisted his knapsack and walked on. The sun was hot on his face and arms, and he touched the top of his head, felt his warm hair, no hat. He wished he had a cap.

He had a sense of urgency, of getting away fast, yet there was also another sensation, a tugging, like he couldn't leave. He had the feeling there was something he was forgetting, but he couldn't remember what it was. He was forgetting what he was forgetting. He imagined a Möbius strip with the word *forgetting* written in a continuous line around it, meeting up with itself again. Forgettingforgettingforgetting. The road he walked on could be one side of the Möbius strip. There was a curve up ahead. Eventually, he might meet up with himself. The heat was unbearable down here off the mountain.

His head felt stuffed, packed with cotton. It was as if he'd left his body, floated up above, but when he looked down to see the boy on foot, there was a dense vapor, obscuring him. He couldn't see himself down there. A few cars passed, but he forgot to turn around and hold up his sign. Once, when he heard a car coming, he turned and lifted the sign to nothing. No car. The car had passed minutes ago, but maybe the sound was lagging behind it.

His father's face was suspended before him now, his hang-dog expression, his ridiculous hope. A burn started in Tobin's chest. Another car passed, close to the shoulder, whipping air at him. Rage. It scraped its way through him, under his skin, blistering. His blood was gasoline on fire. He wanted to pound his fist into something, a tree trunk, a boulder. His father kept saying that she wasn't the same as before. That the medication she was on kept her even, calm. She wanted to come home. His father said, "Forgive her." Tobin loathed her. He didn't want to help take care of her. How could he find even a shimmer of kindness for her?

The sky was just beginning to brighten by the time he had made his way home from the lodge. He'd snuck upstairs to his room and dug out the old cardboard sign. The writing had faded. "I-93" was barely visible. He'd have to find a marker and darken it. He packed a knapsack, put the sign under his arm, and left. He refused to be around when his father brought her back. *She doesn't mean to do it, Tobin. Please forgive her, T.*

Why must he forgive her? She was treacherous.

Before he left, he crossed the yard to the barn, swung open the doors, went in. The pigs were sleeping, lying back to back or with heads draped over one another. Pigs were supposed to be smart, good pets. Loyal. He'd fed them their own kind and they'd eaten greedily. They'd trotted with their fast, short legs toward the trough, small blank eyes intent only on food. Tobin unlatched the gate to the sty. The pigs stirred, grunted, snored. He'd left the gate open, and then also the barn door.

As he walked, the memories of Ben with Mary—sitting on her front deck, coming down from the summit, taking her hand—bothered him. Then Mary's father-in-law. You could see the pain and helplessness in the man's eyes—a father who'd lost his son.

He remembered how Mary sat on the eave that night, kicking her legs back and forth, alcohol on her breath. He'd put his arm out to protect her. He needed to keep her safe. He'd put his hand on her leg. Then last night, she sang, like coming back to life. Maybe he could play piano again, too, especially if Mary could. He recalled when he was a kid and they'd taken turns at the piano, the song he'd made up for her. But he was leaving. He wouldn't be there when his father brought his mother home.

He stopped walking. Cars whizzed by. The heat rose off the tar, making the air ripple. Then other images edged into his mind, hazy, dreamlike. A naked girl in the middle of the field. Callie. He didn't know what to make of it. It confused and thrilled him. Thinking of her mouth on his, his hands on her breasts, gave him prickles in his stomach and his cock grew.

When he'd felt something touch his leg, he nearly jumped out of his skin. She'd giggled, then taken his hand, tugged him down to the grass, against her body, her softness, her breasts.

"Callie?" he'd whispered, but she'd hushed him by touching her finger to his lips. She ran her fingers through his hair and so he did the same in return, his fingers combing through her long, blond hair and down her arms. Fingers coming to her waist, then up to her breasts, and she let him. He'd never touched breasts, and they felt like he'd imagined. Amazing. Her nipples were hard and he fingered them gently, kissed one. Careful not to put too much weight on her, he rolled on top of her. His erection poked her near her crotch and he felt her stiffen, her legs closed tightly, and though he wanted to part her legs, lie between them, he knew from her tensions he should not insinuate himself like that. It didn't matter. He was touching her body. She was touching his.

They kissed and kissed, tongues moving around each other's; her hand on his neck, up under his hair. Her fingers reached under his shirt, touched his nipples. He remembered his body trembling, shivering out of control in the warm air. He tried to calm his nerves, tried to focus only on her, on her kisses.

Now it seemed like a dream. But it had happened. They might have stayed there, lying in the grass, touching one another until the sky lightened, but then he realized her face was wet. She was crying, though she still pressed her mouth against his. He pulled away. "Are you all right?" he whispered. She shuddered and a small sob came loose as she pushed him away, sat up, and grabbed her shirt. She'd struggled to get it over her head, and he almost reached out to help her but sat back on his heels, watching. Then she was up and running toward Lo-House, leaving him alone, raw and bewildered.

Cars zipped by, coming toward him. After Callie left, he'd lain in the grass, staring at the sky until it lightened. He remembered another sky, and lying on his back on the ground, numb, looking up at the barn roof where he'd just been standing. His mother was up there, kneeling on the edge, looking down, ropes of black hair dangling over the eave. Her mouth was open as if she was shrieking, but Tobin couldn't hear anything, until his father's footfalls rumbled down the stairs in the house and came across the yard.

Damn his father. How could he bring her back now? Then it came upon him with clarity: he couldn't leave. Callie might want him, need him. And Mary, too. There was too much at stake to leave Cascom now. He crossed to the other side of the road and stuck out his thumb.

CHAPTER 39

IT SEEMED TO MARY that Callie didn't look very well. Her skin was tan, but there was a pale undertone to it, like she hadn't slept in a while. She was drawn, her cheeks hollowed. The boy, Rabbit, had come with her but had stayed outside, waiting. He was polite, said he was too dirty to come in. He had a saw and other tools wedged into the top of his pack, jutting up behind him. He also carried Callie's pack, swung over his shoulder next to his own pack. They'd been on trail-clearing duty, Callie told her, for the last few days. Now Callie was in the bathroom, and Mary waited for her with a Popsicle. Rabbit chose to wait in the yard. He'd put the packs and equipment down at his feet and was intently sucking on his Popsicle.

"Ben brought me these," Mary said when Callie came out. Callie took the Popsicle and unwrapped it, touched it with her tongue, then shivered all over in a burst. Mary wondered if she should offer them a ride back to the lodge.

She wanted to smooth Callie's hair back where a piece of it stuck to her cheek near the corner of her mouth, but she stopped herself. She didn't want to make the girl feel self-conscious or embarrassed.

"I remember clearing trails," Mary said. "It's hard work."

Callie smiled. Her lips had become tinged with purple dye, and she was starting to look revived. Callie flicked the piece of hair away from her own face, leaving a streak in the grime.

"I felt a little dizzy," Callie said.

"The heat?" Mary asked.

"I guess. It comes and goes."

"Sit. Doesn't Rabbit want to come in?"

Callie shook her head. "He won't. He's like that."

Mary opened the screen door. "Rabbit," she called to him. "I don't mind dirty. Please come in."

Rabbit held his Popsicle up like he was making a toast. "It's okay. I'm good," he said, and continued to stand there.

"Are you feeling okay?" Callie asked, almost whispering. She pointed with her Popsicle at Mary's stomach. "I mean, do you ever get morning sickness?"

Mary felt heat go through her. "Callie," she said. "I'm not pregnant. Maybe Mr. Walker confused you, because at first I thought I might be. He was hoping. So was I, even though I got my period. I took a test. I'm not." Mary remembered Clayton's sad, long sigh, staring at the stick, the minus sign, proving she'd been right all along. She was not pregnant. Nothing of her and Michael, no future child.

Callie stared at her, her gray eyes flooding.

"Sweetie," Mary said. "I'm okay. I'm going to be fine."

Callie wiped her tears, glanced at the door. Mary could see Rabbit outside; his face glistened with sweat, and he swatted at drips on his temples. Callie looked back at Mary. "Did you want to have a baby?" she asked.

"I thought so," Mary said. "But it's probably better this way. I'm, you know, alone. Single." It was awful to say the word *single*—a word from her past, now back to label her. Widowed. There was a new word. A horrid word.

Callie nodded, sniffed, and sucked on the Popsicle.

"Ben brought you Popsicles?" she asked.

Mary nodded.

"Can we talk sometime? You know, when no one else is around?" She tilted her head to indicate Rabbit.

"Of course," Mary said. "Any time."

Mary walked Callie outside. Rabbit called out a thank-you, and Mary watched as the two gathered their tools and packs and started off on the road toward the lodge.

As soon as they were out of sight, she heard a footfall on the roof and turned to find Tobin gazing down at her from the eave.

"Why didn't you say something?" she asked, using her hand to shield the sun from her eyes.

"I don't know," he said.

"Well, why don't you come down? Have a Popsicle."

He shrugged and moved to the low eave, sat, and jumped off, landing in a crouch. She noticed a knapsack and a piece of cardboard in the grass next to the house. The cardboard had writing on it—a sign for hitchhiking. She remembered the first night she and Michael had driven up the mountain. Michael had said he'd seen a boy, holding a sign. That night seemed so long ago now.

"Are you going somewhere?" she asked. She made out "I-93" on the sign.

"What was up with Callie?" he asked. "She all right?"

"I'm not sure. She thought I was pregnant."

Tobin nodded, scuffed the ground with one heel, did it again, then with the other.

"I was going to leave, but then I decided not to," he said. "I was going to leave because my father, he's bringing my mother home."

"Oh, Tobin. I know that must be hard."

His fingers began tapping, one by one, against his thigh, a

nervous habit she'd witnessed several times. Sweat streamed down his neck. Now both his hands were in motion, fingers fluttering. It was as if his hands had a mind of their own.

She waited, but when it didn't seem like he was going to stop, she said, "Could you please cut that out?" She hadn't meant to sound irritated.

He looked utterly ashamed, horrified, and quickly crossed his arms, pressed his hands into his armpits.

"Sorry," he said. "I hate that I do that."

"It's okay," she said. "I mean, I'm sure things won't be how they were before."

"I don't want to be like her," he said. "I'm not like her, am I?"

"No, of course not," she said, but again her voice betrayed her. She'd sounded unsure.

He picked up his pack, put his arm through one strap, then tucked the cardboard sign under his arm.

"See you," he said, and started away.

"Okay," she said. "See you."

Then suddenly he was coming back toward the house. He touched the tips of his fingers to the side of the house, like checking for dust, or how you might to see if the paint was dry. He did this several times in the same spot, some sort of compulsive thing.

"Oh, Tobin," she said, now her voice full of pity, but before she could say more, he turned and ran down the hill, gone.

She went inside, feeling awful, feeling that she'd let him down somehow. She could have been more understanding, more consoling. But, hell, she was just a neighbor. It wasn't like she was his mother, or something. The thought, so benign in how she meant it—he wasn't her responsibility; she wasn't his parent—now disturbed her, because *his* mother, the real one, was the scariest person alive to Tobin. He was just a boy, hurt, frightened to death of becoming the person who terrified him the most.

Out the window the mountain seemed to watch her with its composed, bright granite face.

"What do you want?" she cried. The granite face gleamed, serene, unfazed.

CHAPTER 40

CALLIE CAME AWAKE in a jolt. It felt as if she'd been shooting down a steep slope, then snagged suddenly by a tree branch, punched, jerked backward up into the air, and dropped to the ground in a heap. For a moment she lay in the dark, staring at the underside of Marlee's bunk above her, slightly disoriented, wondering if somehow the dream had actually produced the effect of knocking the wind out of her because she was taking deep breaths, trying to make her lungs as full as possible, but the air she drew in still felt inadequate.

She'd been dreaming, she remembered, and in the dream she'd been standing in the cooks' private bathroom in the upper quarters of the lodge, looking at the wand of a pregnancy test. As she stared at the little window in the stick, the color kept changing from blue to pink, sometimes other colors, and then she'd come awake, and now lay here troubled, anxious. She tried to see back into her dream, to know what color it had been. Was it supposed to be pink or blue? She remembered that Mary wasn't pregnant. Mary had thought she was, but then she wasn't. Maybe that would happen to her too, and the thought made her feel better for a second. Then, knowing Mary wasn't pregnant after all made her feel even more alone.

She thought of Tobin. She felt embarrassed, then also a tiny thrill at the thought of how they kissed so deeply, so long. He was so willing. His whole body was trembling. Then she felt sad, dark-gloom in her chest, and now she couldn't even look at Tobin. She didn't know why she pulled him down, why she kissed him, or what to feel.

"Marlee?" Callie whispered. There was no response. She strained to hear breathing, or the familiar creaks of Marlee rolling over up there, but it was silent.

Then a noise came from outside, distant, a splash of water. Then another watery plunk and swash, like someone hitting the surface in a cannonball. People were in the pond. She leaned up on an elbow, listening through the screened windows.

"Marls?" she said, a little louder. But the room stayed quiet, and gradually she realized that Marlee was not there at all. She got out of bed, stood on the bottom rungs of the ladder, and swept her hand across the empty upper bunk.

It was very humid outside, barely a breeze as Callie crossed the yard in the dark. The air was so full of moisture it still felt like she couldn't get enough air into her lungs. She breathed in as far as she could, until her lungs refused more, held her breath for a few paces, then let it out. The grass, recently mowed, was soaked, and clumps of cut pieces stuck to her feet and wedged between her toes.

There was a glimmer of light coming from Spencer's window. It was past midnight; maybe he was waiting for her, hoping for her to come to him.

She neared the middle of the lawn and the noises down at the pond—a swooshing, dripping sound, like when you hoist yourself up onto the raft. Then voices, low, serious tones. Callie stood still, her ears strained. She was shaking.

A giggle. Definitely Marlee. Another voice, maybe two other voices. There was some relief—more than just two voices.

Marlee laughed again, and then a deeper voice rose underneath Marlee's voice.

Her stomach tightened, and heat shot through her, up under her arms, making her sweat. The coarse gravel of the parking lot was cool under her bare feet, but also scattered with sharp pebbles. She walked on tiptoes, saving the bottoms of her feet. There were only a few cars in the lot, not like there would be tomorrow for the weekend crowd. Maybe Marlee's boyfriend had come to visit and was swimming with Marlee now. That made sense. Marlee's days off were just around the corner. Earlier in the summer Marlee had hoped Jack might come get her, and then they could go somewhere for her days off. There was more splashing and Marlee tittered, and said something, and then there was the other voice, then silence.

Callie crept down the short path until she was just above the small beach, and made out the faint shape of the white raft in the center of the pond. Whoever was on the raft was lying down, but it was too dark to see any definition. Her heart beat fast and she still couldn't seem to get enough air into her lungs. Then she heard the male voice say something, breathy and in a rhythm. A lilting, a rise and fall, almost like a New England accent. Tears stung in her eyes. She stood still, her ear turned toward the pond, but no one spoke again. The bodies made one long shape on the surface of the raft; they barely moved. Maybe they were just having a conversation, and now they were lying there thinking, or whispering, watching stars. The two were just friends. God, Marlee wouldn't tell Ben anything about her, would she? Callie walked out onto the beach, her feet sinking into the cold, newly shoveled sand. The dark shapes rolled together as one. Her skin felt hot, as if she were standing too close to a campfire. She was shaky, flustered. Disbelief and irritation, shifting to twitching anger, then the sense that what they were doing was deceitful, worked inside her, but nothing was exactly clear. Ben and Marlee. She didn't know what she should feel, or what she was allowed to feel.

"Hey, you guys," she called out into the dark. "You swimming without me?" she asked, keeping her tone light but feeling the ache in her throat, the tiny twist in her voice that might reveal how hurt and exposed she was. When no one answered, her skin turned to goose bumps. She waited, knowing their silence was guilt, was betrayal.

"It's me," she said brightly, as if to feign the possibility that they truly didn't know it was her, or hadn't heard her clearly. "Callie," she added, bitterly.

"Callie?" came Marlee's voice.

Instantly, the amicable tone of her friend's voice made her feel better. Callie waded into the water up to her shins. Why wasn't *he* saying anything?

"You guys went swimming without me?" She tried to sound fake-mad, but now she was mad, and she knew she wasn't welcome, that yes they had gone without her, very much so.

Then she heard the man say something quietly and Marlee hushed him, and his figure rolled in a way so that she knew he'd been lying on top of Marlee.

"Callie?" came Marlee's voice.

She was paralyzed. A meanness rose inside her. It wasn't fair. Marlee knew she liked Ben. She'd told her, but she remembered Marlee hadn't responded.

"I'm coming out," she said, though she didn't move. She could, though. She could just walk out to her waist, sleeping shirt and all, and swim to them, make them deal with her.

Then the mean feeling dropped, fell right to her belly—her bloated, growing belly. A sob came from her throat.

"Is she all right?" came the man's voice. It wasn't Ben's voice at all. It wasn't Ben. Relief poured through her. Not Ben. Then someone else splashed behind her, throwing cold drops onto her back. She shrieked and turned to find Rabbit making his way into the water.

"There you are," Rabbit said. "I was looking for you. It's king of the raft. Us against the goofers. Marlee's got a new guy friend."

Callie felt the heat of embarrassment. "She does?"

Rabbit waded past her, up to his chest. "Yeah," he whispered. "Some dude, staying in the campsite."

"Is Ben coming?"

"Who? No, he went up to Hi-House hours ago. Come on, let's whip their asses. Here come the recruits," he said, and dove under, just as three people, some college-aged guests she recognized from dinner, came running across the beach, splashing all around her.

Marlee called after her, but she kept going, back across the parking lot, until she was behind the lodge. She leaned against the clapboards, angry, though she wasn't sure why. She felt woozy again. It was everything. It was kissing Tobin when she really wanted it to be Ben. It was being alone. And then she knew she was going to Spencer's. She needed to tell him her fear, that maybe she was pregnant. He would have to be nice to her, comfort her. It was his fault, after all. He should help her.

Spencer's light was out now; probably he was asleep. Down at the pond there was splashing and muffled laughter. She knocked on his door. Nothing. She tried the knob and the door opened. She knew the room well, and began across it in the dark as she'd done many times before. She stepped on something, clothing on the floor.

"Spencer?" she said, toward the movement in the bed. "Wake up."

The light came on. She squinted, trying to adjust her eyes.

She saw him rise up on an elbow, and then she realized that he wasn't alone. Someone lay behind him in the bed.

For a half second she saw Mary—the pale face and cap of dark hair—but then the face wasn't Mary, but a girl.

"Who's that?" the girl said, squinting, a hand above her eyes to shade them.

It was the girl in the photo. The one who Barb and Lewis called "the fiancée." The "chick" Marlee kept reminding Callie to take into account. The girl was spooned against Spencer's back, now looking over his shoulder with a disconcerted, ticked-off expression. She pushed hair away from her cheek and pulled at Spencer's shoulder so he'd look her in the eye. Spencer glanced at her, his mouth open as if to indicate complete ignorance.

"What's *she* doing here?" the girlfriend said, and she said this as if she knew something about Callie. As if Callie had been discussed.

Spencer turned his still half-awake eyes on Callie and his lips came apart, almost a snarl.

"Get out of here," he said, and swiped his hand through the air as if to push her away. She walked backward, stepped on the clothes on the floor. She looked down to see a lacy yellow bra, lying on top of jeans. She glanced up again at Spencer, his eyes narrowed on her. She turned, got through the door, pulling it closed behind her, and ran.

She made her way quickly along the road, shining her flashlight on the ground. She ran for a ways, then hiked fast. She was pregnant, and she was alone. She just had to get to Mary's. The game of king of the raft had still been under way as she went back to her room, dressed, and hurried out.

Soon she came to the bridge, the brook gurgling down there in the blackness. She shivered and ran fast across it and dug in, trying to keep the pace as she started up the sharp grade. Her throat ached. The hill was steep, and she had to slow to a walk. The woods seemed to close in more on either side.

She reached the top of the hill and shone her light across the cracked sign that read "Hall," then turned onto the logging road, directing her light back and forth in front of her feet. There was the swampy smell of the frog pond, and then the opening to one side that she felt looming where the stagnant water sat. It was eerie. Bullfrogs grunted, deep as the twang of a bass string. She didn't dare shine her flashlight over there. She tripped on a rock and her heart flew into a rapid pulse, but she didn't fall, regained her footing and continued on. She wished she had that thing bats had, echolocation, Tobin called it.

Finally she reached the ledges and started up, feeling better as the granite opened and her feet were on firmer ground. Then at the top and starting down again, she hurried, eager to see the lights coming from Mary's house, but there were none. The house was dark, and when she rounded the corner into the driveway, the house looked ominous, hunkering.

The truck was there, looming and white. She shone her flashlight on it, then toward the house. The windows sucked her light inside, and she imagined how scary it would be to be inside and have a beam pass over you, like a searchlight. But Mary was probably in her bedroom, asleep. She knocked lightly on the screen door, then pulled it open and held it with her hip as she knocked on the main door. She felt terrible, for having to wake her, but she had to. She couldn't go back now. Still Mary didn't come.

"Mary?" she whispered, then tried the knob. It opened.

In the living room she turned the overhead light on and her flashlight off. The house was quiet and strange feeling. She went down the hall to the bedroom.

"Mary?" she called again, hearing the crack in her voice, and how close sobs were. The bed was empty. She sat on the end of the bed. It creaked and gave under her weight.

She was alone, alone in someone else's house where she didn't belong, and it was so quiet and still and sad, and not like when she and Marlee slipped inside houses, full of excitement and mystery. Marlee wasn't with her. And Mary, too, wasn't here. Gone. It made her queasy with worry and mistrust. Then, maybe Mary had gone somewhere with Mr. Walker.

She went outside, adrenaline pushing her, and headed toward the woods, toward the mountain, the Clark Trail, and Ben's. He would invite her in, comfort her.

CHAPTER 41

IT WAS EARLY EVENING when Mary reached Hi-House. Ben was hammering nails into bright new boards on the far side of his cabin. She watched him for a minute, not wanting to startle him. He wore no shirt and his muscles stood out in his arms and were firm across his tanned back. When he finished with one nail, he reached into a coffee can on the sill for more nails. He put one between his lips and readied another for the hammer. Under the hammer, the nails drove into the wood with the reverberation of high notes to low. She waited, watching, until finally he turned and saw her.

He grinned, taking a nail from between his lips.

"Hi," she said. "I just happened to be in the neighborhood."

He laughed. "And you couldn't resist my fresh-made bread."

As soon as he said it, she smelled a warm, yeasty waft coming from his kitchen. It seemed miraculous—the smell of bread up here, the sun now gone behind the mountain and the granite cooling after a hot day. A breeze came through the junipers and up over the tops of the studded trees that edged one side of his cabin, and on, she imagined over more trees, and down into the darkening valley, like a messenger delivering night.

Inside, Ben washed his hands under the water jug tap. He ran a wet cloth over his forehead and face, and quickly into each armpit. From his tiny closet he took out a crisp white shirt and drew it on. As he started to button it, bottom toward top, closing up the smooth surface of his chest, she found herself moving toward him. He stopped buttoning when she placed one hand against his chest.

"You're not going to hit me again, are you?" he joked, dropping his arms to his sides.

She shook her head no, knowing exactly what she was doing, even if she still felt unsure. Sliding her hand across his chest, she looked into his eyes. When he put his hands on her face, on either cheek, and gently pulled her forward, she didn't resist. His lips touched hers, and she opened her mouth to him. They kissed slowly, tenderly, and Mary thought about who they were and who they'd lost. How loss had drawn them to this place, to this strange point in time, on this mountain. As his hands moved over her, around the back of her head, fingers through her hair, down her back, they kissed harder. She did want this. She did. Thoughts came in bursts, then vanished: Michael, the toy fawn, the kids at the lodge, Tobin's floppy hair always over one eye. Tobin's hands. Anna Kimball, suddenly, and her beautiful, pale face, her long white hair, and her loss—the dead boy on the trail.

She pushed the shirt off Ben's shoulders and he helped, letting it fall to the floor. His hands were on her face again, pulling her mouth to his. Then she felt his hands at the hem of her T-shirt tugging it up, and she put her arms straight up over her head so he could pull it off. She reached behind herself and unclasped her bra, let it fall. He watched, hummed, put his hands on her breasts. Warm. It was like a rushing brook, flooding over her. The current pushing, pulling. She unbuckled his belt, worked the zipper down, put her hands on his hips, and then they stood apart to undress themselves the rest of the way.

When they were both nude, they paused, looking at each other for a long moment. Tan line at his hips, the lighter skin of his thighs, legs. His full erection. Then, in a fury, they were together again, clasping tightly, skin against skin.

Mary let herself go. She didn't want to think anymore. This was necessary. It felt necessary. There was no reason not to let grief slide away for this. They were just two people, two bodies. Two aggrieved. Grief side by side, diminishing each.

CHAPTER 42

WHATEVER HEAT HAD CLUNG to the ground, trapped under the leafy limbs of trees, had left. The air had thinned, growing colder, and gusts of a strong wind huffed through the trees, coming down from the upper reaches of the mountain. All the moisture in the air was gone; the wind had dried it out. The waning moon made shadows, but not nearly as sharp as the other night when it was full. Callie kept her flashlight on the ground just in front of her, just before her feet, afraid to raise it, afraid to see anything on either side or too far ahead. The flashlight beam made an oblong shape, pushing on ahead of her. She worried that the cat's-eye in the middle of the light was growing. That dark sliver was starting to eclipse the light, and she knew the batteries were getting weak. The faint beam made odd shadows inside hummocks and behind rocks and exposed roots. At times the shadows appeared like pools of dark water, and she found herself stepping wide over spaces that were probably not anything. There was no point. Her feet were already soaked through from where she'd accidently sloshed through a puddle. The bottom of her jeans felt heavy with water and dirt, and her socks squished in her sneakers. She'd come too far to turn back.

The trees on either side of the trail blended together in one dark mass. If she turned her light in there, tree trunks and branches were illuminated in the hazy tunnel of light. The trail was narrower now, and brambles swiped at her arms and jabbed into her legs. Then the trail opened and she moved on for a few yards, until suddenly the path vanished, and she faced a curtain of trees. She turned around, shone her light on the ground where she'd just come. No clearing at all. She rotated in a tight circle, shining her light slowly, looking for anything that might resemble a trail. One side gave way to what seemed like an opening farther ahead. If she bushwhacked through a few feet of snarled branches, maybe she'd hit the trail again. She started forward, carefully lifting and holding back whiplike limbs so they wouldn't snap back at her, but one caught her in the face and she yelped, stopped, and put her hand over her injured eye, waiting for the sting to pass. Her hand felt wet, and she wondered if she was bleeding. She didn't want to waste the batteries on anything but the woods in front of her, so kept moving.

She knew, though she didn't want to believe it, that she'd gone off the trail. It was so ridiculous. The sting of embarrassment and confusion pushed her on. Spencer with that girl. Marlee on the raft, making out with some new guy. Mary—wasn't it late to be out with Mr. Walker? She plowed through the brambles, letting them scrape across her body, using the flashlight as a shield as much as possible. She kept going up, thrashing at stinging branches. Keep moving, she told herself. Don't stop. Stopping meant hearing the sounds of the woods, which made her feel more vulnerable than just beating her way through it. And the bugs, the mosquitoes, incessant in her ears and trying for her skin; she flailed, rushed on.

Again she came to a wall of branches. This time it was pine trees, heavy with needles. She smelled pitch and felt the stickiness on her free hand as she pressed bushy branches aside. The sweet smell of pitch made her hope she'd discover freshly sawed branches, a sign of a trail. She shoved her way through, letting the needles sweep her arms and over her head, walking blindly, hands swimming ahead, as if looking for the opening between heavy drapes. The grade began to get steeper, and it made sense to head uphill rather than down, or horizontally through the wilderness, which could take her anywhere. She had to get her bearings. Up was the only way.

It was just the forest, just like in the day. It was just trees and boulders, and the animals that lived in it, like birds and fox and deer. Bear too and moose, but didn't they sleep? And besides, animals would smell her and stay away. Animals were more afraid of you than you were of them, she remembered people saying. They were always saying that.

The growth was dense on every side, and she moved forward inside the blackness, pushing it back with her dimming light. Really, it was just the same woods she knew, only night was inside them. How horrible it would be to come across the hulking figure of a moose. Find a pair of shining eyes staring back at her in the dying flashlight beam.

The toe of her sneaker caught under something and sent her flying forward. She landed on her knees and hard on one elbow. It hurt and knocked the wind out of her. Her heart was going so fast it almost seemed as if she could hear it, hear the squeeze of blood pumping. It was like a distant drum, far off, echoing, only it was inside her own chest. She still had a grip on the flashlight, and its faint light made a murky pool over the ground, illuminating the stems of a clump of green ferns, and then the white bark at the base of a cluster of thin birch trees. She sat up and turned the light on her arm. It was smudged with dirt and also scraped open, some blood. She wanted to cry, but crying wouldn't help. She was too afraid to cry. She turned the beam back on the undergrowth and ran her light up the birch trunks, showing their markings, thin dashes of black freckling the white peeling bark. She followed the tree trunks up to their branches and then further. The beam was so weak now that it disappeared quickly into the bits of dark sky between leaves above. Then she ran the light down to their bases. Somehow the trees, so familiar and bright, comforted her, until she remembered where she was.

She shone her light on the toe of her sneaker and up her one outstretched leg. Her jeans were muddy at the ankles, wet at the knees. She shivered hard in a burst. Then the light wavered and went out. She shook the flashlight, rattling the batteries inside. The light flickered and came on again.

Fear clutched her, tightening her muscles. There were sounds, trees creaking and high-pitched squeaks as if furniture was being moved across a slate floor. Leaves burst into flutters as a wind came up, shooting over the tops of the trees and weaving down between them, bringing everything alive in movement, and cold over her skin; then it stopped, and fronds at her feet wavered lazily, as if someone had just brushed against them, leaving them in motion.

She knew that you were supposed to stay in one place when you were lost. That was the rule, but she couldn't stand to be in the woods. Things had turned in another direction—there was danger in what she was doing, and in where she was, and with wet feet and dying flashlight. She thought of Peggy the cat who'd disappeared and how Spencer said she'd probably been caught by a coyote or a fox. She shouldn't be afraid of animals, but how large was a coyote? How dangerous or hungry? Mary had rescued a fawn from a bobcat. How ferocious were bobcats?

She rose, stamping her feet to bring them alive again, and started up. She had to get to Hi-House.

She went on, exhausted and shivering and cold, straining her body, pushing it to go faster. Her arms stung with cuts, and she was pretty sure there was a good scrape across her cheek where a branch had caught her. The flashlight flickered. She shook it hard until it came on again, but then the faint ring of light seemed to collapse in on itself; the cat's-eye enlarged, and then the flashlight was dead.

Trying not to fall, she batted at things, swinging the flashlight like a sickle. Her throat was dry and achy. She jiggled the flashlight, the batteries clacking, but it wouldn't come on. Useless.

She went a few more paces. This was useless. It was all too black, completely black. Her eyes could have been closed or open, there was no difference. She sat down, her back against a tree, and drew her knees up, hugged them. Mosquitoes whined, and she put her hands over her ears. Her body shook in a spasm, and she thought it was a good sign, or not exactly good, but better than not shaking, or suddenly feeling warm, which could signal hypothermia.

Images tumbled through her mind. The girl with Spencer and their angry expressions. Tobin. At first it felt exciting kissing him, then something inside her shifted and she felt overwhelmed, couldn't bear it. Mary. Where was Mary? She wanted her mother, suddenly. So badly. She wanted to feel her mother's arms around her.

She felt sick, like she could throw up, but she was also thirsty. Dreadfully thirsty. She imagined a huge glass of water, felt it go down her throat, and she swallowed, but her mouth was dry. She shut her eyes and imagined lying down on the bank by the brook, putting her lips on the surface of a pool, pulling that cold water into her mouth. Then the brook was roaring, she could hear it. It was right there! She got up and walked a few feet and knelt down, smelled lush, wet dirt, wet ferns. But then she hadn't moved and she'd only imagined this.

Her knees tapped together, out of control with shivering. It felt as if there were pads of felt glued to the bottoms of her feet.

She stared into the woods and up toward the sky. When she looked back to the woods, it seemed her eyes had adjusted; she just made out the shapes of tree trunks. She hugged her knees tighter and closed her eyes. If only morning would come. She willed the night to go by quicker, longed for the sky to brighten, make her eyes useful again.

Then she heard something. A tree creaking? Terror surged through her, making her so weak that it felt as if she'd come right out of herself. Then there was a moan, a long whimper, not like a tree bent against wind. An animal sound. It was definitely vocal, from a mouth, a throat. Again, a high moan, long and wavery, rose up. It came from below her in the woods, but how far down she couldn't tell. She held her breath, made herself smaller. Then the whine rose in pitch and volume, turned horrible, scratchy, and stopped abruptly. She stared into the blackness. Her mind spun, trying to make sense of what it could it be.

Then the sound of something solid moving through branches, snapping them back, and then a tramping sound, like feet hitting dirt hard, running a short distance, then silence. She clicked the flashlight on and off, but got nothing. She held it like a club.

Her limbs felt weak. A branch broke in the woods closer by, and then more footfalls on the dirt, but from behind her this time. She thought she might be fainting, but fought it, hugging herself tightly. It was just as Marlee had told it. It was like the ghost girl was all around you, closing in from either side. She strained her eyes, but couldn't see anything. Her ears, too, felt like they would burst as she tried to determine which direction she'd last heard the sounds. She raised her hands, ready. The bushes shook hard below her, and then a shape, a figure, moved. She could barely see it as it came forward, hunched over, slowly coming toward her through brush below. There was a quick glow of something pale.

Oh God, oh God. She cringed, trying to be invisible, a part of the tree she leaned against. She held her breath, then said, "Please," her voice barely audible, "I can't help you."

Everything stopped. It heard her. Perfect stillness, until she detected breathing. It was soft, then grew heavier, deeper, erratic. It came from below. She strained her eyes, kept her hands out, ready, but her arms were shaking. Her back, even though up against the tree, felt exposed. She could not punch out everywhere if it came at her from all sides. The breathing was there, a tone in it now, like a voice, like words, and she felt her inner ears beating, nearly cracking with trying to hear the words, to make sure she understood, because it felt like her survival depended on it.

It rushed forward. It came on hands and knees, fast. Callie ducked, then scrambled into a crawl, then to her feet. She ran, plowing through bushes and branches, letting them whip and stab her. And then something got her across the waist, knocked her to the ground. On her knees, she doubled over, no air. She willed herself to move, keep running, but she couldn't get her lungs to work. Then air came down her throat, like sand, and she bent over, coughed. When she looked up, it was right in front of her.

CHAPTER 43

YESTERDAY, TOBIN HAD left his father a note, saying he was leaving, that he wouldn't be there when he brought her home. Then, after trying to hitchhike away, he'd returned. Last night he'd snuck into the lodge and slept on a couch in the boot room. No one was around. No one knew. He was up and out early, back to the woods.

Now he lay on the boulder he used to call the Hemingway. He didn't know where to go or what to do. Across the way, the boulder called Moby sat as it always had. It was harder to understand how he'd ever envisioned its shape as a whale. It was just a boulder, left by glaciers. Last night he half hoped Callie would find him in the boot room. He imagined crossing the field again, finding her there, but then he'd fallen asleep quickly, exhausted from everything.

With the memory of Callie, tingles zipped through him, followed by humiliation. He'd only followed her lead; his mind didn't play tricks with him, telling him to tap or count, and he'd felt so released, except that his body would not stop shaking. He had no idea why she was naked in the field in the first place. Nor did he have any idea why she'd suddenly broken away, run off in tears. He wished he could talk to her, but everything was so confused. So wrecked with his father's stupidity.

When his mind turned to Mary, it felt like his body was collapsing, folding up on itself. Mortified. That look on her face—pity, disgust. It was all bad luck. Bad things would happen. Bad things were happening—his mother, returned.

There was his father's truck parked next to the barn. His mother, then, was on the premises. The air had turned sour, murky, as if her presence was already leaking toxins into it. He'd stolen up behind the barn and now stood at the corner. His gut was tight, and acid came up his throat to mix with spit, burned, and went back down. His temples felt compressed.

Across the yard he heard his father's voice in the studio. Tobin pictured his mother, already standing on the modeling platform, arms dangling, the pink shawl uselessly swirled around her feet, breasts hidden by her long, dark hair. Her eyes piercing the air. His father, the artist, forgetting her, not really seeing her, only a figure and form, a structure to follow. The familiar outline, the swell of the belly, and the shadow of the muscle running down her thigh, along the bone, where one leg would be placed forward and raised, her bare foot on an old, squat milking stool.

Tobin remembered how she was like a cow in her stillness, patient, but for the eyes that flickered with little pulses, a turmoil of crazy thoughts slithering around inside her head. He cringed, thinking of the times he'd glimpsed her posing nude, and then, of course, she was everywhere in his father's paintings.

Now Tobin moved along the side of the barn, glancing up toward the roof. He reminded himself that he was older, taller, stronger.

He crossed the yard, making a wide arc so he came up behind the studio, where he might be able to see inside without being seen. As he crouched below the back windows, his stomach tightened.

Inside, his father spoke in a string of light notes, almost as if coaxing a dog. Nothing came from her in return. His father went on and on in a burble of various tones. His ears refused to understand the sounds as having any meaning. The pitch was low, flat, muted, like when you press an organ key without pumping the bellows hard enough.

His back was stiff and his leg ached. The pain ignited him with anger. He sat down in the dirt, leaned against the wall, stretched his legs out, and the pain subsided instantly.

Another voice in the studio rose up. Recognition of it sent him into a panic; his eyes blurred, and his jaw trembled. Her voice, that level airy sound when she was holding back, when there were explosives lodged in her chest and she was just barely keeping them settled. It amazed him that his father still couldn't hear this.

The screen door on the other side opened and swung shut, and he thought they must have left the studio. Perhaps his father wasn't painting her yet. No, of course not. His father would be reacquainting her with the place, reminding her, letting her absorb it all again. He wondered how long they'd been back.

He rose slowly, staying low until he peeked over the sill. She was there. He ducked, then looked again. It was her. She sat in the chair, facing away toward the screen door. Fat. She was fat. Flesh hung from under her arms and flattened against the arms of the chair. White hair, shiny, short, blunt cut at the back. Of course, he should have expected her to have aged. It had been at least four years since his father had made him see her at the group home in Concord, but still it astounded him. The skin on her arms, the bit of face he could see, looked pasty, not the oily hue of olive it had once been. He was surprised to find himself mildly disappointed. It was unfair that she should have transformed into this. This lumpy dough. Where was her sleek black hair, her taut, sharp edges?

She lifted her arms, sat forward. He ducked below the window. When he looked again, she was gone. Panic swept through him. His father shouldn't have left her alone. She was dangerous. His skin prickled, and he couldn't help but turn around, survey all sides behind him, nearly expecting her to appear there, lurch out of nowhere, fingernails going for his skin. Then he realized that she'd gone into the adjacent room—the storage area, where most of the old portraits were. He slid along the wall to the window there, and rose slowly, quietly.

She stood for a while in front of a painting of herself, the tallest of them that leaned up against the wall. She might have been looking into a mirror of her former self. Slumped now, roundish, the baggy smock of a blouse and skirt grazing her thick ankles—it almost couldn't be her. It was as if her spine had contracted. She reached out, put one hand on the edge of the painting. Then she let her arm drop and stood there, staring at the painting. She reached for the canvas again, this time with both hands, and hoisted it up, lifting it away from the wall. It leaned toward her precariously, and she grunted, then let it down, turning it on its side. She began to shove it through the doorway into the other room. Tobin moved quickly back to the other window. As she came through from the other side, he got the first real look at her face. There, yes, there she was. He could see who he remembered again, though camouflaged in puffiness—her nose less prominent, her jowls sagging. She was homely, not frightening like before. There was a new blandness to her, but it was still unmistakably her. The fierce eyes, the way her lips narrowed, and then peaked in a scallop below her nostrils, and how her mouth opened slightly, then closed in a slight exhalation that was hers, hers alone.

She tipped the canvas over on its back on the floor, then went again to the other room. In a second she returned with two more of the portraits, smaller ones, one in each hand, dangling at her sides. She laid them on top of the other and went back. She returned in a second with another.

This strange nonmother worked, bringing painting after painting from the other room. When the pile got too high to easily place the next on top, she began a new stack alongside it. Why had his father left her alone?

Then she hesitated and stared at her construction. Her hands plunged into the large pockets of her skirt. She jerked when his father passed by outside the screen door. He carried buckets in each hand, and didn't look in. He called in to her, "Be back in a moment, Delia." He was heading toward the barn.

She didn't respond, and then, to Tobin's horror, as if she'd known he was watching her all along, she turned her head slightly, then her eyes followed, and then she was looking directly at him.

CHAPTER 44

IT WAS A COOL MORNING when Mary went outside, and onto the granite in front of Ben's cabin. He came down the steps to see her off. He put his arms around her, and he smelled good, his cotton T-shirt and the warmth of his chest coming through it, and sweat, nearly sweet smelling, from the night.

"Mary," he whispered into her hair. "Thank you. I hope you're okay with this. I feel good."

"Me too," she said. She did. She felt fine, unconcerned. There was nothing to define, to discuss or delineate. It just was.

The sun was coming on strong. It was a beautiful day, and she felt a lightness she hadn't felt in a while as she went down the mountain. The woods in their intricate, twisted, disheveled, entangled order, the trees, this wilderness, calmed her. The crisscross of the branches overhead, and the way the leaves of the hardwoods formed a lacy ceiling and made it cooler underneath. The silence, such stillness, no wind today at all, yet stalks and fronds and foliage swayed or ruffled, sometimes as if all on their own. The sunlight penetrated the leaves, making shimmering nets, woven over roots and rocks and the brown, leafy floor between the trees.

The trees, so firm, immutable, even the old and rotting ones, even the felled ones, their roots ripped from the ground and reaching like tangles of arms, tentacles feathered with hairy rootlets and hanging on to clumps of dark, rich dirt. Even long-lying blowdowns, punky and flaking, turning back to soil, sprouted saplings and offshoots. Nurse logs, her father had called them. Grief was like a nurse log, she realized, lying heavy and dark and sinking into earth, while all the while life kindled inside, insisted on itself, and grew from it, sweet and new. The trees owned this land. When she was young, she used to imagine that instead of growing up from the soil, they'd arrived from above and dug their roots in like fingers.

Her father told her how a forest managed itself perfectly—all relationships with animals, insects, plants, in a balance, supporting each others' complex systems, needs, and of course maneuvering for the best light, using what was available and plentiful from one year to the next in a constant state of survival. Here were birch, growing tall and straight in their struggle to reach the light. Surrounded by lofty spruce and other hardwoods, they'd shot up toward the sky, no room to branch out, lean, arc. These birch, crowded among other trees, had been less vulnerable to the ice, using their neighbors for support.

She loved the woods, spending so much time as a girl, isolated, dreaming, roaming. "What do you think, Mary," her father might say as she emerged, finding her parents sitting on the deck, sipping beers at the end of the day. "Shall we cut that stand of spruce, open it up a bit more?" he'd ask as if she'd been there all the while, part of an ongoing conversation. The mountain had raised her as much as they had.

Self-reliance was absolute, the aim, perhaps. Their affection toward her was in the form of intellect—discussion, information. She'd once confessed to Michael that her father had never kissed her in her whole life. Michael had been taken aback—a piece of her past he hadn't expected, not quite fitting the hero father she usually portrayed. But she had kissed him, finally: it was when he lay in his hospital bed, hooked to tubes and breathing apparatus, that she'd summoned the courage to kiss him on the cheek. Her lips touched his stubbly skin, and his eyes turned wet instantly. And then he'd looked at her so solidly, eyes drowning, and she realized how much it moved him. Why had she waited? All those years of longing to be noticed, held, hugged. Something more than praise for good grades and a good mind.

Now both her parents were gone. Was she still hoping for their eyes, their approval? Maybe this was why she'd come back to the mountain in the first place, and why she held on to it now. To re-create the life she thought they'd be proud of, recognize, finally see. To emulate their perfect, romantic isolation, because that's what she believed love should be. Useless ideas now. They were dead. Now Michael, too. People, she thought, should have family. Lots of family. Being an only child was too lonely. Poor Tobin, he too. She would talk to him about what was going on with him— the quirks, his fears. She would try to help him, find him some sort of counseling. His father was clearly oblivious, preoccupied, or perhaps simply didn't care enough.

The brook grew louder as she neared the bottom. How many years, how many hundreds of times, had her feet fallen on this very ground? There was Mary—the child, the girl, the young woman—trudging over the same trails, same dirt and hemlock needles, same worn roots, the same dreams and wishes in her head. The fulfillment of those dreams began with Michael but, she saw now, would not end with his death either. Now, Mary— the child, the girl, the young woman—was on her own once more, and determined to live her own life.

When she got down from the mountain, Clayton was just pulling in to the driveway. He was headed back to the Cape, he said.

It was time to return home, but he wanted to say good-bye. She invited him in for coffee.

"We should keep in touch," he said. "If you want."

"Okay," Mary said, though she couldn't imagine that they would. "Sure."

They stood a few feet apart, locked in place it seemed, by the inability to say anything that might make sense or mean anything. When they heard voices on the logging road, they turned away. Through the screen door she caught flashes of arms and legs, and the colors of their clothes, as people passed behind the trees, then came into view. It was the crew from the lodge, probably on some sort of work detail, perhaps on their way up the mountain, but then they turned toward the house, cut between her truck and Clayton's car and came across the yard to the door. Callie wasn't among them.

They stopped talking when they saw her. She held the screen open, and they nodded to her with serious expressions as they filed past her and to the living room. When they saw Clayton, they went to him. Clayton shook Rabbit's hand, then Spencer's; he nodded firmly at Marlee. It was as if they all knew each other well, saying hello with the familiarity of old friends from his time at the lodge. When Marlee turned back to her, her eyes wide and sad, Mary realized even more acutely that there was something wrong.

"We were hoping to find Callie with you," Spencer said. "Have you seen her?"

"I haven't," she said. Panic surged through her. "Why?"

"She seems to be missing," Spencer said.

"Missing?" Clayton said.

Marlee cleared her throat. "She was upset, I think. She might have come over here last night."

"Last night?" Mary said. "I wasn't here. I just got back this morning."

Clayton glanced at her, then he said, "I'll look around," and started down the hallway toward the other rooms.

"What upset her?" Mary asked. At once, they all looked at the floor.

It was Rabbit who spoke up. "I think she got her heart broken." He spoke with a hint of anger, and turned to look at Spencer as if to point him out.

"She's just *sixteen*," Marlee said. "A kid."

Spencer coughed and looked down.

"She's been gone all night?" Mary asked.

"We think so," Rabbit said. "We think she might have come looking for you. Maybe when you weren't here, she went somewhere else. Maybe it's nothing, but remember the other day? She wasn't feeling well. I'm worried she's still sick, or something."

Marlee nodded, her eyes full of fear. She glanced at Spencer, then back to Mary.

"If you weren't here," Marlee said. "She might have gone up to Ben's."

"Ben's?"

Marlee nodded. "Yeah, well, she sort of has a crush on him."

"Oh?" Spencer said, but Marlee rolled her eyes at him, and he didn't continue.

Mary felt a chill, then dread, as she paced to the front window, looked out, saw nothing, her mind scrambling to make everything clear. Callie was looking for her, needing her. She felt awful, angry with herself. And worse, if the girl had climbed to Hi-House last night, she may have looked through the window. Callie might have seen her with Ben. She remembered the door rattling at Hi-House, but no, it rattled all night; it was the wind.

Spencer stood with Clayton, speaking in authoritative tones, and Mary heard the phrase, *Organize a search party*. She heard the words: *radio the fire tower, notify rangers,* and then, *heatstroke* and *hypothermia.*

Marlee took her arm, led her aside. "Mary," she whispered. "There's something else. Callie said, well she thought she might be . . . she told me that her period was late."

The girl stopped talking, waiting. Mary looked into Marlee's surreal blue eyes. She remembered how Callie had asked about morning sickness.

"Please don't tell anyone," Marlee said.

Mary put her hand to her forehead. "Callie."

"This is all my fault," Marlee said. "I haven't been a good friend. I should have watched out for her better."

"It's going to be all right," Mary said, but her face felt hot and her temples pulsed.

Marlee leaned closer. "No one else knows," she whispered. Marlee's eyes flew to Spencer and away.

The blue knapsack sat behind the couch. She snapped it up and barreled past Marlee, past Clayton and Spencer, and into the kitchen, where there was a water bottle and a first aid kit.

"Mary?" Clayton said, but she couldn't answer. She slammed a cabinet shut and opened another, searching for the water bottle.

They should stop talking, get moving. This just couldn't be happening.

"She's out there," Mary said. "We have to find her."

CHAPTER 45

His mother's eyes—small and round, cold as pigs' eyes—found him, pierced him, stayed on him, her hands moving around inside her pockets, and the skirt, hanging over her protruding stomach, the hem rising a little, showing widened ankles. Then one hand came out of a pocket. She didn't look at what was in her hand, but kept her eyes on his face.

It was as if he was looking at a scene on a television set, the window screen making a gray, snowy grid over her image. She hadn't even flinched at seeing him outside the window. Her eyes were fixed on him, challenging him almost. He began to think that maybe she didn't actually see him. Maybe the light and the screen in the window obscured him somehow. But then her mouth started to change, to open until she was grinning widely.

"Toby?" she said softly, childlike.

The sound of his name coming from her mouth made him queasy. But her tone was not what he remembered. Not caustic or brusque or like sandpaper grit, but feeble, pitiful. He leaned his forehead on the screen. And then he surprised himself.

"Mom?" he said. His voice came out changed too—a higher pitch, the eagerness of a child.

"My smart boy," she said. Her voice was wistful, as if he were only a memory to her, not at all real, or standing a few feet from her behind a window screen.

"They gave me these," she said, and pulled one hand from a pocket to show him what was in her palm. He couldn't see anything in her hand, and then she snapped her fingers closed and shoved her hand back into the pocket.

"To keep me below," she said. "So I won't come up. I don't like it here."

"Here?" he asked.

"There," she said. "I don't like it there."

"I'm sorry," he said, wondering at himself. He wasn't sorry. But he felt like he was talking to a small child, and apologetically, as if partly responsible for her demise.

"Here, there," she said with a sigh.

Now she looked down at the pile of canvases she'd made at her feet—her portraits, laid out haphazardly on top of one another. She gazed at her construction, her hand rummaging again in the deep pocket of her skirt.

Though he knew it was his mother, she was so changed—fleshy and old, her chin doubling, her eyes smaller from the weight of the skin sagging around them—that he began to feel cheated. This was not the same mother. Now he had to pity her. He had to absorb her ruthlessness, accept her instability for what it was, for what his father had always told him it was—an illness.

This was not the mother he wanted to hate, and so a different fury started inside him. He'd been deceived. How could he hold the same contempt? He wanted her to be the tall, dark, cruel mother she'd been, so he could approach her now, make her understand what she'd done to him. That mother was gone. That mother had tricked him, moved on without him. That mother was cunning, a trickster. To the end she slipped away, dodged back into the dark closet or straightened herself flat behind the door, and ultimately receded into the depths, never to be seen again.

He was light-headed, sick. Now he felt sorry for her. And with that, he began to see how his father had worn the mask. His father had been the most ingenious trickster, the most artful impersonator, hidden behind an appeasing, kindhearted demeanor. The oblivious, gentle-seeming fraud who'd allowed her abuse to continue under the guise of sympathy for her. Never, *never*, had he apologized to Tobin. Never had he put a stop to it, nor acknowledged it. Not until she'd almost killed Tobin, and outsiders had, by law, been brought into their concealed world. No, the ire seeping through his skin now was not aimed at her. His father was the one. He dug his fingernails into the windowsill. It was all his father's doing. His fault.

Now, this new, pathetic mother who stood before him, now pulling a pack of cigarettes out of her skirt pocket.

"Do you have a light?" she asked, tapping a cigarette out of the pack. "Before he comes back. He won't like it. I've been dying for a cigarette."

His father, Tobin knew, was still in the barn. He moved around to the front of the studio. The barn doors were wide open. His father would have discovered the open sty, the back gate open, too. Maybe the pigs hadn't gone anywhere, stupid as they were. Or maybe his father was just now discovering their absence. Tobin moved stealthily toward the barn. As he came closer he saw his father in there, standing next to the gate that Tobin had left open. His father was immobile, staring into the empty pen, the slop pails at his feet. Seeing his father, the ridiculous thin ponytail, the sweaty pate of his head, his chubby arms, baggy corduroys, disgusted him. He reached out with both arms and took hold of the two doors.

"There you are," his father said, turning, but Tobin had already swung the doors. They slammed shut, and he threw the cross beam in place, locking his father inside.

Then he turned, went back across the yard to the house. In the kitchen he found a box of wooden matches, then headed back toward the studio, remembering how when he was a child she would sometimes ask him to light her cigarettes; it was an honor.

Now she placed the cigarette between her lips and leaned forward as he struck a match and held it to the end of her cigarette. She inhaled, exhaled. Sometimes, when he was a boy, he'd hold the lit match until the flame nearly touched his fingertips before shaking it out.

"Thank you," she said. "I was dying for a cig."

He heard his father talking to him from the barn, using even language, trying to reason with him to come open the door, but he could climb through the sty and out the back if he wanted to.

Suddenly a flame whooshed upward near his hand. She made a noise, startled. Tobin stared in disbelief. Some rags, probably full of turpentine, hanging near his hand had caught fire. His fingers still held the match, and he shook it, tossed it on the floor. The flames jumped to more rags; one fell on the floor. His mother came toward him, putting her arms out like she meant to embrace him, but instead she took his arm and pulled him away.

Outside he heard his father's voice, angrier now, still inside the barn. The doors rattled, and she glanced over there, stopped walking, seemed to contemplate the situation—her husband shut in the barn.

There was a loud crack, something exploded in the studio, and they both turned to look. The flames had crept up the legs of the easel, and also covered the modeling platform, igniting rags and cans of things there. The windows in the storage area flashed, and now the sound was louder, crackling and ticking, whooshing.

His mother turned to him, her face full of worry, her eyes wide.

"Oh God," Tobin said. "Shit." He looked around for what to do. The hose. A shovel. A fire extinguisher somewhere in the house.

His mother hurried past him, heading toward the barn door.

CHAPTER 46

THE SKY HAD BEEN A PALE BLUE this morning, but now it was heavy and gray, rain coming, and this was not good. Mary walked faster, hoisting her pack. Clayton kept alongside her, matching her stride. She carried the blue pack, filled with extra clothing and food and water. She had a flashlight and extra batteries. She was not going to come back without Callie.

The trees at the edges of the fields seemed cast in a soft mist, the grayness of the sky seeping down between their trunks. Panic was a rock wedged in her chest. Callie just had to be all right. There were those steep ledges and overhangs. The *cliff.*

The crew had gone back to the lodge to organize and spread out. They'd keep Ben notified by radio in the tower.

"How well does she know the mountain?" Clayton asked.

"I don't know," she said. "She's cleared trails, but if she went off-trail, that's another thing." Clayton had insisted on coming with her. He didn't think she should go on her own. He said he was fond of Callie, too, and wanted to help. Mary was glad for his assistance and concern. Hearing his footfalls, his breathing, was comforting, and his presence, these past days, the shared grief, made him seem more familiar somehow. It was as if she'd known him for years.

It was noon already as they crossed the brook a second time and started up the Clark Trail. Now they were ascending the inside wall of the valley, headed toward the summit. It was nearly the opposite route Mary had taken on her own in search of Anna Kimball all those years ago.

They stopped on a rise and scanned the woods, looking deeply into the trees, then Mary called out Callie's name. She yelled in three different directions. The hollow echo returned, boomer-anging, half pronounced, so much like the bleat of a fawn. It frightened her.

"Spencer said that if she didn't turn up by afternoon, they'd see if they could get a helicopter to do an air search," Clayton said through breaths behind her.

The wilderness from above would appear like a dark blanket, thick, impenetrable fur; if Callie was deep inside the woods, she wouldn't be visible. Mary remembered how Callie had wanted to ask her advice, and the overreaction, the empathic shock, when Mary told her that she'd never been pregnant at all. Sixteen was no time to be pregnant. The phrase *dark-gloom* came to mind, and she worried about Callie all the more.

"Why would she do this?" Clayton said after a minute. "Take off in the middle of the night?"

Mary was hit with a wave of shame; again she imagined that Callie might have seen her with Ben. She thought about the cliffs, not far to the north of Hi-House. *Please, please*, she said to herself, *don't let anything happen to her.*

"She might be . . . pregnant," Mary said. "Marlee just told me."

Clayton stopped hiking and she turned to look at him. "No," he said. "By whom?"

Mary shrugged. She didn't know. She guessed it was the crew boss, but she had no proof.

Clayton looked angry. "Jesus," he said. "She's just a girl."

Finally, they came out at Hi-House and stopped. Clayton tugged at the pack on her back, and she let him slide it off. He drew out the water bottle, took a drink, handed it to her. The tarpaper on the roof of Hi-House flapped in the wind, the door padlocked from the outside while Ben was in the tower. She knew he would be up there, communicating with other search parties by radio, or else he'd be out, scouring the other side of the peak. She thought of Ben last night—after they'd exhausted each other, she'd lain with her head on his chest, his arms around her. In the morning they'd made love again, twice, ferociously, and Mary cringed to realize now, that all that time Callie was hurting, maybe in danger, somewhere out there.

"Pregnant," Clayton said. "Sixteen. Just awful."

Mary wondered if he was thinking of Michael in high school and the girl he'd gotten pregnant.

"Was Michael very upset?" she asked. "About his child being put up for adoption. Never knowing his kid?"

Clayton tucked the water bottle back into the pack, and then hoisted the pack onto his back. She let him take it.

"Of course he was."

"But did he ever, or you ever, consider keeping it, raising it?"

"It was the best thing for everyone to let the child go." Clayton stooped to retie his boot. "Water under the bridge."

Mary doubted that it was ever as simple as that. Poor Michael. *Callie, oh God.*

They had a choice now, to head straight down from here into the brambles, or cut across to the trail and toward the ledges. The sky was the color of granite, mottled grays, and darker in some more distant areas where the clouds were filling up, holding on to showers. A turkey vulture flew lazily in an arc overhead, wings spread. And then another swooped across the other's path, and another, making rings and figure eights, gliding. She shivered. The world just couldn't repeat itself, couldn't turn itself around and go backward.

"Callie!" Clayton yelled. Then she yelled too, and they waited. It was silent, except for a light wind rustling through scrubby spruce and junipers. She turned into the wind, yelled once more.

"Callie!" The echo came back—a nonsense sound, a flat syllable with no definition at beginning or end.

The air, heavy and still, also held the slight musty smell of rain on its way. She looked up at the sky, the cloud cover darkening in places like bruises, bluish black, and pooled in swells inside the overhanging gray.

Then her feet were taking her down the sloping granite and toward the edge of the thick black spruce that cut a sharp line across the rock where they stopped growing, almost dead on, at some invisible boundary that was timberline.

They continued along tree line, moving slowly, canvassing the growth where it met the granite. From here the line wasn't really such a clear cut, or so abrupt, as it appeared from above. Junipers grew lower, flatter to the ground, their limbs reaching like vines over the rock. Scruffy trees had jumped the line, finding pockets of soil, filling crevices, trying to regain the land they'd lost long ago in the forest fire. At the memory of it, she thought she felt the sting of smoke in her nostrils. She sniffed, turning at angles, but it was gone.

Clayton squatted, looked closely at brambles, then rose and moved along the edge of the bushes. She followed him. It was slow going, and she was careful to keep her eyes moving, looking for any color that might be Callie's clothing.

"Do you smell that?" Clayton asked. "Every now and then, like smoke?"

"I thought so, too," she said. "But now I don't."

Clayton shrugged and continued along timberline.

As she went after him, a burst of frantic energy shot through her. She remembered herself as a little girl, standing alone in the field, challenging the universe to find her, challenging her father to find her, knowing exactly where she was, then into dizzying fear. Not really lost, but paralyzed, stuck, unwilling, unable to move. It was as if she felt Callie's terror. Terror that would pin you to one place, rendering your limbs useless. Your body and your mind, your rational mind, refusing to cooperate.

Now they were on the trail that wove through the dense spruce of the Cathedral Forest. It was dark and cool here, and it just seemed impossible that anyone could be inside the mass of dead, piled trunks and nests of dry, sharp branches that spanned either side of the narrow trail.

A part of her wanted to run uphill again. She remembered that pull, that desire to ascend again to Michael, to make sure he was still there, unchanged.

"We should go back," she said. She'd stopped in the middle of the trail, and turned around to face Clayton. He halted, sweating, breathing deeply, his thumbs tucked under the straps of the pack at his shoulders.

"The cliff," he said.

Mary nodded, and they reversed direction.

CHAPTER 47

H E CLIMBED FAST. The tower was the highest place. The highest place is where no one can get you. He had to get there. He imagined himself running up the clattering metal stairs, grabbing the rails to pull himself up faster, and as he hiked he realized he was already using his arms and hands as if the rails were there, but he was only grabbing at the air on either side.

As he came out on the ledges, he stopped, bent over, breathed. His eyes stung, and he lifted the hem of his T-shirt to wipe them, smelled the smoke in the cloth; it made him shake. He'd stomped the grass with his feet when some sparks pranced through the screen door. When he'd glanced up, he saw that she had reached the barn. There was a crackling, whooshing noise in the studio. His father's work of years, burning up. She'd wanted to smoke; let her take the blame. An accident. His fault. He hadn't put the match out. Had it been a command in his head? *Don't put the match out yet, let it burn down to your fingers.* He couldn't remember. Just the startling eruption of flames.

He started on again, passing Hi-House—it was locked—and up the sheer, open granite toward the summit. Ben would probably be up there in the tower.

He didn't follow the zigzagging cairns, but made a straight line toward the top. He rested, noticed the overcast sky, bulging with dark clouds. The top of the tower rose above the curve of the rock dome, poking its roof into the sky. Then the steel girders came into view, their feet forking into huge blocks of concrete, cemented to the granite and the metal stairs between them. There was the whir of the tiny power windmill attached to the tower buzzing loudly in the stiff wind, and the protruding shelf of solar panels just below the windows. Ben was inside, holding binoculars, looking out toward the valley, toward Four Corners, toward the fire, then lowering the binoculars to the granite below, to him. To Tobin, who went fast, over the granite, coming toward the base of the tower, because he had to get up there. Had to be in the highest, safest spot. Up above all the world. Above the body of the boy who was down there, coming over the granite. The boy who'd let madness loose.

Ben was on the radio as he came up the metal stairs and hoisted himself through the hatch. Scratchy voices answered Ben. Tobin heard a metallic voice on the radio say, "Gough Farm." Ben's eyes ran over Tobin, then away, as he wrote something down on a pad full of scribbles.

Tobin stood on one side of the round geodetic map table that sat in the center of the small room, waiting for Ben to say something. To tell him what was happening down there in the valley. Ben looked at him, eyes full of worry, maybe suspicion, as he listened on a radio.

"There's a fire at your farm," Ben said. His voice was too calm. Tobin stared at him, feeling the moisture on his forehead grow cold, then hot again. "Do you know what happened?" Ben pressed on. "Are you all right?"

Tobin let the air go out of his lungs. His eyes watered. Shame swelled, remembering, and he looked away from Ben to the window. Smoke, black, billowing rose from the valley, from Four

Corners. He was amazed at what he was seeing—so much smoke—and looked at Ben for help, but then Ben was talking on the radio again.

Tobin's throat was dry and hard. "What's happening?" he managed to ask. "What are they saying?"

Ben wrote on his pad. He told whoever was on the radio the names of trails, and Tobin didn't know why that was necessary until Ben said, "Callie is missing. We think she might be lost."

"Callie?" Tobin felt panic in his chest. "Where?" he said, hugging himself.

Ben said, "Don't get crazy, now."

Crazy? Was he crazy?

"We don't know," Ben said. "She was upset last night, apparently, and went looking for Mary. For some reason she may have tried to come up the mountain in the dark."

Callie. Out there. What did this mean? "Why?" he managed to ask.

"Mary had come up," Ben said.

"Mary . . . here?" he squeaked, a tangle of jealousies erupting, then fear. The fire. Callie out there?

The radio was full of sound, people talking. He thought he heard his name, *Gough*, again, and also, *Cascom Mountain Road. Four Corners. Engulfed. Barn. Spreading. Back field engaged. One hurt.*

"What did it say?" Tobin yelled.

Ben shook his head at Tobin, a look of fear.

"What did it say?" He waved his finger at the radio, trying to make Ben understand.

"Four Corners is on fire," Ben said. "The barn, they said, and spreading."

Tobin's head felt compressed. *No, no, no.*

"No," Tobin said. He took a step back toward the hatch. The studio had been on fire, but nothing more. Just the studio.

"The barn?"

"Try to be calm," Ben said.

"Someone's hurt?" His voice was barely a squeak.

Ben nodded. "They said that, yes."

"Who?" Tobin's eyes blurred. He'd just wanted to let her smoke a cigarette. *The barn on fire? The house?* "Who's hurt?"

Ben shook his head. "I don't know, Tobin."

Tobin looked out the windows toward the valley. The sky, already gray and heavy with rain clouds, made it difficult to see where the clouds ended and the smoke began.

His heart felt like fingers drumming rapidly on his chest. He looked back at Ben, not sure what to do. He was high above the rock, where it was safe from fire, from *her*. There were black smudges on his hands. He'd seen his mother go to the barn. She was supposed to let him out. His father would have put the fire out.

He moved toward the hatch, and began to lower himself through.

"Wait!" Ben said. "Stay here."

But Tobin was already descending the metal stairs to the granite. Rain began to pelt his arms and face, and the granite turned dark in a second, sending up a metallic smell. He looked up once to see Ben, looking down from above. Then he ran.

CHAPTER 48

THE SMELL OF SMOKE evaporated as they moved on, but every now and again it hit Mary's nostrils, faint, hardly discernible, but clearly there. She shuddered. The woods were dry. A fire could eat up the mountain in a second. Trees like matchsticks. They had to find Callie, and soon.

"I came this way with Callie," Clayton said. "Should we continue, then cross over on the top of the ledge, or just cut below the cliff? What do you think?"

"I don't know," Mary said, feeling tears sting. She didn't want to go to the cliff.

Clayton stopped climbing, turned to look at her.

"Don't stop," she said. "Keep going."

"No," he said. "Let's rest." He raised his chin, peered into the woods.

"Do you see anything?"

"There's an outlook." He pointed to a place where the low spruce parted and ledge showed. "Let's take a break there. Maybe we can get a full view of the valley. Maybe we'll see something."

Clayton tromped off-trail toward the opening. She didn't want to rest, but she followed him anyway. Seeing him lead, his leg muscles prominent, mud spattered up the backs of his calves, made her heart ache.

Clayton held branches aside, and she slipped through out onto the small opening. She'd been here before, she was sure of it, though the view seemed fresh to her. This outlook was far lower than the cliff, yet it still gave a dramatic view. The summit of Firescrew was visible across the valley. It was several hundred feet shorter than Cascom, but looked impressive with its long, gradual expanse of open granite. From its summit the ridge lowered steadily, angling down into firs and ending in the flat near some lakes. From here the whole Cascom Range was like a giant chair, its two arms curving out, and she and Clayton stood on the opposite arm from the Firescrew side. Cascom's summit itself wasn't visible from this angle. Mary looked out over the hills and into the cup of the valley, then down. The red roof of Lo-House showed through the green down there.

She scanned back up the valley, until her eyes found the cliff. Yes, there it was, strangely shortened, the extreme of its sheer drop hidden from this angle.

"Little girl, where are you?" Clayton said to himself, his eyes roving over the valley.

Mary looked at him, remembering the logger who'd found her in the field, called her *little one*. She watched drops of sweat trail down Clayton's cheek.

"I'm so sorry," she said, without thinking. She meant for Michael, for his death.

Clayton screwed the cap back on the water bottle, then, without looking at her, put his hand on her shoulder, squeezed. Her eyes blurred, and she turned away from his gaze.

It started to rain, large pellets beating against her arms, darkening the stones below her feet. Callie, Callie, Callie, she thought with each breath.

"What the hell?" Clayton said, his voice incredulous. He was wiping his eyes, and she thought he was commenting on the rain. A chill shook her as she followed his gaze toward the cliff, every muscle tightening at once when she saw that someone was up there, close to the edge.

CHAPTER 49

FROM THE HIGHEST POINT you are the safest. Get high up, and then you can see who's down there and who's coming. It's always better to be above than below. Tobin held his arms out to his sides and felt the breeze, cool on his skin. The air was fresh, no smoke smell here, as if the heavy rain had washed it away. His clothes were soaked from the downpour, but now the rain had stopped. The sky was whitish, but there was a heaviness, the thickening of clouds, dark-bottomed clouds out there everywhere, hanging just under the ceiling of white, ready to open again.

There were the gray-olive lakes in the distance, and mountains barely visible at the horizon, seeped in haze. The sudden smell of smoke tinged his nostrils, faint, but there. *One hurt.* Was his father hurt? His mother? Callie?

He shut his eyes, imagined the luminous golden field, full of light-colored straw, surrounded by brilliant poplars, and a little boy, safe in his other country, way down there on the earth. Then the same boy, but running across the dirt yard toward the barn. It was late at night, and he was panting, and then he was scrambling, trying to be quiet, reaching for the low roof, up to the ladder. A thump where his toes hit the clapboards, pulling himself up, and to the peak of the barn.

The boy heard his mother gasp as she struggled to pull herself onto the eave. He stood on the peak, put his arms out. The wind tapped gently under his chin, came under his arms. He was ready to lift out of his body and rise high above the roof, above her, so he could look down on them from a position of safety. But then something different happened. He didn't leave his body. He took it with him.

Now, the sting of smoke came and went, carried in the breeze. He remembered how his nostrils would burn when she smoked in the car. Her eyes in the rearview mirror, watching him. Then, this new mother in the studio—the determination in her face, in her eyes, as she piled up all the paintings. Maybe she didn't ever want to be who she was, or had been. Maybe she wanted to destroy everything of herself, and maybe, when he was little, that began with him. He was a part of her.

On top of the cliff, looking out over the valley, he wondered what Mary's husband thought, or realized, in that last second before he fell. Perhaps nothing. Nothing but fear surging through him. Tobin imagined Mary standing behind her husband, watching, shocked as he lost his balance. There one moment, then gone.

His mind said, *Take two steps back.* He did. *Now*, his mind said, *take three steps forward*, but he didn't.

Eyes shut, arms out, like flying. He remembered Mary had demonstrated how to fly. How to lift your arms, make them wings. He remembered the piano and Mary, melancholy, listening to him play. The song, the one for Mary—the lullaby that was for her desolation over the missing girl—came to him, softly, briefly. Callie missing now. Then a horrible dissonance rang in his head, as if his mother had slammed her hands on the keys.

Take three steps forward. He took one.

"Son!" A voice behind him. "Dear God, son. Get back. You aren't safe."

Then it was as if his body lifted without him. The air shot out of his lungs, and his arm was wrenched behind his back. He was being pulled backward roughly, painfully. He landed hard, on top of something, someone underneath him. The person made a *huff* sound as Tobin's weight came upon him. A man who had his arms locked, a firm grip around Tobin's middle, so tight Tobin couldn't breathe. He couldn't move, so he didn't struggle, even if he'd cared to. He let his neck go slack, and his head fall back over the shoulder of the person. The man, Mary's father-in-law, whose eyes were scrunched shut, like he didn't dare to look, breathed into Tobin's face. The man was moaning, and not letting go, his chest heaved underneath Tobin's weight.

Tobin relaxed all his muscles and waited. The man loosened his arms a little, and air came back to his lungs. He felt the heels of his boots on the granite, his legs straddling the man's legs. He waited; the man held him, not letting go. He looked up into the gray-white sky. Then Mary, green eyes, sorrowful face, appeared above him.

"Tobin," she said, tears in her eyes. She knelt next to him, smoothed her hand across his forehead. "Tobin," she said again, touching his chest, his cheeks, his arms, as if checking for broken bones.

CHAPTER 50

SHE'D NEVER BEEN SO THIRSTY. For the first time ever, she understood what Spencer and the first aid books said about always carrying water for emergencies. She stumbled along, arms ranging back and forth, hands pushing away prickly spruce branches, imagining a cold can of fizzy orange drink, gulping it down. Then a milkshake—vanilla ice cream and milk mixed up in a blender. At home sometimes she'd make that, then sit in the hammock out back of her house in the shade, sipping, one foot on the ground, rocking. Thick, creamy ice cream shake. And water. Delicious, cold water.

It was light, though the sky was overcast, the woods still eerie. She wove toward any areas that looked more open than others, though none produced anything like a trail. Any trail would be good to find. She stopped every now and again to listen for the brook. Sometimes she thought she heard it, and other things, like cars on a highway, a low hum, far off. A plane booming in the distance once.

Glasses of water. Ginger ale would be really good. Her arms felt heavy, weak; she had to keep moving, though. Her legs were tired, kind of shaky, but not like last night when every muscle was tight and filled with weakness at the same time, curled into a fetal position. The fear. The ghost girl, but then not the ghost girl.

Fetal. The word in her head, the idea of it, and nausea waved through her stomach and up her throat as she trudged on, trying to swallow. There was an embryo inside, a baby. She sobbed, then made herself stop. Must keep moving, focus. Thirst. Thirst was everything.

She struggled up the side of a valley. It was steep and she had to use her hands, digging her fingers into the dirt, grabbing hold of roots, pulling herself over downed trees. Her throat felt narrowed, aching. Thirsty, like a cotton ball stuck in the back of her throat. Everything inside craved, yearned, spoke of getting something to drink. Maybe on the other side of the ridge there would be a brook, or pond. Oh, how she wanted to dive into the pond next to the lodge, mouth open, swallowing mouthfuls of it.

At the top of the ridge, still under tall trees, a smell hit her nostrils and stung. The odor rushed at her again, startling her, but it was only a whiff. She peered down the hillside, between the trees, searching. A rupture of wind shook the leaves overhead, then the odor came seeping back, invisible. Adrenaline prickled in a quick burst under her skin. Definitely smoke. Fire.

At the base of some trees down the hill, a hazy mist of gray smoke, creeping up. She sniffed the air, straining to see it again, unsure if she was imagining it, crawling along the ground, moving toward her. Maybe it was mist, but then that odor again. She stumbled as she spun around and ran, back into the valley she'd just climbed up.

She kept on, heading up another incline. Her mouth was dry, and her tongue felt swollen, sticky, as she breathed, panting through her mouth. At the top of the next ridge, she stopped to test the air again. The smell was gone, and she began to doubt herself. She tested the air in each direction. Nothing. Each uphill gave way to another downhill. Uphill might give her a view of where she was. Downhill might be water.

She wanted her parents. Just wanted to be home. Away from this endless forest. Water was all she needed. Simple. Another waft of smoke odor hit her, and she felt suddenly light-headed, like she might faint. She leaned over, hands on knees. Her eyesight went blurry.

As if she'd conjured it, the sky let loose, and rain pelted against her back, cool, penetrating her clothes. She tipped her face toward the sky, opened her mouth to it. Drops fell against her tongue and she swallowed, opening and closing her mouth like a fish. When she opened her eyes again, she saw the dome of granite, the tower, Ben standing there, smiling at her. She stumbled, fell to her hands and knees. The tower and Ben disappeared, vanished, as if they had been plucked from the summit. A mirage, perhaps, created from thirst, from hypothermia. The word scared her. Soaked through, still thirsty. She felt cold. Skin icy. Tired. If she just closed her eyes for a while, then she'd try again.

CHAPTER 51

"CLAYTON," Mary said, gently pulling at his wrist. "It's okay, now. You can let him go."

Clayton released Tobin slowly, then pulled himself out from under Tobin's limbs, sat cross-legged next to Tobin, one hand still on Tobin's chest. Tobin didn't move. He lay on the granite between them.

"Oh, Tobin," Mary said. She gazed into his confused face, smudged with dirt and ash. "What were you thinking?" she said. "How could you even—"

"It's my fault," he said. "I think my father is hurt."

"What do you mean?" she asked.

"I locked the barn," Tobin said. "I thought she let him out. My fault."

"Hush," Mary said. She lay her hand on his forehead, looked into his eyes, watched tears pop out, roll down his temples into his dark curls.

Clayton stood up when they heard voices below; it was the crew hiking up. Marlee, Rabbit, and Spencer came out on the ledge. They all stopped when they caught sight of Tobin lying there between her and Clayton.

Clayton got up, went to them. "Any news?" he asked.

"We haven't found Callie," Spencer said. "But I just heard from Ben," he said indicating his radio. "They're still trying to contain a fire at the Goughs'. The rain helped, but buildings at Four Corners are destroyed. I'm sorry, Tobin. Really sorry."

"Is anyone hurt?" Mary asked. It seemed to her that Spencer was hesitating, hedging.

"Your mother was taken to a hospital," Spencer told Tobin. "I'm not sure what her condition is. And a fireman got some burns."

"My father?" Tobin asked, and Mary heard the desperation in his voice.

"That's all I know."

Tobin nodded, stared into the sky.

They were almost to the road that would lead them into the parking lot in front of the lodge, and still no sign of Callie. Mary felt dizzy with anxiety. It was hard to get a full breath, as if moss, heavy and saturated, was expanding in her chest. It was too familiar.

Eventually the trail turned them out onto the wider dirt path, then the narrow dirt road. She caught up to Tobin's side, walked with him. He stared straight ahead, afraid, it seemed, to look to her.

She glanced back to see Clayton walking next to Spencer and Marlee. Rabbit behind them. Everyone was quiet. Here was this road again. She'd been running on it last time, frantic, trying to get help, leaving Michael behind her.

She began to hope that they'd find Callie at the lodge. Callie would have made her way down and would be sitting there with guests, waiting for them. Or maybe, she hoped, Spencer's radio would crackle to life, and Ben would tell them that Callie was safe, he had her at the tower. She hoped and was afraid to hope because it hadn't done any good before.

"I didn't want anyone to get hurt," Tobin said.

"Of course you didn't," she said.

"I must be like her," he said. "I must be nuts."

"I don't think so," she said. "Maybe you just need someone to talk to. Maybe you have some sort of compulsive disorder, or something. Lots of people do."

Tobin looked at her with what seemed like relief, then back to dread.

From behind, Rabbit said, "I think we should get some food, make a plan, then head back up."

"We can take the Wilderness Trail," Spencer said. "Maybe Marlee and Rabbit can take the Back Eighty around."

"Let's get Tobin situated," Mary said. "Then I'm with you."

They were in the parking lot now, the old lodge to their left, the pond to the right, the surface glinting in the sun. The white raft floated in the middle.

Someone was in the water. Mary stopped walking. Her heart thudded in her ears. Tobin, too, halted next to her, and exhaled a quick gasp as a girl, long hair dripping, emerged from the water, clothing plastered to her body.

The sound of Callie's voice, as soft as a chime, "It's me. I made it back," made Mary's heart soar. There was her beautiful face, a sheepish smile. An inflamed scratch ran from the corner of one eye to her jaw.

"Were you guys looking for me?" she said, cavalierly, though a break in her voice gave her away. Her chin trembled. "I was so thirsty. I thought I could drink the pond."

Marlee squealed and ran to Callie, threw her arms around her.

Spencer sighed, his shoulders dropping as if he'd just removed a heavy pack.

"Thank God," Clayton said. "Thank God."

Callie looked over Marlee's shoulder, laughing a little, then lips trembling.

"I was lost," she said. She smiled at Mary. "But I found the way out."

Marlee kept an arm around Callie as they came up the path. Callie looked tired, worn.

"Tobin," Callie said, "you won't believe what I saw. I thought it was the ghost girl at first. I was so scared."

Tobin looked up, eyes wide, surprised, no doubt, that Callie had addressed him specifically. But Callie didn't finish, overcome with tears.

Mary went to her, weakened with relief, with joy, marveling at Callie's easy entrance, her remarkable return from the wilderness, all by herself.

CHAPTER 52

Mary stood on the front deck, gazing out at Mount
Cascom. The upper slopes were gray, stark, bare branches.
The trees in the lower valley held their leaves, an occasional brilliant red, but mostly yellows and browns from such a dry summer. The branches seemed weary, slumped heavily, and ready to let
go of their leaves. None of the burn at Four Corners showed from
here, but just the thought of it made her think she smelled smoke.
In the spring the land would revive itself—saplings would shoot
up, ready to take over again.

Behind her, the truck was loaded up.

"I'm going," she told the mountain.

She was deeply sad, but ready.

The temperature had dropped dramatically. She'd had a fire
in the woodstove every night for a week. Last night she'd rolled
her sleeping bag out in front of the hearth and put the screen on
the woodstove so she fell asleep watching flames. She'd let herself cry for a while, thinking of Michael. Everything was still
painful, and she knew it would be for a long time.

Down below sat the pile of brush, never taken care of, and

Tobin's neat stack of birch logs, now depleted from her many fires these last weeks.

The autumn air smelled fresh and wonderful. Earlier that morning, far off, and whining out of the valley, she'd heard a chain saw start up—its motor strident, clear, then faint or diffused, as the wilderness allowed it. Someone working the land.

The dome of granite appeared closer, set against the bright blue sky. The fire tower was empty now. Ben had retreated for the winter, gone off to another job he had with the forest service. He'd come by before he left, hugged her. Perhaps they'd see each other next summer, if he came back, he wasn't sure. Maybe, he'd said, he needed people now, less isolation. "I understand," she'd said. "Maybe me, too."

They exchanged e-mail addresses, though she sensed they'd gotten what they needed from one another. Summer was over, winter would change them.

The lodge now was only open on the weekends for groups to rent out. The young crew, all gone.

Callie had left first. Her parents had come to bring her home. They thanked Mary, and brought her gifts—a basket of fruit and candy—though she explained that it was Callie who'd found her own way back. It was Callie who was brave, resourceful, unwilling to let the wilderness defeat her.

"Where are you going to go?" Callie's father had asked her, and for a moment these two parents were her parents, and they looked at her with love and concern, and she knew they wanted her happiness.

"Massachusetts," she'd said, surprising herself. "Back to Somerville."

You'll be back, the mountain said now.

"I know," she said, sighing, looking at it.

She glanced at the house as if it, too, was waiting for acknowledgment. But it was just a house. She would burn it down in a second if Michael were standing next to her right now.

Maybe he was. Maybe he sat in the truck, buckled into the passenger seat, ready to go with her, bumping down the steep mountain road. Ready to leave this place, watching her, waiting for her. She guessed he would forever. For the rest of her life, probably, she'd imagine him just off to her side, or sitting across a room, or brushing against her, *through* her, in unexpected moments.

Maybe someday another man would lay his arm across her in his sleep and she'd think, just for a moment, that it was Michael, and that they were lying in her parents' bedroom, here at Mount Cascom. That their children were yelling and laughing, tearing around the yard outside. In an instant of forgetting, she imagined herself pregnant again, and all this was inevitable.

But she was not pregnant. And Michael was dead. Nothing would ever be the same.

Still, you couldn't ever let go entirely, you still had to believe that someday, somewhere, all that was missing would somehow appear and come out right. Even when you knew, *you knew*, what you were looking for was just an illusion, a dream, a hope, a myth. And what was truly possible might be in places you never thought to look before. Or had looked, but hadn't seen.

Here was Tobin, coming through the woods. She waved to him, and he lifted his arm in greeting. He seemed better these last weeks. His mother was back in Concord. His father was home, recovering from burns on his hands. The barn and studio had been destroyed. The house, miraculously, had been saved.

Tobin came up the hill. He smiled, but she could tell he was sad she was leaving, everyone was leaving, and he was back to living with his father. Though things had certainly changed between them. Tobin's father had chosen Tobin after all, finally deciding that Tobin's mother was better off, if not happier, living far from the rough country. She had returned to the group home.

Tobin and his father were talking more, especially about where he might go for college. And Mary urged Mr. Gough to take Tobin to see doctors, both for his arthritis and for therapy. Already, she could tell that Tobin was better, calmer. It was as if he'd loosened, his whole body unknotted.

"I'll see you soon," she said.

Tobin grinned, pushed the hair out of his eyes. "Yeah," he said.

"You can call me anytime. You know that, right?"

He nodded. "Safe trip, Mary," he said softly.

She moved forward, put her arms around him, hugged him tightly. He returned the hug lightly, then they released each other, said good-byes again.

Mary climbed into the truck, reversed it around onto the old logging road, and paused to look back once more. Tobin had already started down the hill and away, perhaps hiding tears, she wasn't sure.

Over the roof of the house, the mountain gleamed, sure and unwavering, the god of her childhood, now gray and aging under the weight of fall.

CHAPTER 53

CALLIE TOOK HER MOTHER'S HAND in hers, squeezed. Her mother gave her a reassuring smile and squeezed back. Her mother's smile said, *This is the right thing to do*.

A young girl across the room flipped pages of a magazine. Callie couldn't watch. Everything made her sick, especially anything moving in any kind of rhythm. She couldn't read either. Words made her dizzy.

Out the window she saw a huge maple tree, some of its leaves just starting to turn, but most a dull, murky green. There was music coming from somewhere, a pop song, but every now and again she heard the chants and jeers of protesters on the street across the road from the clinic. When they'd driven up, Callie had looked into those faces, wondering how people could be like that. They called out names—*killer*, and then *mommy*—struggling to find just the right sentiment that would hurt her, get to her, change her decision. She felt sorry for them in a way because they had nothing better to do with their lives than torment people. And she hated them for making people feel bad when they already felt bad.

Callie found that if she stared at the tree outside and thought of other things, she got through moments without feeling nauseated. The tree was old, with a thick trunk and many sturdy branches. She followed one of its branches all the way out and let her eyes travel up a smaller branch that came from it, and she let the tree take her deep inside its layers of leaves. There was much more color in its upper leaves. She concentrated on naming the colors. Red, red-brown, yellow speckles. She let her mind's eye travel inside the foliage. Inside there was olive green, soft yellows, an orange tinge, and the tree was soothing and cool inside its branches.

"You okay, sweetie?" her mother asked softly.

Her mother was being so nice, so kind and understanding. Her father, too, was gentle and had wrapped his arms around her, kissed the top of her head. Though she knew her father wanted to file charges, do something to make Spencer accountable, she and her mother had convinced him to let it go.

Her parents had been summoned to the mountain shortly after everything had happened, and they'd taken her home. She'd missed the last two and a half weeks of work, and it made her feel awful, but not as awful as morning sickness, so she'd been glad to leave. Everyone else would have left the lodge by now, too.

Marlee would be off to Colorado for her first year of college. Rabbit would be back in Hartford, just starting his senior year of high school, just as she was about to start her junior year back at St. Paul's. Spencer would be in Cambridge, strolling the streets, holding hands with his girlfriend on the way to their classes at Harvard. Spencer would never know that she was pregnant. He'd never know, and that was fine, because in an hour there would be no baby. It would be as if nothing ever happened.

But so many things had happened this summer. She thought now of how Marlee had sat at the foot of her bunk, saying how angry she was with herself for that night, for not coming after her and staying for some guy who didn't even matter.

"It's okay," Callie said. She was so tired and scraped up, bandages on her arms and face. She wasn't mad at Marlee, and also she knew that she herself was guilty of many things.

She might not ever see those people again. How strange. People who meant so much to her, and had shared so much, and she might not ever lay eyes on them again. Who knew if any of them would return to Cascom Lodge for another summer? Maybe. Maybe she would, but that was too far away to think of now.

Mary had told her that she'd never again heard from any of her crew members back then. Not even from the crew boss she'd loved. People left, disappeared, or died.

"It's going to be okay," her mother said now.

"I know," Callie said.

She remembered Mary's words, too: she said Callie was young, her whole life ahead—school, college, a career. Someday a husband and someday children. Now, Callie wondered if she'd ever see Mary again. Yes. Because Mary would always be on the mountain, and even if Callie didn't work at the lodge next summer, she could go back to visit. She'd be getting her driver's license this fall. She'd learn stick shift, and she'd drive up there next summer, and maybe she and Mary could climb Cascom together. Maybe Callie would bring her boyfriend. He'd be gorgeous and kind and he'd love to hike and he'd think Mary was the coolest. Maybe Ben would be there, and they'd be friends. And Tobin, maybe she could be his friend, too.

Callie caught herself making up the future. The future that would never, could never, be as she dreamed it, no matter how much she wanted it. Maybe it was better not to imagine it. Let it come however it would. Don't expect much, and you won't be disappointed—this was one of Marlee's dictums.

Things were never how you thought. Like that night in the woods. The Goughs' pigs. They were just pigs, but she'd felt something else emanating from them. They'd come toward her, brushed against her, snorting and screeching. She'd felt their bristly skin on her arms as she pulled her legs in, making herself as small as possible. They grunted and circled her relentlessly. Maybe they were just domesticated pigs, but that night they were something else, wild. Wild, free, full of their truer nature. The next day the pigs had been herded up and brought in, but one pig was missing, and later found dead at the bottom of some steep granite.

And in the woods, lost, thirsty, the scary smell of smoke in her nose, she'd prayed for water. Miraculously, it had come, filling her mouth, but she was so tired, she'd lain down, shut her eyes. Dangerous, but it was only for a moment. She felt dizzy, cold. The rain was persistent, like soft bullets thumping on her chest. For a second she thought it was Tobin, and he'd come to lie next to her, smoothing his fingertips over her arms as he had the night they'd kissed. "Callie," he said. "Open your eyes," and her eyes had snapped open. She'd sat up, alone, but once more determined to move on.

"Think of other things," her mother said now. "Imagine some-place peaceful."

She saw the sky from the top of the mountain. It was blue and gorgeous, and she felt blue-kindness. And there was something way up there, like a balloon, and it was her baby, floating off, and it terrified her. But then she saw that there was a string unwinding from her wrist. She followed the string with her eyes, and it went up into the sky, disappearing as it grew thin and distant. She let the string spin out, so high she couldn't see anything anymore, but she knew that when she was ready, maybe many years from now, she could reel it back down.

EPILOGUE

OVERNIGHT, HEAVY SNOW FELL, filling the roads, covering cars parked on the narrow streets of Somerville. In the morning, she wanted nothing more than to stay home.

"Stay home," Paul told her on the phone. "No one's coming in. Listen to some *good* music." He'd been getting more sarcastic, given the many bad musicians they'd worked with lately. "Even Lisie stayed in bed," he said of his hardworking wife.

So she stayed home from work, pulled out her guitar and notepad, began to strum, jot down words as they came.

A beagle mutt named Clark, rescued from the pound, was asleep at her feet. His paws twitched, chasing rabbits in his dreams. It had been Tobin's suggestion to get a dog, and she thought of Tobin now, up there on the mountain, so thankful to have him there, keeping an eye on her place. She hoped that he was healing, finding relief.

Earlier she'd called him, reminded him to shovel off her roof if it got too deep.

"How's your father?" she'd asked.

"Good, painting again."

"How are you?"

"Great!" he said brightly, almost too enthusiastically, and a wash of concern came over her.

"You're sure?"

Tobin breathed into the phone. She thought she heard tapping, fingers tapping rhythmically, felt a chill, worried, almost afraid to ask.

"I'm applying to MIT," he said. "And Harvard."

"That's fantastic. Good for you."

"They're supposed to be good schools."

She couldn't help but laugh. "Yes, I've heard that."

"I'd be close by."

"I'd like that. A lot," she said, and it was true.

"How's Clark?" he asked.

She'd looked down at her sleeping dog, his eyelids twitching in sleep.

"He's dreaming. And drooling."

Tobin laughed. "It's his prerogative. He's a mutt."

"Don't make fun of Clark," she scolded.

"I wouldn't," he said seriously, and she'd smiled into the receiver, sure he was smiling, too. They'd said good-bye, and Mary had felt so happy. Tobin, new and unexpected family.

Now, an e-mail message popped up. It pleased Mary that Callie kept in touch, writing every few weeks or so. This time the subject line was "Private Eye," not the usual "Hi Mary, It's Callie" they'd sent back and forth for weeks without bothering to change.

Are you ready for this? I found this website of this photographer guy who recently had a show at a gallery in San Francisco—all people with albinism. They're really beautiful. Anyway, there's this one woman whose name is Anna Kimball! who lives in

Boulder. Do you think this could be her? See attachment. Big
hugs.
Love, Callie

Mary's fingers hovered over the keys as the image down-
loaded, but before anything more than the top edge of the photo
appeared, she hit delete. No need for resurrection, for going
back. Whoever she was, she'd vanished.

ACKNOWLEDGMENTS

For their support while I was writing this novel, I'd like to thank the National Endowment for the Arts, the Wallace Stegner Fellowship program at Stanford University, the University of New Hampshire, California College of the Arts, Vermont Studio Center, Jentel Artist Residency Program, Artcroft in Kentucky, and the Millay Colony for the Arts. This book was a long time in the works, and I'm incredibly grateful to all the people over the years who've offered editorial advice and encouragement, in particular, my fellow fellows at Stanford. I'm especially indebted to my longtime writer friend Gregory Spatz, who read numerous drafts—more than seems possible—with such an excellent eye and generosity of spirit. Infinite thanks to brilliant fellow writers Daniel Orozco and Doug Dorst, who helped me through early drafts. Also Malinda McCollum, Andrea Bewick, Angela Pneuman, Ed Schwarzschild, Ron Nyren, Bay Anapol, Eliza Harding Turner, and Donna Vitucci. Thanks to bighearted readers Gwen Jones, Karen Dufour, Ronni Radbill, and Art DiMambro. Thanks to everyone at Bloomsbury, especially Kathy Belden, most fabulous editor. With huge appreciation, thanks to Dorian Karchmar at WME. For laughter and keeping me connected to the world I owe a great deal of gratitude to my students and colleagues at CCA and UNH. Thanks to my teachers at UNH, the Iowa Writers' Workshop, and Stanford. For ever present support, thanks to John Yount, Art and Celeste (she is deeply missed), Ted and Janet, Pete and Tamara, and my wonderful mother, Elizabeth Blood Williams.

A NOTE ON THE AUTHOR

Ann Joslin Williams grew up in New Hampshire. She earned her MFA from the Iowa Writers' Workshop, and was a Wallace Stegner Fellow at Stanford University. She is a recipient of a National Endowment for the Arts grant, and is the author of *The Woman in the Woods*, a collection of linked stories, which won the 2005 Spokane Prize for Short Fiction. Her work has appeared in *StoryQuarterly*, *The Iowa Review*, *The Missouri Review*, *Ploughshares*, and elsewhere. She is an assistant professor at the University of New Hampshire.